PASSION'S DEMAND

"Don't be impossible, Caroline!" he demanded.

"Me! Of course, I'm impossible! I'm the spoiled child you have to fetch home to her doting papa." She tugged on her arm, making him hold her tighter. "Well, don't bother! I can get on the train tomorrow by myself."

Rory hauled her against his chest. "Oh, no, you won't. I promised your father I'd bring you home and I will." His hands went from her arms to her waist, and he lifted her until her face was level with his.

"Put me down! I mean it, Rory!"

He laughed as he pushed one knee between her dangling legs. "I may never put you down. I think I like you this way."

"I'll scream," she whispered.

His lips then his teeth tugged at her earlobe, and she sucked in her breath, but not to scream. His mouth covered hers, gently, caressingly, and she felt a jolt go through her body. She melted under its heat. Even her legs became weak, and she felt herself slipping down his legs. The feeling was so delicious, so wicked— wonderfully, wonderfully wicked. . . .

ZEBRA'S GOT THE ROMANCE
TO SET YOUR HEART AFIRE!

RAGING DESIRE   (2242, $3.75)
by Colleen Faulkner

A wealthy gentleman and officer in General Washington's army, Devon Marsh wasn't meant for the likes of Cassie O'Flynn, an immigrant bond servant. But from the moment their lips first met, Cassie knew she could love no other . . . even if it meant marching into the flames of war to make him hers!

TEXAS TWILIGHT   (2241, $3.75)
by Vivian Vaughan

When handsome Trace Garrett stepped onto the porch of the Santa Clara ranch, he wove a rapturous spell around Clara Ehler's heart. Though Clara planned to sell the spread and move back East, Trace was determined to keep her on the wild Western frontier where she belonged — to share with him the glory and the splendor of the passion-filled TEXAS TWILIGHT.

RENEGADE HEART   (2244, $3.75)
by Marjorie Price

Strong-willed Hannah Hatch resented her imprisonment by Captain Jake Farnsworth, even after the daring Yankee had rescued her from bloodthirsty marauders. And though Jake's rock-hard physique made Hannah tremble with desire, the spirited beauty was nevertheless resolved to exploit her femininity to the fullest and gain her independence from the virile bluecoat.

LOVING CHALLENGE   (2243, $3.75)
by Carol King

When the notorious Captain Dominic Warbrooke burst into Laurette Harker's eighteenth birthday ball, the accomplished beauty challenged the arrogant scoundrel to a duel. But when the captain named her innocence as his stakes, Laurette was terrified she'd not only lose the fight, but her heart as well!

Available wherever paperbacks are sold, or order direct from the Publisher. Send cover price plus 50¢ per copy for mailing and handling to Zebra Books, Dept. 2441, 475 Park Avenue South, New York, N.Y. 10016. Residents of New York, New Jersey and Pennsylvania must include sales tax. DO NOT SEND CASH.

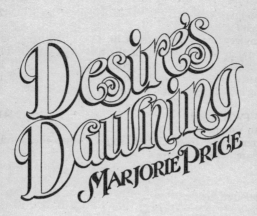

Desire's Dawning

Marjorie Price

ZEBRA BOOKS
KENSINGTON PUBLISHING CORP.

ZEBRA BOOKS

are published by

Kensington Publishing Corp.
475 Park Avenue South
New York, NY 10016

First printing: August, 1988

Printed in the United States of America

Chapter One

With an earsplitting grind of metal on metal, the locomotive halted, sending the unprepared passengers flying from their seats.

In front of Caroline Farnsworth, whose quick reflexes saved her from taking a hard fall to the floor, a child began to cry and a man swore. Caroline hid a grim smile of agreement behind her hand. The nearer she came to her destination, the more intolerant she became of delay. What now? she wanted to scream. Instead, she turned to the tiny matron across the aisle. "Are you all right?"

"Why, I don't know." Mrs. Reed peered owlishly at Caroline from under her hat. It was tipped forward over her eyes, and her parcels were on the floor. "Are we there already?"

Caroline gathered up the packages, piling them on the seat next to Mrs. Reed. Although Caroline was twenty years younger than Mrs. Reed, something about her, perhaps her distracted air, made Caroline feel protective of the older woman. Perhaps, though, it was not so odd. After all, she was the native, the veteran traveler. She was going home, not making her first trip west.

Three long years away . . . Caroline bit back a sigh of longing. She had gone east for two years of schooling in Philadelphia, never knowing she would have to be away for a third year. But Gramma Lunig had broken her hip and never recovered, sending Grampa into a similar decline. She had never thought she could feel so helpless, so useless and so needed all at the same time.

The letter from Hannah, her stepmother, had made it worse. Her father had been injured in a fall from horseback, puncturing his lung, and he lay near death. She had been torn. She couldn't leave Grampa, but she had longed to be home, helping Hannah, helping Papa with the ranch. Just to be there. Home.

And now, soon she would be there. Papa was well again. Hannah had said so. Rory had said so. *He* had said so. But she had to see him to be sure.

Tamping down her anxiety, Caroline answered Mrs. Reed cheerfully. "The conductor didn't warn us, so it's probably just an animal on the tracks. Maybe a herd. This is cattle country." A glance out the grimy window at the flat Kansas prairie confirmed her statement. There was no town yet. Nothing to see but grass and sky.

"How soon do you think we'll get to Dodge City?"

Caroline turned away, one hand reaching for Grampa's pocket watch, which she wore on a chain around her neck. She had answered that question before. Mrs. Reed, who had been her companion since Topeka, had no more sense of time than a child. She opened the watch, steadying herself in the aisle as the train gave a convulsive lurch.

The door behind her opened with a clang to reveal a man dressed in black. She sat down hard, her mouth agape in surprise. The one touch of color in the man's garb was the red bandana tied over his mouth and nose. She had worn a bandana just like it, as had all the hands on her father's ranch, but never with such sinister purpose. With his hat pulled low over his brow, only his narrowly slitted eyes were visible. They were black, too, she noted. But it was the gun he held that grabbed her attention.

Caroline was not the only stunned passenger. Two rows behind her a woman began to wail, burying her face in her husband's shoulder. The man patted her arm mechanically, his eyes fixed warily on the gunman.

"We're all going to die!" she sobbed.

Caroline immediately rejected that notion. They would be robbed, but not harmed, she was sure.

The man spoke, confirming her thoughts. "No one will be hurt as long as you all do as you're told," he said in a surprisingly gentle voice. For all its gentleness, however, there was a vein of steel in his speech. "My associate is

6

going to come along the aisle and collect your valuables in his sack. Don't try to hold anything back. It won't do you any good, and it might upset him. Or worse—make me angry!"

Incredibly, he laughed then. "Think of it as being in church. You have to contribute to the collection to assure yourself of salvation!"

Caroline almost joined his amused chuckle. Just in time, she stopped out of sympathy for those around her. She wasn't worried about herself. What little money and jewelry she had was sewn into her petticoats for safekeeping. Even if she lost that, she was only going on alone to Dodge City, the next stop. Rory would meet her there and accompany her the rest of the way to New Mexico. Most of the other passengers were carrying all their travel funds on them. They would not fare so well with nothing.

She sat quietly, her reticule in her hands. She would give it up willingly, along with the few coins it contained, but she wished for the gun she used to carry years ago. She had meant to purchase one in Topeka. Instead, she had decided to wait for her father's or Rory's advice. There were new models available now, and living in Philadelphia and placid little Hanford, Pennsylvania, had once again put weapons and their use outside of her realm.

The gunman's "associate," as he had called him, was nowhere near as refined as his leader. He was dirty and disheveled, both thinner and younger than the man in black. His clothes were the sweat-stained common gear of every range rider in the West. His dirty, crumpled hat, pulled down over his eyes, looked as if it had been used as a pillow and fan and drinking cup for years. He was efficient but nervous as he worked his way toward Caroline under his boss's watchful eye. His nervousness worried Caroline. Did he fear them or his boss? Or someone outside?

He aimed his gun at Mrs. Reed while she divested herself of everything she held dear, whimpering miserably the whole time. Anger flared briefly in Caroline's breast before she pushed it down. Better to lose everything and be alive than to provoke this edgy bandit.

7

"Hurry it up," ordered the man in black. He was speaking to the couple behind her, preparatory to leaving. She identified the gentleness in his speech as the remnants of a southern drawl just as she held out her purse to the man with the sack.

Having given up her reticule, Caroline sat back, prepared to dismiss the whole unpleasant incident from her mind. The outlaw had other ideas. He waved his gun under her nose and muttered, "Gimme the chain and the watch."

Caroline looked down in amazement. She had worn the watch beneath her dress the whole trip. Now, because she had been about to check the time for Mrs. Reed, it peeked from between the buttons of her bodice. The gold chain was beautifully wrought and quite expensive. She would have given that up without thinking, but it was attached to her grandfather's gold pocket watch, and she wasn't about to part with that. Grampa had only been dead nine weeks, and it was her only remembrance of him.

She forgot common sense in a moment of blind stupidity that was as much temper as sentiment. She shook her head, her expression scornful and stubborn.

Refusing was bad enough, but then she made it worse. Holding the watch with one hand, she pushed the gun away with the other.

For an instant no one in the car moved as Caroline's audacity registered on the passengers and on the two outlaws. And on herself.

Then everything happened at once.

"Come on. We've got to move!" the leader ordered in an impatient hiss of breath.

His accomplice swung the sack of loot at him without taking his eyes off Caroline's frozen features. "Naw," he said, raking her with a slowly dawning smile. "She's comin' with me."

Caroline hadn't feared the gun, but that smile made her sick with fright. She clawed at her neckline, trying to free the chain and watch. Her attempt only dislodged her hat and gave the man access to her arms. Before she could scream, he had hauled her into the aisle. She fought his

8

hands, aided briefly by the man in the row behind her, who deserted his cringing wife to grapple for Caroline.

"Leave her!" the man in black yelled.

Caroline saw him backing from the passenger car, his gun on the other passengers and the sack under his arm.

For a moment it seemed Caroline would escape. The man's grip on her loosened long enough for him to turn and deal with the person attacking his rear. That was Mrs. Reed. She was the only one with the courage — or the folly — to persist in trying to rescue Caroline. The outlaw gave her a sharp push that sent her backward into the seats in a heap.

Concern for Mrs. Reed made Caroline doubly frantic. She tried to elude recapture, but there was nowhere to go. She was stuck in the small space between the now-closed locomotive door and the robber. He dragged her out and opened the door, yanking on her arm as he went. She clung to the back of the last seat with one hand until her grip slipped and she went hurtling out the door that slammed shut behind her. She fell down the sharp drop to the ground after the man in time to hear her captor ordered one more time to leave her behind.

"Naw," he answered again, as stubborn as she was. "She's purty. Look at that hair!"

Caroline groaned inwardly. Her pale silver-blond hair, now streaming down over her shoulders from her struggles, had been an attractive nuisance all her life. Once again it was bringing her the wrong kind of attention, but this time she had only herself to blame. She and her foolish, ill-timed rebellion had set this particular stage for trouble.

"Please!" she begged the leader of what she could now see was a whole band of outlaws. "I can't ride. I'll only hold you back. Let me go!"

"I'll carry her!" a third, moon-faced man volunteered to a chorus of raucous laughter.

"I found her! She's mine!"

"Get her on a horse and let's get out of here!"

Her fate decided, Caroline found herself snatched up, half dragged and half carried to a horse. She dug her shoes

9

into the loose dirt, resisting all the way. When she screamed, the man in charge yelled, "Shut her up, Walt!"

Walt grabbed her by the hair and planted his fist on her chin. Caroline collapsed at his feet, quiet at last.

Chapter Two

Even before he heard that the train was late, Rory had a bad feeling about Caroline and this trip. He didn't discount his feelings, either. He had learned not to. He was still alive, thanks to hunches like this. But hunches about other people and their safety weren't much good. He couldn't act on them. He could only stand around, stewing in his own juices.

He glared down the rails, trying to no avail to conjure up the cinder- and-ash spewing locomotive. The tracks remained empty; only the depot was filled with people, all speculating about the delay.

Delays weren't uncommon. In fact, they were almost customary, hardly surprising given the nature of railway travel. A hundred things, from mechanical breakdowns to animals on the track, could foul up the schedule. Nevertheless, in his heart Rory knew this time the train had been stopped by outlaws.

Unwilling to listen to the talk buzzing around him, he strode from the train yard and crossed the broad, unpaved expanse of Front Street. It was quiet, as was the whole town this time of year. The spring cattle drive was over, and all but a few unsold steer were gone from the stockyards outside of town. Without the cattle, there were few cowboys in Dodge City, which left the town to the local populace, mostly farmers and merchants who were busy at work this time of day. He stepped from the narrow board sidewalk into the dim interior of the almost deserted Long Branch Saloon.

As Rory took the seat opposite Zeb, the wiry little man silently shoved a drink in front of him. He took a bracing sip and noted the inroads Zeb, never much of a drinker, had made in his own. "You've heard," he said.

11

"It's jest late. Don't mean nothing."

"If it were anyone else on board, I wouldn't worry," Rory said. "But Caroline! She's such a hothead."

Zeb shook his head, setting the unruly tangle of black hair around his face into motion. "She's a cool one, and you know it. She'll be fine. Jest mad as hell to be kept back."

Rory didn't argue. Neither of them knew for sure what she would do, and conjecture was futile. Besides, Zeb was as fond of Caroline as he was. "At least Jake isn't here. That's something." He took another swallow of liquor, his lips curling back from his teeth as the fiery liquid slid down his throat.

While Zeb studied the bottles arrayed behind the bar, Rory studied him. He'd known Zeb for eleven years, as long as he'd known Caroline, but unlike her, Zeb never changed. He was as close to being ageless as a human being could be. Except for his hair, he was pure rawhide, thin and tough.

Rory didn't want to upset Zeb, but he couldn't keep himself from asking, "Do you suppose she heard about Blackie?"

"Hard to tell. It's been in the papers, and God knows she reads the print off'n anything she gets her hands on."

Rory gave a silent laugh. "But back east she might have missed it." He swirled the liquid in his glass and put the whole thing aside, determined to keep his wits. "I just wish I knew whether it would be better if she knew her enemy was out there or not."

"Wouldn't make no difference," Zeb said fatalistically.

Rory thought that, too, but it didn't help. He rubbed a hand over his smooth-shaved jaw, setting it at a more determined angle. "We both know it would be worse for her if Baltimore Blackie knew *she* was within his reach. A man who'll take on the whole Santa Fe Railroad just to avenge the fact that his old crony was taken from it and lynched would go to no end of trouble because of her. She was the one who put Belasco behind bars to start with!"

Zeb's expression didn't change. "Don't do no good to think on it," he said flatly.

"But Blackie couldn't know she was on that train, could

he?"

"Don't see how."

"Could he have access to passenger lists, do you suppose?" Rory pursued.

"Don't see how," Zeb repeated, refusing to be drawn into the conversation.

"He probably doesn't even remember her—or know her name. That was *years* ago!" Rory exclaimed, trying hard to convince himself.

Baltimore Blackie was the name on everyone's lips along the route of the Atchison, Topeka and Santa Fe Railroad because of the series of daring train robberies he'd recently executed. His stated purpose was indeed revenge, although few people could understand why he held the railroad responsible for what the citizens of one town had done.

Vigilantes from Cottonwood Falls, a town not even directly on the railroad line, had ridden out and stopped a train carrying Baltimore Blackie's longtime partner in crime, taking him away to hang him for the murder of one of their people in a bank robbery years ago. Kid Belasco, the dead convict, had been in transit from one prison to another at the time, but the reason he was in captivity at all was Caroline Farnsworth, and Baltimore Blackie had to know that fact as well as Rory did.

At the time, Caroline had been a child of almost ten years, on her way to New Mexico with her father, Jake. Although Jake had made the actual arrest, it was Caroline who had spotted the holdup in progress and supplied the loaded gun for her father to use. She had prodded him into action, and that fact had been duly noted in the newspaper accounts of the time. Baltimore Blackie had undoubtedly read every word printed about the Farnsworths. Like the people of Cottonwood Falls, he, too, wouldn't forget. The fact that he was harassing the railroad now was proof of that.

"He don't hurt the passengers anyway," Zeb offered by way of encouragement, adding, "If'n it *is* him."

Rory pushed down his anxiety and got to his feet, leaving the rest of his drink untouched. "It probably isn't. It's

13

probably just a dead cow on the track, and Caroline is helping the crew haul away the carcass. And if it is Baltimore Blackie, he'd be a fool to mess with her. Just look what she did to his pal — and that was before she spent eight years riding the range."

Zeb grinned. "Jake and Hannah are expectin' her to come back all ladylike. Me — I'm countin' on Caroline bein' as harum-scarum as ever. Whatcha wanna bet?"

Rory clapped Zeb's shoulder in parting, inexplicably cheered by the picture he painted. "Come over when you hear the train. It shouldn't be long now."

He was stopped at the door by a hearty "Well, well, Mr. Farnsworth! What brings you to Dodge City today?"

Rory wasn't really a Farnsworth. His family name was Talmage, but he'd lived so long as a sort of adopted son to Jake Farnsworth that he answered to either name. He turned to shake hands with cattle broker Miles Caldwell, one of Jake's many business acquaintances along the cattle trail. "Just meeting the train today. A pleasure trip, you might say."

"I hope it turns out to be a pleasure. Rumor has it the train was held up."

"Delayed, certainly," Rory said, frowning. He didn't want to hear any more about rumors.

"The railroad will have to take steps to stop these robberies, or there'll just be more violence," Caldwell declared, warming to the subject. "Why, I just heard that the robber has vowed to lynch someone from each train he stops from now on. I say hanging's too good for a man like that!"

Rory had no idea what he said to break off the conversation and make his escape. Fortunately, as soon as he reached the depot it was obvious from the murmur of anticipation in the crowd that the train was coming at last.

If he lived to be a hundred he would never outgrow the clutch of excitement that gripped him whenever a train bore down upon a station, but this time his anticipation was extreme. Caroline was coming home after three years. She had left as a girl; now she would be a grown woman — soon to be twenty-one years old.

14

He hardly knew what he wanted, the harum-scarum girl Zeb hoped for or something else he couldn't name. She was unique in his life, part sister who was no relation at all to him, part pest he had alternately teased and protected. But everything about her was special because she, above all others, was responsible for making the Farnsworths into a real family.

Motherless from birth, Caroline's early life had been enough to make any child harum-scarum. Jake had taken her from place to place along the frontier states, giving her his abundant love and the best care he could manage, but not much else. She had not known a settled homelife or real schooling until Jake took her to stay with her mother's parents in Pennsylvania while he fought in the Civil War.

Once mustered out, he postponed his desire to reclaim Caroline immediately and took on a dangerous job for the backers of the Union Pacific Railroad in Nebraska in order to earn enough money to stake them to a new home in the territory of New Mexico.

While he was in Nebraska he met and fell in love with Hannah Veazie, but not even that experience could deflect him from his chosen path. His daughter came first with Jake, not because he didn't love Hannah, but because Caroline was a child and dependent upon him. Hannah had been forced to pursue Jake and insinuate herself into the very fabric of his relationship with Caroline before he would give in to her—and to his own needs and desires.

To Rory, who had accidentally come upon Hannah and Jake late in their relationship, the strength, purpose and love binding the three Farnsworths stood as the prime example in his life of all that was good. But he knew better than most that none of it would have worked out if Caroline had been either selfish or jealous.

Other girls in her position, reunited with a beloved father after years of enforced separation, might have played the pampered princess, daddy's little girl restored to her throne at last. But not Caroline. Much as she delighted in her father's company and attention, she had been wise enough to know that sometimes less is more. She had wanted more:

a mother for herself and a wife for her father.

And, even more remarkable, she had also wanted him— Rory—as part of her family. Jake and Hannah had set the tone for his acceptance, of course, but Rory knew that Caroline had determined the degree of his welcome as an honorary Farnsworth.

Because she had made him—a totally unrelated person with no claim on anyone's affection or purse—into her brother, she had also made him her slave. He'd hidden his devotion behind gruff words and horseplay, but it was there, as much a part of him as his brown eyes and sun-streaked brown hair. Anything that happened to Caroline, anything that hurt her, was his responsibility.

Rory stood apart, dismissing one agitated passenger after another as the train disgorged them, his eyes scanning each new face that appeared at the top of the steps. Finally, he could stand the tension no longer. He pushed forward, searching for someone in authority.

The people at the foot of the steps were anything but authority figures. One woman wept, the other woman looked dazed and crumpled. The man was little more composed.

"I'm looking for Miss Farnsworth," he said to them all.

The man and the weeping woman folded in on each other, leaving the smaller woman to answer Rory. He drew her aside gently, hoping she would hold up better alone.

"What happened?"

"They took her away," she began in a wavering voice. "She wouldn't give up her watch and . . . the one with the bag and the . . . gun . . . well, he took a fancy to her."

Rory realized he was crushing the poor woman's arm when she cringed from his grip and tried to break away. "I'm sorry," he offered quickly. "Go on."

"She fought him something fierce and I . . . tried to help." She caught her breath and hurried on with the story. "That one pushed me down and dragged her away. None of the men would go after her. Not even the railroad men! They didn't have horses, they said," she finished scornfully.

"Was she the only one taken?"

16

"I believe so, but I don't know about the trainmen."

"How many robbers were there?"

"The conductor told me six, but he may have been exaggerating. I saw two in our car."

"There had to have been more up front," Rory said, thinking aloud. To the lady he called out, "Thank you!" as he sprinted away.

"You go after her, young man!" she yelled after him. "And good luck!"

Rory learned nothing more from any of the men. By the time Zeb joined him he was beginning to appreciate Baltimore Blackie's desire for vengeance against the ineptitude of everyone connected with the railroad.

None of the crew had thought to pursue the kidnappers or even to mark the railroad bed to indicate where the incident had occurred. They agreed to a man that the gang had ridden back along the tracks toward Kinsley, the previous stop, but most also assured him that pursuit was impossible.

With the Arkansas River on one side of the rails and the trackless plain on the other, no one, they vowed fervently, "not even an Injun," could trace their escape. Having confirmed that the culprit was indeed Baltimore Blackie, they were content to leave the matter in the hands of the law and go on, excited by their own harmless brush with danger.

Rory took possession of Caroline's baggage, storing it with the stationmaster while Zeb went to get horses and supplies. Impossible or not, he and Zeb would find Caroline or die trying. He wasn't much of a tracker, and there was truth to the men's assessment that the river in particular complicated their task.

He took comfort from the fact that the men had gone back along the tracks instead of heading for the river. It told Rory they didn't expect to be pursued. Perhaps they would be cocky and leave an easy trail. They were, after all, old hands at stopping this railroad line. By now they knew what to expect. They had never before abducted a passenger, but they probably didn't mean to keep her long.

A muscle twitched in Rory's clenched jaw at the unwelcome thought. He told himself the same thing he'd been

17

saying all along: Caroline was smart. She would be safe.

He didn't listen to the other voice in his head, the one that said she hadn't been smart enough to give up the watch in the first place and stay out of trouble altogether.

But that was Caroline, brave and foolish and clever and . . .

Damn it, God, he half-prayed, half-threatened, completely unaware of either irreverence or irony, *keep her safe until I can get my hands on her!*

Chapter Three

Nila Jasper had saved her stop at Hannah Farnsworth's for last. *The best for last,* she said to herself, getting down from the buggy with a pleased smile. She was already awash in tea from her other visits, but even another cup would not be amiss with a good friend like Hannah.

Young Lincoln Farnsworth came running to lead her horse away. He gave her an engaging grin with his greeting. A tall boy for his eight years, he reminded Nila of her son Ted at the same age. Of course, Ted had her dark coloring just as Lincoln had his mother's red hair, thereby earning his knickname of Rusty, but Nila, who liked to see parallels between the Farnsworths and Jaspers, saw this as another link joining their two families.

"I'll rub her down good for you, Mrs. Jasper," Rusty promised, looking over the horse with a knowing eye. "You must have driven a long way."

"I did," she told him. "I've been to all the neighbors today, and this is my last stop. I came to tell your mother that we're having a party next week."

"Oh, boy!" Rusty launched himself straight up into the air, startling the mare. Fortunately, she was too tired to bolt, for she did have a tendency to be difficult.

Here in New Mexico, parties were called fiestas or sometimes even fandangos, but Nila couldn't bring herself to use those terms. Let others take up the native customs. She was from New England, and blending in was not her role. Still, she enjoyed sociability and laughed to see Rusty's reaction. Whatever it was called, a party out here was an occasion for the whole family, and Rusty would be as much their guest as his parents.

The door opened to her before she could raise her hand to

knock. She smiled at Maria, the daughter of Hannah's housekeeper, Lupe Martinez, as Hannah herself came to the foyer with outstretched arms. "Nila! How wonderful to see you!" Hannah did nothing by halves. Her greeting was as warm as the fiery highlights in her rich auburn hair. "What brings you out in this heat? Something happy, I can see."

"Happy indeed," she laughed. "I've come to invite you all to a party."

"A party!"

Her mother's words brought Abby Farnsworth running to her side. Usually a bit shy at only six years old, Abby let herself be lifted into Nila's arms in her excitement.

"For that we'll have to have some lemonade," Hannah said, turning back to address Lupe with her suggestion. But Lupe had already faded away to the kitchen, anticipating the request with her usual efficiency.

"I'll take care if it," Maria said, stepping forward.

Hannah didn't smile in response. Instead she suggested with just a touch of reproof, "Perhaps you could take Abby so Mrs. Jasper can sit down and rest."

Maria moved as if to take the child, who only hugged Nila closer, to no one's surprise. Although Lupe Martinez was a treasure in every way, her daughter, recently returned to the Farnsworths after the death of her supposed husband, was her mother's complete opposite. Except for her sloe-eyed beauty, which was in reality another problem for everyone around her, Maria had little to recommend her. She was irresponsible and possibly unkind to Hannah's children, prone to pushing herself forward at every turn, looking for attention.

Knowing all that, Nila hugged Abby back and simply carried her along to the cool, spacious parlor. "Nonsense, Hannah," she scolded. "Would you reward my invitation by denying me a chance to cuddle this beautiful little girl?"

"Not when I know what a frustrated grandmother you are," Hannah teased in return.

"Oh, please. First we have to find a wife for Ted."

Hannah led her friend to the sofa, giving her a wide smile.

"I'm sure he has but to ask and any young woman would leap to accept him, Nila. He's just the handsomest young man."

Nila accepted the compliment, knowing it was sincere. Still, she wondered if Hannah would want her stepdaughter Caroline to accept Ted in marriage.

That was the match her husband wanted. It was, in fact, the reason Dwight had proposed to celebrate their wedding anniversary with this party. He certainly wasn't sentimental about their marriage, and it wasn't sentiment that made him eager for Ted to marry Caroline.

Dwight looked at marriage through the eyes of a feudal prince. He wanted to forge an empire. When Frank and Ellen Colby gave up ranching, which they were sure to do any time, Dwight would buy their acreage. But in the meantime, why shouldn't Ted, who was overdue to settle down, marry Jake Farnsworth's daughter and join the two most prosperous ranches in the area into one? Especially since Jake was no longer well?

The marriage would serve all their needs perfectly. Ted and Caroline were well suited, both attractive and young. Jake, who doted absurdly — in Dwight's opinion — on Caroline, would bind her to his side and to the land they both loved. Married to Ted, she would stay in New Mexico.

Jake would also gain the help he needed managing the ranch. In Ted's name and through his son, Dwight would extend aid unstintingly, all the while cleverly concealing that fact from Jake. Although Nila didn't doubt Jake's intelligence, she above all others knew how wily Dwight could be when he wanted something. And Jake still suffered from his accident. He was thin and weak. His need and Caroline's timely return played perfectly into Dwight's hands.

Nila worried that Dwight oversimplified the case, as he did sometimes in the grip of great desire. There were two drawbacks Nila could think of. Rory Talmage was one. He wasn't Jake's son, but he was treated like one. Where did he fit into the inheritance picture? He seemed not to have an avid interest in Renegade Ranch, yet that could easily change. What if it did? Would Jake make him an heir?

Then there was Rusty Farnsworth, Jake's own son. He was only eight. Even if Rory never became Jake's heir, Rusty would be.

Typically, Dwight preferred to see complications as challenges. He had overlooked facts not to his liking before and doubtless would again. Nila would not thwart his will in this instance, because it fit so well with her own, and probably with Ted's too. Caroline had gone east soon after they had moved to the ranch abutting Farnsworth's southern acres, but Ted had his father's eye for a lovely face. He could not have forgotten her beauty and charm.

"The party will be next week, on Saturday," she said, putting aside all of her tiresome thoughts for a time.

"How perfect!" Hannah exclaimed. "Caroline will be home again by then, and we'll all be in the mood to celebrate."

"That's what we'll do, then." She couldn't tell Hannah that that was Dwight's true reason for the party, but it was. Instead, she said, "It's our thirtieth anniversary on the following Wednesday."

Hannah's eyes widened. "Thirty years. Oh, my. How lucky you are to have had so many years together. I hope Jake and I have as many." Then she laughed, her expression still clouded by the worry that never left her lately. "No, to be honest with you, I'm terribly greedy. I want at least a hundred."

"I'm sure you'll have them, then, my dear." She didn't tell Hannah that her thirty years already felt like a hundred. Hannah and her Jake had that rare relationship, a true love match. She could never believe what life was like for others. "When do you expect Caroline home?"

"Rory is joining the train at Dodge City today," she answered with glowing eyes. "I've been thinking of them all day. He and Zeb had business in Ellsworth, Kansas, so they rode from there to meet her. You can imagine how excited Jake is. It's been so long."

"Over two years at least, isn't it?" Nila asked. "She left

22

after we first moved here."

"She did, but it's been more than three years. She kept putting off going east to school because she loves the ranch so much. Of course, she also loves books, so when we insisted, she was willing enough to go. Then her grandmother in Pennsylvania fell and broke her hip. She wanted to help, especially since she had been spending her vacations with them rather than make the long trip back and forth here every summer. We thought that might be dangerous. Then, too, we were afraid if she came all this way home she'd want to stay."

"And you'd want her to stay," Nila added gently.

"Yes. You know me so well, Nila. She's too bright not to get a good education, but we're selfish enough to want her with us. Having made the break once, we were afraid we'd never be able to do it again."

"It was good of her to nurse her grandmother."

"I'm sure it was hard. Mrs. Lunig was a gruff woman, but if she loved anyone it was Caroline. And they cared for her while Jake served in the army. Caroline felt the obligation, and we were proud that she did her duty."

"There was no one else to help?"

"Neighbors and friends, of course. It's well-settled country there, and everyone was good to them. Her grandfather helped," Hannah said softly. "But when Martha died, he had no will to live at all. I think that bothered Caroline most. He just gave up."

"Some couples are like that," Nila said. "My parents did it the other way around. My mother faded away after my father died."

"That I can understand," Hannah said soberly. Then she forced herself to laugh. "My, aren't we cheerful! One would think you'd brought us bad news instead of an invitation to a party!"

Maria brought their lemonade and served it with an obsequious smile for Nila. She frowned, trying to think why Maria was paying her court when Hannah wasn't looking. The smile was definitely for her, not for Abby, whose

23

attention was on the tray of cookies before them.

"What can we do to help you?" Hannah was asking.

"Help me?" Nila echoed, seeking to bring her mind to task. "You'll be guests, my dear. It's your job to look lovely and smile and dance with your handsome husband — especially now that he's well again," she said, falling back upon years of social conditioning to buy herself time to think.

Then it came to her. Maria was interested in *Ted*.

She took a sip from her glass and put it down, focusing intently on Maria while pretending not to see her. "Perhaps there is something," she began hesitantly, with a quick glance to Hannah.

"Anything at all."

"Perhaps Maria could help with the food. Not the cooking, of course. Just serving."

Busy policing Abby's cookie, Hannah answered without knowing that Maria still lingered behind her. "I'd have to ask her, of course, but I can't think why she'd mind."

Nila watched Maria's expressive face go carefully blank and inward-looking. *Curious.* She made a great show of noticing the young woman's presence and said to her, "Would you be willing to help out, Maria? We'd be happy to pay you for your time."

"Of course, Mrs. Jasper," Maria said. "I'd enjoy that."

"Thank you. Perhaps you could come for a while the day before as well. I know we'll have a lot to do."

Maria's slightly downcast gaze as she departed could not hide her flushed look of triumph from Nila, who was left trying to figure out what it meant. She cut her visit as short as courtesy permitted in order to think it out.

Maria had been back for several weeks now, and Ted, who was no saint, could have been bedding her for most of that time. If that was so, it would have to end. She would have to find out what was between them. When Maria came to help, Nila would see that the girl had enough rope to hang herself. Ted's courtship of Caroline couldn't afford to be cumbered by an embarrassing relationship with a maid in her own household. No woman would put up with a situation like

24

that!

Nila would handle this for Ted and pray that it was the last time. She had no illusions about Ted, God knew, but oh, she did have hopes. And no little piece of dirt like Maria Martinez was going to get in her way.

Chapter Four

"What's your name, girl?"

Caroline opened her eyes, then shut them quickly. Her head hurt, especially her jaw, and the low rays of the sun glared into her eyes. She moved her tongue cautiously along her teeth. Her mouth was dry, but her teeth were still intact.

She gave an anguished cry as rough hands hauled her into a sitting position and propped her against a tree. She clutched her head and bent forward to rest it on her knees. Now everything hurt!

"Come on, honey," the soft voice urged. "What's your name?"

Without looking she knew this was the man in black, not Walt. Walt had slugged her, but this one was no prince either.

He went on to prove it. "You're a well-dressed young lady, still wearing your precious gold watch, I might add. Who's waiting for you at the station right now? Somebody special? Somebody rich enough to buy you back?"

With names jumbling through her aching head—Rory, Papa, Hannah's Uncle Simon—as her mind responded to his questions, Caroline was glad she hadn't been able to answer him at first. What if she'd told him her name? Would he hold Papa up for ransom? He was far away, but the train went to Santa Fe. And if he ever found out she was connected to Hannah's Uncle Simon . . .

She had to think.

"There are half a dozen men waiting to find out what to call you, honey. So unless you want them to practice whispering sweet nothings in your pretty little ear, I suggest you tell me your name."

Lifting her head slowly, Caroline looked at her tormentor's face. It was stubbled with dark hair and seamed around the eyes and mouth with lines put there by years of hard outdoor living. He was as old as her father, but not as lean and muscular. Not as tall, either. It had probably been years since he'd worked at anything. It wasn't a soft face, though. All his softness was in his voice, and that had been put there by an accident of birth. His eyes were cold, not really black but lacking the sparks of humor and intelligence that made brown eyes like Hannah's and Rory's warm.

Fearful of his reaction to her probing stare, she made her eyes waver and shook her head as if to clear it. It wasn't all an act. She had seen two of everything earlier. She wet her lips and croaked, "Twins?"

He laughed the way he had on the train, and she revised her opinion of his humor. It was there, but in a twisted form. He held up two fingers and asked, "How many?"

She blinked and said, "Two."

"Now your name, little princess."

She was prepared now. "Cathleen Farrell."

"Where were you headed, little Cathleen?"

Dodge City was too close. He couldn't think her unprotected, but he had to feel safe from immediate pursuit. "I was going to Sargent." That was at least a stop or two beyond Dodge City, Caroline was sure.

"All the way from where?"

She didn't trust his soft questions a bit, but pretending to seemed a wise choice. "I lived in Pennsylvania — Hanford, Pennsylvania. It's near Gettysburg. I went to school in Philadelphia until my grandparents got sick. They . . . died; Gramma first, then Grampa. The watch was his and . . . I just couldn't bear to part with it." It was easy to give in to the pain in her stomach from lying over the horse and the pain in her head from hanging unconscious upside down that way. Her eyes filled with tears.

"Who was meeting you in Sargent?"

Not her father. Rory. But why? How? "I . . . answered

27

an ad. . . ."

His laugh rang out, full-bodied now.

Pretending offense, Caroline didn't go on.

"A mail-order bride? Is that what we've got here?"

"We've corresponded extensively," she said stiffly. "He's a fine, upstanding gentleman."

"Out in *Sargent,* Kansas?" Hilarity overtook him again.

"He lives in Colorado. He's prospecting for silver. Very successfully, I'm sure."

He rocked back and forth while she fed his amusement with maidenly outrage. "How old is this geezer?" he wheezed, wiping at his eyes with the back of his hand.

"He's twenty-eight years old, sir, and a fine-looking man."

"Sure he is. He's handsome as a prince, I reckon."

"He is," she insisted, sure that if she were really in Cathleen Farrell's desperate shoes she would defend her choice with all her might. "He has light brown hair and brown eyes and stands two inches above six feet," she said proudly, describing Rory.

"I suppose he told you that."

"He told me his height, but as to the other, I have his picture for proof."

"Let's see it," he demanded, still laughing at her.

"It's in my trunk."

"And that's back on the train. Of course." His laughter had ebbed away, but he wasn't willing to leave such an amusing subject behind. "Well, that's a damn shame, Cathleen honey. I sure would like to get a look at this guy."

"When he finds out I've been taken from the train, perhaps you will see him. He won't be happy about this!"

Her words restored his humor. "I'm shaking in my boots, little miss prim."

He was getting to his feet to leave her. Caroline grabbed his hand with no idea what she was going to say. She didn't like or trust him, but he hadn't harmed her yet, and he could have. He was the only one standing between her and all the other men, or even between her and Walt, who

28

seemed to believe he had some right to her.

"'Please, sir, whoever you are, no matter what you've done, please don't let those men . . .'"

His mouth twisted into a smile at the way she couldn't bring herself to name what the men would do to her. "Don't let them what?" he taunted.

Her eyes fell. "You know," she whispered. She could have said the word rape, but Cathleen Farrell wouldn't. She refused to give him any inkling that she wasn't completely cowed by her predicament. She needed him gullible—and on her side. "Please," she begged, looking up at him. "I can . . . cook for you all. I'm a good cook. I'll work and I won't be any trouble. I promise. Just keep the men away from me."

"Walt wasn't looking for a cook when he took you."

She bowed her head. "I know that."

He reached down for her chin and inspected her up-turned face. She had no idea what he saw, but when his hand dropped away and he growled out, "Bind up your hair, for God's sake, and don't let them see those calf eyes," she knew she'd won. A reprieve, anyway. It was up to her to make it last.

She gathered up her hair at the back of her neck, searching for pins to hold a braid there. She found three lost in the tangles. It would do.

"You'll tell them to leave me alone?"

He didn't answer, just strode off.

Blackie had the uncomfortable feeling he'd regret taking Miss Cathleen Farrell's side against his men. She wasn't the meek little maid she played, no matter how those big blue eyes swam with tears. She had guts. He wasn't forgetting that she'd slapped away a loaded gun held to her throat with fire in her eyes just to keep a ten-dollar pocket watch. She was hiding it now, but he knew it was there. He also knew how rare it was, that quality of raw courage. It was as rare as the milk white perfection of her skin. He hoped it was her skin that influenced him, not the other, but he wasn't sure. All he knew was that he'd shoot the first one of those clods who touched just one shining strand of her hair.

The men looked at him with varying degrees of intensity. They had split up the cash and valuables, bartering among themselves as they always did. He left that to them, just as they expected him to leave Caroline to them.

When he didn't speak, they grew restive, then quiet.

"She's mine."

Walt exploded. "No fair, boss! You didn't want her. I did! I saw her first!"

Thinking how much he sounded like a spoiled child, Blackie said only, "Tough. I want her now."

He looked around, testing each gaze. Only Walt's remained mutinous. It went against his grain to bargain with his men. They followed him because he was strong and smart. But he was also fair, and since fairness was important, he decided to compensate Walt for his disappointment. He offered half his cut for her and saw Walt's rebellion melt away into gratitude.

"Her name is Cathleen. She's going to cook for us." With a nod to Walt, he said, "In case the rest of you get any ideas about increasing your stake this way, let me warn you. This is it. The next fool who gets carried away by a pretty face will get himself carried off—feet first."

"What're you gonna do with her, boss?" Moon asked with sly innocence.

"Guess," came the answer from Humphrey before Blackie could speak.

He overrode their laughter, saying, "I'm going to try for ransom, I think. If I do, you'll all share."

"Gonna tie her up?" Moon asked again.

"She doesn't ride. Where's she going to go?" he asked back.

"Weren't what I meant," Moon mumbled, drawing more laughs.

Blackie shot him a cutting look and stalked off.

The trouble with making an exit from camp was that there was nowhere to go. He could check the horses or go

30

back to Cathleen. He chose the horses this time, but after a minute or two there was nothing to do but return to the men and get them busy about chores. They moved, but slowly, keeping an eye on him. He could see he'd lost face with them, but he wasn't sure whether it was because he'd kept them from Cathleen or because he'd paid Walt for her. If the latter, he was in more trouble than he wanted.

The fire was going, but no one had started supper, reminding Blackie that he'd told the men Cathleen would cook. He sent Humphrey and Moon to the river for water, while he went for Cathleen.

She was sleeping or resting with her eyes closed, her pale cheeks looking like peaches burnished by streaks of sunset. He shook her arm, and she came instantly alert, tensed and ready for combat. "We're ready for some home cooking, girl."

"Oh. Yes, of course."

He liked that. She got to her feet, shaking off his offer of assistance and finding her own balance. Her hair was tightly bound and her travel suit as neat as she could make it, the watch and chain hidden away under her clothes. He pushed away that thought—for now. "I sent for water. The rest is up to you."

Her eyes weighed him, then fell modestly. "Thank you."

Caroline concentrated on keeping her back straight as she followed her savior to the clearing. She didn't look at the men, just at the fire and the equipment waiting for her use. She had promised to cook, but short of a miracle of loaves and fishes she had to have some ingredients. She found dried beans, onions, salt, coffee, flour, some leavening powder in a tin, a can of lard, bacon and sausage. It was a start. She could cook the sausage and make biscuits. She set to work.

Once the men saw that she was competent, the weight of their attention dropped off. It never disappeared, but she didn't expect that. Not yet, anyway. Later, when her presence was taken for granted, they would forget to watch her every move. That was her goal, but first she had to win

31

their respect.

She set aside one pail of water for washing and made coffee with another after she used part of it to rinse out each pan she intended to use. She picked up the empty pail and started toward the water.

"Hey!"

She stopped and turned. "Yes?"

"Where you goin'?" It was the round-faced man who challenged her.

"To get water."

"Whadda you need more for?"

"I want to let the sediment settle out, and then I want to put beans to soak overnight. There is also need for more wash water."

"Awright. *I'll* get it, not you."

She inclined her head regally. "I'd be obliged if you did."

He took the pail, leaning menacingly close. "How obliged?"

"Not enough," she snapped.

Although the lout deserved ridicule, Caroline wasn't happy that her words brought such ringing laughter. She didn't want enemies. When he returned with the full pail, she made a point of thanking him. "Shall I always ask you to fetch the water?"

"I'll go next," another volunteered.

"Thank you. I'll remember that. What is your name?"

"Humphrey, ma'am."

Ma'am. Caroline was elated. A man didn't rape a woman he called ma'am, or one he fetched water for.

The meal was only a modest success by Caroline's standards, but the men were effusive in praise of her biscuits. She took the opportunity then to ask if anyone knew how to trap rabbits.

"Why not jest shoot 'em?" the one called Moon asked.

"I know nothing about weapons," she said, taking care to look helplessly distressed. "I assumed you wouldn't want to fire them needlessly."

"Why not? You afraid we'd scare away the birds?"

32

Caroline frowned as the men laughed loudly. She had been taught to be careful and not waste valuable ammunition, but obviously these men were different. Then she remembered that Hannah refused to take any hotel room above the saloon in a western town, not because of the noise but because of the way the men discharged their guns into the ceiling at the least provocation. She was afraid one of the family would be hit by a stray bullet coming up through the floor.

When the laughter died out, Caroline said, "If the rabbits can be shot without damage to the meat, it doesn't matter to me how it's done." Then she added with a delicate shudder of distaste, "As long as I don't have to do it."

"You gonna make pets outta these rabbits we getcha?" Moon asked with a sneer.

"What I do will depend on how many you provide. I had stew in mind."

"With dumplings?"

Caroline turned to look at the new speaker, the quiet one called Ernie. He was young, perhaps younger than she, and very thin. He looked like one of the ranch hands Lupe fed double portions on the sly. "If you give me a hand dressing them, I'll make dumplings so light you'll think they're clouds," she promised.

Ernie ducked his head as if he were embarrassed to have spoken and drawn attention to himself, but he nodded, and Caroline felt she had won another ally.

Blackie watched Cathleen's conquest of his men with growing disquiet. He had meant to keep her from becoming a bone they fought over. Now he wondered if he needed to protect them from her. She was already lining them up to do her bidding like a governess with a pack of unruly boys. Except for Moon, who wasn't as tough as he wanted to be, they were falling over themselves to help her. Next they'd be checking their fingernails for grime, worried about being allowed to eat with her.

Ernie began to fashion rabbit traps out of branches and rope. An old country hand himself, Blackie knew exactly

33

what he was doing. He would have done it himself if she had given him a chance. She hadn't spoken to him since she had asked for his protection. If he didn't do something soon to assert himself, she wouldn't need him at all before long. Already he knew he couldn't rape her any more than he could have left her to Walt. Something about her, something fine, stood in his way. It was the way she talked as much as anything. All those words—rows of them as perfect as her little white teeth. It unmanned him.

Caroline forced herself to sit like a stone as soon as she had finished cleaning up after the meal. She was nervous about the night. She had slept out before as the only female among males, but this was different. She wasn't the ranch owner's cherished daughter out here. She was fair game, if not for all the men, then at least for their leader.

She wasn't the only one waiting, Blackie saw. Until Ernie got up and slipped away with his traps, no one moved from the dying fire. Blackie got up and reached down to Cathleen. "Bedtime, my dear," he said.

He had to give her credit. She didn't make a fuss. He led her to his bedroll, where they both stopped. "You can have this. I have an extra blanket. Do I have to tie your ankle to mine?"

"Tie . . . ?"

He had rattled her at last. "So you don't run away?"

"In the dark?"

He laughed. "There's a moon now and then, but you wouldn't get far."

"I wouldn't move from here," she vowed fervently.

He admired the firm way she had regained control of her tremulous voice.

"But I would like some privacy first," she said, looking around at the trees behind them. They were mostly cottonwoods, filled in with brushy alders.

"Go that way," he pointed. "Ernie's setting traps on the other side."

"Thank you."

She melted away into the brush so quietly Blackie almost

questioned that she had been there. He chuckled. She was something with her polite little thank-yous. Someone would sure as hell want her back. But a silver prospector from Colorado? How the hell could he get ransom from a guy like that?

Caroline was slowly working her way back to the clearing when she heard movement in the undergrowth off to the left. She froze, all her senses straining. The men were dangerous enough; she didn't need to face a wild animal just now.

A voice called out.

"It's me, Blackie," came the answer. "Just Ernie."

Caroline's relief was short-lived. "Just Ernie" was fine, but "Blackie"? *Baltimore Blackie?* She grabbed a tree and held on.

It couldn't be.

Thoughts and images whirled through her head, leaving her knees weak. His soft voice with its trace of the south. His age. He could indeed be Baltimore Blackie.

Caroline breathed deeply, hoping to clear her head. At least she hadn't told him her name. What would he do if he knew she was the child who long ago brought about the capture of his partner in a bank in Independence, Missouri?

It didn't bear thinking about.

All sound except the distant rush of the Arkansas River died away from Caroline. When she and Papa had left Missouri to follow the Santa Fe Trail, she had imagined that they were being followed by Kid Belasco's partner, this same Baltimore Blackie. She'd never told Papa about her half-fearful, half-excited fantasies of pursuit. He hadn't known then about the books she read. If she never returned from this misadventure, he would discover three of her most recent purchases in her trunk and know her privileged education hadn't done a thing to improve her. She still loved dime novels, the wilder the better.

She gathered her scattered wits and took a cautious step away from the sturdy tree. There was a chance—perhaps even a good one — that her imagination was running away with her again. This Blackie might not be the same one. And even if he were, he would never find out who she was. Tomorrow or the next day she would find a way to escape. He'd never know that the prim little lady he'd saved from rape was the same gun-toting girl who'd foiled a bank robbery and helped her father earn two rewards for his partner's capture. She'd be gone.

Again the bushes in front of her rustled, and again she paused.

"Cathleen?"

"Here," she answered softly, waiting where she stood.

Blackie found her clinging to a tree, too frightened to move.

"Thank goodness you found me. I heard noises and I thought it was a bear! Then I didn't know which way to go."

He took her arm and led her back to the clearing. *A bear,* he thought, careful not to laugh out loud at her. He could feel the tension that made her arm quiver like a tightly drawn bow.

She sank to the blanket with a sigh. "Thank you," she said quietly. "I was afraid I was lost."

"Not any more." He tried to keep the sympathy out of his voice. She was so much out of her element, yet so brave about it. "You could have called to me," he reminded her gruffly.

"I . . . never thought. Besides," she added, her spirit returning, "I don't know your name."

He hesitated for the merest beat of time. Then he said in a rush, "Thomas. You can call me Thomas."

Caroline heard both the pause and his following haste. Did he suspect that she knew who he was? In that split second he had made some sort of decision about her, but what was it and what did it mean? Did he already recognize her?

Reason told her he couldn't. Even if he knew the name Caroline Farnsworth, he had no way to connect it with her.

Or to connect her to the child she had been. Her picture had been on the front of the Independence newspaper, but she was different now. Only her hair was unchanged.

She covered herself with the blanket and tried to quiet the clamor in her mind. By now Rory knew she had been taken. He was on his way to rescue her. He was counting on her to remain sensible. She never doubted that she would get safely free, just as she didn't doubt Rory. Like Papa, like Hannah, like herself even, Rory was steadfast and utterly reliable. She wanted to save him from having to take on seven armed men by himself, as he would if he got to them before she escaped and started back to meet him.

Caroline knew exactly where to go and what to do. Only the opportunity to execute her plan was in doubt, but if she were patient and smart she'd have her chance. The fact that Baltimore Blackie held her—no matter how loosely—was a complication, but not an insurmountable one.

Still, her mind stuck on his identity. Thomas, he called himself. Thomas Black? She tried to recall what she had read about him. He was from Baltimore and wore black; wasn't that the whole of it? What had happened to Kid Belasco? Was he here, too?

Caroline almost cried out. She stifled the sound, but not in time to keep the man lying next to her from hearing her quickened breathing.

She was afraid of him.

Of course she was, Blackie reminded himself harshly. What's more, he wanted her to be afraid. Then why did he want to take her into his arms and comfort her? And why in hell had he told her to call him Thomas? *Thomas,* for God's sake. He hadn't been Thomas for fifteen years or more. Not since . . . Priscilla.

He heaved himself over onto his side to face away from Cathleen. She was nothing like Priscilla. Nothing. Her hair was lighter, with none of the wild curliness that had tangled around his fingers. And the way she talked, so precise and proper, was entirely different. But there was something about her voice that had made him want to hear her say his

37

real name.

She sighed softly, and the sound stole over his senses like a caress. He was no different from his men. Like them, he had been beguiled. She was small and soft in a world where everything else was rough and hard. She wasn't Priscilla — thank God — but she was soft.

And that, not her courage, made her dangerous.

Chapter Five

Caroline woke just before dawn, startled by an unfamiliar sound. As soon as her eyes opened she realized she had heard the shriek of a trapped animal. It reminded her that she would have to make rabbit stew today.

She rolled over to look at her captor. Baltimore Blackie looked younger and less menacing with his face relaxed in sleep. He wasn't really bearded, just unshaved of late, although perhaps he was growing a beard. For disguise? It wouldn't work with her. She would know him again under any circumstance.

Before she could get depressed by the thought of how much she was endangered by that fact, she slipped from the bedroll. She had taken off her jacket, skirt and petticoat under the covers, but they were wrinkled and tired-looking.

Like her father, Caroline had learned to move with a minimum of noise. She wasn't totally silent the way he was, but then she had not lived with Indians in her youth as he had. Admiration for her papa had inspired her to imitate him almost from the moment he reentered her life, when she was nine years old. Stealth and economy of motion were just two of the things she had learned from him, but they were perhaps the most useful to her now.

With her skirt held securely in one hand, Caroline made her way to the bank of the river. The railroad tracks had been following along beside the mighty Arkansas River all the way from Hutchinson, Kansas, so she was already familiar with the sight. It was different, however, at close range. She knew that it was swift, wide and powerful, and that it carried the melting snows from the mountains of Colorado to the Mississippi River, but from ground level it was awe-inspiring. Although she could swim and the sight of so much water made her long for a bath, she had no thought of trying it here. The most she hoped for was a side stream or a low place where the water had cut into the banking and perhaps formed a backwater.

Before she set off upstream, which seemed to be the most promising direction, she inspected the somewhat worn path back to the clearing. She wanted to fix the spot in her mind so she wouldn't get lost or, almost as bad, seem to be trying to escape. Villains or not, the men and their horses were still the key to her deliverance.

No matter how she tried, she couldn't be sure she would recognize the beginning of the path. It had nothing to mark it. She began to gather up stones. After a few minutes of that she got smart. Her underpetticoat was in her way, and it would make an unmistakable marker. She draped it over a bush and headed off upstream.

She had nearly decided she would have to go back when she came upon exactly what she wanted. It was both a small tributary stream and a marshy section of land. Unlike the steeply cut banks of the main river, the sides here were low and green. She couldn't bathe, but she could wash and refresh herself. She removed her shoes and stockings and waded into the silty muck.

But it wasn't pleasant underfoot, and the thought of snakes soon sent her back to firm ground. As she picked her way along she noticed the profusion of dandelions. Although it was late and many were quite mature, she picked the smallest she could find, delighted to have greenery for her stew. They might taste bitter, but men who lived on beans and greasy meat would appreciate the healthful change. Or they would if she told them they should. Surely some of them had once had mothers who served them greens every spring for their well-being.

She had picked her skirt almost full of dandelions when she spotted another plant among the weeds. Boneset. Suddenly she saw a whole different set of possibilities. Thanks to Gramma Lunig, Caroline knew quite a bit about medicinal herbs. Gramma had a home remedy for everything that

40

could ail a body.

Caroline picked the distinctive plant and looked around for more. Now that she had her eyes open, they were everywhere, those double lance-shaped leaves so cleverly joined at the base to look as if the stalk pierced the center of a single leaf. She was not mistaken. It was boneset.

Here was her opportunity to get away from the men today.

She picked the plants greedily, hand over hand, while stooping awkwardly so her skirt could hold the harvest. An effusion of boneset applied externally could soothe and heal broken skin, and even help bones mend, according to Gramma's firm belief. Internally, in the quantity she would use, it could all but turn a body inside out. It wouldn't kill, of course; it would just make the person wish he could die and get it over with. It was both an emetic and a laxative, offering the body a total, thoroughly debilitating purge.

She would have to use every onion she could get her hands on to disguise the bitter taste of the boneset and hope the men would accept her story that the dandelions caused it. Then, when the men were too sick to pay attention to her, she would ride away.

With her mind awhirl with her plans, she almost overlooked another plant along the bank. This one was totally benign, but like the dandelion, its presence would help disguise the boneset. It was watercress. Ordinarily she would not add it to a stew, but today she would.

Stopping only long enough to put on stockings and shoes, Caroline raced back along the river, retracing her steps. She went with no particular care because she knew her petticoat was an obvious marker, so when the dark shape of a man stepped from the trees into her path, she screamed in surprise. The sound, to her ears so like the trapped animal's cry earlier, was quickly cut off as Moon clapped his hand over her mouth. He held her until she went limp to indicate that she wouldn't struggle.

As long as Caroline retained possession of her cupped skirt and the greens that were to be her salvation, nothing

41

could frighten her. She was so confident she gave no thought to her isolation or to Moon's obvious hostility. She smiled at him the way she had at Rory when he had tried to frighten her by jumping out at her on the ranch.

"You startled me," she acknowledged, her relief slipping into mild embarrassment as she noticed that he held her petticoat. She reached out for it. "I was afraid I wouldn't be able to find the path back to camp without a marker. This was the best I could think of."

"Where'd you go?" Moon demanded.

"Just upstream a way, and it's a good thing I did. I found some greens to put in the rabbit stew—dandelions, watercress and thoroughwort." The last was another name for boneset, one less common, on the off chance that one of the men knew about its medicinal properties. Whatever she did, she was going to be completely open about it.

His scowl deepened. "What for?"

She laughed. "Why, to make the stew better. The dandelions may taste a little bit *strong*," she allowed, choosing an innocent word, "but they're good for you. Didn't your mother tell you to eat your vegetables?"

She could feel his resentment beating at her like heat from a fire. It was part frustration that she didn't cower from him and part confusion. Most of it, however, was a dangerous mix of lust and thwarted will. Her choice of defense, refusing to acknowledge what he wanted, wasn't going to work much longer, she knew, so she decided to enlist his aid as a guide.

She got out only one word—"why"—before he hauled her against him into a rough embrace. The odor of his unwashed body and the slide of his open, slack mouth on her face disgusted Caroline. She stiffened, shoving against him with her trapped hands, trying to get free. He turned her around and threw her to the ground, and for the first time Caroline worried more about herself than her spilled plants. She tried to get up but couldn't, tried to roll free but was caught by her skirt. She managed a small, breathless cry before the round face that gave Moon his name blotted out

42

everything else.

In trying to roll away, she had twisted her skirt around her thrashing legs so tightly that he was as hindered as she was. He yanked and she kicked, pulling on his arms and digging him as much as she could with her nails, but neither of them had any success.

Then, suddenly, she was free.

She looked up in surprise to see Moon fly past her, propelled by a fist to his jaw. He fell beyond her, momentarily stunned.

Ernie reached down to help her up, and she took his hand, grateful that he was her rescuer.

But while she was getting to her feet, so was Moon. He butted Ernie's back, sending his slighter form sprawling. She wanted to help Ernie, but without a weapon she had no way. She looked for a rock or a sturdy stick while the men were busy. Ernie ran blindly at Moon, who sidestepped him neatly, then chopped him on the back of the head as he went past. By then Caroline was armed. It was only a clumsy length of wood, but it was something. She faced off against Moon, crouched low so she could dive to either side if he ran at her.

He did nothing. An explosion of gunfire startled both of them into looking up.

"What the hell is going on here?" Blackie demanded. He had shot into the air but held his gun at the ready.

"He attacked me—"

"She was running away—"

"One at a time!" Blackie bellowed.

Ernie groaned and tried to move.

Caroline put down her cudgel and straightened up. She was safe. No matter what Moon said, she had Ernie to back up her side. "He's hurt," she said, pointing out Ernie.

"Let's hear it," Blackie said. The dark red color had drained from his face, making him less fearsome. "Moon?"

Caroline, all ready to tell her version, shut her mouth with an audible snap of her teeth. Of course the men would stick together, she fumed. How could she have expected otherwise?

"She sneaked outta camp this morning. I seen her and followed. She was tryin' to escape." He shot her a malevolent glare. "When I stopped her she started undressin'. I was jest givin' her what she wanted!" He bent to retrieve Caroline's petticoat and handed it to Blackie with a flourish, the damning evidence to confirm his story.

"That's nonsense," Caroline retorted. "I left the petticoat to mark the path back to camp so I wouldn't lose my way again. I went upstream to wash and stayed to gather greens for dinner. He made me drop them!"

"And that's it?" Blackie asked. "You're fighting over dropped greens?"

Caroline flushed. "Of course not. He attacked me. I told you that. That's when I dropped them out of my skirt. Ernie tried to save me and ended up getting the worst of it."

Blackie was hard put to keep a straight face. He knew Moon had been trying to rape Cathleen, yet all she could talk about was her salad and Ernie! "Is it too much to hope that you can rescue your salad?"

Caroline moved past both men, giving Moon as especially wide margin, and found the spot where she'd dropped the greens. "They're still here." She knelt to retrieve them, adding happily, "And they didn't even get trampled."

"I'm so relieved."

Caroline ignored his sarcasm and concentrated on reclaiming every dropped sprig from her collection. She followed along behind when Blackie ordered Moon to help support Ernie on the way back, wishing she could spare some of the boneset for Ernie's head. A poultice would help him, but she didn't dare reveal her knowledge of herbs.

Anyway, it was absurd to help him now, when she was going to try to make him sick as soon as she could. The whole business was insane. She was grateful to Ernie and she would try to help him if she could, but as long as he was part of Blackie's gang he was as much her enemy as Moon.

She *would* escape. Nothing, not even her sympathy from someone who had helped her, would keep her from succeeding.

The rest of the morning was anticlimactic. Caroline steeped her precious greens, both the virulent and the innocent, in water. Then she browned the meat of the rabbits over the coals as fast as the men — except Ernie, who was still woozy, and Moon, who was sulking — could skin them for her. Even Blackie helped.

When the stew was assembled and bubbling slowly over the small fire, she sat back on her heels to rest. "Are you all right?" Blackie asked.

She was, but she didn't say so. She winced and looked distressed. Once the men started getting sick, they would immediately suspect her of poisoning them. Being sick first seemed her best defense. It would also give her a way to avoid having to eat the doctored food herself.

"My stomach aches, but I'll be all right."

"Why don't you go lie down? You've had a busy morning."

"Perhaps I will," she said, giving him a brave little smile.

Blackie watched her go. Her hair had fallen into wisps around her face, making her look lovelier than usual. Because of her and her damned stew, he had already changed his plans for the day once. Now he was looking for another way to please her. He'd meant to ride on at daybreak, but with Ernie hurt and the men salivating over her cooking, he hadn't dared give the order to move for fear no one would have gone. It was absurd.

They were probably safe enough right where they were, but he didn't like staying so close to the scene. No one had pursued them before, and probably no one was coming this time, either. Still, he didn't like it.

He didn't like the fight between Ernie and Moon, either. The fact was, Cathleen was a problem. Just her presence created distractions and the possibility of further clashes. He had to get rid of her, and soon.

But how? They couldn't turn her loose out here, miles from civilization. She'd never survive. For all her courage, just one day with them had already taken a toll on her meager strength. If they took her to a town and just released her, she'd have to appeal to the authorities for help. There could be no quicker way to make sure they were pursued again—and by people who knew everything she could tell them about his men. She had seen their faces and knew their names. She could see them all hanged.

Blackie tipped his hat over his eyes and leaned back to rest. He was tired of worrying about Cathleen Farrell. Most of all, he was tired of the way he was making too much of her. She was a problem, yes. But he knew perfectly well what to do about her. He would take her to bed, make her his, and the men wouldn't fight over her any more. What's more, then she wouldn't be able to leave. She'd be damaged goods, with no place to go. Even her silver prospector—if there was such a person—might not want a robber's cast-off doxie.

It was the best solution, perhaps the only one. So why didn't he go after her now? Why did he lie here smelling the oniony aroma of her rabbit stew, doing nothing? He dozed off rather than confront the answer.

A strange noise woke him. He sat up and reached for his gun, looking around. No one had moved. Walt was cleaning his gun on the other side of the fire. He poked his head toward the bushes and said, "It's your girlfriend, boss. Guess she's sick."

Repulsed, but trying not to show it, Blackie began to sweat. He was used to the casual vomit of drunks, but Cathleen wasn't drunk. The retching sound went on and on, all the worse for its quietness. He could imagine her struggle for composure all too well. She was too much the little lady not to feel humiliated by her body's rebellion. He felt sorry for her and panicked for himself. He had claimed her, and before his nap he'd decided to sleep with her. Did that mean he had to help her now? What if she was contagious?

A sudden thought saved him from that worry, bringing instant relief. She was a woman. That was it. She was having one of those female troubles that came and went. All women had them. It would pass, and she'd be good as new in a day or so.

46

"Ain't you gonna help her?"

Blackie confronted the accusation in Ernie's eyes and let his gaze drop away. He ignored the question to ask another. "Well, Ernie, glad to have you back with us. How's your head?"

"It hurts," came the flat answer. "But Miss Cathleen probably feels worse. Ain't you gonna help her?"

"I don't imagine there's anything anyone can do for her," he replied uncomfortably. "Most sick people just want to be left alone."

"Maybe she don't."

Blackie said nothing. What could he say? And anyway, Cathleen had grown quiet.

"If you don't help her, I will," Ernie said.

Blackie just shrugged. He wasn't going to fight for the privilege of playing nurse, and it didn't look like anyone else wanted to. His only concern was keeping peace among the men.

Ernie got up. He moved with difficulty, which only increased Blackie's amusement. What a bunch of chivalrous gentlemen they all were under the skin. It came out in different ways with each of them, but Cathleen Farrell had the key to wind each one of them up in one way or another.

Blackie flopped back down in disgust. She was making toys of his men. Maybe she'd just die of whatever ailed her. Otherwise she'd be taking over this fearless band of outlaws, sending them off to hunt and fish for her cooking pot, all thoughts of robbery forgotten.

Caroline slipped back to the bedroll she thought of as hers. She hadn't thrown up, but the effort of making the right noises had reddened her face convincingly. She closed her eyes, her arm over her forehead.

"Miss Cathleen? Can I get something for you? Some water?"

She sat up in surprise. She hadn't heard anyone approach. "Ernie?"

"It's me. Just Ernie."

"Oh, Ernie, what are you doing up? Does your head

47

hurt?"

"It's all right. Doesn't hurt half as much as your stomach does, I'll wager."

"I'll be fine, Ernie. I hope I didn't bother you."

"Let me get you a drink."

She caught his arm before he could leave. "No. Not right now."

He gave a nod of understanding. "Later, then. You rest."

"You, too. Please. Do you have a lump?"

He put his hand to the back of his head. "Don't think so. My head's pretty hard."

"Good." She smiled and sank back. "Thank you, Ernie. You're nice."

It wasn't surprising that Caroline didn't hear him leave, because he was floating ten inches above the ground from the combination of her smile and compliment.

Blackie watched him return and kept track of each visit he made to Cathleen's side thereafter. He thought of objecting but didn't. *He* wasn't going to fetch water for her, so he might as well let Ernie have the dubious pleasure. But there was no doubt that the boy believed it was a pleasure.

By the time the day was half gone Ernie had worn a path to Cathleen's blanket. She hadn't been sick again, so over his strenuous objections, she pronounced herself well enough to make dumplings for the stew. Blackie hadn't remembered her promise, but everyone else had, and no one except Ernie argued with her.

Blackie had never heard such a to-do over a meal in his life. Cathleen fussed over each man and fussed more about the stew itself, seeking reassurance that she had pleased them.

Wasn't it too salty? No, she was told. She went on and on about the dandelions being too strong until he could have choked her. Walt and Humphrey, and even Moon, fell all over themselves, trying to convince her that it was the best stew ever made. Jeeter and Brock didn't say much, but they ate their share, as did he.

Ernie, of course, watched her like a spaniel, waiting for a

48

chance to serve her in some way. He washed up and fetched extra water from the river. This time no one else volunteered. They'd all eaten too much.

Blackie looked from one to the other and decided an announcement was in order. "Tomorrow morning we're heading east, do you understand? No more of this sitting around listening to stew bubble. I'm disgusted with the lot of you." Before they could call him on the accusation, he added, "Yeah, I know I've been just as bad. Worse, probably. But no more."

He reserved his most scathing glance for Ernie and said, "Since you're so lively and eager to be *helpful,* Coogins, why don't you go check on the horses—that is, if you don't have any more housework to do?"

Caroline felt sorry for Ernie, but she didn't defend him. That would only make things worse for him.

She'd only eaten one dumpling, which had been her reason for making them. The only one of the men whose intake she hadn't been able to monitor was Ernie. He worried her. She didn't know what to make of his devotion. Was it real or not? He seemed kind, but if he was, what was he doing in a gang of outlaws? And more importantly, did he suspect something? Was he helping her or keeping an eye on her?

She had no idea how long it would take before the men got sick or, in fact, how they would react to their symptoms. She hadn't been able to separate them from their weapons. Even sick, maybe *especially* sick, they would be able to shoot. Then there was the trail to worry about. She knew to ride away from the river to find the railroad, then go upstream beside it toward Dodge City, but she couldn't stop worrying. The woods here were thick. What if she got lost?

She let out a moan of anguish, the first she had not manufactured.

"If you're going to be sick again, go back to bed," Blackie said sharply.

"I'm not going to be sick, but I'll be happy to take my unwelcome presence elsewhere." She got to her feet, pre-

49

tending affront. "Maybe I'll go for a walk," she announced, starting off with a flouncing swish of skirts she hoped looked convincingly aggrieved. With every step she expected to be called back.

She wasn't. Instead, he laughed. "Don't go too far," he called out tauntingly.

She knew the other men laughed, but she was already beyond the reach of their voices. She was looking for the horses and the way back to the railroad tracks, hoping to avoid meeting Ernie. She heard the horses first and realized Ernie was still among them. She stood quietly and watched as he took a pail from one horse and gave it to another. He talked to them constantly in the reassuring patter that horse-loving people always affect with their animals.

Ernie reminded her then of Rory with Duchess, his mare. She was too old now for anyone except Rusty to ride, yet Rory would never have her destroyed. He had brought her on the Santa Fe Trail that first time along with Papa's Victor. Victor was dead, but Caroline hoped Duchess was still back on Renegade Ranch, waiting for her to come home.

She tamped down her sudden surge of homesickness, afraid to think about home and Rory now. Thinking about her family could interfere with doing the job at hand, and comparing Ernie to Rory was ludicrous. Ernie was her enemy. He stood in the way of her freedom as much as Blackie and Moon did. She couldn't afford sympathy or sentimentality where he was concerned.

She stepped forward, determined to learn what she could about the men. Just by being here she had already discovered that the horses were kept saddled. That was probably a precaution against getting caught off-guard, but it helped her, too. She had wondered how she could saddle a horse in a hurry. Now she only had to tighten the cinch and be off.

"Can I give you a hand?"

Ernie didn't seem surprised to see her. "I'm almost done. You must be feeling better."

Caroline could see no suspicion in his manner, but his expression was so bland she couldn't be sure. "Yes, I seem to

50

be recovering."

"Blackie don't mind you being here?"

"I said I was going for a walk. All he said was don't go too far," she answered, watching him unobtrusively. She petted a horse, half her mind occupied with picking the one she would ride. "Why do they call him Blackie, do you know? Is his name Thomas Black?"

Ernie stopped in the act of picking out a horse's shoe and stared at her. "Thomas? He told you his name is Thomas?"

"Isn't it? It's what he told me to call him."

Ernie laughed, and the tight lines in his face relaxed. He looked years younger that way, making Caroline realize that only his gangliness had betrayed his youth before. His face had been old as well as watchful and closed. Now he looked even more like Rory, but Rory as she had first met him, when he was sixteen. That was the Rory she loved best. Having been away for three years, she had no idea what to expect of the man he had become in her absence.

"How old are you, Ernie?"

He stopped laughing. "Old enough."

"To do what?"

He turned away and bent to the horse's hoof again.

"You didn't answer my question."

"You shouldn't ask," he sent back over his shoulder.

"I'm sorry. It's just that you don't seem like the others."

She hoped he would take up her invitation to explain himself. When he didn't, she turned away and explored the other side of the woods. She didn't go far for fear that Blackie or Moon would investigate her whereabouts and become suspicious.

As she got to the edge of the clearing she heard the first sounds of someone being sick in the bushes. After a split second of elation, she was overcome by fear. She didn't know what to do. If it was Blackie, she should offer sympathy. If it was someone else, she could just go to her own bedroll and ignore it.

She walked to the blanket and discovered Blackie there. His face was drawn, his eyes closed in misery. She went closer, moving cautiously. His brow was coated with sweat and he didn't move, not even to open his eyes.

"Blackie?" She bent to touch his shoulder. "Can I help you?"

He groaned and clutched at his stomach.

Caroline wet her dry lips and reached for his gun belt, saying softly, "You'll feel more comfortable without this." Deftly, she undid the belt just in time as another spasm struck him. If she hadn't been there, she was sure he'd have been sick right there, but his pride drove him to roll over and crawl away to the nearest brush. He didn't get far, just far enough to give Caroline time to take his guns from the holster. She didn't take the belt, although it would have been useful to her. She was afraid he would miss it.

She looked around the clearing furtively, afraid someone had seen her. There was no one. She held the guns in the folds of her skirt, one to a side, and walked out of the clearing. She didn't take the direct route to the horses, but circled around to avoid the men, including Ernie. She prayed that he had finished there and gone back to camp. She didn't want to have to confront him.

She was in luck.

She went directly to the horse she had chosen and took up the reins. Like most western horses, these had been trained to stay pretty much in place as long as their reins trailed the ground. The horse followed as she pulled it over to a fallen tree she could use as a mounting stool. She put the guns on the ground, tightened the cinch and lowered the stirrups. Already she regretted leaving Blackie's gunbelt. Getting up astride was awkward enough in a skirt without having to hold two guns at the same time.

She was busy tucking her hoisted skirts around her legs when Ernie materialized at the head of her horse. She lifted the gun she hadn't yet secured into a loop of her skirt, aiming it directly at his chest.

"Stand aside, Ernie. I don't want to shoot you, but I will. I'm not as helpless as I look." She was proud that her voice didn't quaver. He had startled and frightened her.

"I know you're not, Miss Cathleen." He held his hands up and showed his spread palms in a gesture of openness. "I want to go with you."

"I don't want you."

"Then you might as well shoot me now. Once you're gone the others will just kill me. They'll think I helped you."

She hadn't thought of that. "Just pretend you're sick, too."

"I can help you. You need me."

She shook her head. "How do I know you won't try to bring me back here?"

"I suppose you don't, but I won't. I wouldn't."

Caroline was torn. She wanted to trust him. Part of her did. But it wasn't smart. She didn't have time to think out all the pros and cons right now. "Stand aside."

He stepped away, following her order even as his eyes pleaded for understanding. "You don't want to leave them all these horses," he said. "They could follow us."

She didn't know if it was the word us, or the sense of his suggestion that clinched it for her. She put the gun between her leg and the saddle. "Do it, then," she said, "And hurry."

She wheeled the horse toward the woods, leaving Ernie to catch up. When he did, he was pulling a string of five horses behind him. That wasn't all the horses, but their loss would put a serious crimp in the men's pursuit of them.

He grinned broadly at her look of astonishment. "The other horses will come along part of the way," he yelled. "They're used to being together. It'll take 'em a good while to catch even one."

Caroline grinned back at him from her position low on the horse's neck. She didn't try to talk to him until they were clear of the woods. Then she said, "Thank you, Ernie. I hope I haven't made a mistake by trusting you."

"You haven't. You're the first person to treat me decent in years. I'll never let you down."

The sound of their hoofbeats carried as a vibration along the ground under Baltimore Blackie. He rolled over to reach for his guns and found the empty belt. He knew then that they weren't under attack. The attack was already over.

He cursed, remembering Cathleen's soft hand disarming him literally as she already had figuratively. His stomach muscles cramped again, and he folded his arms over himself, rocking in misery.

Sneaky little bitch. He brushed sweat from his eyes with the back of his hand and vowed that Cathleen Farrell hadn't see the last of him. Somehow, some way, he'd find her again and make her pay for this.

As another wave of nausea hit him, he thought of her voice, so soft, so treacherous. Then he remembered something else about her voice. He had never heard her call him Thomas.

Chapter Six

Rory took off his hat to mop his face. His shadow stretched out before him, an ever-lengthening stain on the ground that seemed to measure his defeat. Just when he thought they'd found the trail, it petered off into nothing. Now he realized the first one they'd followed had been cattle, not horses. Probably this was, too.

Zeb came out of the stand of trees and shook his head. "There's a camp, but it's old. At least a week."

They rode back to the railroad bed without speaking. They had already said everything there was to say. Zeb advocated pushing on to Kinsley, while Rory refused to bypass a single thicket by the river he judged big enough to conceal his quarry. His way made for slow going. He was frustrated and angry, all the more so for his suspicion that he was wrong. He hated the thought of being wrong, and with Caroline's life at risk . . .

Zeb tried to comfort him with assurances that Caroline was tough, but Rory feared that quality in her more than any other. She had always overestimated her own strength, measuring herself against the whipcord toughness of the lowliest ranch hand, sure she was as capable. But she had been away for three years. Would she remember that? Take it into account? Her performance on the train told him no.

After another half mile, the tracks they were following veered off toward cover once again, and Zeb looked back in question. It didn't look promising, but Rory kneed the horse forward, taking the lead this time. He had barely broken into the shade when he heard something different. He eliminated thunder and rapids in the river before he could admit what it was. Horses.

Zeb heard it, too, and turned back.

55

Even before the second rider registered on Rory he was racing to meet their approach. He had seen that flash of pale hair in the sunlight too many times not to know Caroline. She saw him almost immediately and took off at a gallop from her course parallel to the tracks. Zeb kept one eye on their near collision while he headed off the other rider, stopping him at the tracks.

"I knew you'd come!" Caroline exulted. She sat up in the stirrups, leaning toward him with her eyes shining, ready to launch herself at Rory the way she always had. He would catch her with a careless hug and sit her in front of him to ride for a while that way. She reached out, but her feet never left the stirrups.

He took her hands in his and held them. His grin was broad and mocking, warm as the Kansas sun on their shoulders, but the look in his eyes held her off instead of drawing her close. "So you still need me to get you out of trouble after all this time. Didn't you learn anything back east?"

"Do I look like I'm in trouble?" She grinned back at him, pulling one hand free to indicate her liberated state in a broad sweep of her arm.

"You are if you've taken up horse thievery."

Caroline saw that she hadn't imagined that hint of frost in Rory. She sat back and stared, cutting off the laugh of relief that was bubbling its way up into her throat.

"That was Ernie's idea," she confessed, suddenly almost ashamed that she couldn't seem to let go of his hand or stop devouring his face with her eyes. He was still Rory, her brother and her friend, but he was also different somehow. He was older. A man now.

Was that it?

Well, of course. And he was obviously disappointed in her. After three years Rory expected adult behavior from her, not another childish escapade like this. Besides, she had frightened him. Like Papa, he was always at his most forbidding in relief. Maybe all men were.

Relieved herself now that she had thought it all out, she

smiled at him again.

In the few seconds it had taken Caroline to sort through her quicksilver feelings and impressions, Rory's gaze had moved past her to come to rest on Ernie. "I didn't know anyone else was taken from the train," he said.

Puzzled, Caroline followed his gaze and saw not Ernie, but Zeb. She gave a happy cry and galloped off to him.

Here was the unconditional welcome she had not received from Rory. Zeb hugged her hard enough to break ribs, his button black eyes wet with tears he would never admit to even if he were drowning in them.

"Zeb, oh, Zeb! I'm so glad to see you. I never dreamed you'd be here, too."

"Someone had to come along to help Rory haul you outta trouble."

Caroline groaned and laughed at the same time. "Don't remind me!" She pulled her horse back from Zeb's skittish mount, feasting her eyes on this tough little man who was as much her unfailing friend as he was her father's. Her horse bumped another, setting off a chain reaction that recalled Ernie to her attention.

"Zeb, this is Ernie." She presented him proudly in spite of the fact that she didn't know his last name. "He helped me over and over," she added, giving all the explanation Zeb would require.

Ernie sat forward to clasp Zeb's hand. "Name's Coogins."

Caroline was pleased with him, but she wasn't looking forward to explaining him to Rory, particularly his membership in Blackie's gang. She had already determined that she wouldn't permit him to be turned over to the law. Rory would say he had only acted opportunistically in helping her. She knew better. Defending her had cost him a terrible beating. Now she would defend him.

Sensing Rory behind her, Caroline presented him economically. "Ernie, this is my brother, Rory Talmage. Rory, the man who helped me, Ernie Coogins."

They didn't shake hands, and Caroline knew it wasn't

because of the horses and the distance between them. Ernie did touch his hat, however, so she was satisfied. She had no idea of what Rory did. She didn't look to see.

Then she turned to him. "Perhaps we should go," she said. "I don't think we'll be followed right away, but it would be safer."

"How many are there?"

"Six, but they haven't many horses—if they can catch the ones Ernie left."

She flashed him a bright smile, which he answered with a shy grin. "You mean if they can even walk."

Her laugh rang out, as silvery as her hair in the sunlight. Rory's glower deepened. "What happened?" he asked.

"Let's just ride," Caroline countered. She didn't like taking over, but she was afraid to linger. Rory wasn't himself yet, and she was beginning to wonder if he ever would be again. She needed time as much as he did, time to come to grips with the way he had changed.

She didn't wait for confirmation from either Zeb or Rory, just urged her horse forward into a smooth lope. She knew it was Rory who fell in quickly behind her. After a time, he pulled up beside her and handed her his hat. She took it without breaking stride. It took both hands to stuff her hair inside and keep it from falling off, so Rory took the reins to help her. With that procedure, so like their old times together, some of Caroline's apprehension fell away.

She was almost home again. Everything would be fine.

They stopped for the night a few miles outside of Dodge City. From the moment Rory lifted her down from the saddle, Caroline knew a hundred years wouldn't be enough time for her to understand this new, tight-lipped Rory. He watched her shake out her bedraggled skirt and take a few limping steps. She hadn't been on a horse in weeks and wanted to rub her sore legs and bottom, but not in front of this disapproving stranger. She contented herself with stretching and flexing her shoulders, struggling against suddenly overwhelming weariness.

She stiffened when his hands fell onto her shoulders, but

58

he was only massaging the tight muscles of her back and neck. She relaxed and let her head fall forward in relief.

To Rory, her head looked like a bright flower sagging from a slender stem. He had the most insane urge to touch his lips to the tender skin at the side of her neck. He could see the throb of her pulse there, just under the surface where her hair parted to fall half over her shoulder and half down her back. His hands tightened, drawing a gasp of pain from Caroline.

He let her go immediately.

She turned and looked up at him, her eyes wide and questioning.

"Are you all right?" he asked. Those simple words had to carry so many questions, some he couldn't begin to phrase.

Caroline nodded solemnly. His gentle tone gave badly needed reassurance, but she needed more.

So did he, apparently. "You're sure?"

She smiled then, and some of the bonds around his chest loosened. "Really. I'm sorry, though. I was so stupid." She shook her head, thinking of how deep would be her regret if her folly had brought misery or harm to the people she loved. "Papa doesn't know, does he?"

"I didn't wire him. We can do that as soon as we get to town. Then I'll be happy to leave it up to you to explain the delay when we get to Santa Fe."

She went into his arms then, laughing and crying at the same time. "It'll be worth his temper just to be home." She pulled back to look at him, but her tears obscured his image. She concealed them with a turn of her head and tried to go around him. "I should help Zeb," she said, swallowing back an unladylike sniff.

Rory pulled his pack from the horse. "He wouldn't hear of it, and neither would I. You need some rest." He found a likely spot and unrolled his bed for her. "I'll call you for supper. Until then, you rest."

She watched through half-closed eyes as he led the horses away. She meant to use the time alone to consider what she had learned about this new Rory, but she was too tired to

59

do more than form his image in her mind. She had told her school friends in Philadelphia about her brother-who-was-not-related, but she had forgotten just how handsome he was.

Now she wondered how she could have forgotten.

Caroline resisted the tug of attraction, unwilling to travel down that road. He was *Rory,* for heaven's sake. She closed her eyes, impatient with herself and confused by her jumbled feelings. She was tired, that's all.

But with her eyes closed she could see him more clearly, see and appreciate the classical symmetry of the bone and cartilage that shaped his brow, cheeks and jaw. Even his nose was perfect, straight and handsome. His skin was tanned to a honey brown color like toasted bread, only a few subtle shades lighter than the golden brown of his hair.

She had always envied him his hair. Unlike her own fine wisps, his was springy and full, neither curly nor straight. Tamed only by ruthless wet combing, it would bounce back at will as soon as it dried to frame his face the way petals edge the heart of a flower.

Caroline smiled to herself sleepily at the thought of comparing Rory to a flower. A thistle, perhaps? But no, something about the comparison was apt. It persisted and she relished it. She even imagined combing her fingers through his hair. She wondered how it would feel. Like thick strands of warm silk? It would be lively and vibrant, as warm as the glints of golden light in his eyes.

Today, though, his eyes had held no warmth when he looked at her. Except after he'd rubbed her back, she amended. Now *that* was a warming thought. She clung to that, feeling again the clasp of his hands on her shoulders as she drifted off into sleep.

Although she woke quickly and completely the instant Rory touched her, she was startled by the familiar feeling of his hand on her shoulder. She shook him off angrily, denying herself the easy explanation for her feelings. She hadn't been dreaming, not of Rory, not of anything. She had only been asleep.

Rory stepped back, elaborately giving her room. "Supper's ready. I brought you some water so you can wash up, and maybe *wake* up," he added pointedly.

Caroline let him go, offering no explanation for her surliness. The only rational one, that she'd mistaken him for one of the kidnappers, wasn't true. She'd pulled back from Rory *because* he was Rory. And if she hadn't exactly dreamed of him, she'd put herself to sleep with thoughts of him. What should she make of that?

Nothing, she told herself resolutely. She had just been glad to see his familiar face, glad to be safely on her way home again.

Her mood improved at once when Zeb put a plate of beans in front of her. She smiled to herself after her first mouthful, thinking perhaps she had only been hungry. Ernie gave her a broad wink as he, too, began to eat. She could see that he and Zeb were at ease with each other.

"You notice I didn't start eatin' till you did, Miss Caroline," Ernie said. "The way to stay healthy around her," he explained to Zeb, "is to eat just what she does and nothin' else."

"Is that what you did?" she asked, laughing. "What made you suspicious? Nobody else was."

"I wasn't really unconscious the whole time. And I'm a suspicious cuss by nature. Besides, you were too eager to cook. I watched you cuttin' up those weeds, and I just figured they couldn't be good for a body."

Rory had taken his place beside Caroline. He asked, "What did you use? And where on earth did you learn about it?"

"It was boneset, one of Gramma Lunig's home cures. I used to help her gather herbs. Half of them I'd never know again, but that one was easy. She told me what everything was good for and *not* good for. She had little bottles on a high shelf in the pantry. The boneset effusion was marked with a skull and crossbones, like a pirate flag. It fascinated me, especially when she used it once on Grampa. I thought she meant to kill him. Of course, she explained that it was

61

only poisonous taken internally, and she told me what it did then. She could be rather earthy, so I never forgot it."

"Didn't it taste bad?" Rory asked.

"It's bitter, but I convinced the men the bitterness came from the dandelion greens. I'm afraid I talked about it so much they ate just to shut me up. I was worse than Lupe when she burns the roast."

Zeb and Rory groaned, so Caroline explained Lupe to Ernie. "You'll love her," she added, "but she takes her cooking *very* seriously."

She had not considered how much she was revealing about her plans for Ernie until she felt Rory stiffen in reaction beside her. Zeb covered for him with Ernie, adding his own comments about Lupe's cooking.

Appearing not to notice Rory's agitation, Ernie said, as much to Rory as to Zeb, "No matter what you all think, this Lupe can't make better biscuits and dumplings than Miss Caroline."

Caroline thought she saw a way to change the subject. "I see you've learned my real name. I just hope Blackie never does."

"Then you did know Baltimore Blackie was harassing the Santa Fe Railroad," Rory put in. "I wondered if you'd read about it in the papers back east."

"I didn't. I just heard him called Blackie—by you, Ernie." She sent him a smile before turning back to address Rory. "He wanted to know my name. The way he asked, I knew he was thinking about ransom, and I wanted to protect Papa. Cathleen Farrell was the best I could do. Then, when I heard who he was, I was so glad I'd lied."

"What's your last name?" Ernie asked. "And why would Blackie know it?"

Before Caroline could answer him, Rory interrupted, putting his hand on her arm. "I don't think you should tell him anything."

"Rory!" Caroline shook free of his grasp and said, "Years ago—"

She got no further. Rory jumped up and pulled her to her

62

feet after him. Her protests were swallowed up by the effort involved in keeping pace with her arm as he dragged it behind him. He didn't release her until they were well away from the clearing and the others.

"Haven't you got a speck of common sense left?"

"Rory! What's wrong with you?"

Their questions canceled out each other. Caroline rubbed furiously at her arm, concentrating on the physical pain rather than grappling with what seemed a larger one.

"I don't understand you," she whispered.

Rory pointed back to the unseen Ernie. "You know nothing about that guy except that he's an outlaw—part of Blackie's gang—yet you were going to tell him all about why Blackie might bear you a grudge. Do you know *why* his gang has been stopping the trains?"

"To rob them?"

His black look labeled her a backward child. "Because the Santa Fe Railroad failed to protect Kid Belasco from vigilantes. They took him from a train and hung him. For that—which the railroad had little part in, as I'm sure you'll agree—he and his men, including your precious Ernie Coogins, have been stopping trains right and left and robbing them. And you want to tell him that you're the one who put Kid Belasco behind bars to start with?"

"Belasco must have been released sometime in all that time," Caroline said, appalled. "Wasn't he? That was so long ago."

"He might or might not have been," Rory answered, his voice still harsh with barely suppressed emotion. "How would I know?"

"Well, you know more about it than I do."

"So you admit that, do you?"

"Rory . . ." She looked pleadingly at him. When had he become so implacable? "You've been angry since you saw me. Believe me, Rory, I didn't mean to cause you so much trouble—"

He broke in with a pungent curse.

"I am sorry. I told you that."

63

"That's not the point," Rory said. "You've adopted that guy, I can tell, and—"

"For good reason." She put her hand on his arm. "You don't have to like him, Rory, but I'm grateful to him. He saved me from being raped." The muscles in his arm jumped under her fingers. She squeezed reassuringly. "It's all right. Nothing happened, thanks to Ernie. But he was beaten up for helping me and I can't—I *won't*—turn my back on him now."

"He's a wanted man, Caroline. We have to turn him in."

"No. He can come with us to New Mexico. Papa will give him a chance. He's so young, Rory. I don't know why he was with Blackie, but I didn't see him do anything wrong. He deserves a chance. He won't be the first person to make a new start out there, and he can do it. We're a long way from the law at home."

"That's what worries me," Rory said. "You'd be bringing a known criminal onto your father's ranch. Don't you think Jake has troubles enough?"

"Ernie will be grateful for the chance and completely loyal. Papa can always use another loyal man—*especially* now."

"You know him so well?"

Caroline was puzzled by his half-sneer. "Well, of course I do," she protested. "He's my father."

"I meant Coogins."

"He told me he'd never let me down."

"Wonderful. So we have the outlaw's word of honor."

Caroline saw that she was winning this battle but losing some larger war she hadn't known had been declared. "This isn't just about Ernie, is it?" she asked softly. "You're upset with me. Did you want me to stay back east?"

She had made a wild but not uninformed guess at the problem besetting Rory. Much as she loved him, she wasn't unaware of what she represented to him. She was Papa's own child, as he was not. Her place in the family was secure, while he wasn't anything, not even illegitimate, as he had once confided to her.

64

She understood. He'd been sixteen years old when he met Hannah and Jake. He had been an orphan, running away from his only living relative, an uncle he believed responsible for his father's death. The three of them, Jake, Hannah and Rory, had banded together for mutual aid and protection, and ultimately, with the addition of Caroline, became a family when Hannah and Jake married. But while Caroline knew she belonged, Rory had always felt like an outsider. He had been nearly a grown man, someone who'd had another family and lost it. He could have gone on alone in the world as others his age did with varying degrees of success, but no one had wanted to part with him.

To Hannah, Rory was part son, part younger brother, and all friend. She counted on him and his support. Because Jake was a bit older, he saw Rory more as a son, but a son he could allow to be his friend as well. Between them there was an equality few fathers and sons ever achieved. Because he knew Rory felt insecure, Jake had offered to adopt Rory legally soon after he married Hannah. Caroline knew Rory cherished the fact that Jake had wanted him. Only his loyalty to the memory of his own father, and perhaps his pride, had kept Rory from becoming a legally adopted Farnsworth.

Caroline's soft question rocked Rory back onto his heels. "How can you think such a thing?" Meeting her question with another wasn't a tactic for him to buy more time. He was genuinely shocked that she could ask. Did she think him such a monster that he wanted to keep her from her family?

"I don't know what to think." Her eyes fell away from his as if she consulted some inner vision she wasn't sure she understood. "You were away from home until after I went east," she said, testing his response to what she saw. "Then you went home—but only after I was gone."

"And you thought I was avoiding you, mite?"

It was worth being laughed at to see Rory's smile soften his tight mouth. "It occurred to me." She didn't dare smile

65

back yet. She had to be sure she wasn't right.

He looked away from her, his frown back in place. "I thought you understood why I had to go."

He had gone in search of his Uncle Joseph, a man they both considered as much a villain as Baltimore Blackie. Joseph Talmage hadn't robbed banks or trains. He had directed his enmity toward Rory, his brother's son.

Rory had grown up on a farm outside of St. Louis, Missouri, where his father, Robert, together with Joseph, operated a prosperous foundry. The business did especially well during the Civil War, because they provided materials of warfare, particularly iron for the ironclad warships that soon became vital to both sides.

Although Rory was too young to be directly involved in the business, it was his heritage, and he followed closely whatever his father told him about it. By the end of the war, Rory was sixteen. He might have gone to war himself under other circumstances. Instead, he helped at the foundry and took care of the farm. His mother and younger sister died of cholera, and that loss, as well as their mutual escape from similar deaths, drew father and son closer than ever.

Then, suddenly, his father was dead. An accident, Joseph said. Robert had fallen under a heavy piece of machinery and been crushed. No one else witnessed the accident, but Rory was suspicious. His father and uncle had quarreled about the business and about other matters Rory was too young to understand. Or so his father had told him.

With his father dead, Rory had no protection against his uncle. Joseph sold the foundry and the farm that had been Rory's only home. He told Rory they would go to Oregon and begin a new life there. Although Rory appealed to his father's friends, no one would oppose Joseph, who made much of his affection for his brother's son. All Rory could take of his own on the trek west was his mare, Duchess. When he escaped from the wagon train outside of Omaha, Nebraska, afraid to go farther under Joseph's dubious protection, he took Duchess with him.

From the time Caroline had heard Rory's story, she had understood his need to find his uncle again and win back his heritage. Sometimes she had thought *she* wanted revenge more than Rory did, especially when she had been younger. With her imagination fed from her books, she had been a peculiarly bloodthirsty child. She wasn't that way any more, but she understood how he felt. She prided herself on that.

"I thought I did, too, and if you stay home now that I'm back I'll believe you." She grinned at him. "Otherwise . . ." Her voice trailed off into a shrugged challenge.

"No conditions," he said, trying to look severe.

"That's your trick and you know it," Caroline said, relieved now that Rory seemed to be his old teasing self again. "You've been angry with me from the start. You didn't even hug me properly," she chided.

"Hug you! After pulling a stunt like you did?"

She hadn't thought she'd be happy to have him refer to the train robbery again, but she was. Even being in the wrong was more comfortable for Caroline than confronting her fears about Rory's feeling for her. She didn't want him to resent her. After so long away from home, she wanted everything the way it had always been between them, the way it was supposed to be.

Rory might be the handsomest man she'd ever seen, but he was still her best friend and brother. For now, that was all she wanted him to be. She could stand being wrong as long as she knew she could count on Rory. He was part of her bedrock, her secure base. As long as his place in her life didn't change, she could put up with being in the wrong. Being wrong wasn't unique in her life, and this time she had to agree with him.

"Ah, Rory," she laughed. "Someday you'll understand. It's *after* I've pulled a really dumb stunt that I need hugging the most."

This time he provided it, and she almost wept with joy. She would have, except that she still had to deal with him over Ernie.

She stepped back and looked up to see if his clouded expression was back. It wasn't.

"Then you'll give Ernie a chance?" she asked.

"I'll talk to him," he answered gruffly.

Although he had promised nothing, Caroline knew she had won. "We can give him a new name if he's wanted and say he came with you and Zeb. No one notices the hands you bring along."

She had all the answers, Rory thought, letting her lead him back to the others. She even had some of the right questions as well. He was amazed that she had noticed the way he had made himself scarce from the ranch during her last years at home. He'd done it deliberately, of course, but not for the reason Caroline thought.

Perhaps he should be insulted that she believed him jealous of her place in her own family. At first he had been. But now that the shock had worn off, he was glad she misunderstood. It wouldn't help either of them for her to know the real reason for his absence.

As he resumed eating, he thought back to the day he had realized that he couldn't stay home any more. Caroline was a coltish seventeen and completely unaware that her artless warmth and free-spirited ways made her the object of speculation among the younger ranch hands. Rory knew because he worked among the men and because he was no better than the worst of them when it came to Caroline. Unlike the others, though, he had an unofficial place in her family. The men often forgot that, but Rory didn't. Or tried not to.

Sometimes it was difficult. On one of those occasions, all of his mixed and pent-up feelings erupted into violence. He overheard a lewd remark about Caroline; that was all. It had taken Zeb and two others to pull him off the unfortunate cowboy. Zeb had patched up the cowboy's battered hand and sent him on his way, an object lesson to all.

The lesson had not been lost on Rory, either. Two days

later he left for Oregon. His search for Uncle Joseph provided the perfect excuse, so perfect that no one but he himself knew the real reason for his extended absence.

Rory hadn't found Uncle Joseph, nor had he found peace of mind. Shortly after Caroline went away to school, he'd returned to the ranch, a temporary arrangement he'd intended to end well before she returned home again.

But then Jake got hurt. Rory was needed. He still was — for a while. He wouldn't stay, though. He couldn't. He would take Caroline to Jake as he'd promised, and then he'd leave again. It would be harder to do this time, but that only meant it was more necessary than ever.

Chapter Seven

They rode into Dodge City looking like outlaws. Rory, who took the lead, told Caroline to stay back with Zeb and leave everything to him. He got the names of all of Blackie's men from Ernie, who rode as much at his side as he would allow.

Although Caroline wanted to go directly to the marshal's office with Rory, he wouldn't hear of it. He dispatched Zeb to take her to the hotel, with orders that, once she was settled, Zeb was to fetch her trunks from the depot.

Rory saw them off to the hotel with a small nod of satisfaction. He'd seen the rebellion in Caroline's eyes, but he'd deal with that later. His next order of business was Ernie.

Turning his horse to face the younger man, he asked without preamble, "Is there a warrant out for your arrest, Coogins?"

"Not as far as I know."

"But there could be?"

"I don't see how."

"When you just participated in a train robbery?"

"All I ever did was stay with the horses."

"You were there," Rory said flatly. "The marshal won't make any fine distinctions like that. And neither do I."

Ernie didn't refute him.

"Why were you with them?"

He looked down Front Street, following Caroline and Zeb's progress. "I had my reasons."

"Which were?"

Ernie looked back at Rory. His expression wasn't sullen, just determined. All he said was, "Private."

70

In spite of himself, Rory was impressed. "Give me one reason why I shouldn't turn you over to the marshal."

Ernie just shook his head. He didn't remind Rory that Caroline defended him. He didn't defend himself.

"How old are you?"

"Twenty-two."

Rory sensed a lie. "You don't look it."

Ernie shrugged, saying with his slim body that he couldn't do anything about his looks.

"I'll give you money and a head start," Rory promised. "When I go to the marshal I won't say a word about you. You can be long gone before Blackie's men name you—if they ever do."

With a grim smile, Ernie shook his head again. "They will, but it don't matter. I'm not goin'."

"You're turning yourself in?"

"No, I won't do that. You want me turned in, you're gonna have to do it yourself. But I won't leave her."

"Caroline?" He shouldn't have been surprised. He knew why Ernie was so adamant. What surprised him was that Ernie was open about it.

"I promised her I'd never let her down. She wants me to stay."

"What did she promise you?" Rory asked sharply.

"Nothin'. I just know."

"You don't stand a chance with her, you know." Rory felt compelled to issue the warning, although he knew it was a waste of breath.

"She needs me."

Rory recognized a stone wall when he saw one. No matter how reluctant he was, he couldn't fight his own grudging respect for the man. Caroline had made another conquest. He turned his horse around, pausing only to issue a final warning. "You do anything to harm her or anyone she loves—and that includes a lot of people—and I'll make you sorry you were ever born."

He didn't bother to wait for an acknowledgment from Ernie; the sound of hoofbeats behind him was answer enough. What surprised him was that he felt curiously

71

satisfied with their exchange, at least insofar as Caroline was concerned. Whatever Ernie Coogins was, he meant no harm to Caroline. As long as Rory was sure of that he felt he could handle everything else Ernie did. He would warn Jake and keep his eyes open. The rest was just the normal risk of living.

For Caroline's sake Rory took the precaution of talking to the marshal alone. Rory didn't want Ernie to know about Caroline's childhood involvement with Kid Belasco's arrest, and he was afraid if Ernie were in on the discussion he would learn that Blackie had reason to hate her. Rory's fear about that didn't jibe with his trust that Ernie would not harm Caroline, but there it was. He had no intention of trying to overanalyze his feelings about Caroline and Ernie. He wasn't afraid of what he'd discover; he was just cautious. Caution was never a mistake, he'd found.

Marshal Deger's zeal for pursuing Blackie and his men was considerably enhanced by news he'd received that the railroad was now offering a generous reward for the gang's capture. Learning that Caroline had incapacitated the men for them was the final spur to set a posse into action. On one point, however, the marshal was immovable — Caroline had to stay in Dodge City until the men were brought back. Rory could not change his mind on that score.

Before he left the marshal's office, and without giving Coogins away, Rory determined to his own satisfaction that Ernie had told the truth about being wanted. Marshal Deger's information about the gang gave no indication that Coogins was part of it. The marshal noted each name as Rory gave it, reacting only to mention of Walt Stimpson. Since he was the one responsible for taking Caroline from the train, Rory was grimly satisfied to learn that he was a wanted man.

Ordinarily Rory would have joined the posse, Caroline or no Caroline. But with Ernie around he decided to remain close at hand. He did offer Ernie the protection of an introduction to the marshal under another name, the only one that came to his mind at that instant. "This is Lefty, one of my hands," he said offhandedly.

Ernie shook the marshal's hand, then opened the door for him to go out.

He didn't. Instead he looked at Ernie shrewdly. "Lefty? You're no lefty. What's your real name?"

"Boyd Kellogg," Ernie answered with hesitation. "Lefty's just some cowboy's idea of a joke. I've been stuck with it a long time."

Rory looked from one to the other. Both men had surprised him, Ernie — again — with his smooth answer, Marshal Deger by being observant. Rory had supposed, because the marshal hadn't rushed off after the train robbers at first news of the holdup, that the marshal was either lazy or corrupt. Possibly both. Now he found himself revising his perhaps hasty judgment.

He had not noticed which hand Ernie favored. He'd only used the nickname because it was familiar to him and, he assumed, an entirely unremarkable one. Last year Jake had had a hand named Lefty, but for the life of him Rory couldn't remember whether or not he had been left-handed. As Ernie said, cowboys often exhibited a warped sense of humor in branding their fellows with names. The fact that Ernie also knew that, and had used the information so easily to explain away Rory's gaffe, was revealing. At some time Ernie had been around ranch hands.

Interesting, Rory told himself, filing away the name Boyd Kellogg for future examination. Somehow, he doubted that it was any more genuine than the name Ernie Coogins or Lefty. Was there an outlaw named Boyd Kellogg? Rory intended to find out.

As they walked along Front Street to the hotel Rory took out some of his frustration on Ernie by saying acidly, "You lie rather well, Coogins — if that's really your name."

Ernie gave another of his eloquent shrugs. This one managed to be both modest and unoffended. "Only in comparison to you."

"I just didn't want Deger to remember your name when Blackie's men tell him about the one who got away."

"I wasn't complainin'."

Uncomfortably aware that he'd been put in the wrong

again, Rory opted for silence the rest of the way. He hoped Zeb had finished with Caroline's trunks so he could take over as Ernie's watchdog. Rory had had quite enough of the man's company, but he was damned if he was ready to turn him loose yet. Let Zeb deal with him; it was time he checked on Caroline.

Seeing her might be his duty, as he told himself, but it was one he was especially eager to perform. He needed to test out his half-formed impressions of the way she was now.

Was she still, as Zeb put it, a harum-scarum girl? Or had her years back east changed her? He didn't know. Worse, he didn't know what he wanted her to be. She was older, to be sure, but so far seeing her had been a trip back in time to their first meeting. She had been nine, a colt of a girl, full of humor and zest, capable of trying to jump off a moving carriage because she was angry. From that perspective, nothing about her had changed. Her temper was still getting her into trouble.

But that wasn't the whole story. Even the bedraggled state of her clothing couldn't disguise her essential loveliness. Her smile was as dazzling as sunset over the Saw Tooth Mountains back home, and her heart was still good and kind. She was Caroline. Special. Beautiful.

But was she really grown-up now? Rory thought of Hannah, of the womanliness that made Hannah stand out like a swan among brood hens. Caroline had the height for elegance, but perhaps, given her hoydenish ways, she would always remain merely . . . angular.

Rory went to his room to wash up and change his clothes, still thinking about Caroline. He didn't want her to be artificial, nor did he object to her stature, although he did like curves and femininity, he had discovered.

He looked into the mirror above the dresser and grimaced. He gave his collar a tug before leaving to fetch Caroline. She was probably disappointed in him. He hadn't given her the warmest welcome. He would have to do better, if only to keep her from relying too heavily upon the admiration of men like Ernie Coogins. He didn't think he'd ever marry — after all, what did he have to offer a woman? —

74

but he'd offer himself any day to keep Caroline safe from the likes of an Ernie Coogins. He owed Jake and Hannah at least that much.

Full of good intentions, Rory knocked firmly on Caroline's door. After a surprisingly long pause, she called out, "Who is it?"

A commotion in the hall behind him drew his attention. He turned to look, answering in a low tone, "It's Rory," unaware that what Caroline heard was the voice of the woman next door as she entered her room with a companion.

He heard Caroline invite him in and opened the door, still looking back into the hall, his mind's eye full of the most intriguing bustle he had seen in ages. The door thunked shut behind him as he stepped inside and suddenly found himself face-to-face with a Caroline he had never seen before. It was a sight no man had seen, he was certain, because she sat in a tub of water.

She drew her knees higher and covered her chest with crossed arms and a washcloth, making the water splash musically around her. He knew she had fallen asleep in her bath as surely as he knew he should turn around and leave. Immediately.

He didn't move.

Neither did she.

"You said come in."

"I thought you were the maid."

"I'm sorry. I'll leave."

Rory groped for the knob behind him. It was pressing into his backside, but he couldn't tear his eyes away from her to turn around and grasp it. Carefully, deliberately, he kept his eyes focused on her face. It was flushed and pink, either from the warm water or from embarrassment. Probably both. She had pinned up her hair into a knot on the top of her head, but strands had escaped to droop beguilingly around her brow and neck.

In spite of the way he concentrated on *not* seeing what he should not see, his peripheral vision was excellent. He saw her knees protruding from the water like twin islands, slim, pale, pretty. Even the soapsuds that circled them looked like baubles strung on the surface of the water as ornamentation. He would have killed if she had shown so much of her neck and shoulders in a dress, and now he had the picture of all that bare loveliness permanently etched into his brain.

Finally he succeeded in getting his hand on the doorknob. He wrenched it open and turned, colliding with the maid who was coming in. She squawked in protest as he barreled past her.

"I'm so sorry, ma'am. I was delayed," she apologized in a voice that easily carried to where Rory slumped against the wall outside. "I hope that man didn't bother you."

"Him? Oh, no," Caroline laughed. Her voice came to him faintly, but he could still hear her dismissive tone. "That's just my brother. He doesn't bother me."

Insulted, Rory drew himself up to his full height. Brother! He was absolutely no relation to Caroline, and she knew it. He might have played that role with her over the years, but that's all it was, a role. Once he would have said that pride was a small part of his nature, but not now. He was more than angry that Caroline could dismiss him so readily. He was hurt, too. He was a man, not a eunuch, damn it!

Rory pushed away from the wall and started down the hall, fueled by indignation. After a few steps his sense of humor resurfaced. Just minutes before, he had questioned whether Caroline was grown-up and feminine enough to suit him. Well, he certainly had the answer to that question.

Knowing that, however, wasn't as much help to him as he'd thought. Growing up was more than developing the proper curves. She had to understand that—and so did he.

No matter what he felt for Caroline, from love to pique, he wasn't free to indulge himself as he chose. Her unique place in his life demanded special care. She wasn't his sister, but she wasn't just anyone, either. And she was still in his care.

Jake had trusted him to bring her safely home. Rory couldn't betray that trust any more than he could simply turn the tables on Caroline. Because his pride was stinging, it would be easy, and wonderfully satisfying, to make her as achingly aware of him as he was aware of her.

He couldn't do it. He'd have to do something, though — but what?

He had to think.

Chapter Eight

Caroline had not dismissed Rory as easily as he thought. Not at all. She felt thoroughly shaken by the look she had seen in his eyes. She'd told the maid he was her brother as much to remind herself as to avoid any hint of a scandal.

There had been nothing brotherly about Rory's expression, however. No one had ever before looked at her with such glowing, hot eyes, not even Quentin Makepeace back in Philadelphia, and he had asked her to marry him — three times.

She stepped into the towel the maid held for her and wrapped it tightly around her body, feeling strangely aware of herself. It was as if she had just now developed her womanly shape. Although the bath water had grown cold while she dozed, she felt uncomfortably warm.

Another knock on the door startled her, but it wasn't Rory again. A second maid delivered her dress, freshly pressed after days in her trunk. Such service was a luxury she rarely availed herself of, but today she had felt in need of pampering.

She looked at the frock she had chosen, wondering if she dared wear it. She'd selected it because it was among her most flattering. She had wanted Rory to see that she could look elegant when she wasn't bouncing around on horseback. Now she wasn't sure about her judgment. Holding the towel with one hand, she flipped back the top of the trunk and rummaged for her dove gray shirtwaist. It would give her the no-nonsense look she craved.

"That'll need pressing, too, ma'am," the maid said, looking up from her chore of emptying out the bathwater.

"So I see." Caroline let it drop back and replaced the cover.

She was making too much of Rory's reaction—or of *her* reaction. He had been surprised, that's all. Naturally. He'd never expected to walk in on her bath. It was a momentary reaction, and the critical moment had long since passed. All she had to do now was put it out of her mind and go on as if nothing had happened. Because nothing *had* happened!

She dithered so long about dressing that the maid had finished emptying the tub and was carting it out before she was into her corset and in need of assistance. Hannah would laugh at the idea of lacing her already willowy shape into such a contraption, but the dress was made to fit that way.

Back east, she had conformed. Here she would do so whenever it was convenient. As the maid patted her dress into place over the corset, Caroline decided she liked the armored feeling it gave her. She had a hunch she would need the extra layer of fortification when she saw Rory.

She dressed her hair with equal care, pinning it up into the fashionable rolls she had learned to make at school. Sometimes she thought that was the most useful thing she had learned there. Since her hair didn't curl the way Hannah's did, it took skill and concentration for her too accomplish the same effect. Or so she believed.

The dress was simple and striking. The wide U-shaped neckline was high enough for modesty, yet it set off to advantage the elegant length of her neck and the delicacy of her collarbone and shoulders. Swags of the same sapphire blue as the dress, but in a more substantial fabric than the watered silk of the bodice, were artfully draped at the back of the skirt to approximate a bustle. Being slender, Caroline liked the look of a bustle, but she was too active and sensible to tolerate wearing a veritable bird cage over her legs. Thanks to her clever dressmaker in Pennsylvania, she had the best compromise possible between style and sense.

She could see only a small portion of herself in the mirror, but what she saw made her frown. Her color was too hectic. One look at her still flushed cheeks and Rory would know she wasn't recovered from the shock of having him walk in on her bath. *Oh, for some of Gramma Lunig's talcum*

79

powder, she thought, turning away in disgust. Having none, she stiffened her spine and prepared to leave.

Rory had not come for her again. He knew as well as she did that ladies did not call upon gentlemen at their hotel rooms. He should have returned for her by now. Enough time had passed for her to have prepared for presentation before royalty, and still he hadn't come.

Caroline decided she could devise no better way to demonstrate her unconcern than by calling for him. Unorthodox as it was, it was still something she would have done as an unconscious girl. What better way to assure him that she saw him as her brother still, and as nothing more?

She stood several minutes outside Rory's room before she could bring herself to knock, but once she did, he answered promptly — and opened the door so quickly she knew he had only been waiting inside.

"Caroline!" He grabbed her arm and, after a wild-eyed look up and down the vacant corridor, dragged her inside. "You shouldn't have come here."

"No?" She looked around the room interestedly. It was no different from hers, decorated predominantly by an open valise rather than a huge travel trunk. She gave him a saucy smile. "How else would I be able to turn the tables and catch you at your bath?"

Rory turned the most rewarding red, making Caroline realize that she had never seen him blush before. She watched him struggle for composure, noting how long it was taking his color to fade. Long before he had found his normal balance, she took pity on him.

"Have you decided how to word the telegram for Papa? I don't want him to worry. Do you suppose the passengers who went on to Santa Fe will tell about the robbery?"

"It's too much to hope they won't," he answered, obviously relieved to have another topic for discussion.

"In that case, it's better for us to be honest, don't you think? If we don't mention it and he hears about it, he'll only imagine something worse than what happened."

After agreeing with her in an almost comically distracted

manner, Rory went to the door, opened it and glanced out furtively.

Caroline started past him. "Honestly, Rory," she said, trying not to laugh, "aren't you being rather silly? No one knows us here. We could be a married couple, or we could *really* be brother and—"

Rory clamped his big hand over her mouth and pulled her back inside. "Must you announce your indiscretion to the whole world?" he muttered fiercely at her back. He held her tight against him, one hand at her waist, the other still over her mouth. With both of them jammed into the small space behind the half-opened door, Caroline was too startled even to breathe.

As if he only just then realized what he had done, Rory released her as suddenly as he had caught her to him. She put out a hand to the doorjamb and looked at him with wide eyes. "My . . . indiscretion?" she whispered, her senses reeling. "What did I do?"

Rory plowed his fingers through his hair and glared at her. He had overreacted and now had no idea what to say. He closed his eyes. "Caroline," he began weakly, "you shouldn't come to a man's room."

"You already said that once." She was slowly regaining her equilibrium after what had felt like an assault. She could still feel the press of his hard body behind her, and her mouth felt strange. She wanted to lick her lips to see if she could taste Rory on them. She couldn't do that, not with him staring at her so avidly, but she could—and did—put her hand on her waist where his hand had not rested but *clasped* her.

"Didn't you learn anything back east?"

"I learned a lot of things, just nothing that seems to apply right now."

"I'm sorry I grabbed you."

He was. More than anything, he wished he could rub his hands down his pant legs to rid them of the sensation of her soft skin and dress. His whole body tingled with awareness of her body, and his head was filled with her feminine fragrance. The flowery scent brought back every sensation he had experienced when he walked in on her bath, sensations he had spent the intervening time repressing. In one instant, just by touching her, he had undone all that work. And made it worse.

Caroline smiled uncertainly. His reaction, insofar as it mirrored her own, pleased her. In spite of her years and her education, she had little experience with men, Quentin Makepeace aside. She'd had friends and companions among her father's men, but none of that counted in the way Rory meant.

Her education had been just that, serious schooling provided by the Society of Friends in Philadelphia to prepare her for teaching. It hadn't been a finishing school, nor had she had social connections in the city. Her classmates had been mostly Quaker maidens from good families.

Her own mother, Grace Lunig, had met Jake Farnsworth in Hanford, Pennsylvania, but when Caroline returned there during school vacations to visit her grandparents and later to care for them in their final days, she met no one like her papa. Her two childhood chums, Becky and Alice, were married, one already a mother, the other about to become one.

Somehow, she had not fit in with either group. She had not wanted to. Like her father, she was in love with the West.

Caroline knew about romantic love from books, secondhand. But unlike a lot of people, she didn't distrust what she read. She knew it was sometimes exaggerated for artistic effect, but she made allowance for that. Her reaction to Rory—and his to her, if she could judge fairly from what she was seeing—convinced her that, for certain people, life could be as much an adventure as the most boisterous novel by Mr. Ned Buntline, who was still her favorite author after all these years. Not every chapter of anyone's life was riotous, of course, but she was determined that her own life story would be a romantic adventure.

Instinctively, she had known that Quentin could not be her hero. She wasn't sure yet about Rory. He was handsome enough and he was the right age—older without being *too* old—but perhaps he was too stuffy already. None of the heros in her books ever apologized when they grabbed the heroine. If he were to become her hero, he'd have to get over being so fraternal and protective toward her.

Coming home, she had thought of Rory that way, too. She had thought to return to the unchanged and unchanging past. Now she saw other possibilities for them. Did he see them, too? Was that why they were finding it such hard going to be together?

"I guess I didn't think," she said to him with a more natural smile. "It's an old failing of mine."

Rory hitched at his collar and nodded. "People do know me in Dodge City. I come here often, doing business." He held the door for her without checking the hall this time.

"I'll be more aware," Caroline promised.

Aware. Rory looked at her solemn features, so at odds with the blue sparkle of her eyes. In that dress, he didn't need any more awareness. She was the embodiment of temptation, and she had to know it. Was she playing a game with him?

He tucked her hand under his arm. Resolution straightened the firm line of his mouth. He didn't want to believe that she was toying with him, but what else could he think? She had always been a handful.

Groaning silently at the image he had inadvertently invoked, he tightened his right hand into a fist. He *would* regain his self-control. He had to.

When they got to the railroad depot to send their telegraph message, they discovered that Caroline had become something of a sensation. Stories about her capture and escape already painted her as a daring heroine, but when the men working or lounging there found out that she was beautiful and blond, young and unmarried, her stature grew by the minute. So did the admiring circle of men around her.

Caroline tried to take the attention in stride. At first she was amused. Mostly the furor made her wish she'd worn her sensible gray dress after all.

83

Eventually she and Rory found sanctuary in the telegraph office, but even that had its price. The operator came with it. He was so eager to assist them that they had no privacy. Caroline had wanted to send a full accounting to her father, no matter the cost, knowing she could not put a price on his peace of mind. While they could hardly ask the man to give up his tiny office to them, neither could they discuss their differences about wording in front of him. Not when every word they said was sure to be repeated as soon as they left.

They compromised on a stilted message that satisfied neither of them, hoping Jake would be reassured just to know they were both well.

"He's going to worry," Caroline fussed out loud as they finally made their escape from the depot.

Rory looked behind them. Even now they were trailed distantly by men. "We'll make it up to him later. I didn't want the world to know our plans. Perhaps I can go back later alone and send another message."

"The operator will remember you."

"Maybe another man will be working then."

Pleased with that prospect, Caroline stepped out with Rory onto Front Street. Just as they reached the middle of the roadway several riders appeared at the eastern end of the town. It was early for the posse to be returning, but that was the thought she and Rory instantly shared. He let go of her arm to start toward them, and Caroline turned back, intending to regain the planked sidewalk.

She never made it. Another horse and rider tore out from the corner of the depot, bearing down upon her faster than she could move away. A combination of moves—her own, Rory's to pull her back, and the rider's to avoid running her down—kept her from being trampled under the horse.

The moment the danger was over Caroline felt her knees turn to liquid and give way. Relief made her limp. She clung to Rory, sure she would fall in a heap of watered silk if he let her go.

He did not. He swept her up into his arms and carried her across the street. He was vaguely aware that the men in front of the depot cheered and laughed, but he was too busy, too afraid, too *angry* to care. The store across from the depot advertised "Guns, Pistols, Ammunition; Hardware and Tinware" in foot-tall letters on the front. All Rory saw was the wooden keg where he deposited Caroline. Now that he wasn't busy or afraid, all that was left was his anger.

"What in hell were you doing?" he raged. "Can't you even cross a street without getting into trouble?"

Caroline's eyes filled with tears as she stared up at him, all her sparkling pink color gone. She didn't say a word. Later, she would understand why Rory yelled at her, but now it seemed unfair. She wanted to defend herself, but her mind was wiped clean of words.

As soon as he saw her tears Rory regretted his reaction. He knew she hadn't been at fault. He owed her another apology, but he couldn't speak. He didn't remember ever seeing her cry. In fact, she didn't now. Somehow, either her willpower or her silky, spiked eyelashes held back the tears so they never fell to mar the pale perfection of her cheeks. She didn't sniff either. She just stared, willing him to soften toward her and offer her comfort.

They were on a public street in the middle of a bright summer day, but they had finally found a small island of anonymity. The riders who had distracted him from Caroline now distracted everyone else, leaving them isolated together.

Rory bent his head and touched his lips to hers. His intent had been to kiss her forehead, to soothe away the small knot of anxiety that lurked between her brows, but as he drew near, her lips became his target. They were soft and pink, just parted and moist. Irresistible.

She didn't really kiss him back, yet her lips clung to his holding him, drawing him down to her. He had never tasted such sweetness.

After the longest moment he drew back to find that she was still staring at him. He wanted to laugh, to make a joke, to instruct her—anything to break the tension—but nothing came from him but a soundless sigh of longing.

He cleared his throat and stuffed his hands into his pockets.

"Are you all right?"

All right? She was wonderful!

She blinked and found her tears gone.

"Yes, I'm fine now." She reached up to pat his arm. "Thank you, Rory. You were wonderful. I can't think now why my feet refused to obey me. Perhaps I would have been unhurt anyway, but it was kind of you to be so gallant."

With every word she added she saw Rory's befuddlement grow thicker until it was an intangible morass about him. She had been kissed before, and not just by Quentin Makepeace. She might be inexperienced, at least in comparison to the women in the books she'd read, but she was smart enough to know she had not been the only one moved by their kiss. She also knew Rory wasn't happy about the fact that she had stirred his emotions.

She wasn't mean, and she didn't intend to toy with his feelings, but she didn't want him to think she was going to be easy to win. It had been a very nice kiss, one with possibilities. He had meant to comfort her. What was wrong with letting him believe he had succeeded?

"You're such a comfort, Rory. I'm certainly glad Papa sent you to meet me." She got to her feet, smoothed the front of her dress and patted her hair. "I think now I'd like something to eat. Why don't we go to the Beatty and Kelley Restaurant? I remember Papa speaking well of it."

Their walk down Front Street to the corner of First Street was made in silence. In theory, Caroline had suffered far greater recent trials than Rory, but in fact he was the one most bemused. Inside the restaurant she had to take over for Rory, first securing them a table, then adding Zeb and Ernie to their party when they arrived.

Seeing Zeb jogged Rory back to normalcy. During the meal he joined with Zeb to answer the questions Caroline had not been able to ask until then about her family. Ernie

86

listened attentively to all their stories. Occasionally, Caroline explained a reference for him, whether to a person or an animal, but he asked no questions and offered no comments.

After a time Caroline pushed her plate aside, surprised to find that it was empty. She didn't remember eating. She was even more surprised to find her eyes stinging with tears. "All this talk is making me more homesick now than I was back east," she confessed to Rory's wavering image. "It must be that I'm almost there. If it hadn't been for the train robbery, I'd at least be with Papa by now."

When Rory's glance slid to Ernie, hers followed. Stricken, she said to him, "Please don't take that personally, Ernie. I just meant . . ."

He made a dismissive gesture and smiled. "Hearing about all those Talmages, I can understand why you want to go home. They sound like real nice folks."

"Talmages?" Caroline looked at Rory in momentary confusion. Then she remembered that Ernie had never been told her name. Since he believed them truly brother and sister, he would naturally assume that all her family had Rory's last name.

Rory opened his mouth, meaning to intercede before Caroline could correct Ernie's mistake. When Ernie got to New Mexico—*if* he got to New Mexico—he would learn who Caroline was. Until then, Rory would continue to protect her identity. But before either of them could find their voices, Ernie spoke again, this time to Rory. "Are you all related to that Talmage feller I saw at the hotel this morning?"

Caroline sucked in her breath, and Rory went very still. "What Talmage fellow?"

"An older man," Ernie said. "I heard someone call out to him. I thought it was you, but they called him John—no, Joe," he corrected. Looking from one to the other of them, he sensed their agitation and tried to minimize it. "Probably I got the name wrong . . ."

Caroline reached for Rory's hand. It was as cold as hers.

Joseph Talmage. Could it be that Ernie had stumbled accidentally upon the man Rory had sought for so long? And found him so close at hand? Rory had traveled the Oregon Trail once four years ago in pursuit of his elusive uncle, only to find an innocent man — someone else by the same, not-uncommon name. Since then even Hannah's wealthy uncle, Simon Sargent, hadn't been able to turn up a trace of the man.

Rory leaned toward Ernie. "Tell me everything, exactly as you saw it."

Ernie straightened, concentrating now on what he had begun as only an idle comment. "I was in the lobby, waitin' for Zeb." He nodded at Zeb. "Two or three men came in. They were talkin', you know, like they were goin' their separate ways. One of them spotted this other feller and called out to him. It wasn't much, just the kinda thing a body says when he's surprised to see someone. I only noticed because he called him Talmage. I couldn't see him, so I moved around so's I could. I lost interest when I saw it wasn't you."

"Where did he come from?"

"I don't know." Ernie felt the challenge of three intense faces turned on him. "This really matters to you, don't it." It wasn't a question.

"More than you'd ever believe."

"Try to picture what happened then, Ernie," Caroline urged softy. "Where did the men go?"

He thought a while. "Every which way. The Talmage guy went out. The others went upstairs, mostly. Maybe one went out back. To the bar, maybe?" He looked from one to the other, but no one helped him out.

"What did he look like, this Joe Talmage?" Rory's scorn was plain in his voice.

"Average, I'd say. Not tall; not fat but runnin' that way. Had a hat and a dark coat. I never saw his face."

"They called him Joe?"

"Son of a gun, mostly," Ernie said, trying out a small smile that no one returned.

"That figures." Rory gave Caroline a hard look.

"Do you think he was staying at the hotel?" she asked Ernie.

"Could be. I didn't see where he came from."

After a short, considering pause Rory stood up and threw some bills onto the table. He gave Ernie a measuring look, then nodded to Zeb. "Settle up for us."

By then Caroline was on her feet, going with him. He tried to shake her off, even stopping once to speak to her, but when he left she was at his heels.

Zeb picked up the money and counted it out. He looked up to see that Ernie's eyes were still on the empty doorway.

"They're remarkably close for a brother and sister of that age," Ernie said. "It must be quite a family."

"It is that," Zeb agreed.

He liked Ernie because he felt easy with him. He had asked no questions about why the youngster had been with a bunch of outlaws, and he never would. It wasn't his way. There was a story there somewhere, and like all such stories it would come out when the time was right. Whatever it was, it wouldn't change Zeb's mind about Ernie.

If Caroline got her way — and when hadn't she with Rory or Jake? — Ernie would be going on to the territory of New Mexico with them. He'd find out Caroline's last name then. For some reason Rory didn't want him to know yet, probably to protect her. Someday Rory would learn that Caroline needed protection about as much as a dog needed fleas.

In the meantime, Zeb would make no suggestions. That wasn't his way either. He had learned long ago that there were things a man could do and things a man couldn't do. By now he knew which was which — most of the time. He did what he could and kept his eyes and ears open the rest of the time.

Zeb's lips turned up in a wry smile as he thought of what his father, the *Bible*-thumping preacher Zachary Prentiss, would make of his son's philosophy of life. Or of his life, for that matter.

Perhaps, as his father would say, it wasn't much, but it

sure did make for an interesting time — especially around the Farnsworths.

Chapter Nine

It took only five strides for Maria Martinez to go from the window to the door of the little house. And for this, she thought indignantly, she was supposed to be grateful. Grateful! She felt nothing but contempt for the notion of gratitude either to her mother for "giving up" her cherished bungalow to Maria or to the Farnsworths for providing it in the first place. It was nothing, this wretched little place.

Maria's lips curled back in scorn. She wanted to spit on the floor. The only thing preventing her was the fact that there was no one to clean up after her if she did. Her mother cleaned up after the Farnsworths, as did she when she was forced to, but she had no one to wait on her. Yet.

Soon she would, though, and this time she would make no mistake. She would not be taken in again by lies. It had killed her to have to come back to her mother in defeat. She had been stupid once. She could not afford to be again.

Maria paced to the window and glared out. The moon looked as though one crescent would snag on the ragged junipers and piñons standing sentinel outside the low adobe house, but Maria saw nothing of the clear, bright night. She was only waiting.

This time she waited for Ted Jasper. He said he would come tonight. He had already kept her waiting too long. As soon as she heard his horse she intended to drop her wrap and get into bed. She would be indifferent tonight, hard to wake. He was fool enough to be pleased to think she'd waited for him in bed, so she had to make it clear that she hadn't been waiting.

She wished it wasn't Ted she waited for. The man she

really wanted, the one she knew would be man enough for her, was Jake Farnsworth. He was old, but even sick he was all man. To be Mrs. Jake Farnsworth would mean owning this whole ranch, the best in the territory. If she couldn't have him—and it seemed she couldn't—her next choice was Rory Talmage. He was like Jake, strong and manly, only better in some ways. For one thing, he didn't have a red-headed witch for a wife.

When her mother had laughed at her fantasies about Jake years ago, she had consoled herself that she could have Rory. She still thought she could, but she'd lost interest in him when she found out he was as poor as she was. He wasn't really a Farnsworth. He only acted the son. Now that Jake had his own son, Rory would get nothing. Maria knew how the world worked—only sons counted.

Which left her with Ted Jasper. He was an only son, and that was better than just being the oldest. He didn't even have sisters. The Jasper place wasn't as well run or as rich as Renegade Ranch, but as Mrs. Theodore Jasper she would matter. People would look up to her. She could have servants and beautiful clothes and . . .

She broke off her dreaming with an impatient sigh. How she hated waiting. All her life she had waited. Tonight she would be done with waiting. Tonight she would—

Ted moved so quickly that Maria had to run to get to the bed before he had the door open. She heard his pleased chuckle, and her temper went up another notch. If he touched her while she was feeling the effects of her unaccustomed exertion, he would be even more flattered. She ground her teeth in exasperation and concentrated on lying perfectly still.

After a few tense moments of silence, Maria heard the rustle of clothing and realized that he was undressing. Forgetting all pretense of sleep, she sat upright and launched into a spate of Spanish.

Surprised, Ted paused to listen in admiration, one boot on, one in his hand. Although his understanding of Spanish consisted of *mañana* and *adios,* spoken at half her speed, he had no trouble with the gist of Maria's meaning. He tossed aside the boot he held and took off the other, hopping a bit in the process. When she seemed to be slowing down, he shook his head, chuckled and started to take off his pants.

He wasn't offended by anything she called him or his ancestors. In fact, he was pleased. He took her show of temper as a sign of great passion. In his father, anger was so chillingly cold just his presence when he was displeased could lower the temperature in a room by perceptible degrees. His more moderate mother expressed disfavor by sighing heavily. Compared to such wintery behavior, Maria in the full flower of her fury seemed as rare and entrancing as a tropical storm. Ted was sure it helped that he couldn't actually follow each word, and perhaps in time such torrential outpourings would grow wearisome, but for now it was wonderful. As long as she was crazy about him he was going to enjoy the ride.

Naked and thoroughly aroused, Ted got into bed, offhandedly trying to soothe and calm Maria. "Now, now, honey," he murmured.

She fended off his first clumsy caresses with ease, but she was no match for his size and strength. When the flood of her displeasure began to slow, Ted took it as a sign that he was successfully channeling her protest into sexual passion. He held her legs with one thigh, her wrists with one hand and her head with the other hand. One thing she liked to do that he hated was spit at him. He thought that was disgusting. When she got that look in her eye, he kissed her fast and hard.

Her response was always different from any other woman's. She grew very still. She never kissed back or moved against him, offering her body. She just stopped struggling. Still, it was so exciting to conquer her that he didn't miss the response he expected from others. Maria was unique. She was his little Mexican firecracker. If she reacted to sex as she did to her grievances, her enthusiasm would exhaust him, and he was already tired.

He'd had another discussion with his father. They were always discussions, not arguments, for his father permitted no back talk. He laughed to himself, thinking of that childish term. That's what his father called any response of his except "Yes, sir."

He was collapsed atop Maria, who pushed on his chest, her dark eyes unreadable. All he saw in them was his own miniature reflection, curved and distorted. He moved off her, reacting slowly. His limbs felt as heavy as if they belonged to someone else.

"So you find me funny, do you?"

One glance told him Maria was beginning to get worked up again. If she did, he would leave. What was amusing once was intolerable a second time.

"I find you gorgeous," he said, making what was, for him, a supreme effort to please her.

She snorted rudely, reminding him again of some of her more inelegant ways. He put his hand over her mouth and said, "Don't. Just don't."

Her eyes changed, and for a moment he saw something besides anger in them. She moved against him in invitation, but it came too late to interest him. He laughed and rolled away from her to sit on the edge of the bed. He wanted his pants, but he was almost too tired to get them. He sat with his head in his hands, unable to rally until he felt Maria stir behind him.

Expecting sympathy, he turned back to her, meaning to stem another tidal wave of Spanish. She didn't look sympathetic, but he took no chances. "Look, I'm sorry I was late. The old man was all aquiver over the delay of his great party. It seems the guest of honor has been held up in Dodge City."

Maria found her command of English. "Guest of honor? Your parents are the honored ones, are they not?"

"They are not. Yes, indeed, they are not, little Maria." He stepped into his pants and turned back to her. "Ah, you're confused, little one. That's no surprise."

The room was nearly as light as it was in daylight, brightened by the lanternlike moon outside the window. Whitewashed walls reflected it back to Maria, even showing Ted's shadow as he dressed. She watched him cover his sleek, smooth chest, the one thing about his body she really liked. Other men had hair, great mats of it in some cases, that repelled her.

Her rapt attention flattered Ted. Another time he would have been tempted to undress again for her, but not tonight.

"The real guest of honor is to be Caroline Farnsworth," he explained. "My parent's anniversary is just the excuse he uses because it's not his proper place to hold a welcome-home party for Miss Farnsworth."

"That one," Maria said dismissively.

"Yes, that one."

She looked at him sharply, hearing his sigh, but it seemed the sound of tiredness, not desire, so she was satisfied. She leaned back against the pillow and draped the sheet to fall artfully around her legs. Her coppery skin made the ideal contrast to the white bed linen, and her pose displayed the ripe thrust of her breasts to perfection. She loved to compose pictures with her body and see the admiration flare in a man's eyes.

She would be the happiest woman in the world if that was all it took to please men. If only they didn't have to touch and ram her, too. But they did, and all her wishing would never change that. What she could do, although only occasionally—like now, when Ted was too tired to want her again—was please herself and see that desire grow without having to suffer the distasteful consequences.

Of course, she had to be careful. Already she could see Ted begin to wonder if he was as tired as he had thought. Sometimes she miscalculated. But not, she thought, this time.

She slid up onto her knees. "Hand me my robe," she said, giving him a slow smile. "So your father, too, has a fancy for pale hair. You should warn him that her father will not be pleased. He is simple about that one, I can tell you."

Ted burst out laughing. He couldn't help it. The thought of his father lusting for anything but land struck him as hilarious.

Maria snatched the robe from his hand and wrapped it around herself. He felt punished by her action and knew why. She thought he was laughing at her. His only consolation lay in the fact that she expressed her outrage by pulling the garment skintight to her body.

"No, no, Maria, you misunderstand me," he protested, still chuckling. "I'm not laughing at you, only at the idea of my father and Caroline. Believe me, it would never enter his mind."

She plainly disbelieved him. "You think he does not want a woman?"

The way she put it wasn't as funny, but it didn't bear thinking about. "He wants *me* to marry Caroline Farnsworth. He already has a wife." Ted knew all about the marriage settlement his mother was supposed to have brought, the business her father had managed to run into the ground before Dwight Jasper could get his hands on it. Ted figured his parents' marriage had died the day Perkins and Dunbar declared bankruptcy.

Maria hated Caroline Farnsworth. She always had. From the beginning even her mother had expected her to play with Caroline and be her friend. Pah! She could not be friends with such a creature. She was too tall and skinny and too pale. To Maria, Caroline looked like one of the crawling things that live under dead logs, white and disgusting. She could not understand how everyone stared at her hair as if it were made of gold or silver. It didn't even curl the way the redheaded one's did. That at least was interesting. But straight and fine and colorless? What was so wonderful about that?

Very quickly she and Caroline had agreed to have nothing to do with each other. Caroline rode after the ranch hands and chased cows, doing all the dirty things the men did for money in her father's hire. That, or she sat in a corner with her nose in a book. Even her cast-off clothing was useless to Maria. Caroline was flat as a board in the chest; she even had no hips.

The one thing Caroline Farnsworth had that Maria envied was the security of her father's love and the family place that flowed from that. She was only a daughter, but no one could doubt that her father loved her. By herself she had nothing to make Maria afraid, not even some men's unaccountable fascination with pale hair. But as Jake

Farnsworth's daughter, she could perhaps interest a man such as Ted's father. Ted did not hunger for land the way his father did. He wanted her—Maria. That, too, was why Ted laughed.

Wasn't it?

She went to Ted, pressing and rubbing against him. "You told your father no, didn't you? You told him you do not want that creature for your wife."

Ted didn't make the mistake of laughing again, although he was tempted. She had no idea how utterly transparent she was. There were mysteries about her—as, for example, the rise and fall of her temper—but in this case he knew exactly what she was about.

"I'm in no hurry to get married. He knows that. He also knows I'd have to please Caroline, and that may not be easy. I'll see." He rested his chin on the top of her head and ran his hands down the satiny cloth covering her back. His fingers played along the small laddered bones of her spine until he reached the swelling fullness of her hips. For a moment he lost himself in the response of his own body. Fortunately, the tension in hers reminded him of his purpose. She needed reassurance, and he was happy to give it.

"Nothing will change between us, Maria. You can be sure of that. Caroline's a good sort, and if I have to marry someone I suppose I could do worse, but you'll still be my little love."

"You would marry her?"

"I doubt it will come to that, but I could give courtship a try to please the old man. He's—"

Maria didn't wait for whatever justification Ted would offer. She knocked him to the floor with a sudden body blow. Unprepared, he sat down hard. He fended off her kicks, rolling away instinctively, and caught the boots that rained down upon him. There were only two, but it seemed like more.

If she hadn't been jabbering at him, he might have tried to explain, but all those foreign words made an impenetrable wall around her. He started to get up, then changed his mind as he saw her about to launch another attack. Holding his boots, he ran outside, doubled over to protect his vulnerable underside.

She slammed the door behind him.

He stopped to look back. Hopping on first one foot, then the other, he put on the boots and began to laugh. She was one hot little number, that Maria. He wasn't giving her up, not for anyone, no sir.

That decided, he got on his horse and rode back home.

Chapter Ten

Caroline fixed her eyes on the empty chair in the next room. She sat in darkness in a small office at the jail, prepared to identify the men who had kidnapped her from the train. Although she had been told otherwise, it seemed to her that any man to sit in that chair would be able to see her as easily as she saw him. Rory assured her it was not so. He had checked for himself.

Rory had arranged this whole farce—to protect her, he said. She'd told him and the marshal it wasn't necessary. The men had all seen her before. They knew what she looked like. Why should she hide from them now that they had been arrested? What could they do to her now? It seemed silly to conceal herself behind such an elaborate facade.

She felt Rory's presence behind her. He meant to be reassuring, but in fact all this nonsense was beginning to spook her. She preferred things out in the open and straightforward, yet here she was, following Rory's cautious directions. She wore her darkest clothes and had a dark scarf over her hair to keep her invisible through the partially opened door. It was a wonder Rory hadn't insisted on blackface, she thought, suppressing a snicker.

The marshal squeezed his bulk through the door without disturbing its set. He stopped in front of her, cutting off her view of the reception area beyond. "They're about ready," he said quietly. "Remember now, I'll be right here and the men will be well guarded. Nothing can happen to you."

Caroline had heard it all before. No matter what she told him to the contrary, he persisted in believing that she had been the one insistent upon being hidden away. "I know," she answered, keeping the irritation out of her voice.

"Don't say anything until each man is taken away," he warned again.

She nodded. She didn't trust herself to speak calmly again. Both of them, even Rory, who ought to know better, evidently expected her to scream at first sight of her captors. As the marshal slipped behind her to stand with Rory, she smiled grimly, thinking perhaps she should faint or do something melodramatic so they would feel they'd done the proper thing in protecting her this way.

She almost did cry out when the first man took the carefully placed chair, but only because Rory gave her shoulder a painful squeeze just at that moment. She reached up and patted his hand consolingly. Poor Rory. *He* was the one suffering.

One by one, the men were put in the chair, ostensibly to be asked questions. First came Jeeter, then Brock. Caroline identified each by the only names she'd heard, thinking how ordinary and harmless they looked. The next, Moon, who she knew was not harmless, looked as if he had been asleep. He blinked like a mole in the bright light directed into his face. Remembering his attempt to rape her and his attack on Ernie, she didn't mind at all labeling him a criminal.

Humphrey was another story, though. His face looked drawn with illness still, and Caroline was moved to sympathy. He had paid dearly for so eagerly devouring her stew. Then, too, like Jeeter and Brock, he had done her no harm. Like Ernie, although to a lesser degree, he had helped her. When she gave his name, she tried to explain that fact to the marshal.

Rory interrupted. "What did he do to help you?"

"He fetched water from the river, and he was very polite. He called me ma'am."

The men were unimpressed. Marshal Deger signaled for the next man.

Walt, too, looked innocuous, but Caroline freely admitted that he had robbed the train passengers at gunpoint and abducted her in the face of Blackie's opposition.

The way things had gone so far Caroline felt perfectly comfortable as she watched Baltimore Blackie take the chair. Like the others, he showed signs that he had suffered from the purgative she had put in the stew. His skin was pale and clammy-looking.

But as soon as he took the seat she saw that he was different. He was aware. His eyes glittered as he looked around the outer office. Raising his shoulder to try to shield his face from the glaring lamp, he demanded. "What the hell is going on here? Why are you dragging us out here like this?"

Then, as if drawn by the force of her unseen attention, he looked toward the half-opened door. "Who's in there?"

Caroline held her breath and didn't move. She felt Rory's hand, heavy on her shoulder, reassuring now rather than oppressive. She told herself Blackie couldn't know she was there, no matter how he peered into the darkness.

But he did. Somehow, he did.

"You've got that sneaking, lying bitch in there, haven't you?" He was speaking softly, but with the same curious vocal power she had noticed on the train. Like an actor, he could throw his soft voice with the force of a boulder.

The deputy she couldn't see addressed Blackie, but he paid no attention. His black eyes, filled with hatred, bored into the shielding darkness around her, burning away the protection of Rory's ruse.

"I know you're in there, little Miss Farrell, and I have a message for you." He had to lunge to the side to avoid being grabbed, but it didn't stop him or change the soft menace in his voice. "Don't get too comfortable in your life," he warned, "because I'm going to find you again and make you wish you'd never been born. I'm going to—"

The deputy stepped between Blackie and the door, cutting off Caroline's view and stopping the flow of words. He struggled against the men who forced him away, raising his voice to be heard above their shouts. The incoherent sounds hung in the silence long after he was gone, all the more virulent somehow for being incomprehensible.

Rory came to life before Caroline did, stirred by his

101

bone-deep fury. When she tried to stand, he held her down, and for once she was grateful. He saved her from fainting dead away just as surely as he had saved her from giving Blackie the satisfaction of seeing her terror.

She felt like a fool. She had been so sure of herself, so . . . foolish.

"That was the one the men called Blackie," she said, summoning all her resources just to speak. "He told me to call him Thomas, but I never knew why. I didn't call him that. I didn't call him anything, really. He protected me from Walt at first. I don't think he took me seriously then."

Her attempt at levity brought a smile to Marshal Deger's ruddy face. He looked back in the act of opening the door, his eyes reflecting the gleam from the lamp. "I think it's safe to say he takes you seriously now."

Caroline stood up, restored.

"We'll do our best to see that he never finds out your real name, little lady, but even if he does, he won't hurt you. It won't be long before he swings by the neck."

She shuddered at his words, but shook off the image to turn to Rory. She owed him an apology for her arrogant assumption that she didn't need his care.

He took her arm and addressed himself to the marshal. "We're leaving in the morning. Thank you for all you've done."

"Miss 'Farrell' here did most of our work for us," he said, twinkling at her like a fond uncle. He shook Rory's hand the same way. "Take good care of her, now."

Caroline couldn't bring herself to resent their assumption of her helplessness. She knew she hadn't been helpless when it counted, and so did they. No one, not even Papa, was strong all the time.

She was quiet as they walked back to the hotel in the dark. Along Front Street only the Long Branch Saloon was lit and noisy. She watched men come and go and wondered what the inside looked like. If she asked, Rory wouldn't tell her, and he certainly wouldn't take her there.

Rory heard the small sigh that escaped her. "You're not to worry, Caroline. I promise you, you'll be safe."

Safe. She would be that, all right. Rory would keep her safe, but would he ever understand her? She didn't want to be a man, she just wanted . . . something. She shook her head, impatient with herself. If she couldn't put it into words for herself, how could she ever make anyone else understand?

"I know, Rory. I'm not afraid. His hatred shocked me, but I suppose he feels he has reason. What's funny to me is that he was outraged that I lied to him. He and his men put me in mortal danger, yet I should have been straight and honest with them!" She laughed to think of it.

"That's just the face he puts on it. You're only a slip of a girl, and you beat him. That's what's driving him crazy."

"He underestimated me because I'm female, you mean. Maybe he won't do that with the next one he meets."

"No. He'll take no chances and simply kill the next unfortunate woman. But he'll have to get free first, and that just won't happen."

"I wish I could have found out more about the others, particularly Humphrey. I'm sorry for him. I think he's like Ernie."

"Or the other way around," Rory muttered under his breath.

Caroline heard him and tried to withdraw her hand from the crook of his arm. He countered her move by trapping her hand between the bulging muscle of his arm and his side. "I don't understand you," she protested. "I would expect you to be grateful that he helped me. Do you know he offered to spare me this ordeal tonight by volunteering to turn himself in and tell what he knew about the gang?"

She was stretching the point. What Ernie had said was that he *wished* he could spare her. He hadn't really offered.

Rory was unimpressed anyway. "He knew he was safe as long as he did his volunteering to you. He certainly didn't tell me that. Or Marshal Deger."

"I wouldn't hear of it!"

"My point exactly."

Caroline gave up the argument. They differed and neither would change. As they approached the hotel, their steps slowed by mutual consent. Inside, they would have to separate. Inside, there were other people.

"You haven't told me what you're going to do about your uncle," Caroline said. She had not been tactful on the subject earlier. She'd made a lot of suggestions as soon as they'd learned his uncle was in the area, none of which he had appreciated. Now she trod on slippered tiptoes.

"Because I don't know."

She knew that wasn't the whole story. He probably *didn't* know, but if he had, he still wouldn't have told her. Not any more. "Remember the schemes we used to dream up about him?"

They had stopped walking altogether, and Caroline leaned back against the support of a post. Her wistful tone brought a smile from Rory. "They were your schemes, pretty much. You were the one with the imagination."

She grinned. "Courtesy of all my years of reading adventures. You thought some of them were pretty good, though."

"Boiling him in oil?"

Caroline enjoyed his rich laugh. He didn't laugh enough now that he was a man. "That would be hard to arrange these days," she admitted, hating to be brought back to reality. "Do you ever wish you'd been born in the days of knights and castles?" Her question was only half-serious. "Things were simpler then. You could have challenged your uncle to a fight and vanquished him forever."

He shook his head at her, smiling but less amused. "It wasn't any simpler then than it is now. Besides, they had lice and vermin in those days. I don't think I would have cared for all that armor, either."

She fought his unromantic vision, putting forth her own but trying to match his light tone. "But you'd make such a handsome knight. I could give you my scarf to tie on your sleeve—"

"If you'd lived in those days you'd be stowed away in a dark dungeon by this time in your life for being an unnatural female."

"Not so! Not by Papa!"

His teasing smile took on a stern cast. "Perhaps so. God knows, Jake would have been Jake then, too."

"You think I'm spoiled, don't you?" Caroline was too stunned to keep the hurt out of her expression. She saw Rory struggle for a way to explain himself. She waved it away. "Never mind," she said curtly. She pushed away from the post to walk by him. She had felt it before, this . . . jealousy of his because of their family positions. She understood, but it hurt. Oh, God, it hurt.

Yesterday he had kissed her and she had begun to dream about them . . . together. Rory and Caroline. But it was impossible. Other people might try and fail at romance because they didn't know each other well enough, because they didn't have enough in common. She and Rory had the reverse problem. They had too much history. They knew each other too well.

Rory felt like an outsider in the midst of their family. Still. He was loved, wanted, admired. But it wasn't enough. He didn't feel secure . . . or something. He saw the love she reveled in as indulgence and saw her as a pampered brat.

It was wrong. It was unfair. But it was his version of the truth, so how could she fight it? And did she even want to?

Right now, with him holding her arm to glare down at her, the answer was no.

"Don't be impossible, Caroline," he growled.

Her temper snapped. "Me? Of course I'm impossible! I'm the spoiled child you have to fetch home to her dear, doting papa." She tugged on her arm, making him hold her tighter. His fingers were already bruising her upper arm. She welcomed the pain, because it gave her something external to focus on. "Well, don't bother! I can get on the train tomorrow by myself."

Rory caught her other arm and hauled her against his chest. "Oh, no, you won't. I promised Jake I'd bring you home, and I will."

"You've done enough. Just go off and chase your uncle. It's what you want to do," she flung at him, knowing it was the truth—another truth about Rory that hurt. She was an impediment. He felt bound by his promise to Jake, when he

105

wanted more than anything to ride off to Ellsworth after his Uncle Joseph.

"Can't you stand to think that I might resemble one of your knights of old after all? You do admire men of honor, don't you?"

"But I don't need you to escort me. You can go. Zeb will take over."

"And Ernie?"

"Yes!" Let him think what he wanted about Ernie. She was sick of his jealousy. It was petty, and she didn't like to think of Rory as petty.

"No!" His hands went from her arms to her waist as he forced her back against the rough siding of the building. She hadn't been shouting because they were on the street, albeit one dark enough for a measure of privacy, but her tone had been scathing. His was more so. Deep and rough, it flayed her, removing another protective coating.

He lifted her, his hands spread to span her waist, until her face was level with his. Tall as she was among women, she always had to tilt her head to look into Rory's eyes. Now she didn't. She had often wanted to erase that particular disparity between them, but she wasn't enjoying this. She didn't feel equal at all. She felt helpless. It was as though he had hung her on the wall. She wasn't afraid of falling. There was no chance of that, not with his hands holding her, not with his body pressed against hers.

She felt her mouth go dry and nervously ran the tip of her tongue over her lower lip. His face was so close she could feel his breath on her cheek. If she turned her head . . .

"Put me down."

His laugh was a puff of warm air on her skin. He laughed because she sounded afraid.

She tried harder. "I mean it, Rory."

But her firmness only made him bolder. He pushed one knee between her dangling legs. The contact with his body was shocking enough, but he made it worse by easing his grip on her waist. Instinctively, to keep from falling, she gripped his thigh between hers the way she would a horse.

He chuckled smugly and said, "I may never put you down. I think I like you this way."

"I'll . . . scream," she whispered.

He nuzzled her cheek and found her ear. The damp heat of his breath made her head swim. "Go ahead," he urged. "Scream."

His lips, then his teeth tugged at her earlobe, and she sucked in breath. But not to scream. She had never felt anything like the jolt that went through her body. She melted under its heat. Even her limbs became flaccid, and she felt herself slipping lower around his leg. The feeling was so delicious. It was wicked — wonderfully, wonderfully wicked.

Remembering herself, Caroline stiffened and tried to pull her head free. There was only one way to move, toward Rory. The building wouldn't move. When she turned, his mouth covered hers. It was a firm mouth with expressive, warm lips. She had been about to speak when he caught her, so she immediately clamped her lips together in order to kiss him properly.

He let her, contenting himself with just the soft texture of her lips, moving his mouth gently, caressingly. Letting her kiss him back. She looped her arms around his shoulders to do so, pressing her breasts tightly against his chest.

When he lifted his mouth, she followed until she remembered not to.

"Open your mouth for me."

His words, as dark and sweet as molasses, seemed to come from her own mind. Without thought, she obeyed. Later she would rationalize that she had been about to protest and he took advantage of that fact. Now she was unable to put two words together. She only parted her lips slightly, then responded to the gentle rub of his tongue along the rim of her lower lip. Her quick intake of breath seemed to draw his tongue deeper.

Rory hovered on the edge of complete loss of control. Touching Caroline had been an impulse. Her taunts had ignited his usually cool temper, and now he was in danger of forgetting himself totally. He could feel the heat of her body surrounding his thigh and the soft weight of her breasts pressing his chest just above his spread hands. A few more inches . . .

Her breath was as ragged, as erratic as his. He lifted his head to look into her face. It was pale, an almost featureless oval, like the moon in a dark sky. He knew her features better than his own. He'd studied them for years and watched her grow from a gamin-child into an almost-woman. But there was no almost about the woman he held. She was sweet and sweetly responsive.

This was the Caroline he'd never dared hope to find.

It didn't seem fair that he should find her now, just when he would have to leave her again. It had been hard to go away years ago, but this time it would be worse. Then she'd only been a promise. So many things could have changed between them in the interim. He could have found another to love. So could she. But they hadn't.

Last time he'd left her, his search for Uncle Joseph had been little better than an excuse to put distance between them while she grew up. Now he needed his heritage more than ever. Without it, what did he have to offer Caroline? He had to go, no matter how bad the timing was. And it was a great deal more than bad.

One thing he knew. He should never have kissed her, not like this.

Slowly she opened her eyes and let him see her confusion. She wore the soft, unfocused look of arousal—and doubt. Her scarf had slipped to her shoulders, and the shingled building had caught tendrils of her hair, tugging them free of their confinement.

"Caroline—"

He had no idea what to say. He should apologize, reassure her . . . something.

Ashamed of himself, he was gruff. Tightening his grip on her ribs, he pulled back his leg and set her onto her feet. The only way he could think of to make amends was to replace her scarf, but in doing so his hand collided with hers. He dropped the scarf instantly.

"Fix your hair." Although he spoke softly, his hoarseness

made the words sound ugly and demanding.

Caroline felt as though she had been dropped from the heavens into a vat of cold water. She swayed on her feet, unable to find her balance. Even her temper had deserted her. She lifted shaking hands to her hair and made the only decision she was capable of forming. She wouldn't fix her hair. She wouldn't do another thing Rory told her to do. Ever!

"I hate you."

"Caroline, I'm sorry. I didn't . . ." He cleared his throat and tried again. "This isn't the place for . . ." Oh, God. He was making it worse.

He certainly was. Caroline wrapped the dark gray scarf around her head, tight enough to choke herself, and backed off from Rory, facing him furiously. He took a step toward her, his hands spread in a placating gesture.

Rory could see that she wasn't going to be soothed, but he believed he had to try. He'd made a complete botch of a moment that would live in his heart forever. Somehow he had to rectify it. "I meant you no dishonor, Caroline."

So far, so good. He took another step.

Before he could react, she delivered a furious kick to his shin and marched away on her sensible, solidly shod feet. The kick and her escape caught him off guard, particularly because he'd had his eyes on her hands, thinking she might try to slap him. He should have known better. He'd been kicked before, by horses, mules and cows—miserable creatures all—but this was different, and she wasn't going to get away with it. He wasted no time hopping on one foot or rubbing his leg.

He caught up to her in the lobby and matched her stride for stride as she sailed for the wide staircase. It was late enough so that the lobby was nearly deserted. The desk clerk ignored them to read a newspaper, while another man dozed in a chair over his. The only one to notice their militant march was the man cleaning out the spittoons. He stopped work to watch until they were out of sight.

Caroline hadn't been able to shake his hand from her arm, but she refused to let that disturb her. She had the key

109

to her room. Soon she'd be inside. Nothing mattered except her goal of total privacy.

A man left his room at the end of the hall on her floor and scurried to the back stairs as if he were hurrying to get out of their path. All the other doors remained tightly shut as Caroline reluctantly gave up her key so he could open the door for her. She wanted to refuse but didn't quite dare challenge the locked severity of his jaw. He looked formidable as he held the door open for her to pass.

She didn't move. "My key," she said, putting out her hand. The demand she intended to be imperious came out sounding breathless. Her heart beat like an overwound clock, its spring about to jump out of her chest. Exertion, she told herself. She had walked too fast.

Rory took her hand and drew her toward the door. He didn't give her the key, but she could feel it in his hand. "Inside," he said, standing aside.

She resisted, distrusting his stance.

"So now you've the good sense to be afraid," he laughed.

Her chin rose sharply. "I am not afraid!"

He drew her away from the wall. "You should be. I said I was sorry once, but if you ever pull a trick like that again I'll make *you* very, very sorry."

Outraged, Caroline snatched back her hand, forgetting about the key, and swept past him into her room. She moved quickly, but not fast enough to avoid the perfectly timed downswing of his broad hand. The stinging smack caught her by surprise in spite of his warning, burning through the cloth of her skirt and petticoat as if they weren't there. It was enough to make her wish for a bustle.

She wheeled on him, just in time to see him toss the key at her feet and shut the door. She also saw his smile of satisfaction.

The smile didn't last long. As angry as he was with Caroline, Rory was more upset at himself. Not for the swat. She'd deserved that; but she hadn't deserved the way he'd hurt her down in the street. That had been unconscionable. His only excuse, that he'd been unable to control himself, didn't wash. He was experienced; she was not. His experience should have shown him how to ease her gently back to earth with her confidence in herself—and in him—intact.

He hadn't done that. Instead, he'd gotten caught in the web of sensation she'd spun around him. Then, panicked at his own lack of control, he'd ripped the whole subtle construction down around their heads, injuring her more than he cared to realize.

He pushed through the lobby, telling himself he'd make it up to her. She was tough, as Zeb was always reminding him. She had resilience. With such indefatigable spirit, she would bounce right back up again. But Rory could not forgive himself for causing her pain. She was half overindulged child, half emerging woman and—sometimes—all termagant, but she deserved better, especially from him.

Next time, he told himself. Next time.

Rory disappeared into the Long Branch Saloon, but the man following him kept going. Finished with his work back at the hotel, he went to the jail, where he liked to visit with his cousin. Ollie would still be awake for a while, and the man was curious to see the new prisoners. Dodge City was no stranger to excitement, but today had been a doozie.

Ollie had the checkerboard set up on the battered tabletop, as if he expected company. Willard Perkins gave it only a glance. "Where's them new fellers?"

"Now where do you think they are?"

Willard paced the corridor, looking into each cell. "Which one is the great Baltimore Blackie?" he called back to Ollie. He knew he was disturbing the men who were trying to sleep, but they were behind bars now. He was safe. "I wanta see the great outlaw who got foxed by a *girl!*"

Ollie's chuckle echoed down the bare hall. "He's in there, all right. You oughta be able to pick him out."

"He's famous, ain't he, Ollie? Why, everyone in town's buzzin' their heads off 'bout how that slick little filly had him eatin' outta her hand."

"And pukin' up his guts, too!" Ollie joined him at the cell door, finding Willard's sport irresistible.

"He don't look dangerous to me." Willard spoke to his

cousin confidingly while they both stared at two men inside one cell. "Looks like a weasel, though. Sneaky," he pronounced.

"That one's Stimpson. Blackie's next door."

As if they were at a zoo, they moved on to the next barred door.

Blackie had not been able to settle down after his return to the cell he shared with Moon, and he was in no mood to put up with the comments he was hearing. Once proud of his self-control, he had rarely been violent in his life. Now, in the aftermath of his oblique confrontation with Cathleen Farrell, he was. And frustrated. His eyes, as he met Willard's childishly curious gaze, glowed with malevolent fury. He couldn't do what he wanted to the miserable excuse for a man on the other side of the door, but he could enjoy reducing him to a slack-jawed imbecile with just one potent stare.

Against his will, Willard's breath leaked out in a sigh that was half fear, half satisfaction. Here was what he had come to see. It frightened him, but it was also curiously pleasing. In that moment he had everything he wanted. To see, and perhaps touch, something evil. To do it from safety. His eyes locked with Blackie's, and it took all his self-possession not to look away in fear.

He might have been satisfied that he won that battle, except for the contempt on Blackie's face as he looked away from Willard. It made him feel dismissed.

Willard refused to be dismissed. He stepped closer to the bars and spoke softly to Blackie, imitating the drawl he'd heard was Blackie's signature. "I reckon you didn't hear yet about the statue folks are gonna put in the depot. It's gonna be a girl and a stewpot," he laughed, warming to his inspiration.

Ollie plucked at his arm, urging him back from the door, but Willard paid no mind. Blackie had his back to them, and Willard wasn't finished yet. He extended his hand inside in an expansive gesture. "Yes, sir," he continued in a soft singsong, "and on the bottom it's gonna say, 'To Miss Caroline Farnsworth, the girl—' "

112

Blackie whirled on Willard, grabbing him before he could bring his hand back to safety. "What did you say?"

The pain of Blackie's grip made Willard's body sag against the bars, putting him in peril of being choked to death. With Blackie's fingers at his throat, he was incapable of answering, even if he'd known what to say.

Ollie alternatively struck at Blackie through the bars and tugged on Willard's shirt, but nothing could pry his cousin loose.

"What did you call her?" Blackie bellowed. For emphasis, he shook Willard against the bars. "Her name!" he demanded.

In the shaking, Blackie's grip slipped from Willard's neck. He didn't get away completely, though, and when Blackie wrenched his arm against the bars Willard screamed out, "Caroline . . . Farns . . . worth!"

Chapter Eleven

"Did she hear about it?"

"Not from me."

Rory frowned, not at Zeb, who answered plainly, as always, but at the picture Caroline made with her pale head only inches from Ernie's. They looked out the train window together, Caroline pointing out something, Ernie leaning over to peer out with interest. *Just as if there were something to see out there,* Rory thought scornfully.

"Did he tell her?"

"Not that I heard."

"Did *he* hear about it?" Rory didn't know why he persisted in questioning Zeb. He was as informative as a wall. All Rory ever got back was the echo of his own voice. But he had to talk to someone or burst, and there was no one else available. If only Jake or Hannah were here . . . no, not Jake.

The thought of Jake waiting in Santa Fe was enough to make his palms sweaty. He'd have to tell Jake he'd failed to protect Caroline. That he'd tried wasn't good enough. He'd failed, and Jake would be worried when he still looked as though the weight of a feather added to his broad shoulders would put him six feet under the ground.

"I didn't have him tied to me," Zeb said with a nod of his head to Ernie, "but he wasn't far away, either. I 'spect I'd've heard about it if he had."

"I don't know how he didn't," Rory concluded glumly.

Rory had been sitting quietly at the bar, hoping to drink himself into oblivion, when word came to the saloon that all hell had broken out at the jail. Baltimore Blackie was on a rampage.

Rory followed the crowd to the jail, wondering if he was

becoming part of a necktie party. He wasn't drunk at all. He hadn't had time yet, but others were not so sober. Nor had the others his intense interest in Baltimore Blackie. To them, Blackie was only a curiosity, a source of excitement. They hadn't his hatred of the man or his fear. They sought diversion, while he was driven by the need to know what Blackie was up to. If he'd escaped . . .

He hadn't. He'd broken a man's arm in two places, but he remained in his cell—or had been put back there again. Only Rory, apparently, wondered how Blackie had managed to assault a free man from the confines of his cell.

Rory never had a chance to find out if he would have tried to prevent a mob lynching. Marshal Deger moved quickly to disperse the crowd, making sure it never became a mob. For his part, Rory was pleased not to be put to the test. He believed in justice and law, even for Blackie, but with the men around him muttering that Blackie had been yelling about "the girl," he doubted that he could have forced himself to speak up in opposition to an impromptu execution.

"Who was hurt?" he asked the man next to him on the edge of the thinning crowd.

"Just old Willard Perkins," came the answer between squirts of tobacco juice into the dirt.

"He lives here?"

"More or less. He cleans the depot and the hotel, sort of. The man's scum."

"Was he in jail?"

"He visits there."

Rory wasn't sure what that meant. "He's a drunk?"

"Sometimes."

That explained how Blackie got close enough to harm Perkins, but not why. Perhaps there was no why. Blackie had been taken to his cell ranting at Caroline. Probably the man had just been unlucky enough to get in his way.

It all came clear to Rory later when a deputy took the seat next to him and shook his head apologetically. "We tried," he said ruefully, "but there's always some fool with a big mouth."

Then Rory heard the story complete, and the fine hairs at the back of his neck stood on end.

"He went berserk," the deputy said of Blackie. "I can't see the difference between two names, but Blackie sure can. It won't help his case any, of course, to have shown such enmity to a mere girl, even if she did trick him. What did he expect her to do? Wrestle him for his gun?"

Rory pounced on the alarming part of the man's statement. "You don't really believe he has a case, do you? No judge would set him free." It was his next to worst fear, right up there with the chance of Blackie's escape.

"Well, no. They've got too much on him. He'll hang unless he gets a miracle."

The idea of a miracle for Baltimore Blackie continued to plague Rory. He would have to tell Jake the whole story, but at least he could keep it from Caroline. She had been shaken by Blackie's hatred. She would feel worse if she knew he had made the connection between Cathleen Farrell and Caroline Farnsworth.

It wasn't as though being warned would do her any good. There was nothing anyone could do, beyond what they were already doing—putting miles between Caroline and Baltimore Blackie. She would be safe in New Mexico.

Outside the train, Kansas slipped by. They were almost to Sargent, the last stop before the Colorado border. Rory would be glad to see the last of Kansas for a while. He would, of course, be back. Uncle Joseph was in Kansas, and he had business yet with Uncle Joseph.

He kept his eyes on the back of Caroline's head. If he hadn't had to escort her back to Jake, what would he have done about Uncle Joseph? Nothing, he hoped—yet. For now it was enough to have a fresh trail to follow. He didn't want to plunge in without a plan of action. How strange to have found him like that, unexpectedly, and in his own backyard, so to speak.

His glance moved from Caroline to Ernie. He'd have to thank Ernie for finding him. He wondered what Caroline had told Ernie. Plenty, it looked like. They chattered like squirrels.

116

Zeb noted with sympathy the obsessive direction Rory's eyes took. Caroline had come back looking like a new penny. She'd always been a pretty little mite, all sparkle and smiles. Now she made a man's eyes hurt. It didn't take a genius to see she'd set Rory back on his heels pretty hard.

Wanting to help Rory some way, Zeb dredged his mind for some distracting topic of conversation. All he could find was a question. "What did you find out about Joseph Talmage?"

Rory answered without taking his eyes off the couple three seats ahead of them. "Not much. He comes from Ellsworth. Or at least that's where he says he's from."

"Is he the right one?"

"I don't know. He had checked out and gone."

"What are you gonna do?"

"I don't know."

Zeb could think of nothing else to say. And anyway, it hadn't worked. Rory was still boring holes with his eyes in the backs of their heads.

After a pause, Rory asked in obvious exasperation, "What do they find to talk about like that?"

Zeb gave a quiet chuckle. "You're askin' *me?*"

When the train stopped in Sargent, Caroline and Ernie prepared to leave the car. They started forward, but when Rory got to his feet as if he wanted to protest, Caroline came back to offer an explanation. With it, she gave Rory his first smile of the day. It was impudent, challenging Rory to object.

"I can't resist the chance to see Sargent. I told Blackie I was being met here by my future husband."

"Your husband?"

Her eyes danced with mischief. "I told him I had answered an ad from a silver prospector in Colorado. I described you, but Blackie thought I had been misled by an old codger. He wouldn't believe anything good could come out of Sargent, Kansas. Now I want to see for myself if he was right."

Rory didn't know what to say. He recognized the look in her eye and knew she was still angry about last night. He

117

would have to apologize sometime, but this wasn't the time or place for it. Feeling surly, he snapped, "Don't miss the train."

Not deigning to respond, Caroline turned back to the waiting Ernie and made her way outside.

Without the obliterating noise of the moving train, the interior became unnaturally quiet, exaggerating sounds that leaked in from outside. There were few other passengers, and those who remained seated inside had little to say. After several minutes of strained silence, Rory said, "Perhaps I'll stretch my legs a bit."

Zeb was behind him when he stepped down onto the platform. A glance at the tiny depot, little more than a shack, lettered on the side, told Rory he agreed with Blackie about the settlement. When he didn't see Caroline immediately, he began to search for her in earnest.

Zeb noticed and said, "She's inside." He nodded to the building behind Rory.

He turned to look and saw the opened doorway, clustered with men. His mouth tightened to think of Caroline at the center. Because he wanted to go and pull her away, he paced off in the opposite direction. Zeb trailed him distantly, stationing himself midway between Rory and the depot like a dog torn by loyalties to a master and mistress.

Caroline came out without Ernie. She strode toward Zeb, and then, seeing Rory, marched in his direction.

"Why didn't you tell me?" she demanded.

Rory didn't have to ask what she meant. Out of the corner of his eyes he saw Ernie force his way through the men in pursuit of Caroline. At the same time he saw Zeb intercept his path and, like a clever cow pony, herd him away from them onto the train.

"Who told you?"

"What difference does it make? *You* should have told me."

Rory only wanted to know that Ernie hadn't been the one. Or maybe that was what he hoped for. Logic told him it was one of the trainmen who had been talking to Caroline, not Ernie; otherwise, why would he have waited so

118

long? But logic played little part in Rory's feelings about Ernie.

"I didn't want you upset."

"He broke a man's *arm* when he found out my name?" There was horror in her question and an unspoken need for reassurance.

Rory took her arm gently. "It sounds worse than it was. The deputy marshal told me about it. I'm not condoning what Blackie did, but the man asked for it, Caroline. He was baiting him the way kids do with a chained dog. He taunted Blackie about being outwitted by a girl."

She resisted his touch, regaining her normal spirit. "Why does everyone make so much of that? Just because I'm female, I'm supposed to be helpless? And stupid?"

"Of course you're not," he soothed, steering her toward the train. "We both know Hannah would have done just as well, but most women—most *people*," he amended emphatically, "wouldn't have. Think of all the men on that train you were taken from. No one helped you. No one chased those men."

"Mrs. Reed tried," Caroline said.

"Mrs. Reed?" He helped her up the first steep step at the entrance opposite the one Zeb and Ernie used.

"She sat across from me on the train. She was half as tall as I am and half as sensible—most of the time, anyway. I took care of her on the trip. She was coming out to join her husband. She kept losing things, dropping things. She asked as many questions as Abby. But she was the only one who lifted a hand to help me when I was being carried off. She attacked Walt Stimpson from behind. He pushed her down, and I worried that he hurt her. I suppose I'll never know."

Rory urged her into a seat near the back and sat next to her. "I know who you mean. She's the one who told me you were taken. She was fine. I remember now how disgusted she was that the men wouldn't go after you."

"Well, you see?" Caroline asked with a satisfied look.

Rory had no idea what she meant. He had been concentrating on getting her seated well away from Ernie. Their conversation had been incidental, but he was glad to see that she felt better.

Loud clangs and slams announced the start of the train again, and he was reminded that there was another issue between them, one he didn't want to grow out of proportion and poison their relationship. Now that he had the opportunity for privacy, however, it seemed indelicate to bring it up again. But he had to.

He cleared his throat and said, "About last night . . ."

Caroline's face colored faintly, and she shifted on the seat. Her eyes darted to his, then away as she lifted her chin. "I suppose I had it coming."

For a second Rory was puzzled, and then he laughed, unconsciously fingering his bruised shin. "Not the swat. You certainly did deserve that." He enjoyed the way her blush deepened, but then it was his turn—again—to be uncomfortable. "Before you kicked me," he said, struggling to find the appropriate words. "I'm sorry for before—"

She glared at him, and his grasp on his intent slipped loose.

"I shouldn't have—I mean, I *should* have—"

"You had it right the first time," she snapped. "You had absolutely no right to touch me, and if you ever do it again I'll—"

"You'll what?" He pulled her around to face him. There was no one behind them and no way for the people in front of them to hear their intense but low voices. He wanted to kiss her again right now. Her lips were parted enticingly over the indignant words she was about to hurl at him. If he kissed her, they would soften and bloom under the pressure of his mouth. . . .

Instead, he put his thumb over them, vertically, and held her chin with his fingers along the delicate rim of her jawbone. She was too surprised to move away, although she pulled back slightly as if she wanted to snap her teeth over his thumb.

"Caroline," he said with soft insistence, "I am not apologizing for kissing you. I'll do that any time I want to—

including now." He tightened his hold on her in warning. Her mutinous look became a blush, whether of anger or mortification he couldn't tell. He smiled gently. "Sorry, sweetheart, but that's the way it is. Those aren't the things a man apologizes for. I *am* sorry for being abrupt with you afterward. I never meant to get so carried away, and I didn't let you down gently—as I should have."

Embarrassment won the war in Caroline over anger. She didn't have experience enough to know how rare Rory's concern for her was. She only knew he was talking out loud about something that was too painful for her even to think about. Last night he had assaulted her person; now he was doing the same thing—with words—to her soul.

She pulled back, stricken to the core, then pushed her way past him out into the aisle of the swaying, shuddering train.

With her heart clamoring as insistently as the flywheel driving the locomotive, she stumbled into the empty seat behind Zeb and Ernie, where she knew she would be safe. She'd never be able to erase his words—let her down gently, indeed!—but she wouldn't give him another opportunity to humiliate her again. As if she had *wanted* him to kiss her and touch her so intimately!

It hurt so very badly, and all the more so because it was Rory doing and saying such things. He had always been her friend. She had trusted him. Now she didn't know or understand him at all.

She curled in upon herself in the hard, high-backed seat, pressed to the window side. Her chin and arm still felt warm from his touch, touches she was determined to wipe from her mind.

She almost yelped when he took the seat beside her, startling her into taking one quick look at him. Fortunately, he didn't look at her, but his profile was as hard-edged as a relief carving in bronze. She held herself stiffly away from his unwanted presence and pretended to sleep.

It was such a long way to Santa Fe. How would she stand it?

She would have been pleased to know that the trip was as

intolerable for Rory as it was for her. He followed to sit with her, unwelcome or not, because he wouldn't let her dictate what he could do or where he could sit. He didn't understand his offense this time, so he dismissed it — or tried to.

When she got up to walk outside at the next station, he didn't follow. And when she resettled with Ernie, he ignored them. He did note, with a certain grim pleasure, that though she sat with Ernie, she didn't talk to him the way she had before.

Perhaps, after all, he had accomplished something.

The carriage Jake handed Caroline up into was the finest Santa Fe had to offer. Like everything Spanish, it was ornate and handsome, sacrificing nothing to utility. Caroline sank back into the seat with a sigh of pleasure. It was her first totally natural act since their arrival, and as such, it was twice the relief it seemed. She wasn't much of an actress.

At the last minute, as Jake had first come into view in his tall buff hat trimmed with a jaunty red feather, Rory had stepped in front of Caroline to warn in his most ungentle tone, "He looks like hell, Caroline, but don't you *dare* cry!"

She had needed the warning. Everything about it, his timing, words and tone of voice, had been calculated to rouse her temper. She might not know Rory any more, but he knew her. He knew once she saw her father she would need every ounce of starch anger could give her.

The essential Jake Farnsworth was still there. He was still tall and broad-shouldered, still darkly handsome, and his eyes were still like circles of sky that warmed with love at the sight of her. But the changes — dear God, she had wanted to scream at those.

She still did. But the only person she could abuse was Rory, and it wasn't his fault. She felt lied to, though, and betrayed. Especially, she felt guilty that she had so easily accepted their loving lies. They had meant to comfort her, and she had let them do so instead of clinging to her

122

suspicions and worries.

Jake got in beside her and immediately took her hand in both of his. "It's all right, punkin," he said, giving her hand a squeeze. *"I'm* all right now, I promise."

Caroline summoned a smile, hoping it didn't look as unnatural as it felt. "I'm so glad, Papa. I knew you had to be better or Hannah wouldn't have let you out of her sight."

"I had to come, honey." His voice thickened dangerously. "God, but I've missed you!"

He was breaking her hand, but she managed to squeeze back. Just as she had not dared run to him earlier for a hug, now she didn't dare lean on him. She touched her head to his shoulder briefly, making do with fleeting contact out of deference to what seemed his skeletal condition.

His words told her that for all her attempt at self-control, which had been mammoth, she hadn't hidden her shock well at all. Hating Rory's quick look of sympathy as he took the seat opposite her, Caroline vowed to do better.

"They don't make carriages like this in Philadelphia, Papa." She patted the worn plush with an appreciative hand. "Now I know I'm back where I belong."

"Back to stay, I hope. You'll never know how I worried that some young man back east would make you change your mind about coming home."

"A couple tried to, but I'm like you. I felt crowded back there. I think I would have even if I'd never moved out here with you. I remember always feeling restless in Hanford, wanting something more that was 'out there' — somewhere. I didn't understand it then, but now that I do, I don't think I could go back to stay."

Caroline wasn't proud that she had mentioned her suitors or that she had done it to spite Rory, but it wasn't a lie. And now that she had assuaged her pride, she put pettiness aside. She was truly back to stay. She would help Papa and work the ranch and live here forever. Rory would go off chasing his uncle, but that meant nothing to her any more. Papa, home, family, New Mexico — everything she wanted was right here.

123

Their trip home would be grueling. Papa had come with Frank and Ellen Colby. Weary though she was from her train ride, she knew the last leg home would be worse. It was, surely, the reason Papa looked so bad. A wagon pulled by oxen moved ponderously in the heat. She pushed down a flare of anger and disbelief that Hannah had allowed Jake to come. She knew it hadn't been Hannah's choice, but why had she not come, too?

She gave Rory a magnanimous smile of forgiveness. Once she was back at Renegade Ranch everything would be perfect. Home was heaven to her, and didn't the scriptures promise that in heaven she would know and understand everything?

Chapter Twelve

"Have you seen Rusty?"

Lupe looked up at Caroline from the bowl she was stirring. "Lincoln? Why, he was just here a minute ago. Perhaps he went to talk to Zeb. He said something about Zeb, but I wasn't paying attention."

"I can imagine. You have plenty to do without keeping your eye on him," Caroline laughed, reaching for the bowl. Lupe was helping Mrs. Jasper feed her many guests, not an unusual arrangement in their area. No one could have a party without Lupe's refreshments; it was unheard of. "Go on. You do something else," she offered. "I can stir this."

"But this is your party, too. You're not supposed to be working. You're supposed to be dancing."

Caroline won the battle of the bowl and pulled out a stool to sit on. "I'm resting my feet. Those cowboys have no mercy." She wiggled her feet, pulling up her gown to show the scuff marks on her shoes.

"They have big boots," Lupe agreed.

"Big feet. But oh, do they love to dance! It's funny. Back east the men all say they hate to dance. They act as if dancing is something only for women. They should see these men dancing with each other for lack of a female partner."

"Then you should be out there." Lupe spoke around a spoon. She said her cooking depended on tasting, not on recipes, and she was her own best advertisement.

"I'm only interested in dancing with my brother. I told him I'd make him do a set with me."

"So that's why he's hiding!"

125

"The little devil said I'd have to catch him first, and so far he's led me on a merry chase." She helped herself to a hot tortilla, filled and rolled it expertly. At her first bite she sighed noisily. "Umm, this is heaven! You can't imagine how I missed your cooking!"

"Of course I can. You've told me with every bite you've taken this week."

"And I've taken a lot of bites, haven't I?" she said complacently. "Soon I'll be popping out of my clothes."

"There's another I wish would eat more," Lupe said darkly, speaking more to herself than to Caroline.

"Papa." She let her hand fall, and only Lupe's quick action saved her dress, an airy confection of scallops and lace the color of a deep blush, from being decorated by a blob of sauce. She frowned, barely aware of Lupe. "He's still so *drawn*-looking."

"But he's better now that you're here," Lupe soothed, obviously unhappy with herself for bringing up the subject.

"Do you think so? I'm not sure I agree."

"Of course I think so. You are his right arm!" Lupe insisted. "Always, he says, 'I need Caroline here. She's my right-arm man.' "

Her imitation of Jake's deep voice and the mangling of his wording made Caroline laugh with delight. She half suspected that Lupe did some of her mangling on purpose, knowing the value of a good laugh. She hugged Lupe anyway and picked up a tray of food to take with her, saying, "Thanks for letting me borrow your stool. If you see Rusty, don't tell him I was here. Keep him as long as you can, and I'll be back."

A string of paper lanterns led Caroline from the kitchen along a path to the decorated patio at the side of Jasper's house. She put down the tray on a table, smiling as everyone converged upon it. Music and the sound of laughter tried to tug her back to the dance, but she didn't succumb. Her game with Rusty thoroughly engaged her interest. He was such a rascal. She was going to outwit him and love every minute of his defeat.

Rounding the corner of the house on the next leg of her

pursuit, Caroline surprised two people embracing. She hurried on, determined not to be able to put names to the bodies who so unwillingly reminded her of Rory and herself back in Dodge City. The woman was pressed against the house, imprisoned by her suitor's arms. Did that man also press his knee between her legs as Rory had done to her? And did she mind?

Her footsteps faltered at the invasive memory. It was shameful, wasn't it? Then why did she think of it so often? She wasn't the kind of woman who liked being shameful. At least she hoped she wasn't.

Pushing aside the thought, she walked on, only to be brought up short by a call from behind. She whirled, checking the shadowed building first. The couple was gone. Had Rory—?

He caught up to her in two strides of his long legs. "You were looking for me?" he asked.

Had he thought she was spying on him? "Certainly not," she said sharply.

Before she could turn away, he took her arm as a gentleman does the lady he's escorting. "But you were. Everywhere I go I heard that Caroline is looking for me."

"I'm looking—"

"To dance?"

"For Rusty," she said firmly.

"Then I'm not the brother you want?"

Caroline didn't care for his emphasis on the word brother. "You're not my brother at all."

"Then you remember that, do you?"

She stumbled on the darkened path and felt his hand steady her. "This is the wrong direction." They were headed toward greater privacy, the last thing she wanted with Rory.

"You want to dance after all?"

The thought of his arms around her made her shake her head.

"Then this is the right way. Unless," he added significantly, "you were avoiding me."

Because she had been, she wanted to deny it. But that was what he expected of her. He wanted her to rise to his

127

challenge and prove she wasn't afraid to be alone with him. But she was. It seemed simpler, and more sensible, to admit it. She couldn't quite do it, but her silence was eloquent.

Rory took Caroline to the shelter of a large cottonwood. They had no need for the shade it would provide in daylight, but there was a gnarled bench to sit on. He knew it was wrong to seek out Caroline, but he couldn't help himself. She drew him. Then too, having her avoid him so obviously made him feel like a despoiler of virgins when, in fact, he'd only kissed her. Tonight he meant to prove to both of them that they could still be friends in spite of the attraction that flashed between them like lightning jumping from peak to peak in the Sangre de Cristos.

Caroline pulled the overflow of her skirt to the side so he could sit beside her, unsure whether or not she could trust his relaxed manner. But he only asked, "Now that you're back again, how do you feel? Strange? Or as if you've never been away?"

She didn't even have to consider her answer. "Both. At the same time." Then she laughed. "That doesn't make sense, does it?"

"It does to me. I've been away, too. I felt the same thing when I first came back. The familiarity and the strangeness." He shook his head.

Mention of his trip to Oregon and California reminded her again that he would soon leave them once more. She seemed to need the reminder. "I'm worried about Papa — and not just his health. He's . . . different."

"He's never a good patient, Caroline, and this was worse than anything he's ever suffered, even being shot. He almost died and he knows it. It's made him aware of his mortality."

Caroline was glad this Rory was the old comfortable one. She badly needed to talk about Hannah. "I understand that. I even understand that sometimes a person's brush with mortality doesn't *improve* him, but I don't understand the way he is with Hannah." After a pause she added, "Or how she stands it."

If Caroline saw the gulf, too, then it was real. Rory had hoped he'd only imagined it. Unlike his own parents, Jake

128

and Hannah were volatile; their emotions were close to the surface. They argued, sometimes fought, but more often showed the great tenderness and love they had for each other. Although his own nature was more pacific than Jake's, he'd decided long ago that he preferred their fireworks to his parents' rigid "peace."

When Rory didn't speak she went on, feeling her way blindly along the pathways of her mind. "I didn't see it on the trip. He wasn't so . . . cold then." She chanced a look up at Rory. "He was charming to Ellen Colby."

He winced, embarrassed to remember. Frank Colby was nearing sixty. Like Zeb, he had been in Jake's army unit and served with him in Nebraska in the renegade troop Jake operated there in aid of the Union Pacific Railroad. Before the war, Frank, a widower, had married Ellen, a woman only marginally older than his grown-up children.

Although Ellen had often made immodest overtures to Jake, and probably to other men nearer her age, Jake had never encouraged her. He would not, as much out of respect and affection for Frank as for love of Hannah. Ellen was a lovely woman, but she paled in comparison to Hannah. On the trip Jake hadn't done anything at all reprehensible, but he had treated Ellen to more of his charm than she deserved.

And Caroline had noticed.

"I don't think that matters."

"It matters that he's sharp with Hannah, though."

"Well, yes, it does. I think that will pass in time." To himself Rory added, *When Jake has proven to himself that he's still in charge of himself.*

"It had better," Caroline muttered darkly.

Rory laughed. "She treats him like a child, you know. That can't help."

It didn't, but it was very easy to see why Hannah was overprotective when Caroline had to fight down her own urge to cosset Jake.

"I was asking about you, though," Rory reminded her. "Are you happy to be back? Is it still what you remembered and wanted?"

"Yes, everything!" She said it too quickly, as if she were

129

afraid to admit to the smallest doubt. Doubts had a way of growing bigger until they towered over what was certain, diminishing it.

"Then I envy you."

"You could stay here, too." She could barely admit to herself how much she wanted that. "I know I always urged you to avenge your father's death, but I don't think that's so necessary any more. No matter what your uncle has done, I don't believe it's profited him in any real way. Evil has its own evil reward, I think."

"'As ye sow, so shall ye reap,' perhaps?"

He looked so amused that Caroline felt herself blushing like a child. His power to alter her behavior that way aggravated her even more. "Something like that," she said, her tone lofty.

"I'm afraid I don't believe that. What I want is simple justice and my own place in the world. No more, no less. You have yours here. That gives you security. That's what I want for myself. That's all. Just what's mine."

"But you could lose the things you already have in trying to grasp that."

"I know. It's like climbing a tree. Sometimes you have to let go of your safe hold and lunge for the higher branch."

"You could fall."

It was ironic that Caroline should now urge restraint just when he needed more than ever to reclaim what was rightly his. He laughed because he had to. She was too close to describing his deepest fear. "How did you get to be such an old lady, Caroline? Did your grandmother take over your soul when she died? You never talked this way before."

Caroline tried to laugh with him. "I don't know. I just don't like to think of you in danger." That was only part of it. The idea of separation was worse. She had only just returned to her loved ones. All of them. She wanted them to stay together, with her.

As before, Rory was weaving a spell around her. She could feel his warmth and the weight of his attention. He drew her the way the sun draws moisture. She turned to look up into his face and found his eyes intent on hers.

130

"Don't be afraid of me."

She shook her head. She wasn't afraid. She was curious. She wanted to investigate the feeling that grew between them when they were close. She had such a need to touch him. Of their own accord her hands rose from her lap and collided with his chest. She started to retract them, then laid them flat.

His muscles jumped under her fingers, and she could feel the thumping measure of his heartbeat. She slid her hands higher, to the crests of his shoulders. "Will you teach me to kiss? The right way?"

He made a noise deep in his throat and covered her mouth. She had remembered to part her lips, but after that, her last conscious thought, instinct took over — instinct and her own warm response to Rory. His lips were softly parted and gentle, creating a small void, a hesitation between them. Her breath caught in her throat as his hand came up to stroke the line of her cheek from brow to chin. She tightened her grip on his shoulders as if he were her only anchor to earth. Something elusive gathered within her, urging her to lean into Rory.

More, it urged. And still he withheld it from her. She never doubted that what she wanted lay within Rory's power.

Her frustration mounted as he moved his lips softly over hers, causing a ripple of sensation. She followed it with her tongue, tentatively touching his lips, and then, as he reacted, reaching for him more surely. His breath sucked her tongue into his mouth, there to feel the softness of his inner lips, the smooth evenness of his teeth and, finally, the parrying slide of his tongue against hers.

Overwhelmed, Caroline gave herself over entirely to sensation. The boundaries of her own body had been expanded to include another, one whose body was not hers but was almost an extension of herself. He was different, complementary; he supplied what she lacked, completing her.

Her hands stole from his shoulders to his neck. One came to rest against his face, and the other found its way to the back of his head. He felt warm and vital. Even his hair had

131

life. She could feel the pulse of blood at his temple and the close-shaved texture of his cheek.

The kiss Rory had begun to prove to himself that he could handle Caroline's appeal was threatening—again—to get completely out of hand. He had been clumsy the first time and hurt her. Now he was in danger of doing it again. He had to retreat while he still could.

One by one, he willed his tensed muscles to relax. At least he was sitting down. . . .

He withdrew from her mouth and changed the character of his kiss, holding her chin in the spread of his fingers until she understood. He kissed her brow and rested his face there against her while he brought his ragged breathing under control.

"Rory?"

Her breath teased his throat, and his hands tightened on her shoulders in reaction.

"Did I do something wrong again?"

"Again?" He drew back to look into her face. "I told you before that was my fault."

"Did you? I guess I don't understand." She sighed. "You make me feel so . . . I don't know. I can't find words for it."

"Nor can I—and we're not the first."

She moved closer, nestling contentedly. "I guess that's good."

Rory had to agree. She felt so good in his arms that he didn't move away. He was too happy, too pleased that he had managed to extricate them both this time before they went too far. It would have been so easy. . . .

Her voice came to him as if from far away, drifting dreamily. "Rory?"

"Hmm?" He rubbed her back, moving his hand in a lazy circle.

"What does it mean? This feeling between us?"

"Mean?" he repeated stupidly.

She had not meant to ask that question. At least not now and not in such bald terms. If he had not been holding her so sweetly and with such affection, his hand rubbing idle circles on her back, she would have guarded her tongue.

132

Now she wished she'd cut it out of her head.

With any other man she would have kept her silence. But he was Rory, and she had never had a thought she was unwilling to share with him. If only tonight he'd been difficult . . . if he'd been the way he was in Dodge City . . .

His slackened arms had fallen away from her, making it easy for her to get away. He was trying to recover, trying to find words that would soothe her, but she didn't want them. Not now.

She was an idiot. A fool. Rory or no Rory, a few kisses didn't have to *mean* anything. She knew that, but she didn't want to hear his patronizing explanation.

Dumbfounded, Rory watched her go, knowing he had bungled again. She had caught him napping when he should have been wary. She was always one for asking the awkward — pointed — question. That was Caroline. But he was twenty-eight years old. He'd been parrying the pointed questions of innocent and not-so-innocent females for years. He should have been able to manage her ill-timed question.

He tried to laugh at himself without success. When had he ever managed around Caroline?

She had proved one thing without doubt: his experiment in friendship was a failure.

Caroline had gone only a few steps before her sense of humor began to resurface. She was still annoyed with herself, but when she realized how telling was Rory's reaction to her question she was almost glad she'd asked. Almost.

He'd stammered and stuttered like a blushing boy. Which he wasn't. Since she'd been home she had heard hints and innuendos about Rory's prowess, not all of them well-meant. Maria's certainly weren't. The fact that Rory had offered no glib response told her better than words that the feeling between them *did* have meaning. He might still, part of the time, see himself as her protective older brother, but he hadn't kissed her as a brother. And next time, well . . .

She rounded the corner of the house wearing a mischievous smile. Absorbed as she was in her own thoughts, she missed seeing the dart of a slight, short figure into the shadows next to the house.

But the juniper bush shook as she drew near. She stopped, and after the faintest tremble of branches, the bush, too, was still.

Without regard for her dress, Caroline dove into the bush and pounced on Rusty. He dragged his feet as she pulled him out, saying some naughty words in Spanish that Caroline pretended not to hear.

"Where'd you come from?" he demanded as she bore him off toward the dance floor.

Laughing, she told him, "I just decided to stop chasing you and let you catch up to me."

He straightened his thick auburn hair after she ruffled it and tried to keep his aggrieved expression. He couldn't. "I guess I'm glad you caught me now. I've been wasting my time looking over my shoulder all the time. After this I can start to have fun again." But his grin said that everything, even dancing with his sister, was fun for him.

The dance was a wild, foot-stomping romp they both enjoyed. He stepped on her foot occasionally, but no more than any other partner. Two fiddles set the pace. One after the other, they raced through the music as if determined to get to the end first. Caroline's skirts bounced and flew, kicked and whirled, and she was red-faced and exhausted when it was over.

The music changed immediately. One of the musicians put down his fiddle, put a harmonica under the dolorous droop of his mustache and began to play languidly. The other sang in a nasal Spanish that made the words incomprehensible.

Caroline tried to hold on to Rusty, but when he squirmed to escape she let him go with a grin. Mouthing the words, "Next time," she turned away and found Ted Jasper waiting with outstretched arms. She walked into them, still smiling.

"I've been looking for you all evening," he said.

Over his shoulder Caroline met Rory's intense brown gaze. He wasn't dancing. He looked as if dancing were the farthest thing from his mind.

She looked away from him.

"I've been busy," she told Ted with a deepening smile. She matched her step to his careful one, thinking that at last she would make it through an entire dance without injury to her toes. Or to anything else. He was not as tall as Rory, so everything about him was comfortable, including his friendly smile.

Soon she was laughing again. Not because Ted was particularly witty; he wasn't. But he was amiable and charming the way the less serious men had been back east.

She wasn't surprised when, at the end of the dance, he put her arm through his and led her away to the refreshments. He filled her plate so full she protested, "I'll have to hunt up Rusty again to help me eat all this."

They found his parents sharing a table with Jake and Hannah. The men rose politely, then seated Caroline between them while they continued talking about cattle, horses and Apaches without concession to her presence. Jake knew she was interested; Dwight Jasper didn't care.

He was an enigma to her. Like Jake, he was lean and sundarkened. Except for his build, which was average, he seemed not to have bequeathed much to his son. Ted had his mother's raven black hair and interesting light gray eyes. His father looked uniformly iron gray and desiccated, as if the dry desert air had sucked from him all liveliness and color. His lips were thin and bloodless; they barely moved as he spoke and rarely smiled. When he did smile, the expression never reached his eyes to make them sparkle or soften. They, too, behind hooded lids, were not so much black as lacking in color.

Across the table, Caroline could watch Ted with his mother and Hannah. He had a way she very much liked. Miriam Makepeace, Quentin's younger sister and Caroline's friend, would call him a ladies' man. That seemed unjust to Caroline because it smirked and hinted at impropriety. Instead, she saw that Ted genuinely liked women and enjoyed their company. In his family it would be difficult not to prefer Nila Jasper to her dour husband. Perhaps that

135

accounted for Ted's ease. Whatever caused it, Caroline could find no fault with the result. Like his mother, who was Hannah's best friend, Ted Jasper was easy to like.

Something in her father's voice suddenly brought Caroline's attention back to his conversation in time to hear Dwight Jasper say of the Apache, "What they ought to do is shoot every one of them. They won't stay on the reservation, and they won't stay in Mexico. Every time they go back and forth between the two places, every ranch in New Mexico gets hit by the marauding thieves."

Caroline saw Hannah's alarm and knew Jake had reached the end of his limited ability to keep silent in the face of such intolerance. She didn't wait to hear what Hannah might say.

Affecting great agitation, she cried out imploringly, "Oh, Mr. Jasper, surely you're exaggerating the danger just to frighten the ladies present here tonight! And I must say, I don't think it's at all kind of you." She softened her words, which bordered on the impertinent, with the kind of arch smile she hated when other women used it. Hannah never did, and from her look of surprise, probably Nila Jasper didn't either.

But it worked. Although Dwight Jasper gave her a disgusted look, he didn't pursue his discussion. In fact, no one said anything for several seconds. Ted and Nila were busy gauging Dwight's reaction to her interruption, while Hannah and Jake struggled with other emotions on their way to relief and gratitude to her for averting a possible scene.

Again Caroline stepped into the breach. She lifted her glass. "Papa, I think you should propose a toast to Mr. and Mrs. Jasper."

"Yes, Jake," Hannah chimed in. "To their thirty years of marriage." Her smile fell warmly on Nila, then included Dwight out of courtesy.

Once the toast was over Ted took her away to dance again. "Very nicely done," he said as soon as she was in his arms.

Caroline hadn't expected him to comment on her ploy. She didn't know how to respond, especially since she knew nothing of his sentiments about the Indians. "I hope your father wasn't offended, but I could see that he was upsetting

Hannah." It was the best excuse she could think of.

"You're close to her, aren't you? Didn't you ever resent having a stepmother?"

It wasn't the question she expected. Again, she was surprised, but pleased. She didn't want to discuss Indians. Jake had never denied his heritage, but neither did he vaunt it, especially now that he was far from his Pawnee relatives. This was Navajo, Zuni and, increasingly, Apache—not Pawnee—territory.

"My mother died shortly after I was born," she told Ted. "When Papa came to bring me out here after the war, we had been separated for years. More than anything, I wanted to live in a real family the way all my friends did. We all came together at the same time: Papa, Hannah, Rory and me. I've never felt other than lucky to have such a wonderful family. It's as if we chose each other. And now we have Rusty and Abby to make it complete."

"You didn't want to stay back in the States when you went back?"

"Oh, no. I love it here. This is home. I missed it terribly." She read the look of puzzlement on his face. "Is that so hard to understand? Don't you love it here?"

His answer was slow in coming. "I don't think I'll ever leave here."

Caroline chose to ignore the fact that his statement wasn't much of an endorsement. "Then I envy you," she said, smiling warmly. "I'd like to think that's my fate, too."

Across the dance floor Rory saw the smile and looked away, his jaw clenched. He wanted to snatch Caroline away from Ted. As the dance ended he saw his opportunity to do just that and started toward her.

Maria Martinez stepped into his path so neatly he knew it was intentional. She took his arm and favored him with a sultry smile. "Ah, Rory," she purred. She had a way of pronouncing the *r*'s in his name that made it sound exotic. "You were coming to ask me to dance, weren't you?"

She gave him no chance to demur, moving into his arms and beginning to dance.

Like everyone in the Farnsworth household, Rory regarded Lupe with a mix of affection and awe. She, more than Hannah, had played mother-substitute to him and to Caroline from the beginning of their life on the ranch. With everyone but her own daughter Maria, Lupe was both wise and warm. With Maria, however, Lupe lost all perspective, enabling Maria to manipulate her mother as dexterously as the mariachi musicians played their instruments. Her threat was real. It gave her power over Lupe and thus, to some degree, over others.

Lupe's estranged husband, Miguel Martinez, was a man of influence in one of the villages outside Mexico City. It was to him that Maria turned whenever her mother would not acquiesce to her demands, returning to Mexico for extended visits that drove Lupe crazy with worry. After years of playing her parents against each other, Maria had learned to be totally selfish and irresponsible. For that reason, if not for her promiscuity, Rory had never been attracted to Maria.

Nor was she attracted to him, he was sure. With Maria he had learned to look behind the obvious to find her true purpose. Now, with Ted Jasper and Caroline within view, she undoubtedly wanted one of them, or perhaps both of them, to see her dancing with him.

He could have refused her overture, but he chose not to. For once, her purpose suited him as well. He wanted Caroline to suffer some of his uncertainty. Not for long, of course; just long enough for her to get a taste of what he felt, seeing her with Jasper.

The sinuous rhythm of the dance gave Maria ample opportunity to show off her dress, which in turn showed off her voluptuous body. She wore black faced with red and peacock blue. Tight diagonal strips of those outlandish colors wrapped her hips, ending in a huge, flowery knot at one side of the skirt.

From his height he had a virtually unobstructed view of her breasts, framed by the low-cut bodice. Although he made no attempt to look away from her display, he found himself wondering why her obviousness so completely undercut the effect she desired. Was he perverse?

By the time the dance was over he had decided that it was Maria's self-involvement that frustrated her purpose with him. She danced, dressed and lived for herself, not for him or for any man, in effect making him and his response redundant. Compared to Maria's bold self-assurance, Caroline's hesitant touches and breathless kisses had become his definition of sexual excitement.

Before he could extricate himself from Maria and her line of eager partners, Ernie Coogins had claimed the next dance with Caroline. Rory used the time to take turns with hostess Nila Jasper and with Hannah.

"Do you dislike him so much still?" she asked, noting the direction of his gaze.

"Coogins?" Rory started, unaware that he had been so obvious. "Did Caroline complain that I've been unfair to him?"

"Just because you're sending knives into his back with your eyes?" Hannah teased.

"Not very effective, is it?" He smiled, giving in to her humor. He pulled his eyes away. If Hannah saw through him, he was being too open. He didn't want Caroline to feel him staring at her. She appeared to be absorbed in her conversation, but perhaps that, like his dance with Maria, was subterfuge.

"She's grown up to be a lovely young woman, hasn't she?" Hannah said musingly. "As beautiful inside as outside."

Rory chuckled, then laughed aloud at Hannah's affronted look.

She joined in finally, giving up her composure. "I'm not very subtle, am I?"

"Perhaps we're alike that way." It was worth being laughed at to see Hannah lose the tight, unhappy pinch to her mouth.

Their carefree laughter drew Jake's glance as well as Caroline's. They both smiled in sympathy. Jake stood to welcome Caroline and offer his arm when the music changed once again, becoming an easy tempo that would not tax his stamina. Since Rory and Hannah were still dancing, Jake said, "He's good for Hannah. I'm glad he's back for a while."

His "for a while" choked Caroline. "Yes" was all she said.

"And you're good for me, punkin. We need you here."

"I need to be here, Papa."

Across the floor Maria danced with Ted, her flamboyance drawing all eyes, including Caroline's. Was she envious? She didn't think so until she saw that Rory also watched Maria. His expression was tight with displeasure, but she couldn't find solace in that. Probably he envied Ted.

"Don't worry about her, honey," Jake said. "She's not the kind of woman a man marries. I think Ted's very taken with you."

Caroline started, temporarily losing the rhythm of the dance. "Ted?"

Jake was pleased. It showed that she wasn't indifferent to young Jasper. "He's a good man. He has a real feel for ranching, I've found."

Rory danced closer, moving Hannah along a path that intersected her gaze at Ted and Maria. He caught Caroline's eye and winked, making her stumble once again. "Sorry, Papa. I guess I've had my feet stepped on too many times tonight."

He smiled at her, looking remarkably like his old self, and Caroline's heart felt light again for the first time tonight. "But not by me," he said proudly.

Nor by Rory, Caroline added silently, painfully aware that he was near. He brought Hannah around with a comical swoop, presenting her to Jake.

"Your lovely wife, sir," Rory said.

Again the pattern of the dance changed. She was with Rory. But for how long? She was committed to home, to New Mexico. Rory had to go. Commitment to his father drew him away just as her destiny held her close at hand.

Rory's strong arms folded around Caroline, and for a few timeless moments she had no doubts. This was where she wanted to be. They moved together as one.

The same sense of unity enveloped Jake and Hannah as they danced away. Under the spell of the music and the gaily colored lanterns, Hannah forgot that Jake had been grievously injured. He held her tightly, feeling the soft sway of her hips against his. She tilted her head up to him, the message in her eyes unmistakable.

"Ah, Hannah," he murmured. "You make me feel like sweeping you away to bed."

"I feel very sweepable."

His hands slid to her hips and he laughed. "That you do, but think what a bad example we would be."

She shook her head. "We'd be a good example. The best." Her sigh was heavy with longing. They were here for the night. Leaving would mean rousting Abby and Rusty from their borrowed beds. It seemed to be her bitter fate that only now when it was impossible did Jake want her after such a long time. She moved closer, her arms high around his broad shoulders. "The feeling will keep," she promised softly, hoping it was true.

In answer, Jake smiled against her cheek. She felt the smile as his lips moved. "It always has."

Tears filled Hannah's eyes, and she had to will them away. Jake had seen too many from her lately. She wouldn't spoil this moment. "Yes."

Then she proceeded to do exactly that. Pulling back the slightest bit from Jake to smile at him, she caught a glimpse of Rory and Caroline. She turned to follow their progress. "They make a handsome couple, don't they?"

She was totally unprepared for Jake's reaction. He recoiled from her as if she had struck him. "Couple? They're not a couple. He's her brother, for heaven's sake."

Hannah stared at him, the color draining from her face. "He's no more Caroline's brother than you are mine."

"Not technically," he retorted, "but in spirit, he is. They grew up together."

"Yes," she said. "And now they're both grown-up." She looked pointedly from Jake to Caroline and Rory, challenging him to see them as they were.

He looked, but he saw what he wanted to see, not what was there. He saw the daughter he would keep near and the almost-son who would not stay.

Bringing his eyes to rest on her whitened countenance,

141

Jake returned her challenge, ripping away her joy and her peace of mind with his next words. "Ted Jasper will make her a much better husband. And she's already attracted to him. I can tell."

Chapter Thirteen

Rory left for Kansas three days after Jasper's party without speaking to Caroline again in private.

With her return to the family, he had gone back to taking his quarters in the bunkhouse with the rest of the hands. At first Caroline had thought little of it. He had lived there off and on throughout their years at the ranch. In fact, as a child she had envied his ability to shuck his Farnsworth identity and become just another of the men. But when she saw that he was avoiding her — or so it seemed — the issue of his choice of a resting place loomed large in her mind.

When she learned by accident that he was leaving for Ellsworth the next morning, she stayed awake waiting for him to return to the bunkhouse, hoping for a word with him. He had gone with some of the men to Rio Mogollon, the nearest town large enough to have a saloon.

Presuming it to be a farewell party of sorts, she had gone to her room after dinner, determined to wait as long as she had to for him. She read, knowing no one else would be disturbed no matter how late she stayed up. The house grew quiet around her, and for a time she stretched out on the bed. She didn't worry about falling asleep and missing Rory. Her nerves were stretched too tight for sleep.

The waiting grew insupportable. Then she paced her room, a white-clad wraith in a white room. She had taken off her dress and petticoats to be comfortable, but now she was cool. She wrapped in a colorful Mexican shawl and went on pacing.

She could not see the bunkhouse from her window, but she had been certain she would hear the horses return. Or the men. Often she heard them singing or shouting as they came back from a night of drinking.

Now she worried that she would miss Rory. It was almost one o'clock. Perhaps he had left the revelry early, aware that it would be foolish to start a trip suffering from a hangover. Perhaps he wasn't going at all. She'd only heard one of the men say so. Perhaps he was alone in the bunkhouse. . . .

Unable to stand her tiresome thoughts, Caroline exchanged the shawl for her plain gray dress and slipped out of the room. The heavy back door obeyed her hand soundlessly, and then she was on the well-worn path from the kitchen to the bunkhouse. At their elevation even full summer nights were cool. There was no breeze to stir her hair or move her dress and no moonlight to reveal her hurried steps.

It took all her nerve for her to open the door and peek inside. She had helped Hannah and Lupe turn the bunkhouse on its ear during spring cleaning, and as a child she'd been welcomed there at times, but this was different. Men would be sleeping or, worse, playing cards. She would have to explain, ask for Rory. . . . She hovered at the doorway, unable to move ahead or retreat until she identified the sound that had stopped her heart. Snoring. She nearly laughed in relief.

Two men were revealed by the lantern on the table in the middle of the room. The snorer lay sprawled in a lower bunk with his arm flung out to drape to the floor. The second man, known as Happy Jack, also slept, but at the table, using his folded arms as a pillow. She couldn't see into all the upper bunks. If Rory was in one of those, he was safe from her. She backed out and let the door fall shut, appalled that she had actually gone so far in her pursuit of Rory.

How could she? Was she crazy?

Evidently.

Caroline leaned back against the building, her knees too wobbly to support her. She had been lucky. No one had seen her. Now she had to get away from the building. She waited in the shadows until she could function again. Once she was away from the bunkhouse she could explain, truthfully, that she hadn't been able to sleep and had gone out for a walk. She was dressed. It would be fine. . . .

She ran across the open yard. Instinct made her want to run inside, but she forced herself to wait until her breathing returned to normal. Strange, that a dash of so few yards could have her panting. It was nerves. She had been foolish, so foolish. While she calmed herself by taking deep breaths, she paced back and forth by the kitchen door, her arms wrapped around herself. At least she wasn't cold any more.

Choking back a sound between a laugh and a cry, she stepped into the dark kitchen. Except it was no longer dark. Jake had lit a lamp. He was sitting at Lupe's chopping table, drinking a glass of milk.

"Papa!"

He took in everything from her unbound hair to her bare feet and frowned, bringing his eyes back to rest on her flushed face and guilty expression.

"I couldn't sleep so I went for a walk." She spoke too quickly and too urgently, thrown by his silence and his piercing stare.

After a terrible pause he said, "You don't look as if it did you much good. Perhaps you should try my cure instead." He gestured to the milk.

Caroline laughed, relieved and sounding more normal to herself. "I think you're right. I got sort of spooked out there, and I ran back to the house. Then I was ashamed of myself."

How good it was to be able to tell the truth, even if it wasn't the whole truth. She had never been able to lie to her father. His eyes seemed to see right to her heart. She'd never had his fondness for milk, but getting it and having it to drink would give her something to do.

She wanted to ask Jake about Rory, but she couldn't just come right out with her question about his trip. Papa wasn't stupid. He would know she had gone to see Rory, or tried to. And he wouldn't approve. Hannah might have chased after him years ago, but that—he would say—had been different. He was probably right. It *had* been different.

Hannah had told Caroline their story, or most of it anyway, years ago. She knew that even then Papa hadn't approved of Hannah's pursuit. He was a rather rigid person, at least in comparison to Hannah. Pursuit was the man's prerogative. He forgave Hannah because he loved her. He would forgive Caroline, too, but not without a fight, and she didn't want to fight with him.

She took a sip of milk, concealing a shudder of distaste. "I'm chilly. Let me get a wrap and my slippers." She got up, promising, "I'll be right back."

Her slippers were doeskin. Made for her by Many Buffalo's wife, Bright Star, they were one of her most cherished possessions. Because Gramma Lunig had disapproved of them and of everything that tied Jake to his Pawnee cousins in Nebraska, Caroline had not worn them in Hanford. Now she could enjoy their comfort again.

As she returned to sit with her father she gave no thought to the slippers or to the Mexican wrap she wore over her Quaker gray dress. Nor did Jake see the various strands of her heritage in her apparel and think how like her beloved territory of New Mexico she was—an Anglo woman warmed by Spanish and Indian articles of clothing.

He saw her only as Caroline, his much-loved daughter who had, incomprehensibly, become a woman long before he was ready to give up her childhood. Especially when he had been deprived of her company for so many years. She wasn't twenty-one yet, and she had lived away from him for more than six of those all-too-brief years.

How those years loomed in his mind as he watched her take her chair again. Would he know her better if she hadn't gone away? Or was she a mystery to him now because she was a woman? He didn't know. All he knew was that he wanted her here now, with him, near him. To stay.

Hard as it had been to send her to her grandparents as a child, it had been worse to send her back east to school as a young adult. Necessity had played no part in that decision. He had been tormented that he would lose her to the

146

civilized east her mother Grace had loved so deeply. Hannah had preached her doctrine that love meant letting go, but she had never lost in quite the way he had. And Caroline was half Grace, wasn't she? He had only to look at her to see that she was. Wouldn't some man back east fall in love with her pink-and-white blond delicacy? Wouldn't she choose to stay? He could scarcely believe she hadn't.

She was back home now, and he wanted to accept his good fortune and rejoice. He did. But instinct told him the battle wasn't over yet. She was troubled by something that told him he had not yet won. She could still go. He — *she* — wasn't safe yet.

He searched her face for a clue to her unhappiness, seeing doubt in her expressive eyes. "What's keeping you awake, punkin? Do you miss being back east?" He felt brave for having asked the hardest question first.

"Oh, no, Papa. You mustn't worry about that." She reached for his hand and gave it a squeeze and a pat.

Relieved, Jake captured her hand to hold. "I guess I'll always worry about that, so I thank you for your assurance. Let me give you some in return." He watched her face carefully, looking for a way to ease her distress. "Perhaps I shouldn't tell you this, but I think it will make you happy. Ted Jasper asked me for permission to call on you."

A flicker of surprise, followed by puzzlement, crossed her face.

"I know it's an old-fashioned thing to do, but it pleased me. It shows he has honorable intentions toward you. He's a fine young man, someone you'd have a lot in common with. He's done well with his father's stock, and he has some good ideas for improving the breed. A good hand with horses, too."

Caroline was finding it hard to make sense of his words. She had been about to blurt out her love for Rory, and now he was talking about Ted.

Her father's praise was generous. If she'd thought at all about how he would react to a suitor for her hand, she would have expected hostility. A father traditionally believes no man can be good enough for his daughter; Jake Farnsworth was bound to take tradition several steps further. Just last night she had been thinking how wonderful not to have to worry about that with Rory. Jake already loved Rory.

But here he was, speaking for Ted Jasper.

She withdrew her hand to take up her glass and drink several quick swallows. "I like Ted, Papa, and I'm glad you do, too," she said carefully. "But I love Rory."

"Well, of course you do. He's your brother."

"No, Papa, I don't mean like that." Caroline paused, unsure how to express her meaning. "I mean, I do love him as a brother, but there's more now. And I think he feels the same way about me."

"He does, honey. I'm sure of it. You've always been special to Rory, and it's wonderful that you've taken up your special relationship again."

"But it's more than that," she insisted. "When we were in Dodge City . . . he . . . I . . ."

"He didn't dishonor you, did he?" It was more demand than question.

"You know he wouldn't, Papa." Her face was growing hot. She didn't know how to make him understand without betraying too much.

"Honey, I'm not going to make excuses for Rory, but you have to understand the way men are. Rory may have kissed you and made you feel special—which you are—but he's not going to marry you."

Caroline misunderstood his meaning. "Why would you object? You love Rory. He's—"

"Of course I do. I'm not *objecting*, sweetheart, I'm explaining how it is with a young man. He's not ready to get married. He's single-minded. You know that. Much as he cares for you and may even desire you, he has only one thing on his mind now. He wants to chase down his uncle. And I don't blame him for that."

"Neither do I," Caroline said faintly. She felt as though she were drowning in hot oil. How casually her father brushed aside the possibility that Rory desired her. As if it

148

weren't important! But it was.

"Then you understand," Jake went on smoothly. "Rory's life has been different. Until he gets this business with his uncle settled, *he* can't settle. It's just the way he is."

Feelings churned through Caroline without giving her any way to express them.

"Did Rory promise you . . . anything? *Say* anything?"

All the hot color in her face drained away. She looked down at the empty glass. She shook her head, wondering when she had drunk all of that. Maybe it was the cold milk in her stomach making her feel sick. She truly hated milk.

"You know he's going away in the morning?"

Caroline nodded without looking up. It didn't seem important any longer to keep him from guessing why she had been outside.

Jake reached for her hand. She pulled away, not wanting his sympathy. In her haste, she knocked over the glass. It didn't break, and Jake put it upright out of their way.

"Sweetheart —"

She got to her feet quickly and came around the table to kiss his cheek. "It's all right, Papa. You don't have to explain any more. I love you."

Jake sat on at the table long after her nearly silent footsteps died away. He wanted to follow her to her room. Was she crying? He wanted to protect her, but he also wanted her to be happy.

He tossed back the milk left in his glass as if it were whiskey, wishing it were.

Caroline wasn't crying in her room. Neither was she sleeping. She heard the men and horses return just as she expected she would, but she didn't go outside. Lying in her darkened room, listening to the men's comical attempts at stealth, she knew her earlier impulse had been stupid. She didn't know what to believe about Rory. She loved and trusted him as she loved and trusted Papa. How could she choose between them when they told her opposite things?

Then she remembered. Rory hadn't told her anything. He had kissed her and made her want something more from him, *with* him. But he had kept his silence, carefully —

even when she had impetuously asked for some assurance of meaning between them.

It was late when Caroline finally fell asleep. She never undressed, because even in her hurt and confusion she intended to be up with the family to see Rory off. But the men were quiet in the morning. She didn't hear them leave, nor did she hear Rory as he came to the house to say good-bye.

He looked for Caroline, but when Hannah noticed her absence and started to send Abby to wake her sister, he called, "Abby, let her sleep. I don't want to disturb her."

He lifted Abby for a second hug to hide his feeling of shame. Coward that he was, he was almost glad not to have to face Caroline this morning. How could he leave her with so much unsaid between them?

Rusty wanted to shake his hand, man to man, instead of hug him. He complied, then grabbed the boy up anyway. He was glad to see that Rusty seemed relieved that he had insisted. "Take care of your little sister for me," he said, putting down his already squirming body. He wanted to add other names to the list, but he knew Rusty took his responsibilities seriously. He could not protect Jake — maybe no one could — and he might feel guilty if he failed when Rory had asked it of him.

Rory's head hurt too much for him to prolong his good-byes to Jake and Hannah, but he did kiss Hannah a second time in order to whisper, "Tell Caroline I'll write to her."

He meant what he said. He even tried to do it. Twice. Each time he balled up the paper and threw it away. Words didn't come easily to him, especially not the words he had to use.

He had been wrong to leave without telling her what he felt. At the time he'd told himself it wasn't fair to obligate her to a man who had no place in the world to call his own. It had been easy to convince himself that he had to settle the score with Uncle Joseph before he declared his love. Self-respect seemed to demand it of him.

But now that he was away he realized that he'd been afraid to speak up. What if he'd misread her response?

Giving her time to grow up had become a habit, one his natural reticence had exaggerated into procrastination.

The realization that he'd made a mistake only compounded the difficulty of putting his feelings into words, especially words he had to put onto paper. He decided it was impossible. He wanted to see Caroline and hold her while he told her what was in his heart.

He would wait.

Caroline waited, too. She had taken heart from his message. It meant that he did care for her. She had her share of regrets as well. If she had only been sensible and gone to bed as she did every night, she would have been awake to see him off. She had done it backward. In the morning, knowing they would be parted for a long time, Rory would have found a way to speak to her in private.

She was not faint of heart. She would wait.

Chapter Fourteen

A month later Caroline was still waiting. Her birthday had come and gone, leaving her feeling strangely stranded on the shores of womanhood. For the sake of her family, who had given its celebration their all, Caroline had pretended to be perfectly happy with her birthday.

It annoyed her that she'd had to pretend when, in fact, she had everything she had wanted last year. She was home, in the midst of her family. Last year she would have viewed Rory's absence as a minor blemish on perfection.

She was determined to regain that perspective.

She urged her nimble little buckskin mare up the slope of a swale toward a juniper thicket. "Good girl, Fortune," she said, reaching down to confer a pat on the mare's neck. As soon as they gained the shade she stopped and took off her hat to mop her brow on her sleeve.

Turning the mare, Caroline looked out over the valley she had just traversed. Her riding today had a purpose. She was covering a remote section of the ranch, looking for "sleepers," calves that were earmarked but not yet branded. Each ranch had its own earmark, a distinctive shape cut into a calf's ear, and as such they were respected—more or less. But earmarks were easily altered; a nip here or there and the calf, taken from its mother and weaned, belonged to someone else. She had already found one maverick, a calf already weaned that was neither branded nor earmarked. That was like finding gold.

The gold spread out before her was more tangible. It lay in bright yellow patches of snakeweed on the floor of the valley, interspersed with splashes of crimson Indian paintbrush and lavender verbena, all under a turquoise sky. She sighed with pleasure and lifted her hair from her back to let it slide through her fingers.

Feeling restored, she had just reached down to take up the slack on the reins when she heard the whicker of another horse. Fortune's ears perked up as a file of Indians rode out of the timber behind her. They rode tough little Indian ponies, with an occasional full-sized horse to add variety to the line. The men wore buckskins and feathers, their long hair loose or braided.

Caroline had no time to be afraid. Her eyes met and locked with the puzzled gaze of the leader in a moment that, for her, contained only recognition, not alarm. He rode slowly in a great circle around her, followed in perfect formation by the rest of the men, one Indian behind the other. She thought of Many Buffalo and Sees Far, knowing only that these were not Pawnee. Were they Apache? Reason told her to be frightened, but she couldn't manage it. They merely looked at her with grave interest.

Then she realized that they were fascinated by the color of her hair. Probably they had never seen a blond woman before. When the leader passed in front of her a second time, she thought to count the men as the silent circle moved around her. She started just in time, for then the leader broke from the ring to resume his original course. All twenty-six Indians followed him in perfect order.

Caroline watched them until they were gone from sight, knowing the experience and the awe she felt would never leave her. She put her hat back on, wondering what they would have done to her if her hair had been covered. She was armed, of course, but at those odds her six-shooter would have been useless.

She went on with her chore, slowly at first, then with renewed vigor. She had another story to tell her grandchildren one day. That was three stories: the bank robbery in Independence, the train robbery in Dodge City, and the Indians. At least this one was not violent.

She frowned at the thought of the two robberies, reminded against her will of the one letter Rory had sent home. But not to her. Hannah tried to soften the blow, but no amount of pretense could alter what Rory had written.

153

The letter told primarily of his frustration to find that Joseph Talmage was not in Ellsworth any more. He had been there, but only briefly, and he was not known there.

Caroline tried to find her old sympathy for Rory's disappointment. Every terse line of the letter, addressed to the family as a whole, resonated with his sense of impotent impatience. What she felt was more personal. She had been rejected, given only the same regard as each other member of the family. He had remembered her birthday, but in the most offhand way — in a post script. "By the way, Caroline, happy birthday. Now you're really all grown up."

She prodded Fortune into a ground-eating lope, determined finally to outrun her thoughts. The crisp, dry air made an invigorating breeze as the game little mare ran. Caroline took off her hat again, the better to feel it in her hair.

Within seconds her joy was gone. Fortune stumbled and fell, throwing Caroline to the ground. She rolled clear of the downed horse, winded and shocked. In the few moments it took her to gather her wits she realized that Fortune had not been so lucky. She was not going to be able to rise. Her right front leg was broken.

Caroline got to her knees slowly, horrified.

"Fortune!" she cried. "Oh, my God!"

The agonized mare screamed with pain, flailing her head and hind legs in the effort to rise. She had fallen onto her right side. In her struggle to get up she was compounding the terrible pain of her injury as she thrashed about, trying to clamber up onto the shattered foreleg.

Crying so badly she couldn't see, Caroline crawled to the horse's head. She wanted to soothe the distraught animal and take away the pain. There was only one way to do that, but her mind recoiled from the necessity.

"Oh, Fortune," she sobbed. "Please, God . . ."

But there was no one to help her, no one to do the hard, terrible task for her.

She took out her gun. Her hands were shaking so badly she was afraid she would not manage the job cleanly. She swiped at her eyes and drew a deep breath.

"God help me," she whispered hoarsely, still on her knees.

As if the ___ understood that Caroline needed her to lie still, Fortune put her head flat to the ground. Caroline placed the cold gun barrel just below the forelock, her left hand resting softly on the buckskin face. She patted once, then concentrated all her strength into squeezing the trigger. She screamed out her own agony as the recoil tore up her arm, then rolled away to be thoroughly sick to her stomach.

In time she crawled away from the horse and curled into a ball of anguish and guilt. Her horse. Her beautiful little mare. Papa's birthday gift. She had killed Fortune only four days after her birthday.

She was still crying when another horse pulled up beside her. She lifted her face in time to see Ted Jasper dismount.

"Are you hurt?"

She shook her head, unable to speak. He needed no explanation for what had happened. Kneeling between Caroline and the horse, he silently offered his handkerchief. She had one she had not had the wit to use. She shook her head and groped at her pants. Like Hannah, she wore the same jeans the men did when she worked, only she didn't have to alter their slim-hipped shape. They fit all too well.

"Take it," Ted said, putting the handkerchief in her hand. "Let me play the gentleman. My mother would be thrilled to think her training hasn't been in vain."

She gave Ted a watery smile, then blew her nose with unladylike force. It was just what she needed to make her laugh. But laughing at all renewed her guilt. Her eyes filled again with tears.

"Don't," Ted said gently. "You did well. No one could have done better."

"But I was running her . . . I shouldn't have . . ."

He pulled her into his arms and held her there. "You can't know that. It happens, Caroline. It's not your fault."

"But it is." She would never forget that she had been racing to outrun her unhappiness over Rory. Unfairly, she blamed him almost as much as she blamed herself.

"Where's your hat?"

Puzzled, she frowned, trying to think. "I took it off." Stupidly, she patted her bare head. "I must have lost it."

Ted got up and urged her to her feet. "We'll find it. Come on."

He used his body to shield her from the sight of the dead horse, keeping himself in her way all the time. She tried to sidestep him. "My saddle—"

"I'll send someone for it and get someone out here to take care of the horse, too."

"But I should—"

Ted attached her hands to his own horse's saddle. "All right. I saw Indians a while ago. They might come back to strip the horse, so I will. But don't watch," he ordered.

Caroline had no intention of watching. She could picture every move he had to make, willingly or not. To keep her mind busy she said, "How did you find me so fast?"

"I was up in that stand of aspens. I saw the Indians go by and then I heard the shot. You screamed, too. Sort of together." His voice deepened to a grunt with the effort of freeing her saddle from the body. "I followed the sound, afraid it was an Indian after you. A laggard, maybe."

"No." She clung to Ted's saddle and rested her head there, keeping her senses full of the smell of living horse-flesh. "I saw them. They circled me. All of them. It was strange. They didn't speak, just stared." She laughed self-consciously. "Finally, I figured out that they just wanted to look at my hair."

She felt his hand on her back before she heard him. He lifted strands of her hair, sifting them through his fingers. "Who says Indians are dumb?"

Caroline stared at him in amazement. He wore the strangest expression. She moistened her lips and tried a smile. "They aren't."

He looked at her without comprehension.

"Indians," she prompted. "They aren't dumb."

"If you say so."

"Thank you for getting my saddle." She saw that he

wasn't holding it and turned to see where it was. He moved to interfere and they collided. Since her father had told her Ted wanted to court her he had been coming to the house to visit, but before today he had never touched her. His visits had not seemed like courtship to her. They had spent little time alone and that sitting awkwardly in the parlor.

His hands fell to the sides of her waist. For a moment she thought he would retreat, but he didn't. He grasped her and pulled her close. "You're lovely, Caroline."

She stood stiffly, not knowing how to react. She welcomed his comfort and wanted to yield, but he seemed as awkward as she was. It struck her then that Ted was more like her than Rory was. Perhaps he, too, had no experience with the opposite sex. Unlike Rory.

The thought pleased her, and she softened toward him. She smiled into his gray eyes and saw that they sparkled. He squeezed his hands on her waist and gave in to the laughter he was suppressing. "These pants of yours are something. It gives me a start every time I think of it."

Caroline had to laugh with him. "I hope that doesn't happen too often."

"More than you'd think." He turned her and said, "Up you go."

"I can walk."

"We'll just go to the line shack and leave off the saddle. It'll be safe there, and then we can ride double the rest of the way."

Nodding, Caroline mounted up while Ted put the saddle over his shoulder. She couldn't resist a last look back at Fortune before she turned resolutely away. She wouldn't give way again to her misery. Not in front of Ted.

After they were well away from the body, Caroline got off his horse to walk with Ted. He put the saddle up and they continued, side by side, leading his horse. Since their moment of intimacy, so to speak, Caroline's mind had been awhirl with her first serious thoughts about Ted.

It occurred to her that this was the best opportunity she would have to find out what Ted was like as a man. He had told Papa he wanted to court her—with marriage in mind.

157

She found the idea startling, but also intriguing. Her relationship with Rory had been so formless, so tenuous. She knew he cared for her, loved her, but perhaps what he had done had been motivated by curiosity or — Papa's choice — brotherliness. How could she tell? She meant to ask him, but perhaps she'd never get a chance.

Ted was easy to talk to. Their conversation as they walked left her mind free to consider her options. He walked slowly, as if he expected the exertion to exhaust her. Surprisingly, by the time they reached the shack Caroline was tired, but only mentally. Thinking about Ted and blocking out her feelings about Fortune had made her steps slow. They dragged more the closer they got to the shack.

If Ted knew what she was thinking . . .

Caroline covered her smile, feigning fatigue.

Ted dumped the saddle on the floor of the single room, looking around in dismay. It wasn't dirty, just dusty, but it smelled stuffy. It was also a most improper place to be alone with Caroline. He left the door open and frowned, hesitant about what he should do for her. Any other woman would have had hysterics several times over by now. People said she was different. Evidently it was true.

The shack stood on the line between Farnsworth and Jasper land as an emergency shelter for the men. It was kept stocked with rations, water and fuel. There was a single rough cot, a crude table and two chairs. He gestured to one of those. "Maybe you'd like to sit down?"

She would. He found the jug of water and a tin cup. Blowing the dust from the latter, he poured her a drink. She took it with a smile of thanks that included understanding of the lack of amenities in their situation.

"Have you ever stayed here in a storm?" she asked when she'd taken a drink and given the cup back.

"Here? No, but I've stayed in others and been glad for them."

"I always wanted to camp out in one, but Papa wouldn't let me."

He sat back on his haunches. "Wise man."

As he lifted the cup to his lips Caroline said, "I think so.

He tells me you want to marry me."

Ted choked on a swallow of water. He stood up, gasping, and turned his head as the liquid threatened to come back up.

Caroline jumped to her feet and pounded his back.

He flinched away and got control of himself before he turned to look at her. His eyes were wide with disbelief. "My God, do you do that often?"

She backed away. "I'm sorry. Did I hurt you?"

"Not *that*." He made a dismissive gesture. "I meant, do you just say whatever comes to mind?"

"Yes, I guess I do—once I know someone a bit." She smiled serenely, pleased somehow by his equally frank question. "I've found it saves a lot of trouble—sometimes. Of course, there are times when it *causes* trouble," she acknowledged. "When people don't understand. I have to work out the timing a little better. That's all."

"Did you really incapacitate a half-dozen train robbers by making them sick?"

Caroline laughed. "Yes, I really did. I was terribly scared, though, and it wasn't as funny as it sounds."

"I'm sure it wasn't," Ted said.

They resettled at the table. She clasped her hands together tightly and said, "You didn't answer my question."

"It wasn't a question."

If she had disconcerted him before, he was retaliating. "Actually, I guess Papa's words were that your intentions were honorable. Doesn't that mean marriage?"

"It makes it a possibility," he admitted. "I like your father. I didn't want to upset him."

"He likes you." Caroline wasn't making much progress. "But you do want to get married?"

He grinned. "Is this a proposal?"

"No," she snapped. "I'm just trying to understand. Why me? Why now?"

Ted shrugged carelessly. "Why not?"

Caroline shook her head and looked away from him. Obviously she wasn't going to get her answers this way. All she had done with her frontal attack was destroy their

159

earlier ease, and she missed that already. "I'm sorry. I shouldn't ask, I know. Even Hannah would be horrified."

"And she doesn't horrify easily, does she?"

"No. She's always tried to help me fit in better, without really trying to change me. I think that's why I feel so at home here. There's room for me to be myself."

"You should be yourself. You're interesting."

It was something, perhaps, but not enough. She made an impatient gesture and started to rise. "I think we should go now."

Ted caught the hand she put out and drew it across the table to cover it with his other hand. "I'm frustrating you, aren't I?"

"You're not the first." Rory came to mind—again. She pushed him away and concentrated on the way Ted held her hand. He wasn't as overpowering as Rory, but he offered solid comfort. She *liked* him.

"It's habit of mine. A way of protecting myself."

Caroline didn't understand the statement, but she liked the fact that he was trying to explain himself. She didn't pull her hand free.

"Not your fault," he went on cryptically. He looked at her hand—addressed it, in fact. "I am thinking about marriage, Caroline. I think it's time."

"How old are you?"

"Twenty-seven. Your father married younger and so did mine."

"I'm already considered a spinster. My friends back east all have children by now."

His mouth lifted in a smile. "A match made in heaven, wouldn't you say?"

Ted was handsome. He hadn't Rory's sculptured features and sun-kissed golden glow, but his smile was heart-stopping. At least this kind of smile was. Now that she'd seen more of him, she realized that he had many different kinds of smiles.

The easy ones didn't touch his eyes. In that he was like his father. In company he smiled often but lightly, without real amusement. Now and then, however, an expression moved over his face the way the wind ripples the pale green of gamma grass. Then his eyes changed, lighting with genuine amusement. She had a feeling she could help him experience that more often.

She laughed with him. "Maybe so. I should warn you, though. My skills don't extend to the usual feminine accomplishments. I sing like a tree frog and have no patience with sewing. I'm a good cook and a wonderful ranch hand, most of the time." Her expression darkened with misery as she remembered why they were there. "I've never abused an animal before and I never will again."

"That wasn't abuse."

"Too much like it. I'll never forgive myself." She slipped her hand from his and got to her feet.

He was beside her instantly. He meant to comfort her, but when she looked up at him the question in her eyes made him want to throw her down onto the cot. She dressed like a man and asked her questions the same way. Her mouth was soft and tremulous under his, though.

After a moment of surprise she began to respond. Her body was tall enough to meet his directly at every essential point, and suddenly he let himself go. He cupped her bottom in the tight pants, pulling her against his arousal, feeling the press of her breasts at his chest. He'd thought of marriage with Caroline, but not with this as part of it.

Now . . . God!

He groaned, trying to break away. She wasn't clinging, but she held him, not backing away from his passion. He moved his hands to her waist and up the side of her body. As he neared her breasts she stepped back, and he lowered them to her waist again.

"It's these clothes of yours," he said harshly.

Caroline stared. Here it was again, that rejection; different but the same. She tried to laugh. "I did warn you that I'm not very feminine." She didn't believe that, didn't *feel* that. But the proof was irrefutable, wasn't it?

"Not feminine? My God, woman, I can feel every inch of you!"

"I'm sorry."

Ted caught her chin and lifted her face. "You really don't know, do you?"

Caroline saw his wonder, mild though it was, but what she really liked was his pleasure. She saw it as approval. There had been a wild hunger in his kiss that made her feel accepted, wanted. It was a heady feeling. She hadn't melted in Ted's arms; she had grown stronger, more sure of herself.

Years ago she had asked Hannah how she would know when she met the man she should marry. Over the years it had become one of her favorite questions to ask women who were happily married, or seemed to be. Her friend Becky had gone all dreamy-faced and foolish. With a sigh, she had said, "You'll know. You'll just . . . *know*." Alice, always more practical, answered, "He'll be the one you can't pass up."

Typically, Hannah's response was complex, containing equal parts of the practical and the romantic. "It's not easy to know sometimes," she had admitted from her experience of one bad and one good marriage. "You must like the man first, even if he makes you furious. You must respect him as a person. You have to consider yourself, too. What are you like when you're with him? Are you a better person, stronger and more complete? Or does he, even unintentionally, reduce you and belittle you?"

The words ran in her head now as they had so many times before, like music she was learning to sing. In real life when she sang the sound was appalling, nothing like what she heard in her mind's ear. Maybe love was like that. It existed in one's mind and heart as an ideal, a perfect melody that people sang and played as best they could.

Of course there was more to Hannah's advice. "Then there's the physical side of love, Caroline. Don't *ever* underestimate the importance of the physical in love."

She thought of Ted's hands approaching her breasts and retreating. She wanted to know that feeling of closeness and possession. If he had touched her would she know her heart better?

"I don't know, Ted; you're right. But I would like to learn."

162

The look he gave her made her believe perhaps she could sing after all.

"Not here. Not now," he said.

Taking her hand, he led her from the shack.

Chapter Fifteen

Priscilla Talmage was going to a hanging.

She wasn't alone. Far from it. Her son Gabriel rode with her, their box lunch, purchased from the hotel, on the floor of the wagon between their feet. Priscilla had wanted to rent a grand carriage for the day, but they had missed their chance. All the carriages were gone. She was annoyed by their humble conveyance, although, in truth, she would have walked before she would miss the occasion.

Thomas Yarborough, otherwise known as Baltimore Blackie, was to hang at noon. Two of his companions, Walt Stimpson and Benny Voss, better known as Moon, were to hang with him, but it was only Thomas that Priscilla came to see.

The gallows had been built next to the jail, a low, square building of heavy planks. It pleased Priscilla to think that Thomas had been able to watch what was to be the instrument of his death in the making. He had practiced insouciance all his life. He would need every bit of it today. Every fall of the hammer must have assaulted his nerves.

She only wished she could let him know she was here to watch him die. She had thought of sending him a message, but it was too risky. Gabe was already too curious. She had wanted to come alone. Now she was glad Gabe was with her. Joseph insisted she shouldn't be alone in the midst of what could be an unruly crowd. If she couldn't inform Thomas that she was here, she could at least enjoy the irony of having his son at her side. For Gabriel Talmage was really Gabriel Yarborough, although neither he nor his "father," Joseph, knew the truth.

But Thomas knew—for all he cared.

Did he think of Gabe now, and in his ruminations on

mortality and immortality, did he wonder what had happened to the child she'd carried? She hoped not, because the knowledge that a part of him lived on might comfort his last hours. She wanted him comfortless and bereft, as lost as Boyd had been when that mob from Cottonwood Falls had taken him from the train and strung him up in a dry wash.

It made her sick to think of it. Her brother—killed for a murder he didn't commit, just the way he'd been caught in that bank in Independence, doing Baltimore Blackie's dirty work. Stupid, gallant Boyd! He'd been proud to be considered dangerous. He'd even been proud of his nickname, "Kid" Belasco. The name had been apt, though. He'd been a kid, playing with guns and chasing his hero, Thomas. And *she* had brought them together.

Gabe kept the plodding horse in line with all the others, casting a concerned eye now and then over his mother's face. She was flushed under her plum-colored bonnet, and her eyes glittered strangely. He hardly knew what to make of her lately. She wasn't the kind of woman to go in for Roman circuses and gruesome spectacles. At least, she had not been until now. Yet there was no doubt that coming today was all her own idea. Both he and his father had tried to talk her out of it. His father had even forbidden her, to no avail.

"Do you feel faint, Mother? It's awfully warm."

"I'm fine."

She didn't look fine. "We could pull over and find shade," he offered.

"Keep going. Don't lose your place in line. We're going to be far back as it is."

Gabe blanched under his weathered complexion. She wanted to be *close* to the gallows! "What are these people to you?" he cried. "I don't understand this." He'd said the same thing before, but now his voice was tinged with desperation. What if he were sick? How could he *not* be?

"They're criminals. Scum. They deserve to die."

165

She didn't look at him, and he gave up trying to understand. Her vehemence repulsed him. He wondered if he could ever again think of her as he had until now. Would his image of her forever be tainted by this aberration?

Priscilla was too full of the past to wonder about the future. She had once loved Thomas Yarborough with all the fervor of her young heart, but it had not been enough. Not then, not ever. She had followed him from Virginia, shamelessly dragging Ida and Boyd with her. She was all they had and Thomas was all she wanted.

She got more, of course. She got a child he would have nothing to do with. By then she also had Joseph, thank God, or where would she have been? But Joseph was not Gabriel's father.

Priscilla chanced a look at him, seeing the look of Thomas in him. His voice was so like Thomas's it was uncanny. If she closed her eyes and just listened to him she was back in Virginia again. Joseph liked Gabe's drawl, thinking he got it from her. Perhaps he did, but she believed it was more that, like Thomas's voice, it could not be rushed. It was soft and sleepy-sounding, yet for all that softness, it carried, packing a powerful punch. Her speech was just slow.

"This is as close as I'm going," Gabe said.

She nodded, looking around avidly. After today she would be safe, *Gabe* would be safe and Boyd would be avenged. She was satisfied. She bent down to get the box and put it on the seat beside her.

Opening it, she asked Gabe, "What would you like to eat? Fried chicken?"

He looked away from the food wildly. "No, thank you," he whispered.

He would never be able to eat fried chicken again.

Across the dusty road, Rory watched the carriages, wagons and carts crowd into the limited space around the gallows and decided if he didn't leave immediately he would be trapped. He had come back to Dodge City for Caroline's sake: not to witness Blackie's death, but to assure himself that no rescue would be mounted for him. The law was well represented in the area, he found, and he began to work his way to the back.

It was unexpectedly hard going. He was a fish swimming upstream. Most people were glad to let him pass, but dodging around the animals was another story. There were horses of every description, mules, dogs, and even a cat sitting on the back of a wagon. Except for the grim rise of the gallows above them, the occasion might have been a church picnic or Centennial celebration. Children played on the backs of wagons and darted, much as he did, under and around the horses, flowing like water through a sieve.

Rory thought he understood that death was part of life as well as most people did; still, he could not help feeling shocked that people would bring young children to an execution. What lesson did they hope to teach? Obedience? Respect for law?

He had almost made his way to the edge of the crowd, but he had to stop when two dogs, inspired perhaps by the bloodthirsty atmosphere, began to fight off to his left. A ragged ring formed around them, closing off the lane where Rory hoped to pass. The dogs were of no particular breed, one larger by half. The smaller, however, appeared to be getting the best of the match, and the men watching quickly began wagering good-naturedly on the outcome.

The circle around the dogs moved as their conflict did, sending people here and there to avoid becoming part of it. It ended as suddenly as it had begun, when both combatants, as dogs sometimes will, stopped snarling to wag their tails and face off differently, their noses inches apart. As if at a signal, they each turned tail and ran away.

The cleared space they left was directly in front of the wagon next to Rory.

"Now we can move up closer," said a woman into the

moment of unexpected quiet.

Something about the voice, its slow-burning intensity, drew Rory's eyes up to the wagon just before it lurched forward to fill the gap. The woman's forehead was shaded by the brim of a purple flower-trimmed hat, but nothing could hide the avid glitter of her eyes as she looked steadily forward to the gallows. She held a partly eaten chicken drumstick in one hand, and with the other she reached out to clutch the driver's arm in excitement.

Rory turned away, sickened by her. Her voice followed him anyway. "Oh, look," she said, "there are the coffins. Three of them, piled up there waiting."

He broke through the rest of the crowd then and walked steadily away from the scene. Like the saloons and cribs that generated the crime to feed it, the jail stood on the wrong side of the railroad tracks. The town wasn't large for all that it was the county seat. Stores were closed up and down Front Street, either for lack of business or because the owners were among the crowd outside the jail. They would open to rip-roaring business as soon as the hanging was over.

As he walked Rory tried to compose the letter he would send Caroline. Again he would avoid mention of anything personal to themselves, but this time he could do so in good conscience. A declaration of love, even if he could bring himself to write one, wouldn't be appropriate to this letter. Which didn't mean it would be easier to write. But he had to let her know what had happened to her enemies.

Rory was sure Caroline would be upset about Blackie's death. Unlike the ghoulish woman he'd just seen, she was not a person to rejoice in anyone's death. Even Blackie's wild-eyed threats hadn't convinced her that he was really her enemy. She persisted in remembering that he had saved her from Walt and the men and treated her, mostly, with gentle courtesy. Rory wasn't so naive, but he was glad that she saw the best in people. He could not have admired her otherwise.

She would be glad, he supposed, that Humphrey had received the lightest sentence and even happier to know that no reference was ever made in the speedy trial to Ernie Coogins or to the presence of a seventh man. That puzzled him somewhat, but it saved him from feeling that Ernie constituted a danger to Caroline or to the family.

Rory would not have been so sanguine if he had been privy to Thomas Yarborough's last thoughts as he went to his death. He, too, was pleased to know that Albert Humphrey would not die at his side. In all his dealings with the law he had done everything he could to be sure that Humphrey was not implicated as more than the lowliest of accomplices in his crimes. He wanted Humphrey to go free as soon as possible.

Blackie had thought long and hard about how he could, even from the grave, get even with Cathleen Farrell-Caroline Farnsworth. Humphrey was his weapon. He was not, thank God, as innocent as he seemed. Like Thomas himself, Humphrey had been a friend of Boyd Belasco's. His relationship had been different, but like everyone who had known Boyd, his attachment ran deep. Boyd had not been the brains of the gang—he hadn't been smart enough. Instead, he had been the one everyone loved. Feckless and devil-may-care, Boyd had been their heart and soul.

If there had been times when Blackie had resented the way Humphrey eluded the law, always seeming to be somewhere else when trouble found them, he no longer felt that way. Humphrey would live to hunt down Caroline Farnsworth, and Ernie Coogins, too.

Because he knew that, Blackie was content. He had never pictured himself as an old man with his exploits behind him. He had expected—hoped—to die in the midst of a gun battle, cut down while his thoughts were somewhere else. He minded the *knowing* how and when he would die more than death itself. At least he thought he did.

As the moment approached he was glad he had passed up his last meal. Moon had eaten with stomach-turning gluttony that Blackie had to block from his mind. He smoked a cigar and looked forward to the glass of whiskey he had requested instead. So fortified, he intended to walk tall. His regrets were few: Boyd, because he had not been able to save him; Caroline Farnsworth, temporarily beyond his reach; and Priscilla, because—

She was unfinished business, too. Unlike Caroline Farnsworth, she was truly beyond his reach. He didn't know where she was. She had gone west, to Oregon it was said, after the Civil War. She was part of Boyd, too, but much more. First he would join Boyd in Hell, he thought with a dry laugh. Then Priscilla would join them both there—if she wasn't there already.

So thinking, Baltimore Blackie followed Walt's shaky steps out into the glaring noon sunlight. His small smile stretched wide as he saw the sea of faces before him. A scattering of applause greeted his grin; then everything stopped as the black hood dropped over his face, precursor of the final blackness to follow.

From snatches of conversation he heard going back to the hotel later, Rory learned more than he wanted to know about the hanging. Blackie, Moon, and Stimpson had gone to their Maker. No gang had ridden into town to rescue them. He was free to go on about his own business once he had written his letter to Caroline.

Faced with the blank paper, Rory forgot the comforting phrases he had rehearsed earlier. His account was brief and factual. He knew it was cold, but didn't know how to modify it. He sat for twenty minutes, turning over and rejecting one sentence after another before he added his only personal note.

It read: "I have made no further progress tracking down Uncle Joseph. Unless I discover something soon I will have

170

to give up again and come home. I hope it doesn't come to that. I trust that you are all well, especially Jake. Remember me to everyone with love." He considered adding "Love, Rory," then decided that was redundant. He signed it quickly before he could change his mind.

He was already packed, so he took his valise to check out on his way to post the letter. As he waited his turn at the desk he mulled over the decision he had made earlier to return to Ellsworth. On the one hand, he felt certain he had exhausted every possible lead there. On the other hand, where else did he have to go? He couldn't go from town to town. It would take forever. Uncle Joseph had been in Ellsworth once. Someone there had to know something about him.

A man in the crush ahead of him jostled him out of his reverie, then turned to apologize in a soft but peculiarly carrying Southern drawl. Rory smiled to show that he was not offended. As he looked away, his idle gaze fell on the purple-hatted woman from the wagon. She was standing guard over a pile of luggage near the door.

He turned away quickly, unwilling to look at her. Her face had lost its look of unholy fervor, but he wanted to forget everything about her and the day. Baltimore Blackie and the execution were behind him. He wanted them to stay there.

He waited behind the dark-haired man who had bumped him, ready to give up his room key and pay his bill. The man presented his two keys to the harried clerk.

"Tell the man to hurry," the woman in purple called out. "We'll be late for the stage."

The clerk sent her a thin-lipped smile. "It will wait, ma'am." He ran his finger down the log, muttering to himself, "Twenty-eight and twenty-nine. Oh, yes, here we are. Mrs. Joseph Talmage and—" he looked up—"Mr. Gabriel Talmage."

He turned the book sideways to make his calculations. By the time he announced the total, Rory had read off the name of his new destination.

Colorado. He was going to Colorado.

Chapter Sixteen

Abby came running from the house as soon as Caroline rode into the yard. She had been visiting Nila Jasper. Mrs. Jasper was kind and sweet, but hard to get away from. She made no secret of her hope that Caroline would marry Ted. The notion no longer seemed strange to Caroline, but she wanted to be sure marriage with Ted would be right for both of them. And today she'd been eager to get home. It was Abby's seventh birthday. She had things to do to get ready, and here was Abby already.

She caught up the streaking child and twirled her around and around in her arms. "Hello there, birthday girl," she said, giving her soft cheek a kiss.

Abby hugged her tightly and squealed, "I thought you'd never get back!"

"I thought so, too, sugarplum." She put her half-sister down, noticing with a pang of sadness that Abby was already losing her little-girl roundness. She measured her height against her own with one hand flat on the top of Abby's silky black curls and said, "Do you know? I think you've grown taller since yesterday."

Abby bounded with joy. "Have I really?"

"I think so." She bent to hug her one more time. "I'm sorry I left this morning without saying happy birthday, but you were sound asleep."

Abby scrunched her pretty face into a disgusted look. "I know. I missed Papa, too. I was so excited last night I couldn't get to sleep on time."

Caroline laughed. "It's probably all to the good. This way you don't have so long to wait for your party."

They started for the house, Caroline swinging their joined hands. Then Abby stopped dead and clapped her other hand over her mouth. "I forgot! I came to tell you there's a surprise inside."

"I'm sure there is. Probably more than one."

"No, it's for you!"

"But it's not my birthday."

Abby looked indignant. "I know. That's what I told Mama. Why should Rory write to you when it's my birthday!" Again she covered her mouth, this time in dismay. "I wasn't supposed to tell!"

Reassuring Abby gave Caroline time to assess her own feelings. Rory had been gone for weeks—seven of them. Except for the one general letter, he had sent no word at all. She didn't know what to think. She decided she was glad to receive this warning before she had to face Hannah. Hannah alone knew that Rory had promised to write to her, and Hannah was much too astute not to see that this letter, after such a long silence, was important to Caroline.

"He probably remembered your birthday, Abby, and wanted to tell you so."

"Do you think so?" Abby's blue eyes grew wide and intense. She adored Rory. "Mama said he might not. She said men don't do that well. But Papa does and he's a man."

Caroline regretted raising the issue. She had been deflecting attention from herself, but now she feared that Abby would be hurt. "Sometimes they do forget, honey, but just when they're far from home."

"Like Rory is," Abby concluded. "I wish he'd come home again."

Caroline didn't agree, at least not out loud. She was waiting to read this letter before she committed herself to any sentiments about Rory. She missed him in the most dreadful way—literally. He was a question mark in her life. One she wanted answered. Like Abby, she wasn't patient. She wanted things settled.

Abby ran ahead of her inside and came back with the letter. Caroline paused just inside the door and let the cool inside air refresh her. She half expected Hannah to appear, then realized that wasn't her way. She would give Caroline

174

privacy.

"Aren't you going to open it?"

Caroline smiled down at Abby. "In a bit. But first I'm going to change my clothes and wash up."

"You're taking a bath now?" Abby asked incredulously.

"Just a sponge bath. It won't take long." She bent and kissed Abby. "I'll tell you what he said later."

"You promise?"

"I promise."

"Then I'll go see if Lupe has my cake done yet."

"That's good idea. Is it to be chocolate or lemon?"

"I don't know," said the disgruntled child. "It's another s'prise."

"Oh, dear," Caroline sympathized. "You'll like it either way, though." When Abby brightened at that Caroline took the opportunity to scoot away, satisfied that her sister's pestering of Lupe would give her some time alone with Rory's letter.

She needed every minute of it.

Rory's concern for her appeared in every line of the letter, but no matter how many times she read over the words she could find nothing personal there. No message from his heart to hers. He had manfully carried out his terrible duty to her, no matter how hard. And it had been hard. She knew that and appreciated it. He didn't rejoice in Blackie's death any more than she did. He wrote, not to gloat, but to let her know she didn't have to worry about Blackie's threats any more.

She put down the letter and undid her bodice. Half-in and half-out of her dress, she paced back to look at it again. It was three weeks old. Had he been coming home, he'd be here by now. Or was he on his way?

She took off her dress and brushed her hair, thinking about his stated unwillingness to return. Naturally he didn't want to fail again, but couldn't he have said he'd like to see her? Or that he missed her?

Evidently not.

Caroline washed at the basin, then poured water from the pitcher into one hand to douse her face. She was proud

175

of her composed expression in the mirror. Papa and Hannah would read the letter and understand that she was upset about the executions. Anyone would be.

But if she was careful, even Hannah wouldn't be able to see how Rory had put paid to her foolish dreams of something more with him. She was glad to know now so she could finish putting away that part of herself and get on with her life. She had been holding Ted off with one hand, waiting, needing to be sure. Now she could be.

She took up the letter once more. Already she had committed every line to memory. She tried to find some sign that he held back some tender feeling, but there was nothing to hint at that.

There was also, she saw then, no mention of Abby's birthday. Weeks ago that wouldn't have been on his mind, but Abby wouldn't know that. She took a pen and added the necessary lines. Abby could read her own name, even in script, and would want to see where Rory had written it.

Her satisfaction felt hollow, but she dressed again and sought Hannah, Abby and Lupe, carrying the letter along. She found them in the kitchen.

Hannah smiled, her eyes busy trying to read Caroline's reaction in her face. At her instantly suppressed distress, Caroline feared that her disguise wasn't working. She tried harder. "Come and see your birthday wish, Abby," she called, spreading the letter on the table and taking Abby into her embrace.

"A-B-B-Y," Abby read, her face radiant. She gave her mother a triumphant look. "See! He did remember!"

Hannah saw too much, but she smiled fondly at both of them. "So I see. That's wonderful, darling. I trust that Rory's well?"

"Yes. You can read it for yourself." She started to hand it to Hannah and when Abby protested.

"It looks different where he says my name, Caroline. Why is that?"

"See these letters, P.S.? That stands for post script. It means that was added on after the rest of the letter was done." She had imitated Rory's style of writing well, but the combination of a different hand and different ink was telling, as she had feared it would be.

"That means he *almost* forgot, doesn't it?" Abby questioned.

"But that only makes it nicer that he didn't," she answered firmly.

"Yes, indeed, Abby," her mother put in. "It's very nice. And you, my pet, must learn not to be so greedy."

Caroline couldn't stand to see Abby scolded, however mildly. She gave her a kiss and put her back down. "But a little greediness is allowed on your birthday—which reminds me that I have some secret things to attend to in my room now." On her way past Abby she gave Hannah the letter to read.

She had two special packages to wrap in the tissue paper she had used to pack around her best gowns. She wrapped the small spurs she'd had Pete Fuller, the farrier and smith, make last week. Although they were blunt, in every other way they were replicas of the ones the men used, scaled to fit on Abby's new riding boots. Like Caroline, she was getting a new mount for her birthday. Hers was a pony, the first horse she would own.

Filled with remorse for what she had done to poor Fortune, Caroline put the box aside and began to wrap Abby's second present, a small beaded purse she had brought from Philadelphia.

Hannah knocked, then came in. She stopped before Caroline and asked gently, "Are you very disappointed?"

"I expected they would be sentenced to death," Caroline said, deliberately misunderstanding the question. "I can't say I'm sorry about it, but I'm not happy either."

"I'm sure you're not." Hannah's expression said she understood Caroline's refusal to talk about the more personal issue of Rory.

Caroline let her hands fall idle. Somehow it seemed wrong to talk about death while she wrapped a birthday present. "I never really felt threatened by Blackie, even when I heard what he said. I don't know why not. It was frightening enough at the time."

177

"Jake will be relieved to hear this. Even with you here, he's been worried that someone would harm you."

"I know. I seem to be such a care."

"Such a joy, you mean. It's so good having you home again. We all feel it."

"Papa does seem better, doesn't he?" She asked for confirmation even as she knew Hannah was no more an unbiased observer than she was.

"Oh, yes. He's even beginning to put on weight at last."

"I thought so."

Hannah admired Abby's gift, absentmindedly turning it over and over in her hands. "It was good of you to add to Rory's letter. He wouldn't be thoughtless unless he had a lot on his mind."

Caroline knew Hannah was speaking to her disappointment as well as Abby's. "I know. It must have been wrenching for him. I hope he didn't see . . ."

"He wouldn't have to, or want to." Hannah reached out. "Don't think about it."

"I won't. It wasn't my fault. I know that."

"The letter took so long coming Rory could be on his way here right now," Hannah said.

"Oh, I hope not," Caroline burst out in her honest way. "It's not what he wants."

"I think he'd find that there are compensations here," Hannah said lightly.

"No, he wouldn't. He'd only be coming home to lick his wounds before he went off again. Better he should stay away than do that any more."

"Be a little patient with him, Caroline. He needs to find his place in the world."

Caroline bent her head. She smoothed the paper, pleated it, then smoothed it again. "Why can't his place be here? This is as much his home as it is mine. We came here together."

"Would you respect him as a man if he gave up this search for his uncle?"

Her head came up. "Of course I would."

"Then tell him so," Hannah urged. "Sometimes men

178

have to be told things straight out, just the way we do." With a laugh, she added, "Rory's a lot like Jake, you know. A man of principle. It's almost impossible to be too direct with them. Sometimes it takes the direct application of a thick board to the back of the head to get your message across."

"Hannah, I did tell him. He just said I was turning into an old lady. I can't change him."

"You could join him."

Hannah had just put into words Caroline's second dearest wish, the one she repressed hardest. She pushed it down again, ruthlessly. Envy of Rory's adventure would do her no good. She was where she wanted to be, where she was needed.

"He doesn't want me. He's given me absolutely no encouragement. Ever." It hurt Caroline to admit the truth out loud, especially to Hannah.

"How do you feel about Ted? Really?"

"Really? I like him." She smiled. "He has the most wonderful disposition. He's just . . . easy."

Hannah nodded as though she had absorbed a blow. "I know. I like him, too." She gave back Abby's purse with a frown of concentration. "I'm not telling you what to do, Caroline, or offering advice—"

"You can do both, Hannah. You know I'd consider anything you say."

Hannah nodded again. "Maybe that's why I hate to offer. But I hope you'll keep in mind that you're a strong person, and sometimes easy doesn't go well with strong. Not for the long run. Just don't rush into anything with Ted. Don't let him charm you into a physical relationship and use that to bind you into marriage."

Caroline almost laughed. "He's not like that. He's very . . . respectful, I guess. Oh, he kisses me, but he's restrained. It's kind of funny, actually."

Hannah didn't respond to her amusement as she expected. Her frown deepened and she seemed puzzled about what to say. After a moment of struggle she said, "I won't ask for a promise, just consideration for what I say. But I hope you'll give Rory a chance to come home again before you make any commitments."

"A chance," she repeated. She wrapped the gift as she thought how open-ended that was. But it was what she wanted, too. "That makes sense, Hannah. I love Rory, you know, but I just don't know if it's the right way. I don't think he knows either. It's so odd what we share. There are feelings between us that nothing can change. It's the other feelings I don't know about."

"You're young yet. Give yourself time. Give Rory time." With those heartfelt words Hannah gave Caroline a smile and a squeeze of the hands and left.

Caroline tied blue hair ribbons that matched Abby's eyes around the package and thought over Hannah's admonitions. She was to give Rory time, but what was she to give Ted? Didn't he count for anything?

Chapter Seventeen

When Ted came to visit after Abby's birthday party, Caroline still hadn't found any answers to her questions. They stood at the corral fence and watched Abby ride her pony around and around. As she came near them he called out. "What are you going to call her, half-pint?"

"Shadow," Abby answered instantly, halting to pat the pony's neck.

"Because she's black?" Ted asked.

"Some, but mostly because she's going to go with me *everywhere!*" She kicked Shadow's sides with her new spurred boots, laughing at the miniature buck she produced.

"What a heartbreaker she's going to be someday," Ted said with feeling, shaking his head. "As bad as you, but different."

Caroline had never thought of herself in that light, so she just laughed.

"Different for sure. She doesn't promise to be a beanstalk like I was . . . am."

Before Ted could reply, Lupe claimed his attention from behind. "Mr. Jasper—"

He turned with a smile. "Call me Ted, please, Lupe. Mr. Jasper is my father. What can I do for you?"

"I wondered if I could put some packages in your carriage for Maria." Maria now lived at the Jaspers' and worked for Nila Jasper, an arrangement that had done much to restore peace and harmony to the Farnsworth household.

"Of course. I'd be happy to deliver them."

"No need. She will know to look for them. I thank you."

"Do you have a message for her?"

"No message, only perhaps you could remember me to your mother? She's a fine lady."

"That she is, Lupe. Thank you. Mother will be pleased to hear from you."

Lupe paused, turning away, to ask, "Maria? She is doing good? Your mother is pleased?"

"Very pleased, Lupe, and so is Maria as far as I can see."

Caroline saw Lupe's knot of anxiety ease just a bit and called out, "The cake was wonderful, Lupe."

She scurried away, laughing, "I do not cook for you. You would eat anything, little pig!" Caroline didn't translate Lupe's name for her, which she said in Spanish.

When she was gone, Caroline wandered over to where Jake and Hannah stood with Rusty. She didn't want to be tempted to say anything about Maria. Her move to the Jaspers' was proving such a blessing to Lupe that Caroline would have ripped out her tongue rather than say anything to upset the arrangement.

Lupe would never be totally free of her anxiety about Maria until she was happily settled somewhere, preferably far away, but until that unlikely time the new situation was a godsend. Lupe had her little house back, and she didn't have to put up with Maria's constant complaints. Nor did the rest of the family. Caroline considered Nila Jasper a saint for what she had done. And it had been her own idea. Hannah would never have foisted Maria onto a friend.

Nila was also responsible for the visit she and Ted were about to make to the Colbys'. She had sent a note to Hannah, along with a small bottle of light scent for Abby, asking if Caroline could accompany Ted while he did an errand for her. Put that way, how could Hannah refuse?

Not to be outdone, however vaguely, Hannah was sending some of Abby's cake to Ellen and Frank. Such excess of propriety amused Caroline when she knew her tomboyish habits, riding astride *in pants* and working like a hired hand, met with disfavor from everyone but Jake and Hannah. But Nila Jasper was determined to approve of her for Ted, and that was that.

"You should take up a regular delivery route," Caroline teased as they drove out, giving a rueful look to the back of the carriage.

182

"With you to keep me company it might not be so bad."

As they rode to the Colbys' they watched the sun set like an orange ball behind distant mountains tinged with purple. Coming back, the nearly full moon rose in the blue-black sky, a teasing promise that was ever withheld, no matter how fast they rode to meet it.

"You're quiet tonight. Is something wrong?"

Caroline told him about Blackie's execution. As she talked, Ted brought the carriage to a stop, securing the brake to let the horse forage.

"You don't blame yourself, do you?"

"Not really, but there's a kind of guilt involved that's hard to shake. I didn't start him on a life of crime, but he was there because his partner was taken from a Santa Fe train and hanged by a mob. And *that* man was there because Papa and I caught him in a bank holdup years ago."

Ted whistled appreciatively. "That makes you one dangerous lady to be around!"

She had to laugh. "Only if you're a robber. You're not one, are you?"

He grinned and made a gun of his fingers, like a child, to point at her ribs. As soon as he touched her, he flattened his hand to slide it around her waist. His other hand tipped her chin up to his mouth.

For the first time ever, Caroline stiffened in protest at the touch of his lips to hers. She wasn't in the mood. Talking to Hannah had brought Rory alive in her thoughts again, and she felt strangely disloyal to him. That made her angry at herself, because she had no illusions that Rory wanted her loyalty or felt any to her in return. In all that welter of emotion there was little room for responsiveness.

Her resistance set off a spark in Ted, surprising him. Except for the day he'd rescued her from her fallen horse and taken her to the line shack, he'd had no problem keeping his courtship every bit as "respectful" as Caroline called it. But Caroline grew on him. He liked her spirit. Her beauty was summery and clear, like the cloudless sky her eyes increasingly reminded him of. She wasn't sulky or stormy; she was warm and perhaps even genuinely passionate.

Whatever his first thought had been when he touched her—comfort, perhaps?—it was gone now. Having her withhold what he had come to rely on, that sweet, natural warmth, made him determined to regain it. Knowing it wasn't a game she played, he wanted to win her over. She had love to give. What would it be like to win that love?

Fighting every instinct that told him to push against her resistance, Ted drew back and let her go.

As soon as he did, Caroline was annoyed. She had felt that first spark of real desire in his kiss, and she was disappointed that he had given up so easily. Rory didn't want her. Now Ted didn't want her. Was this to be her fate? She didn't want to be good old Caroline any more, every man's chum and little sister. She wanted to be loved, to be desired.

She glared at him.

He glared back. "Caroline—"

"I'd like to get down." It was the first thing that came to her mind.

After a small considering pause, Ted got down from the carriage and put his hand up to help her climb down. When she did, he stepped neatly into her path, boxing her in next to the tall wheel.

Caroline stood her ground, perversely aware that she was confused about what she wanted from him. If he kissed her again she was going to struggle. If he didn't, she would be disappointed. She had just enough sense remaining to feel sorry for Ted—for any man. If she didn't know what she wanted, how could any man hope to please her?

He didn't touch her. Neither did he move aside to let her pass. He hooked his thumbs into his belt and laughed. "If I were a robber, I'd be real worried about my neck right now."

The bright moonlight fell on the side of his face and exaggerated the slight depression of his chin, making it look like a cleft. "You should be worried anyway." She tried to put real spirit into her answer, but his laughter had disarmed her.

"I don't think so," he said softly.

184

He leaned forward just enough to touch her lips with his. She could feel the backs of his hands where they rested at his beltline, but he didn't move them to draw her closer. He did that with his kiss.

Caroline wanted to laugh. It was so right. She didn't have to struggle because he wasn't holding her. He wasn't disappointing her either. The fact that he wasn't touching her made her ache with possibilities. His hands were right there. He could move them at any second. That he didn't increased her suspense.

Her lips parted with his, admitting the exploration of his tongue. She clenched her hands into fists at her sides to keep herself from reaching out to him first. His tongue withdrew slowly, tempting hers to follow. She didn't allow it, but she didn't pull back either. He ended the kiss and then took her hands in his.

Ted pried her fists open and lifted one hand to his mouth. "Were you going to hit me?"

She let go of her pent-up breath. "I thought of it," she lied.

He laughed against her palm, his breath warm and moist. She tugged on her hand, but he held it fast. He kissed the sensitive skin and touched it with his tongue while he watched her face. Without letting go, he said, "I think perhaps I'd like to marry you after all."

"After all?" They way he put it surprised her. "I thought that was the idea behind your honorable intentions."

"Not quite. The honorable part was to assure your father that I wasn't going to seduce you. Not every courtship leads to marriage. We might find we're not suited."

Caroline had her hand back and room to move. She took advantage of it. "You think we are? Suited, that is?"

"I see signs of it."

"I'm an unconventional woman, Ted. I'd want to be a real partner to my husband. I'd want him to let me share his life in every way."

"You mean you want to ride around in pants the way you do now?"

"That's not the way I'd put it, but yes, I do."

"You'd have me laughed at?"

"Hannah does the same thing, and no one laughs at Papa."

"I've never seen her out the way you are."

"She doesn't so much now, but at first she did everything she could stand to do. She doesn't really like cattle, though, just horses. And now she has Rusty and Abby."

"You're offering me hope, then? If we have children, you'll stay at home?"

"Why would you want me to? I'm knowledgeable and I'd be on your side. Not everyone who works for you would be. It seems to me any man can use another set of eyes and ears and another pair of hands, especially loyal ones."

"What if I had other uses for your hands?"

"His grin told her he was taking none of this seriously. "Cooking for you? Sewing? We can hire someone to do those things —"

"But hired people are so disloyal," he teased. He saw the quick rise of her hand before she was conscious that she wanted to strike out at him. He pulled her up against him and wrapped both arms around her, trapping her arms at her sides. He kissed her until she was breathless before he eased his grip. She could feel the drumbeat of his heart against her breasts.

When she could speak, Caroline went back to her argument, if only obliquely. "You don't take me seriously."

He put his hand over her breast in a gesture of possessiveness. "I take you very seriously. So much so that maybe I should withdraw my good intentions."

"Not like that."

He moved his hand coaxingly. "You don't like that?"

She did. She just didn't like the way he was using desire as a smoke screen. And Hannah said he wasn't strong enough for her! He was certainly wily enough. She pushed on his chest and felt his hands drop away to her waist where they slipped to her back, holding her against his lower body. She turned her face when he started to kiss her, so conscious that he was aroused that she was afraid to let him. He found her neck instead.

"Maybe there's something to be said for those pants after all," he said softly by her ear. He was sliding his hands down over her hips, there to encounter the many layers of her petticoats.

She had to laugh. "I knew you'd see reason."

He released her and stepped back with a smile. "Maybe I'll also see your father again," he said in the same light, teasing voice he'd used all evening.

"I haven't said I'd marry you," she reminded him pertly.

"But who else would have you? Who else would put up with such an unnatural woman?"

"You didn't think I was so unnatural a minute ago!"

Ted laughed and made no comeback. They drove the rest of the way in a strange sort of silence that was neither companionable nor strained. Caroline was busy examining the truth of his statement that no other man would put up with her. It was, she feared, all too true. Ted wondered at his reaction to Caroline. He'd begun his "courtship" as a way to placate his father's demand. He expected to like her and he did. He hadn't expected to want her—not really.

His parents' marriage was no kind of model for an ideal marriage. The only one of those around was Jake and Hannah Farnsworth's. If that was Caroline's model, and logically it was, it complicated the whole thing. He'd thought that *if* he married Caroline, she would be like his mother. He could not imagine his mother being extra eyes, ears and hands for his father. Her only opinion about cattle was that they smell and attract flies.

Then, too, he'd thought to have Caroline at home and Maria somewhere else nearby. He didn't love Maria, but he enjoyed her. He didn't think he wanted to give her up. And yet . . . it was Caroline's body he pictured now, slim and pale. There was something about her honesty and directness that appealed to him. She called herself an unnatural woman, but she wasn't. She wasn't lush of body, but she had passion. She kissed him back. She was warm—

Damn, but she confused him!

She directed him to stop by the back door, between the kitchen and the bunkhouse. He handed her down from the carriage and drew her into his embrace. Feeling her stiffness, he gave her a little shake and kissed her until he felt her respond. For some reason he had to have that. He held her against him and rocked her from side to side.

"Think of me," he murmured, putting her away to peer into her shadowed face.

"What should I think?" she asked. In another tone of voice the question might have been saucy.

He laughed and kissed her nose. "Good things. All good things."

Ted drove out without looking back to see that she went inside. Caroline felt that, for him, she had just ceased to exist. She walked slowly to the corral. She was thinking about Ted, but her thoughts were muddled. He smiled and laughed, but he wasn't easy. He wanted to marry her; he even desired her. She should be happy, shouldn't she? If Rory didn't want her, someone else did, a handsome, desirable someone. If only she could *know.* . . .

She sighed, then started as a man stepped out of the shadows next to the bunkhouse.

"It's me, Miss Caroline. Just Ernie. Don't be frightened."

"Ernie! I didn't see you." She walked a few steps closer. "I wasn't frightened, just surprised. I'm glad to see you. I haven't talked to you for so long. Are you happy here? Do you still like it?"

"Oh, yes. This is a good place. Your father's a fine man."

"I think so, too. Is everyone treating you well?"

"Sure thing. I just came out for a smoke." He indicated his cigarette, one of the hand-rolled specials the men smoked.

Her momentary happiness to see someone she considered a special friend faded quickly as she remembered her letter. "I have some news for you from Rory. About Blackie and his men." She watched his guarded face. "There's no easy way to say this, Ernie. He and Moon and Walt are dead. They were hanged three weeks ago. Rory's letter was slow getting here."

"I see."

What did he see? she wondered. She could see no change

188

in his expression. "The other three got prison sentences, Humphrey the lightest, as I understand it. I was glad about that at least, and there was no mention of you at the trial, Rory said. I'm sure he didn't attend, but he wanted you to know that."

Ernie nodded, his face hidden behind his hand as he drew on the cigarette.

"Does that make you feel safer, Ernie? I wish you could feel secure here." Then she was struck by another thought. "Or you could leave if you wanted to. I never meant that you *owe* us anything! Please don't feel you have to stay here just because we're glad to have you. You must do what's best for you."

Ernie said nothing. He couldn't have forced a word past the lump in his throat if he'd known what to say. Unwittingly, Caroline had bound him tighter to her side. He would leave, he vowed, only when she did. Then he would follow her and stay as close as she would allow.

She touched his arm. "Are you all right?"

He tried to speak and coughed instead.

"You shouldn't smoke those things. They can't be good for you."

"Yes, ma'am." His mother used to say that to Uncle Boyd. He would laugh and pat her shoulder, saying, "Yes, little Idy."

"Not ma'am, Ernie. Please," Caroline laughed. "I hope we're friends. I only liked Humphrey to call me that because I figured a man would never hurt the woman he called ma'am. It made me feel more comfortable. But you're different."

Ernie thought of Humphrey with a twist of his thin lips. He was very much different from Humphrey, who was, to Ernie's mind, the most treacherous of Blackie's gang. "Thank you, Miss Caroline. I 'preciate the news."

Caroline cocked her head to the side and asked, "I don't suppose I could convince you to leave off the 'miss,' could I?"

Ernie shook his head, but he smiled, too, and Caroline left him, feeling happier than she had since morning.

By the time she was ready for bed, her mind mercifully blank at last, Ted slipped into his bedroom, carrying the packages Lupe sent to Maria. He had decided against leaving them in the carriage. In his room they would provide an excuse for Maria to be there, too. And she would be. She made a point of coming to him whenever he spent time with Caroline.

He was always ready for her then. She liked that, the silly bitch. She took it as a compliment to herself that he wanted her after seeing Caroline. She would coo over him and imply that Caroline wasn't woman enough for him. He wasn't sure about that. He wanted Caroline, no doubt about that. But he'd have to marry her to find out. She was a woman to marry, maybe even to love.

Wouldn't that be something?

He bit back a groan as his body reacted to the thought.

Maria stirred in the bed. "You are late," she whispered.

He put down the packages and moved toward her. Caroline . . . Maria . . . the two were so mixed and intermingled in his thoughts he didn't think he could ever separate them. Somewhere in the back of his mind he knew the day would come when he'd have to, but not tonight.

Not tonight.

Chapter Eighteen

Caroline blamed herself.

If only she had gone with Papa instead of haring off after a mired calf. If only Zeb or Ernie had gone with him—anyone but Rusty, she thought frantically. Rusty was too young. Too young to bear the crushing guilt he would feel if they failed Papa.

But he had done well. He had done everything Zeb or Ernie could have done, with one possible exception. He hadn't killed the mountain lion. But who could say anyone else could have managed that?

She rode a paint cowpony, giving the smart little horse its head to follow Rusty's breakneck pace. Two men followed, to help them and Jake. Caroline wanted to yell at Rusty to slow down, because she was afraid he would fall headlong under the horses. At the same time she silently urged him forward, cursing their slowness.

Rusty said Papa was conscious. He said he was armed. But he was immobile, and there was a wounded mountain lion loose. . . .

They were in the broken countryside near the border of Jasper land. Caroline winced in memory. Did everything bad happen near Jasper land?

Finally, *finally*, they found Jake. Rusty streaked ahead to leap heedlessly from his mount beside his father.

"Papa! I've got Caroline!"

Heartening news, Caroline thought, putting herself in her father's shoes. They both knew she wouldn't be strong enough to lift him to his horse—if they ever found that animal again. Horses that had been spooked and possibly mauled by a mountain lion weren't known for hanging around afterward.

"And I've got two strong men with me, Papa."

He was conscious. Just barely. His eyes were bleary with pain and confusion, but he recognized her. His attempt to smile reassuringly wrung her heart.

By Rusty's account, Jake had been knocked from his horse by the leap of the lion from a tree. Rusty's yell, the horses' screams, the fall itself, and finally Rusty's shot from his own bucking mount had sent the big cat skittering away. She could see blood on the ground, more than she wanted to believe had come from her father.

"Can you ride, Papa?" She lifted Jake's head to put her hat under it.

"I'll go catch Monty," Rusty said.

"No!" Caroline reacted swiftly, catching her brother's arm. She would not let him go off again into the path of danger.

"Whistle," Jake whispered harshly.

Caroline met Rusty's eyes with a start. In her fear she had forgotten that Jake had trained Monty to come in response to his whistle. Rusty shook his head in despair. He couldn't whistle the way Jake did, piercingly, between his teeth. At another time Caroline would have laughed. Rusty had spent hours trying to emulate his father's whistle. She could do it, by putting two fingers in her mouth.

She patted Rusty's arm, stood and gave what sounded to her like Jake's signal. She could only hope Monty would think so, too.

"Are you bleeding?"

"Hurts," Jake said. "Back."

Could he be paralyzed? The men, Hank and Eli, flanked Caroline, peering at Jake with stupefied expressions that Caroline suspected were mirror images of her own. What must Papa think of her? She had to pull herself together.

She knelt before him. It was starting to rain. "See if you can help him sit up." She had to see his back. "Easy now," she murmured, helping, moving around to his back.

192

There was a wicked-looking gash over his shoulder and back that had bled profusely, soaking his shirt and coat. Fresh blood oozed out from their movement of his body. He hadn't moved of his own accord.

Petticoats, Caroline thought. She had heard the story more than once of how Hannah had bound him up with strips torn from her petticoats. She, of course, was in pants. She pulled off her coat and the second heavy shirt she wore under it. It was clean. The sleeves could bind the folded body in place to stop—or slow—his bleeding.

She wanted to weep and scream. Papa was just beginning to be his old self, strong enough to work the fall roundup. Why now? Couldn't anything go right for him?

She folded the shirt, then let Eli cut the body free from the stitched seams for her, improving the padding.

"Do either of you have any whiskey?" She had not thought to trap either man because drinking on the job was forbidden. She hadn't even remembered that Papa had reprimanded Eli twice for doing so. She barely noticed his shamefaced look as he produced a flask. "Oh, thank God," she whispered. She soaked the pad and tied it over Jake's shoulder, being careful to close the wound as well as she could. "You're a saint, Eli."

"Here's Monty," Rusty said.

Caroline had lost track of Rusty while she worked on her father. From his look, he had gone afield to catch Monty, but as long as he hadn't been harmed she couldn't scold him. She threw him a grateful smile and said, "Hold him."

"Lift him as much by his hips as you can," she directed her father's props. "Let's see if we can get him up."

"Papa! We're going to get you up on Monty. Try to help if you can." She saw him fight to rally and help them. "Good, good. That's wonderful, Papa," she encouraged.

The rain had become steady. All day it had threatened, with clouds boiling up over the mountain rim until the sky had lowered to a thick gray presence above them.

193

Hank put his poncho over Jake and took his place at one side of him, with Eli on the other.

"We won't let him fall, Miss Caroline."

They started off slowly, Caroline leading. "Keep your eyes lively behind you, Rusty," she called back, reminding him of the mountain lion. Eli's horse was nervous, frequently prancing sideways away from Jake and Monty. The smell of blood? Caroline wondered. Or the mountain lion?

"Caroline, I should ride over to Jasper's and warn those men."

Rusty hadn't mentioned the lion, but she knew what he meant.

"We'll send over a couple of men when we get home. And a couple to track him," she called back over her shoulder. "We need you riding shotgun." That was a sop to Rusty's pride. She hoped he wouldn't realize that. She felt guilty that the trail might grow cold—or more likely be washed away by the rain—before she sent men out after the wounded beast, but she wouldn't let Rusty go by himself. He was only a child.

The trip home seemed to take hours. She talked to her father constantly, trying to keep him alert. He answered with an occasional monosyllable when he could. Once she was within sight of the ranch Caroline rode ahead to warn Hannah so she and Lupe could be ready for Jake. Hannah grew pale at the prospect of sewing up Jake yet another time, but she was far more concerned that he was cold and wet. He had always been susceptible to fevers and could ill afford pneumonia after his recently punctured lung.

Caroline helped as she could, and then she and Rusty took charge of warning the men and starting the lion hunt. She let Rusty go to Jasper's on the condition that he return to help Hannah and not join the hunt. He begged for his chance, but accepted that his mother needed him. She took Eli, their best tracker, and went to find Zeb. As foreman, he was in charge. Men from Jasper's and Colby's would join them.

Caroline did not attempt to lead the hunt, only to coordinate their efforts and make the necessary decisions. While the men might respect her knowledge and ability with cattle and horses, hunting a wounded mountain lion was something else. She would not assert herself foolishly. She spared a moment for regret that Rory was not there, then did what she could.

By the time Ted and his men found them she was about to order the hunt over. The rain had washed away what little trail they had found. She happily gave him the power to decide. After a word with Eli, he nodded to the circle of men, all armed with rifles as well as their normal six-shooters.

"We're not doing any good here," he said. "Either the wound has stopped bleeding or the rain has washed it away, probably a bit of both. We'll double up on guarding the stock we've got penned and be alert. That's all we can do. Thank you all for helping."

Caroline felt pleased to have her judgment vindicated. Had she dismissed the men, someone would have suggested that she had given up too soon, particularly if the animal reappeared and did damage. Ted had taken her off the hook.

"How is your father?" he asked, coming directly to her.

"I don't know. Alive. I'm more worried about his lungs than his wounds, although he lost a lot of blood."

"I'll come home with you."

Caroline followed him to her horse, numb with gratitude.

"Rusty wasn't hurt?"

"No, and he did so well. If only—"

"So did you," Ted said, cutting off her second guesses. He gave her a leg up and a smile. "Don't worry now. Everything will work out."

With those few words, he restored her confidence and will. He spoke to the men, quietly dispersing them, handling all the details that had suddenly seemed formidable. She had been tired, cold, wet, worried and inade-

195

quate. Now she was only tired, cold, wet and worried.

Ted took her home and turned her over to Lupe while he talked to Hannah, then—briefly—to Jake.

Bathed, warmly dressed and swaddled in a shawl-blanket at Lupe's insistence, Caroline sat alone at the kitchen table, sipping hot chocolate with cinnamon. She had seen her father and even relieved Hannah at his side for a while. She was bone weary, but too upset to sleep. The hot chocolate was Lupe's cure for sleeplessness, but it reminded Caroline too much of Papa and his glass of milk to be effective.

She heard steps behind her and asked without looking, "How is he?"

"He's sleeping. The doctor has seen him," Ted answered.

Caroline turned in surprise. "Ted! I thought you'd gone." She shrugged off her shawl. She wasn't dressed for company, but she was well covered from head to toe. "Let me get you something to drink. Do you like hot chocolate?"

"Just some milk. My father doesn't approve, but I've always loved milk." He sat down heavily.

"So does Papa." Caroline got the words out around the thickening lump in her throat. She buried herself in the cupboard, searching out a glass until she felt in control enough to face Ted.

He took her hand, not the glass, and drew her back to the chair. "He's going to be all right, Caroline."

She nodded. "I just feel so helpless." She took back her hand and put it around the mug. "Last year I thought nothing could be worse than being so far away when he was hurt. I was sure if I were here I'd be useful . . . somehow."

"You are. You managed everything just right today. Jake's very proud of you."

"But I didn't—"

"It was an accident. Things happen. It could have been Rusty or you or anyone."

She bowed her head. "I know."

"He asked me to take the herd to market next week for him. I was going anyway. Zeb will go, but he doesn't handle the sale. Your father was going to do that."

"I know. He was looking forward to it. Last year he couldn't, so Rory did it."

"He'll be well again for next year, and Frank Colby's sending his herd, too. We'll be fine."

"You don't mind?"

"I'm glad to help. I admire Jake. He's already done the hard work of roundup. I'm just sorry he won't be with us. We'll take some extra men."

"I . . . hadn't thought of the drive. I just hadn't got that far." It was a poor excuse. It proved once again today that she wasn't tough enough to run the ranch alone. Even wounded and sick, Papa had been thinking of the herd and of his duties. She had only been thinking of him. It wasn't good enough. *She* wasn't good enough.

"Your father and I talked about one other thing, Caroline. I told him I want to marry you, and he approved. This probably isn't the time to ask, but it's on my mind and I'd like it settled before I leave. I hope you'll agree."

Caroline stared at Ted. She had known a proposal was coming—some day. But now? Like this?

Oh, grow up, Caroline, she told herself angrily. But she didn't speak.

Ted pried her hand from the empty mug and held it between his two palms. "I'm not doing this right, am I? You deserve moonlight and flowers." His thumb rubbed over her wrist, chafing as if to bring her back from her stupor. "You can't be surprised, Caroline. I've made no secret of what I want. I want you—in every way. I . . . I love you and I'd be proud to be your husband."

He loved her. He wasn't teasing and light any more. He was serious.

"Oh, Ted."

He let go of her hand and stood up to come around the table. "Say yes."

He loved her. He said so, answering the question she never dared ask. He was so good, so dependable.

"Then think about it," Ted murmured, drawing her up into his arms. "Sleep on it and tell me tomorrow." He kissed her gently. "Or the next day."

Caroline drew back from his second kiss and smiled. "I don't have to do that. I know the answer." Ted was the answer. She knew that now.

He stopped her lips with his. "Think on it."

"No, I don't need to. I'll marry you, Ted. You've made me very happy."

"You're sure?"

"I'm sure."

"So am I. You're good for me and I'll try to be good for you."

She pulled back, laughing. "What do we do now?"

"I have to go home. I'm tired and there's a lot to do." He patted her back. "This helps, believe me."

Caroline felt that was true. "I'll tell Papa." Somehow that was the most important thing to her. "Be careful going home." Her eyes clouded. Now there was someone else she had to worry about.

"I will. You go to sleep now." He kissed her lightly. "Dream of me."

She didn't. She went to tell Jake, reassured only when he squeezed her hand in answer to her questions, "Are you happy, Papa? Does that please you?"

She thought he smiled but wasn't sure. She didn't tell Hannah, excusing the omission because Hannah was busy right then. In bed she repeated over and over to herself, "I'm going to marry Ted Jasper," hoping to dispel her feeling of unreality.

Apparently, her dream of marrying Rory and living here with him was to be just that—a dream, the true unreality of her life. She had to recognize that now. It was no more real than her innocent belief that her presence at home could somehow keep her father safe. Today had taught her otherwise. Papa was hurt again and she was going to marry Ted. That was reality. She had grown up at last to face the truth. Rory did not want her for his wife.

Traces of the dream were still there in the morning, but she pushed them away. Ted deserved better from her. She had made her decision and she would stick by it, particularly when it was the one she had known all along she would make. The cloud on her happiness was Papa's injury, not anything else. In spite of everything Hannah and Dr. Harper could do, Jake had developed a fever during the night. Caroline and Hannah and Lupe took turns nursing him, sitting by him and trying to keep each other's spirits up.

Ted came every day to see Zeb and oversee preparations for driving the herd to market, and to see Caroline. He could not convince her to leave home long enough to visit his mother, so Nila sent Caroline a note of welcome and best wishes. She sent one to Hannah also which Caroline kept. She told herself Hannah was too busy to be bothered by anything unrelated to Jake. In truth, she dreaded telling Hannah that she was committed to Ted. How could she explain her decision?

The day before Ted was to leave with the cattle, they walked out to the corral where Abby was riding Shadow. The sun felt warm on Caroline's back, and she stretched, rotating her tense shoulder muscles.

"You look tired, Caro," Ted said in concern.

It was a new nickname, one Caroline didn't especially like. She blamed herself for that as she did for everything, including the violet smudges under her eyes. "If only I could sleep," she murmured.

"Does Jake need that much care?"

"No. It's my fault. I can't seem to relax."

"I wanted to make you happy, but it hasn't worked out that way, has it?"

"It's just Papa." Was she using her father as an excuse? She didn't know herself now.

"I understand." After a lengthy pause, he suggested, "While I'm gone perhaps you can tell my mother what your wedding plans are. She's eager to get started."

"I don't have any," she said too quickly. "I mean, *we* don't. I . . . can't think that far ahead."

Ted laughed. "I'd like to be married before winter sets in, you know."

"I thought . . . well, next year—" At his sharp look she blushed and added, "Spring?" She couldn't begin to explain to Ted that she still hadn't told Hannah their plans a week after he had proposed. If she did, she'd have to explain her practically unforgivable lapse. Since he was not an undesirable suitor, how could she expect him to understand?

"Maybe you can wait that long," Ted said lightly, "but I can't. Now that we've decided and we're sure, why should we wait? Do you want a huge wedding?"

"Oh, no. It can be very small. Just family."

"Well, then, between Hannah and Mother that will be a breeze—although I do understand that Jake has to get well first." He put his arm around her reassuringly. "And he will. I keep telling you that. Are you going to be the kind of wife who never believes her husband?"

Each kind, affectionate word struck Caroline like a blow. She turned within his embrace, ready to lash out at him. She took a deep breath—and heard Hannah call from the house.

"Caroline! Come! Abby, too!"

Caroline broke free from Ted, starting for the house. She remembered Abby and turned back for her. Ted was helping her down from the horse. They ran raggedly, responding to Hannah's urgency. Caroline was sure her father was dying. That knowledge made her steps heavy but fast. She had to see him, be with him. . . .

But it was joy that raised Hannah's voice to that pitch of frenzy. She rushed at them, practically dancing. "He's better! Oh, children, he's going to live! He's awake and he wants to see you."

They tumbled down the hall like eager puppies, Abby first, then Caroline. She felt suddenly shy, conscious of Ted hanging back, unsure what to do. Caroline wanted to shout her relief or cry or *something!* She managed to confine her tears and went to restrain Abby before she could hurt Jake with her exuberance.

Jake's eyes found hers over Abby's head. "Caroline." He lifted his hand to grip hers and looked away in order to control his emotions. He spied Ted at the doorway behind Hannah. "Ted," he called, "come in, come in, son. Let me see you."

Caroline saw Ted flush with pride as he stepped forward to take Jake's hand. As she looked from one to the other, her expression softened with understanding. In Jake, Ted had found his true father, the man he could look up to and hope to emulate. Although he never complained about Dwight Jasper, the little he said and her own observations painted the picture of a cold manipulator, not a real father.

Jake caught her look of understanding and chuckled. "I see how it is between you two. You asked and she said yes."

His question was for Ted, who must have answered. Caroline couldn't speak. She was paralyzed by her awareness of Hannah standing next to her. She felt Hannah grow rigid and still with shock.

"Hannah, isn't this wonderful?" Jake said, obviously buoyed by the news. "We're going to have another son — after the wedding."

Caroline's moment of joy was gone. She had hurt Hannah and been disloyal to Ted already. And they weren't even married yet. She would never be able to separate her father's recovery from her own treachery. How could she have acted so badly?

Whatever her own feelings, Hannah was equal to the moment. She smiled at Ted as if she had known all along and, for Jake's sake, sent them all away. In spite of his obvious happiness, Jake was pitifully weak.

Abby's excitement more than covered Caroline's quiet agony. "Is that true? Are you going to be my brother?"

Ted was too kind to chide Caroline for keeping her news from Abby. "That's right, as soon as Caroline and I get married."

"When is that?" she wanted to know.

"You'll have to take that up with your sister." He sent Caroline a sly look. "See if you can make it real soon—especially now that your father is better."

"You're not going to be the kind of husband who says 'I told you so,' are you?"

Ted laughed, pleased that she was teasing him. "Only when I'm right." With Abby gone to catch her pony and continue her ride, Ted drew her close. "Now will you send me on my way with a smile?"

Her eyes filled with tears instead. She was happy and relieved. Why couldn't she stop wanting to cry? She brushed her eyes with the back of her hand like a child and gave Ted a watery smile. "I'm sorry. It just . . ."

"I know. It's been a hard week for you. I'm glad I was here. Now I can be sure he's all right, too." He bent to kiss her gently. "Tell him not to worry. I'll take care of everything for him. I promise."

"I know you will, Ted. I . . . trust you." What had she meant to say?

Her hesitation, or her odd choice of words, drew Ted's quick and too-discerning glance. He frowned. "Don't be so damned grateful, Caro. We're going to be married. Us. The two of us."

His kiss was suddenly hard and demanding. It called to her passion, but that was too deeply buried within her to emerge. She tried to respond but only succeeded in making it worse for herself. Ted, fortunately, didn't seem to notice. He drew back first, his silvery gray eyes heavy-lidded.

He gave her a satisfied pat and said, "Soon, honey. When I get back. You make the plans and I'll show up. Thank God that's all a man has to do."

When he was gone Caroline lingered to watch Abby ride, postponing the need to face Hannah. She had not promised to wait for Rory's return, but how could she explain her decision when she didn't understand it herself?

Hannah used the time it took to settle Jake again to

202

get herself under control. She felt an icy rage that frightened her. It was all out of proportion to the situation. Her feelings were much too strong. They would be appropriate to murder, not marriage.

And toward whom was she directing her fury? Ted? No, she couldn't blame him for wanting Caroline. She couldn't even blame Caroline or Rory for their youthful confusion. *She* knew better. She knew how right they were for each other, but they were pulled by other loyalties.

She was angry at Jake. He had encouraged Ted and played on Caroline's tender sympathy and devotion. He had been selfish.

Think of it! Jake. *Her* Jake. Selfish.

She straightened the covers over his chest and fought down tears of anguish. If only he were well. Then she could tell him off. But he was sick, and he needed her and Caroline and all the love they all could give him to recover again. Just the lack of comforting bulk to his body tore her heart to shreds. He was wrong about Ted and Caroline. She knew it, and if he were well, he would know it, too.

For that was the crux of the situation. This . . . aberration was yet another symptom of his frail health. Jake, the real Jake, would never think to wed his precious daughter to Ted Jasper. And for that reason, she couldn't hate him.

Hannah bent and kissed Jake, smoothing back a fallen wing of his black hair. She barely noticed the habitual gesture, which was sometimes maternal and sometimes passionate but always caring. She loved Jake, right or wrong, and because he was sick she would not fight with him on this issue.

But she would fight. She would fight Ted and the Jaspers. She would even fight Caroline and Rory, but *for* them, although they might not know it.

Caroline had to hunt for Hannah, not because she was hiding but because she was restless. She had put her anger to use, striding through the house, accomplishing many of the chores she had put off doing all week to sit by Jake.

"Hannah, I'm sorry I didn't tell you," she said from the door of the sewing room where she had finally run Hannah to ground. "I wasn't slighting you, believe me. I wouldn't do that."

"I know that," Hannah said gently.

"I would have told you if I'd thought you would be happy for me."

"I'll always be happy for you. That's not the issue, darling girl. Don't you see? I want *you* to be happy for you." She didn't move, although she ached to gather Caroline into her arms.

"I am happy."

Hannah smiled at the obvious lie and added her own. "Then so am I. When did you decide to accept?"

Caroline shifted her stance. She thought of it as relaxing because Hannah wasn't angry. Hannah saw it as wilting—especially when she heard Caroline's answer. "Ted stayed here a while the night of the accident. He'd talked to Papa . . . and . . . I did, too. That's why he knew."

She seemed to be choosing her words with such care. It doubled Hannah's feeling of dread for her. "I'm glad he knew, darling. You're so important to Jake."

"I didn't mean to—"

Hannah waved her hand impatiently, interrupting. "The important thing is that you and Ted love each other deeply. I care so much because I had another kind of marriage before I met your father. I don't want that for you. Life is hard enough even when you have love."

Caroline nodded, looking more and more numbed and defeated. She said, "I know," thinking of what she knew of Hannah's early life. She had lost a four-year-old son of her first marriage to scarlet fever. Even with Papa her life had not been easy. She'd had at least one miscarriage that Caroline knew of, perhaps more. And Papa's accident . . .

"Do you have wedding plans?"

Caroline's guilt grew by leaps and bounds. "Ted says soon. When he gets back."

Hannah smiled broadly. "The eager bridegroom. Well, we'll see." She was not mocking either of them, only looking for a way to help Caroline. She thought she saw it. She would not oppose the wedding, not directly. She would only try to show Caroline, subtly, that she didn't feel what she ought to feel for the man she would marry.

But she would not start her campaign right now. Caroline needed understanding first.

"And now you're feeling sad and mixed up." She embraced Caroline warmly, remembering the child who had needed love most of all when she had done something she regretted. "It's all right to feel that way now, don't you know that? Everything will be wonderful. Your papa is geting well and Ted will come back. And in the meantime we can both use a good cry."

Chapter Nineteen

With Ted gone, taking with him the attendant pressures of roundup and cattle drive, Caroline found that she could relax and almost forget that she had promised to marry him. Almost.

She divided her time, neatly, she thought, between outside and inside. Outside, there was the ranch work and her friendship with Ernie; inside, she alternated between entertaining Papa and lessons with Abby and Rusty.

It was a pleasure to put her education to use with pupils as bright and dear to her as her young brother and sister. Through her teaching she got to know both of them in ways closed to anyone else.

Rusty, for all his quick temper, had dogged patience and practicality that boded well for the future of Renegade Ranch. She learned that no mathematical problem was beyond his grasp if she posed it in terms of cattle, acreage and feed. His strength — and weakness — lay in his persistent determination to understand everything, step by step.

Abby, on the other hand, was a free spirit, imaginative and impatient. She thought with her heart and was passionately involved with all animals, not just her pony, Shadow. Her true shadow, in fact, was a rooster she named, in defiance of all logic, Miss Penny.

Next to teaching the children, Caroline liked talking about them with Hannah and Jake. It amused her to compare her insights with theirs. She loved to trace the crosses of characteristics from parent to child—Jake's dark hair and blue eyes to Abby, his straight hair and stature to Rusty.

Twice, however, those conversations led her to disquieting moments. She expected that with her father, for he loved to remind her of her pending marriage. The date was now set for early November by agreement between Nila Jasper and Hannah, who were in seemingly constant communication about the wedding.

She had been telling Jake about one of Abby's illustrated stories when he suddenly gave her one of his luminous smiles and said, "You'll be a wonderful mother."

For the first time, Caroline understood—really—what her promise to Ted meant. She and Ted would have children who shared, as Abby and Rusty did, their parents' intermingled traits of character and appearance. Suddenly her marriage was real. And frightening. She didn't know Ted well enough to marry him. She had given her word to a stranger.

That moment, like so many others with Jake, passed finally. But the one with Hannah was worse. It reminded her of a truth that she had been suppressing for so long—that she loved Rory.

Then, too, she had been talking about Rusty and Abby, babbling about their splendid characters. "They both have such a firm sense of *justice,*" she said, turning over the idea in her mind. "They want everything to be fair, and not only for themselves. I suppose they get that from you, Hannah. Papa doesn't even expect fairness, it seems to me. Maybe because he's seen so much wrong done to the Indians. But both children just blaze up at the very idea of injustice."

"Oh, I think they get that from Rory, not me," Hannah commented in an offhand way.

"From Rory? But he's not related to them?"

Hannah's attention fixed on her. "Not everything is inborn, Caroline. Rory has been a great influence on them, and he will be all his life. Surely you've seen how

207

like him Rusty is. It's as though Rory provides a stepping stone to manhood for Rusty. His father is older. He supplies the ultimate goal, but Rory is closer to him. Rusty can more easily imagine himself as Rory and aim to be like him. He's been a wonderful influence." She looked away from Caroline's stricken face and delivered her final, most telling blow. "And when he comes back home and lives here again—which he will—his influence will continue."

Caroline had no idea what she said in answer or how she made her way to her room. She sat on the bed and stared at the familiar walls around her. Rory would return. He would live . . . here?

And where would she be? Nila Jasper expected her to live with them.

She could not imagine it.

The next afternoon Caroline and Jake took a walk, her father's most ambitious to date. Knowing that he hated being hovered over, Caroline merely kept him company and stayed alert to his needs as unobtrusively as possible. In that spirit, she sent him on to the house by himself while she pretended to some business at the stable when he had had enough of the outdoors. As soon as he left her sight she put down her make-work to watch his progress to the house.

Once he was safely there she decided to put her restless energy to work cleaning out a storage closet. She took off the cloak she had wrapped herself in so Jake would not object to his heavy outerwear and got busy. She heard horses arrive, but gave them no thought. Even with so many hands away on the drive, horses came and went constantly.

"So this is where you're hiding."

Her head came up suddenly under a shelf. Rory's quick intervention—his hand above her head—saved her from a sharp knock.

Rory.

She had time only to gain the impression of golden brown warmth . . . his hair, eyes and voice. Even his clothes were honey brown. Then she was in his arms and he was kissing her in the shameful-wonderful way of the dreams she had come to believe were nightmares.

Caroline told herself he wasn't real as she kissed him back. His strong arms around her. His hands pressing her flat to his straining body, then seeking her soft breasts, stroking, squeezing, caressing. And his mouth — hot and devouring. She flamed like a curl of piñon to the rasp of a flint.

Rory, Oh, God, *Rory!*

He smelled of horses, leather and the fresh canyon wind. His skin was cold over warm living flesh. For one long mad moment she clung to him, filling every sense with his presence before she let her mind accept — and reject — his reality.

She pushed on his chest. "Rory," she gasped. "You're here."

He gave her the space she desired, laughing down into her upturned face. "I'm here, sweetheart, and oh, God, but I missed you!"

Everywhere she had burned now felt cold. "How did you get here?"

He hugged her exuberantly. "I came with Uncle Simon. I went to see him and we decided to come here. I have so much to tell you."

Indeed.

Caroline could only stare as he framed her face with his big hands and looked her over like a man deciding where to begin eating a delectable cake. "You have a smudge on your nose." He kissed the spot tenderly.

She pushed away, this time managing to move beyond his reach out into the stable.

He dropped his hands to his belt, resting them there while he took in her militant stance. "You're angry at me."

Caroline closed her eyes. If only it were that simple. "I'm sorry I didn't write you."

"But you did."

He wasn't fooled. "That didn't count. I didn't know how to write what I wanted to say." He moved forward and she retreated. He leaned against the doorjamb, staring at her the way he looked at a chessboard while he figured out his next move.

"It doesn't matter now." She started to say more, but he caught her arm, pulling it free from its mate folded over her chest.

"But it does," he insisted. "I wanted to hold you and see your face when I told you how I—"

"Don't!" She put her hand over his mouth, desperate to stop him from saying what she couldn't bear to hear. "Don't say anything! It's too late, Rory."

He shook off her hand and hauled her to his chest. "What's too late? What are you talking about?"

"I'm going to marry Ted Jasper next month."

"What?!"

She didn't repeat the statement. It seemed to be bouncing from wall to wall around the stable like an echo gone crazy, pelting them from every angle.

"I don't believe you," he whispered.

She endured his incredulous stare in silence.

"Why?"

But when she opened her mouth to answer he brushed by her, almost knocking her over.

"Never mind," he snarled over his shoulder. "I don't give a good goddam!"

Caroline sank to the floor, her mind utterly blank. What had she been about to say? She had no idea.

Rory had spent over a week walking a wide circle around Caroline. He had gone from raging at her to raging at himself and back to her until he was as mindless as a mule in harness, plodding round and round to power a thresher. With her avoiding him in return, he almost began to see humor in the situation. If she was sitting with Jake, she would leave when he came in.

Always with an excuse. She was thirsty or tired or just remembered something she had to do.

After their conversation in the stable he had gone directly to Rio Mogollon to get drunk. Having started so early in the day, he was well on his way to success when Ernie came to fetch him home. He remembered greeting Ernie with appropriate belligerence that somehow became camaraderie, undoubtedly based on his perception of Ernie as another of Caroline's disappointed suitors.

He didn't remember returning to the ranch, only waking in the bunkhouse, still in Ernie's matter-of-fact care. Since then he'd been unable to resent Ernie as before, even finding himself seeking him out in Zeb's absence. It was, however, the last night he slept in the bunkhouse. Hannah insisted that to do so now would be rude to Uncle Simon, although he had stayed there during his many other visits.

It didn't matter, though. No matter where he slept there was no peace for him. He could not forget that Caroline was lost to him because he had waited too long to tell her he loved her.

Or had he? After days of pondering every nuance of conversation between them since Dodge City, Rory finally let himself recall the pent-up passion of her kiss in the stable. That had not been the kiss of a sister. Nor had it been the kiss of a woman committed to marrying someone else. She had answered every demand he made without resistance or restraint. True, he had taken her by surprise. But that only meant her reaction had been honest. She had responded, even letting him touch her breasts, because she couldn't help herself. To stop him, she'd had to remember her anger and hurt at his neglect. Then, finally—last—she'd remembered Jasper.

That wasn't the Caroline he knew and loved. Or rather, it was. But it meant that she loved him, not Ted Jasper. Her plan to marry him was a terrible mistake, but it wasn't irreparable. Or it wouldn't be unless he wasted more time before he showed her how wrong she was.

He wasted two more days plotting his approach, then

ignored his plans when chance handed him an unexpected opportunity.

He was going out the back door as Caroline came in. At a glance he took in her pallor, temporarily burnished by fresh air and wind, as well as the faintly darkened circles under her eyes, and decided their time had come. He had been on his way to check Abby's pony for Jake; he had seen something odd in Shadow's gait. But that could wait.

He caught hold of Caroline's wrist and swung around to accompany her inside. She gave a small cry of surprise and tried to pull free. He ignored her. Mentally running down the list of people who might disturb them, he realized he might never have a better moment. Jake and Hannah had taken Uncle Simon and both children to the Colbys' for dinner. Lupe had gone to her house, leaving food for their informal supper. Given a choice, Caroline probably would have gone to the Colbys', too. He had declined, and she had stayed out too long to be included.

It was late. He had already cleaned up, and he knew that was Caroline's intention. Another time he would have gone his way and given her time to bathe and change into a dress. She would not like being at a disadvantage with him, but if he waited she would realize that they were alone and find a way to elude him. He wouldn't take the risk.

He led her, protesting all the way, to his room. It was small, containing only a single bed, chair and chest, all of them covered with cast-off clothing. He wasn't neat. Even the bed was unmade. Her room would have been a better choice, but he didn't want her to be able to order him to leave. He closed the door and leaned back against it in dismay.

He had made another mistake. She was blazingly angry.

She was. In her distress, she had taken refuge behind the first protective cover she could find. "If you're looking for maid service, you can forget it."

Rory shook his head. "I just want to talk. You've been

212

avoiding me."

She didn't deny it, just waited with twitching impatience.

"Caroline, you can't marry Ted Jasper."

She had decided the same thing at least forty times since Rory's return, but she didn't give an inch. She couldn't. She had given her word.

Rory took one step toward her, then another.

Caroline backed up as he advanced, then stopped. She was running out of room. She sensed the bed behind her and held out her hands, warningly. "Don't . . ."

"Caroline." He stopped. "I know I was wrong before. I should have made myself clear to you before I left. I should have written. I'm sorry for that, but adding another wrong to the list won't make any of that right. You don't love Ted—"

"I do too!" she insisted.

He forged on, shaking his head in chagrin at his stupidity. Hadn't he called her Contrary Caroline for years? Didn't he know *anything* about managing her?

Apparently not.

"You don't, but that's not the point." He had to raise his voice to drown out her reflexive protest. "The point is, Caroline, I love you. You're right for me the way I'm right for you. In a way I've always known I was waiting for you to grow up. That's why I've never found anyone else to love. I should have told you just as soon as I realized—"

"And when was that?" Her interruption was sharp, sarcastic.

"When I kissed you on the street in Dodge City."

His answer and the small smile of remembrance that lit his face pierced her makeshift defenses. She didn't let him see the strike. "Oh, yes, I remember. That was when you hung me on the wall and then failed to 'let me down easily.' How strange that I didn't recognize that it was such a tender moment for you."

Rory flushed with anger and embarrassment. He had acted like a swine with her. No wonder she was being difficult. "Not then. The first time. And I've told you I was sorry for that —"

"Yes, you have. I've had any number of apologies from you. One for just about every conversation we've had. I suppose tomorrow I'll get another, for today." She was running out of starch. Her voice turned pleading. "It doesn't matter, Rory. I'm sorry, too, but it's too late. I told you that."

"It can't be too late. You're not married yet. You can change your mind."

"No, I can't. I've given my word."

"Your word isn't enough, Caroline. Listen, sweetheart, you haven't given him your heart. You just can't marry someone you don't love!"

"I do —"

"You don't." Rory stood in front of her, so close she could feel the heat of his body. "I know you don't or you'd never have kissed me the way you did in the stable."

Caroline felt her face burn. "I didn't have a choice. You —"

"I surprised you, yes, but that was your heart dictating to you, not me. I know you. If you loved Ted you'd never kiss me like that."

He was teasing her with his presence, with his lips just inches from hers. Her mouth was dry, and he offered refreshment she wanted desperately. She denied herself, and him.

"No, Rory. You misunderstood. I was struggling . . . and surprised . . ."

"And now?" he questioned softly. "Are you struggling now?"

Yes!

But she stood still. She knew he had to kiss her and she had to let him. Worse, she had to give him no sign of her inner turmoil. She held her breath as he stared down into her face. His golden brown pupils were dilated to let him see in the dim room, making his eyes dark. His expression held such yearning that she was afraid she

214

wouldn't be able to hold herself still. She wanted to give him everything he wanted, for always. If only she could divide herself in two, one to stay here with Papa, one to go with Rory. . . .

She concentrated on taking small, steady draughts of air and waited.

He didn't kiss her. He lifted his hand to her face. It hovered, almost touching. His fingers trembled, and he turned his hand to skim her cheek with the back. His knuckles grazed her skin, lightly, like the brush of a leaf falling to earth.

"Caroline . . . sweetheart . . ."

The descent of his lips to hers seemed a act of will — hers, not his. She drew him down to her, all the while promising herself she would not respond. She would be cool and self-controlled.

Overtly, she was. But she could not prevent — or even know — the way her eyes grew dark and smoky, or the way her eyelids drifted down to cover them. And she could not prevent her lips from clinging to his, from softening with desire.

She didn't move, however. She stood woodenly within the warmth of his embrace. His hands gripped her waist, almost meeting around the narrow span before they parted to go separate ways. One slid to the back to ride down the slope of her hips. The other climbed up over her ribs, one at at time. While he wooed her with his mouth, he conquered her with his hands, claiming unprotected territory.

She didn't protest or defend herself. It took all her concentration just to remain outwardly passive under his assault. She curled her fingers into fists rather than let them touch the shelf of his shoulders or press his broad chest. Her heart began to puck up the measure of its throb, like the hoofbeats of a pursued animal.

She had not thought it would take so long.

Savor, oh savor; remember, she told herself. This kiss had to last her forever.

Rory placed his hand over her breast like a man

215

closing on a prize. He held her trembling warmth, possessing it before he began to enjoy his claim. Once he had held her softness long enough to feel the leap of her heart, as if it would jump out of her chest into his cupping hand, he lifted his fingers and brushed the hardened center with his palm. Around and around he went, keeping her nipple in full and complete contact with the flat of his hand. Her response was undeniable, but she pretended it away.

If she admitted that she ached, that her back arched to give him better access, she would have to protest. She would have to stop him from giving her the most delicious feeling she'd ever known.

For the same reason, she let his tongue breach the barrier of her teeth and thrust in and out of her mouth, stealing her breath with each suggestive foray. She was a rock, she reminded herself. Cold, hard, unmoved . . . But only on the outside. Inside, she was molten stone and steam, under pressure.

He lifted his head, scouring her face with reproachful eyes. He shook her once, sharply, his hand hard on her shoulders. "You want me. Damn it, Caroline, admit it!"

Relief made her knees weak, and she swayed within his grasp. It had worked! He believed her. She was safe.

She let her hands fall to her side, slack, and concentrated on holding herself upright. She shook her head. "I'm sorry, Rory."

"I felt your heartbeat, Caroline."

"You frighten me."

"I do? God, I'd never hurt you—"

"Not that way, no." She put her hand up to his face but let it fall without making contact. She wasn't gone yet. She had to wait, had to make her getaway.

He let her go, his hands at his sides. "I love you. I . . . love you."

His defeated echo tore her heart from her body, but she couldn't let him see that. This was the greater kindness—to be harsh now.

"I love you, too, Rory. I always will. You're my

brother, part of me always." She would never forget the leap of hope in his eyes at her first words or the way she doused it with her last.

Please, God, she pleaded in her heart, *let it stay dead this time. I can never do this again. It hurts too much.*

She left before he could see her tears, while she could still see her way to the door.

Chapter Twenty

"Honey, we'd like you to join us," Jake said after a tap on her closed door.

Caroline had spent the day on her wedding arrangements, and now she was hiding. She was tired and out of sorts. The last thing she wanted to do was join the family in a discussion of Rory's plans.

She put down her book and got up, brushing down her rucked-up skirt. By herself, she made a point of not sitting like a lady. She curled up in chairs or against pillows on her bed, her legs folded under her. One foot was asleep, so she took small steps and flexed her toes. "Of course, Papa. Is there a problem?"

"No, no. It's just that you're the one with all the ideas. None of us has your imagination."

And look where it's gotten me.

She followed along just as if her heart wasn't breaking. At least she knew Rory didn't want her there either. This was Hannah's doing. Papa might be oblivious to the swirls of emotion between Caroline and Rory, but Hannah was not. And she persisted in trying to bring them together. Not obviously, of course. Hannah was nothing if not subtle.

She took a chair opposite Rory and next to Uncle Simon, shooting a poisonous glance at Hannah.

"I'm sorry, Caroline," she said. "Were you sleeping?"

"Just reading." Escaping, she might have said more truthfully.

218

But she had played into Hannah's hands. "That's why we need you. You're the one with all the plots."

"Not in real life," she argued. But she looked politely at Uncle Simon.

He was one of her favorite people. He was an enormously wealthy and powerful man, but here in the bosom of Hannah's family he was just Uncle Simon, the man who had given Hannah his home and his heart when her parents died. She had been ten, just the age Caroline had been when Hannah married her father. Caroline felt that they understood each other better because their lives had both been torn up at the same age.

Like Zeb, Uncle Simon didn't change much from year to year. His ginger mustache was grayer, but his heavy brows, which grew straight across his nose in a line, were still dark and thick, and his eyes snapped with humor. He was bluff and hearty, a man's man on the outside to cover up for the softness of his heart.

"We're trying to decide on a name for Rory," he told her now. "He can't be Rory Talmage. What's a good alias?"

"Why not Farnsworth?" she asked promptly. "Half the world already believes that's his name."

Hannah beamed. "See? I told you she'd have the answer."

Caroline wished she'd held her tongue.

"But Rory's too unusual a name," Jake said. "His uncle would be alerted by that."

"Make it Royal then. It's close, but different. Then if anyone slipped and called him Rory he could explain the lapse."

"That's a dumb name," Rory objected.

Caroline shrugged.

"I've been trying to remember my first impressions of Rory's appearance," Uncle Simon said. "I can't be sure his uncle wouldn't recognize him."

"He could grow a beard," she suggested.

"A mustache maybe; not a beard," Rory put in.

"You're right. You'd only have it full of spilled food," she said.

Jake gave her a sharp look, but Hannah laughed. "Children, children," she said. "Let's be pleasant."

Uncle Simon grinned and went on. "Voices are distinctive, though. Wouldn't his uncle remember Rory's?"

Caroline thought how she would never forget the deep tone of his voice, but she said, "His voice was still changing when we met him. Don't you remember?" She addressed her question to Hannah. "Whenever he got upset or excited his voice would squawk." She knew he hated the unflattering picture, but it served their purpose well. "More to the point," she said, "would be any distinctive family mannerisms or resemblance to his father."

"Don't talk about me as if I'm not here," Rory said tightly.

Her gaze swung to his and locked. "I'm not. Those are questions only you can answer."

"I resemble my mother's family. Uncle Joseph never met them. As for mannerisms, I don't know. Does anyone ever know the little things he does?"

"You rake your fingers through your hair." As soon as the words were out she wished them back. They showed how much she noticed about him.

"But so does Jake," Hannah put in.

Jake and Rory exchanged looks of surprise that made Caroline hasten to add a less personal note. "Maybe all men do."

Uncle Simon laughed and patted his few wisps of hair. "I don't!"

"But you try, darling man," Hannah said, easing them all into laughter.

"If that's all?" Caroline asked, hoping to take advantage of the moment to make her escape good.

"It's a start, honey girl," Uncle Simon said, beaming

approval her way. "You know," he added in his teasing way, his eyes bright with mischief, "it's too bad you're going to marry this Jasper fellow, Caroline. You'd be such a help to Rory and me. A sister would really throw Rory's uncle off the trail. And you could get to know his wife. She's the clue to Joseph Talmage, I believe."

Caroline had heard that Joseph was married. It didn't seem remarkable to her. Of course, Uncle Simon couldn't know how his teasing suggestion would hurt her—or Rory.

Their eyes connected again before she looked away. She didn't escape unscathed, however. Rory said, "Let's not forget his son. Caroline could make him fall in love with her and then we'd have old Joseph over a dozen barrels."

"His son isn't a child?" she asked Rory. "Then you must know him—or he knows you?"

"He was news to me," Rory answered. "I stood right next to him without a flicker of recognition on either side, I'm sure. I'd know them both again, but I was just a face in the crowd to them."

"Can you be sure of that?"

"Not totally, I suppose. The son bumped me and begged my pardon. I doubt he even looked at my face. His mother certainly didn't. She was absorbed in herself." He didn't mention the hanging and Mrs. Talmage's inordinate interest in it. The others knew, and Caroline didn't need to know.

"Your father and Joseph were business partners," she said thoughtfully. "Did they keep their private lives so separate that you wouldn't have known his wife and son?"

"I don't see how."

"Then the marriage must be recent and the son adopted?"

"That's what we think."

She turned to Uncle Simon. "Why do you think she's

221

the key to Joseph?"

"I had them investigated—to a point. She and her son were in the wagon train that Rory deserted, but their relationship to Joseph wasn't obvious at first. Her name is Priscilla and he is Gabriel. Until Joseph claimed them, they didn't seem to have last names."

"A secret marriage?" Caroline askied.

"Or a mistress. They live as a married couple now anyway, and she is fond of money, they say."

Caroline didn't need it spelled out for her. With Uncle Simon's help, Rory would offer his uncle a get-rich-quick scheme that would bring financial ruin instead. It was simple. They didn't need her after all.

Lupe interrupted her morose train of thought with her hesitant appearance at the doorway. Hannah jumped up to remonstrate. "I thought you'd gone home, Lupe."

"Beg pardon—"

"No 'beg pardon' at all, Lupe," she scolded. "You're tired. You should be in bed."

Ted appeared behind her, carrying a tray. "It's all my fault," he said, flashing his most charming smile. "I detained her in the kitchen and ate half of your refreshments."

Lupe gave him a worshipful smile. Since the Jaspers had given Maria a home and Ted was going to marry Caroline, he and his mother had become cherished members of her extended family. She ducked behind him to leave as he looked around for Caroline.

He had been back four days, but Caroline had never been more pleased to see him. She gave him her widest smile, thankful to have a graceful exit. With Rory cold to her and Hannah full of contrivances, Caroline felt comfortable only with Ted and her father. With them she knew her role. Now that he was here she didn't have to feel excluded and lost any more.

Her feelings were irrational. As the bride-to-be she was the focus of far too much attention. At the same time she was cut off from Rory's plans—even when she was consulted, as she had just been. Nothing she felt made sense.

She left with Ted, relieved to be away from the people she loved most. She leaned against him in the hallway, absorbing the good outdoor smell of his clothes.

He lifted her face to his kiss and laughed at the fervor of her response. "Do I detect a note of desperation tonight? Too much wedding conference?"

Caroline made a face. "Let's just say your rescue was timely." She took his hand and tugged him away outside. He lifted her up onto his horse, to ride before him as she had done with Rory as a child. The wedding was less than two weeks away. Her calm and calming ride with Ted notwithstanding, Caroline felt that she was on a runaway horse, plummeting to certain disaster.

She did not know that as soon as she and Ted left, Uncle Simon said goodnight and headed for the guest room. Rory, too, took his leave, slipping out the back in order to avoid the happy couple. Of those she left behind, only Hannah saw Caroline's unhappiness beneath the picture of bliss they presented.

She stood at the front door to watch Ted and Caroline, unaware that she sighed. Jake heard and came up behind her, enfolding her in his arms. "Young love," he murmured as his lips brushed her hair. "Does it make you wish you could go back?"

"Not if I have to be Caroline."

As if her words weren't shocking enough to Jake, she compounded the effect by holding herself rigidly erect in his arms. "I don't understand." He stood back and turned her to face him. "What are you saying?"

She closed her eyes in a gesture of resignation, but when she opened them, she blazed at him like the Hannah of old. "Oh, Jake, are you blind? Can't you see that your daughter is miserable?"

"Miserable?" He stiffened with affront. "Why should

she be miserable?"

"Why indeed," she echoed, her voice heavy with sarcasm.

He blazed back at her. "I can do without the dramatics, Hannah. I asked you a question."

She sighed again, this time softly. "You really don't know, do you?" Because an answer wasn't needed, she plunged on. "Caroline doesn't love Ted. She's fond of him, yes. But love? No. She doesn't love him."

"Then why in hell is she marrying him?"

"He caught her at a bad time. You were hurt. Ted was taking your cattle to market. She felt guilty and alone and grateful for his help. She wanted to please you."

"Please me?! Hannah, you're not making sense! What have I to do with it?"

"You made your wishes very clear. She heard. She's like that."

Jake fought her message. He didn't want to accept responsibility for Caroline's possible unhappiness. "I thought it was just bridal nerves," he whispered. His throat felt raw, closed over.

He turned from Hannah to look out into the yard. Caroline and Ted were no longer in sight, but both Jake and Hannah could still see their image. It had the presence of ghost glimmer, hovering like a silent reproach. Their illusion.

No. *His* illusion.

"She loves Rory," he said, putting the final piece into the puzzle.

"Yes." Hannah put out her hand to him.

"He loves her?"

"I think so, but he won't discuss it. They took some tentative steps toward each other when she came home, but he didn't speak up. Ted did."

Jake remembered his conversation with Caroline the night before Rory left. He had also spoken up. Out of protectiveness. Out of love. Out of . . . selfishness?

ACCEPT YOUR *FREE* GIFT
AND EXPERIENCE MORE OF
THE PASSION AND ADVENTURE
YOU LIKE IN A
HISTORICAL ROMANCE

Zebra Romances are the finest novels of their kind and are written with the adult woman in mind. All of our books are written by authors who really know how to weave tales of romantic adventure in the historical settings you love.

Because our readers tell us these books sell out very fast in the stores, Zebra has made arrangements for you to receive at home the four newest titles published each month. You'll never miss a title and home delivery is so convenient. With your first shipment we'll even send you a FREE Zebra Historical Romance as our gift just for trying our home subscription service. No obligation.

BIG SAVINGS
AND *FREE HOME DELIVERY*

Each month, the Zebra Home Subscription Service will send you the four newest titles as soon as they are published. (We ship these books to our subscribers even before we send them to the stores.) You may preview them *free for 10 days.* If you like them as much as we think you will, you'll pay just $3.50 each and *save $1.80 each month off the cover price.* There is never a charge for shipping, handling or postage and there is no minimum you must buy. *AND you'll also get FREE HOME DELIVERY!* If you decide not to keep any shipment, simply return it within 10 days, no questions asked, and owe nothing.

Had he really done that? Interfered?

"Hannah, I don't know what came over me. I was worried that Rory would break her heart. He didn't seem to be ready—" His voice trailed off to anguish. "I've spoiled her life. How could I? No one on earth knows more about the misery of an unhappy marriage than I do."

"We both do," she comforted, going into his arms the way she had refused to before.

"We have to stop her."

"I'm not sure we can. I've been trying. I think she's even tried, but it's picked up momentum." She shrugged helplessly, spreading her hand on his chest. "The plans . . . the wedding."

"Plans be damned," he muttered fiercely.

"She's given her word. You know how that is."

He did. Caroline's word was sacred to her. "I'll talk to her. If she sees that it's not fair to Ted, she'll relent." He clasped Hannah to his heart, feeling suddenly desperate, as if someone might descend upon him and tear her from his embrace. To think of marriage without the feeling he shared with Hannah—it was unthinkable.

He kissed her with the kind of fierce demand he had not known for weeks. She gave, meeting each demand of his spirit with one of her own.

"God, Hannah," he pulled back, holding her hard enough to shatter a weaker woman. "Why didn't you hit me over the head?"

Her laugh rang out, rich and full. Nothing had changed and everything had changed. Caroline was still slated to marry a man she didn't love or want, but she and Jake were no longer adversaries. Together, they could do anything, solve any problem. She was sure of it. "I just did," she said. "How does it feel?"

"Like I'm really alive again."

"Oh, Jake, I love you!"

The last word of her declaration became a squeal as

Jake swept her off her feet into his arms.

"Jake! Don't! Put me down. You'll hurt yourself."

"You're just worried that I'll drop you." He pretended to stagger into the wall as he went down the hall to their bedroom, and Hannah's cries became giggles.

Neither of them looked behind to see that Caroline had come inside in time to watch their departure. They had eyes only for each other.

Caroline stood without moving long after the bedroom door shut behind them with a careless thunk. The sound seemed to echo in the corridor, emphasizing their privacy and her isolation, bombarding her with conflicting emotions. Their happiness. Her father's recovery. She could rejoice at those and still feel her own pain and anger. *Why? Why not for me?*

Especially that.

Without looking, she found her way to her own room. Just months ago she had blithely weighed Rory as a hero for the romance and adventure that was to be her life. She had thought then of storybook characters, believing she would find examples for her life there. Was Rory dashing enough to sweep her off her feet?

Now she knew. He was. He was also more. He was a man like Papa. He was real—full of strengths and weaknesses, fears and hopes.

And she was like Hannah, a real woman. Hannah had taught her what to expect in the physical relationship of marriage, but she'd done much more than that by living her own loving relationship with Papa honestly and openly. They loved. They shared passion and it showed. It always had.

How had she managed to overlook what was right in front of her own eyes?

Ted talked about bedding her, and she wasn't repulsed by him. She never had been. But when Ted touched her she did not feel the exultation she saw in Hannah's face when she looked at Papa.

Knowing that — and knowing that another man *could* make her feel that and so much more — how could she marry Ted?

How?

Chapter Twenty-one

It was Caroline's wedding day.

She lifted her face to the sun and breathed the crisp, cool air. Fall. Back in Pennsylvania the leaves had flamed and fallen. Here the signs of approaching winter were more subtle but still universal, as all of nature slowed and turned inward. Golden-leaved aspens next to the tiny church caught the glint of sunlight and gave it back, intensified by the breeze that made them dance.

Jake, his eyes suspiciously bright, handed her down from the carriage and busied himself with the small train of her dress. She had to smile at the incongruity of such a masculine lady's maid. She found the loop Hannah had ordered sewn into the skirt and lifted the threatened material from the ground.

"You look beautiful, mite."

"Thank you. You look pretty dashing and handsome yourself."

"And I feel like a damned monkey."

Caroline's laugh rang out in the clear air, turning the heads of the few latecomers at the doorway. She waved to Happy Jack and Eli, both looking stiff and uncomfortable in their best clothes. When she turned back to take her father's arm, she found him looking as uncomfortable as the ranch hands.

"Sweetheart, you don't have to do this, you know. Even now it's not too—"

She put her gloved hand over his lips and went up onto tiptoes to kiss his cheek. "I know what I'm doing,

Papa. Please believe me."

Jake accepted the kiss, but the gathering between his brows didn't smooth. He opened his mouth to say more, then closed it. He had said it all—twice.

The words hung in the air between them, as real a his concern and her determination the night he had first come to her bedroom to say them.

One look at his drawn, tight expression as he stood in the doorway and Caroline put down her hairbrush, drawing him into the room. "What is it, Papa? Are you all right?"

He shook his head and his frown deepened. Hannah was right, he thought. She was always concerned for him, not for herself. Why hadn't he seen it before?

"I'm fine, punkin. I just want to talk to you."

The polite lift of her brows and the tension he sensed behind her patience unnerved him. Wildly, shamefully, he wished for Hannah. She was so much better at things like this. He squared his shoulders, refusing to be deflected from his course when she offered him a chair. He preferred to stand. And pace.

"Honey, it's occurred to me lately that you may have felt pressured into accepting Ted's proposal." The words formed a statement, but his tentative delivery and the slight rise of his inflection almost made it into a question. His eyes, so blue, so filled with love and doubt, searched her face.

Caroline held herself still for his inspection with the greatest difficulty. He had surprised her. Completely. She had not expected him to broach the subject at all. Sensing Hannah's hand at work behind the scenes, she felt a shaft of pure resentment go through her body. She was as shocked by that as she was by Jake's leading statement. She had never resented Hannah. Never.

"I can't imagine why you would think that, Papa."

Her composure was a work of art, but Jake saw the small, telltale signs of her turmoil. She held herself rigidly, with her chin tilted at a defiant angle and her hands clenched into small fists. He didn't admit that he hadn't had the perception to see it by himself. Admitting that, even to himself, made him feel like an insensitive brute. "It's like you to put others first, honey, and I did tell you I'd be pleased if you accepted Ted."

"Ted's very attractive, Papa. Accepting him is no hardship."

"No, no. Well, I should hope not." He paced away, aware that he wasn't saying what he wanted to say. He started to rake his fingers through his hair, then stopped, remembering how she and Hannah had mentioned the mannerism he shared with Rory. Now he knew he really did it.

He turned back to look at Caroline and began again. "The point is, Caroline, the only reason you should marry Ted—or any man—is love. Real, honest-to-God love. And I just don't think that's what you feel for him."

"How can you know what I feel?" she challenged.

Jake took two quick steps back to her and took her hands, one in each of his. "I know what you told me in the kitchen one night. And I know what I told you." He held on to her hands when she tried to pull back. "I spoke selfishly. Out of fear that you would leave me and go off with Rory."

His grip on her hands was painful, but nowhere near as devastating as his words. "Papa, I—"

"I wish I'd never said that, never interfered—"

"Do you really think I would change my mind about something as vital as love on the basis of those few words, Papa?"

"I don't know, sweetheart," he whispered. "I've tormented myself for days over this. I shouldn't have said anything against Rory. He's been a son to me, or a brother—I don't know which. But I know I did say he wasn't serious, wasn't ready to be serious. . . ."

Caroline knew she had found a way to reassure him. She had thrown her question wildly, defending herself in

230

the dark, using whatever came to mind. But she had found her mark. "You've tormented yourself over nothing, Papa. Please believe me." She managed a laugh. "Really, I'd think you'd know me better than that. I'm not so faint of heart as all that!"

He wanted so much to believe her that he did half the work of reassuring himself for her. One side of his mouth lifted with the beginning of a smile as he admitted, "You have been known to hold some pretty contrary opinions."

Her answering smile became natural. "And you thought I was being so contrary I was crossing up myself this time!"

He let himself be beguiled just long enough to sample the feeling of relief he craved before he grew serious again. "Let me tell you a story," he offered, drawing her to sit on the bed.

Her curiosity piqued, she sank down willingly as he took the chair and drew it around to face her. She sensed that he needed to sit as badly as she did.

"I want to tell you about your mother and about our life together. Then perhaps you'll understand why I'm so concerned."

"You don't have to do this, Papa. I understand. I really do."

He didn't allow himself to be swayed by her quick sympathy. "No, you really don't. You probably can't and won't, even when I'm finished, but I have to tell you the truth. And you have to know—for reasons that will become clear to you."

His last phrase kept Caroline from interrupting again.

"You probably believe Grace died in childbirth, don't you?"

"Why, yes, I guess I do. I'm not sure who told me, but it's what I assumed."

"She didn't," he said flatly. "Birth and the whole business of pregnancy was a factor in her eventual death, but not the cause. The real cause was her unhappiness

231

with me and our life."

"I don't understand."

"I've told you she didn't want to leave Pennsylvania—the east—and especially her parents?" She nodded. "She did so only because I forced her hand. I told her I was going whether or not she chose to come with me. I already knew we had problems between us. I even knew they might get worse, but I didn't think they would get so bad. I believed our only hope for a real life was living somewhere else, away from her parents."

Caroline could easily understand that. She had loved Gramma and Grampa Lunig, but she knew they had never accepted her father. She remembered their opposition to her going west with Jake, opposition that had not softened with age. They would have fought having their daughter taken from them.

"You probably can't imagine this, given the way you helped around the farm while you stayed with them, but your mother didn't do any of that. She didn't know how to do anything practical. Her mother treated her like a princess. I saw that while we lived there, of course, and I wondered at it. Grace just said it was her mother's preference."

"It was, Papa. She didn't like to have my help, really. Becky and Alice used to tease me about it. They had so many chores and I didn't. I just did those things because I wanted to. I mean, I couldn't just sit around all day—not when they were so old. I felt guilty.

"But when I did something, Gramma would come along right behind me and do it over again. She couldn't help herself. And sometimes, I'll admit, I didn't bother trying to help. It seemed pointless. But I was as bad as she was most of the time. I had to have something to do, too."

"That's the way it was," her father said. "And I could see it when we lived there. I accepted that Grace was keeping the peace. What I didn't realize, though, was that she really didn't know how to do the simplest

232

things, and, worse, she didn't *want* to know how. She wanted to go on having her mother take care of her."

"And you took her away from her mother."

"Yes." Jake absorbed her understanding. "She never forgave me for that. She hated everything she had to do and everywhere we went."

"I know something about that, Papa. I read some of her letters to Gramma. I . . . It was when you came back from the war and I was trying to decide whether to go with you or stay with Gramma and Grampa. I heard Gramma say she had letters, and I stole some of them to read." In spite of all the years since, Caroline still felt guilty about that incident. "I never told you. I didn't read them all because the ones I saw were so dreadful."

"Dreadful?"

"Just one complaint after another. She was tired; she was dirty; she was cold—or hot."

Jake grimaced. "That was Grace."

"How could you have loved her, Papa? I hate to sound . . . disloyal, but—"

He gave a hoot of laughter. "Well, of course you're right. She was pretty unlovable at times. When I met her, though, she was beautiful and smiling and happy. She seemed the most perfect creature on God's earth. I worshiped her."

"Until you saw her in adversity."

"I was frequently disgusted and annoyed, but I didn't stop loving her even then. She did have some cause for complaint. I knew that. And soon after we were underway she found out she was pregnant. She was very sick then."

"Me."

"Not every woman is that sick. You know Hannah wasn't, although she didn't always feel as well as she pretended to be."

"And my mother did feel sick as she pretended to be?" Caroline challenged.

"Perhaps. I'll never really know about that. There were

days I believed it and days I was out of patience because I believed it. What I do know is that being sick became a habit for Grace, one she wouldn't—or couldn't—give up. She ate very little. She wouldn't eat. If I forced her she would throw it up. After a while I realized that she was forcing herself to be sick."

"Forcing . . . ?"

"She would gag herself. Put her finger down her throat. She said she had to, that food made her stomach hurt and it wouldn't feel better until it was empty."

"But wasn't she starving?"

"Literally, yes. That's exactly what she was doing. By the time you were born she looked like a child with a hugely swollen belly. I was terrified for both of you."

"Was I . . . I mean, did I . . ."

"You were small but perfect, and you had an enormous will to live. Grace couldn't feed you, but we already knew that would be the case. We stayed with a family in Iowa and the woman—Margaret, her name was—took care of both of you. She was wonderful."

"And my . . . mother? Did she ever . . . care?"

"She loved you, but by then she wasn't strong. She wanted to die more than she wanted to live, and nothing could change her mind."

Caroline couldn't think of anything to say.

"So you see, honey. I know what unhappiness in marriage can do."

"Do you think for one minute *I'd* ever do that?"

Jake regarded her indignant expression. "No. Not that. You're looking at this too literally. What I'm trying to tell you is that happiness is important—more important than you can believe now. And that unhappiness—for any reason—can be deadly. It was for me too, you know. Being married to your mother made me afraid to marry Hannah. I was sure she'd be unhappy without the wealth she was accustomed to. I was afraid of failing her as I did Grace."

Caroline nodded solemnly, her mind busy with something else. "You told me that so I wouldn't be afraid to have children, didn't you?"

"That was part of it, of course. I've told you how much you look like Grace. It's natural for you to draw your own conclusions from that and believe that child-birth would be a problem for you." He regarded her gravely. "You were not responsible for her death, you know. You mustn't believe you were."

"But you believe you were," Caroline said.

"Not intentionally. Never that." He looked away, and she saw relief mixed with the strain and concern that had driven him to his disclosures. "I've regretted lots of things, Caroline, but never anything that gave me you."

Now as Jake felt her slip from his embrace to adjust her wedding gown, he had no reason to amend his words. To Caroline, they were a benediction, an expression of her father's love. It gave her courage. All her life she had received his love, basked in its presence, felt its weight. Now she was ready to start a new life, secure in the knowledge that, like her father, she was capable of facing up to the challenges it would offer.

She knew now she could give Ted children and share them with him. She had seen his easy affection for Abby. He would be a good father. They would have the bond of children and home, all the interests that tie people into families. She would not be Rory's love, but because he was part of her family she would not lose him, either.

She took Jake's arm and mounted the four shallow steps to the church. Like the larger Catholic church at the other end of Rio Mogollon, it was made of adobe in the Spanish style. The pews were new since Caroline had gone east, and every seat was filled, with people standing along the outer walls to leave the center aisle clear. Organ music filled the sanctuary and eddied out into the tiny anteroom where Abby waited with Hannah and Lupe.

Abby was to be Caroline's only attendant. She fairly bounced with excitement in her blue dress that was almost a duplicate of Caroline's. It had the same lace inserts at the gently rounded neckline and the same swept-back skirt arranged to cascade down the back into a small train. A V-shaped bodice emphasized Caroline's tiny waist, whereas Abby's had a wide sash of a slightly darker shade of blue. Both wore pearls, Caroline's a choker of four rows the color of her silk dress. For Caroline, too, there were tiny pearls sewn into her veil.

"You look like a princess, Caroline," Abby said as her eyes widened to take in every detail.

"That's just how I feel."

"Do you have my ribbon still?"

Caroline touched the spot under her breast. "It's pinned to my chemise, love. I wouldn't be without it." Abby had given her birthday ribbon back to Caroline so she would have something both borrowed and blue. The pearls, a gift from Hannah, came from her mother, Josie Hatch. Both Hannah and Josie had been married wearing them.

Caroline had time to hug Lupe, elegant in the wine red dress Hannah had made especially for her, before Rusty escorted her down the aisle to sit with him. Her brother was trying to be serious in spite of his audience and his stiff white collar. Caroline peeked around Hannah to watch them go, then gave herself to Hannah's embrace.

"Be happy, my love," Hannah whispered.

Abby tugged on her skirt, urging her attention to the front of the church. "There's Ted, Caroline. Doesn't he look handsome?"

Caroline drifted over to the doorway, but her view of Ted was cut off by a wide masculine shoulder.

Rory.

She raised her eyes to his, reluctant to meet his gaze. Since his attempt to change her mind about marrying Ted, he had kept away from home. Twice he had gone to Santa Fe on business for Uncle Simon, returning only yesterday for the wedding. She could see the remnants of pain in his eyes, but his smile was sweet and warm as he took Hannah's arm to walk with her to the front pew.

Hannah gave Rory's arm a reassuring squeeze as she walked proudly beside him. Like Jake, she was as filled with regrets as with hope that time would prove her fears for Caroline wrong. When Jake had come to her, shaking his head in amazement that his talk with Caroline had only seemed to harden her resolve, Hannah did what she had promised herself she would never do. She interfered.

With uncharacteristic hesitance, she pulled the carriage bringing them back from Rio Mogollon to a stop in order to speak. She chose to be forthright. "Caroline, you must know that I urged Jake to speak to you the other night."

"I know," Caroline said. "It was a great comfort to me."

Hannah was aghast. "Comfort! How on earth did you find comfort in that tale?"

"Oh, I know the story was sad, Hannah, but it meant a lot to me to hear it directly from Papa. I know how hard it was for him to tell me."

From her expression Hannah knew there was more. She waited.

"The real comfort comes from knowing my birth didn't cause my mother's death. I guess I've always felt vaguely guilty about being alive. More from Gramma and Grampa Lunig's standpoint than Papa's."

Caroline looked away from Hannah and let her eyes roam over their surroundings. With summer past, it was beginning to look barren to the untutored eye. But she saw more than the spaciousness of the wide turquoise sky where thunderheads seemed to grow up from the distant mountains as they watched. She saw her home.

"I didn't realize that, love. I wish I'd known." Hannah's eyes searched Caroline's face. "I should have known, shouldn't I?"

Caroline put her hand on her stepmother's arm. "Don't berate yourself. You've been a wonderful mother to me. The best."

"Caroline—"

"More than that," Caroline interrupted, "what comforted me most was the assurance that if my mother didn't die in childbirth, I probably won't either." Seeing that she had surprised Hannah again, she added, "Papa always said I look like her, so I assumed that my body might be . . . wrong somehow."

"Oh, Caroline, of course you did. I'm so sorry I didn't tell you otherwise."

"That made me happy because I've always wanted children. And Ted will be a good father." She added the last deliberately, not as a goad but as a statement of her intentions.

Hannah heard the challenge. "And the unhappiness?"

"I won't be unhappy. My mother was . . . different. I'm not like that, and besides, I'm where I want to live."

"Yes, you are," Hannah answered. "But there's so much more to marriage. I was where I wanted to be when I married Daniel Veazie, and he too was a charming, handsome man. I knew him much as you know Ted—socially. Which is to say, almost not at all."

Caroline's temper flared. "Hannah, I know about Daniel Veazie. He was a criminal. Ted is nothing like that!"

"He didn't start out as a criminal, you know. And he was, to my eyes, much like Ted. Charming. Easy. As long as everything goes his way."

Tears sprang to Caroline's eyes before she could stop them. "Why are you doing this to me, Hannah?" she cried. "Can't you let me alone? I want to be happy! I'm not you and I'm not my mother—or Papa! I'm myself! I'm going to marry Ted and I'm going to prove to you all that I'm happy!"

With that, she burst into such great gulping sobs that the carriage shook. Hannah took her into her arms and comforted her. What else could she do?

And what could she do now?

She smiled at Nila and Dwight Jasper, sitting across the aisle, and turned to fix her eyes on the back of the

238

church. She sensed Rory's tension beside her, saw Zeb and Ernie and so many of the men, looking scrubbed and starched. For a moment her gaze fell on Maria Martinez, sitting not with her mother but on the Jasper side of the aisle. She looked tense and pale. Hannah almost smiled at the thought of vibrant Maria looking pale. She would hate to know it.

The music swelled majestically, catching at Hannah's throat. Abby came slowly down the aisle, looking solemn and impish both. She held her mouth pursed as she did in concentration, daring only to dart a shy smile now and again as someone caught her eye. She was so very beautiful and so young, yet in no time at all it would be her time to be the bride. Hannah beat back the thought and the accompanying tears in order to see Jake and Caroline.

They were so splendid. Proud Jake and Caroline . . . *Oh, God,* she prayed, *let her be happy. Let this be right for her!*

Beside her, Rory spared one moment to look at Ted Jasper, waiting with his best man and the Reverend Curtis. He took in the small, pleased smile and let a hatred he'd never known blossom in his heart. *Give her one day's misery,* he vowed, *and I'll give you eighty.*

Then he turned with Hannah, Rusty, Lupe and Uncle Simon to watch as Abby, then Jake and Caroline made their way to the altar. When he'd thought of this moment, he'd believed he wouldn't be able to look at Caroline.

He couldn't keep his eyes off her.

He knew she'd look beautiful and she did. She also looked immensely serious, even a trifle dogged, the way she looked taking on a new horse or chore. There was pride in the lift of her chin and determination in the glint of her eyes. She looked forward, her eyes perhaps on Ted, although Rory refused to check. She smiled once for Hannah, and then she was past them, standing between Abby and Jake before the minister.

Reverend Curtis asked, "Who gives this woman in marriage?"

Jake said clearly, "Her mother and I do."

Rory heard Hannah's small gasp of surprise to be included and was pleased. He wondered if Caroline or Jake had thought of it; either way, it was entirely right. Hannah was all that a mother could be and more. He stepped to the right slightly to make room for Jake beside Hannah, but it wasn't needed. Hannah had moved closer to Jake, not away, and his arm was around her shoulders as they were invited to sit down.

In turning to sit, Rory caught a quick glimpse of Maria Martinez across the aisle, her face contorted and agonized. He was so startled he paused, his motion arrested. *So it was true,* he thought. Maria and Ted. And she was as unhappy as he was.

Then the minister spoke, claiming Rory's attention. He almost groaned aloud when he realized what was happening. Reverend Curtis wasn't going to conduct a simple, brief ceremony. He wanted to talk. In all honesty, Rory had to admit that his intentions were good. He was fond of the Farnsworths and grateful to Jake and Hannah, who had been instrumental in building this church, the only permanent place of worship for the Anglo community in the area. Curtis rode the circuit as most ministers did, going from settlement to settlement to serve his tiny flock. Only here in Rio Mogollon did he have a real church. Naturally, he wanted to reward his benefactors.

As Rory listened to the minister's praise of Caroline and her family, including a few kind words for the Jaspers as well, the tension within him intensified. He could feel the blood in his veins, pumping, pushing, until he felt he would explode. He wanted this torture over. *Marry her to him and let me go,* he urged silently.

Rusty squirmed beside him, drawing his consoling glance and pat.

Then it was happening. The ceremony. The vows.

Starting with that galvanizing challenge. "If anyone knows a reason why this man and this woman should not be wed, let him speak now or forever hold his peace."

Forever, Rory thought. *Such a long time.*

She doesn't love him, Hannah thought.

I love her, Rory thought.

Neither spoke.

Theodore Hobart took Caroline Elaine to wife for richer, for poorer, in sickness and in health, till death do us part.

No, Rory protested. *It should be me.*

Caroline Elaine then took Theodore Hobart to husband. Her voice was sweet, soft, firm. For richer, for poorer, in sickness and in health, till death do us part.

No, no. She can't.

"No! No! He can't marry her!"

The scream shattered the stillness.

Had he spoken? Rory wondered for an insane moment.

The shrill voice reverberated from the walls as everything happened at once.

The congregation broke into startled speech.

Rory turned his head.

Jake leaped to his feet.

Caroline and Ted parted and Mr. Curtis stepped between them.

Maria.

Lupe screamed.

"My child," Mr. Curtis said. "What is the meaning of this?"

"He cannot marry her!" Maria said with harsh intensity. She was in the aisle now, facing Mr. Curtis like a gunfighter squared off in battle. "He has to marry me! Me!"

Curtis stepped toward her. Perspiration bloomed on his face, making him look shiny all the way to the tufts of hair high on his crown that he grew long in order to comb over his baldness. His gestures placated the madwoman he saw before him.

Maria was having no part of it. She tossed her head in disdain. "He will marry me because I am having his baby!"

Chapter Twenty-two

Caroline was in shock.

Like everyone in the church, her eyes were fixed on Maria. She couldn't take it in. Maria, disrupting her wedding. Maria, screaming in church.

When Reverend Curtis stepped forward she moved to the side to keep Maria in view, trying to understand. Maria and *Ted?*

An hysterical giggle rose in her throat, like a bubble, choking her.

Mr. Curtis walked toward Maria, and then Caroline could see Ted. His face was a mask of cold, hard fury.

She heard Lupe sobbing and thought, *Poor Lupe, she'll never get over this disgrace.*

Then Maria made her accusation. Or was it that?

Strange as it seemed, Caroline heard triumph in Maria's voice. That was it. She wasn't ashamed; she was proud. And desperate.

Caroline could understand that.

"That's a lie!" Ted shouted. He pushed up behind Mr. Curtis, trying to shove him aside to get to Maria. "Get her out of here!" he yelled.

"It is no lie!" Maria yelled back. "Always, he comes to me! He spends time with that whey-faced one and then he comes to my bed!"

Jake had Ted from behind, holding him by both arms. No one was restraining Maria.

"The hell I do!" Ted cried, trying to shake loose from Jake.

The stalemated argument might have gone on indefinitely but for two things. Dwight Jasper joined his son in the aisle, his face purpled with rage. "Get that bitch out of here!" he boomed.

Simultaneously, Rory gently moved Hannah aside and bundled Caroline away from the altar and out the side door. It led to a small back room, a combination study and waiting room for the minister.

Rory pushed her down into the only chair and knelt before her. "It'll be all right, Caroline."

She covered her face with her hands. She was shaking all over. They had not closed the door behind them, and the noise from the sanctuary followed them. She could not distinguish individual voices any more, just general confusion. It sounded like pandemonium.

Maria still stood alone in the church aisle, like a leper no one dared approach. She watched Ted try to fight off Jake Farnsworth, but it was an unequal contest. Even enraged, Ted was inches shorter and pounds lighter. And Jake was every bit as enraged. More, it seemed to her.

She had one moment of triumph left before everything turned to ashes. She saw Rory Talmage hustle Caroline away like a frightened mouse. She had won. Ted and Caroline were not married.

But she had also lost. One look at Ted told her that. He wanted to kill her.

She had not thought of that. She had not thought of anything.

Maria hadn't planned to stop Ted's wedding. Even when the minister asked that question and *invited* her to speak, she didn't. She had wanted to, but she had not. Then, suddenly, she had heard herself screaming out her thoughts, and it was too late.

It was done.

She would not regret it, no matter what happened to her. She had won. Caroline would not have Ted. She would have nothing, no man, no husband.

Just like Maria.

Jake spun Ted around and grabbed him by the lapels of his black dress coat. "Is she telling the truth?" he demanded. "Have you been sleeping with her?"

Ted opened his mouth but didn't speak. Jake shook him wrathfully, his anger strong enough to lift the younger man completely off his feet.

"Have you?" he snarled.

Ted's eyes rolled as his head whipped back and forth. "No!"

"Don't lie to me!" Jake thrust Ted away with one hand and cocked his fist, prepared to strike.

Hannah caught at his arm. She had rescued Abby and thrust her into the seat behind her with Rusty. She took a chance touching Jake in his blind rage, but she had no fear that he would hurt her.

The minister, having no such faith, had wisely removed himself from the aisle.

"Jake," she said sharply, needing force to break through to his common sense. "This is a church, not a barroom."

Jake shoved Ted away, sending him flying backward across the aisle. He would have crashed into the side of the pew except that Dwight Jasper caught him and cushioned the force of his fall with his own body.

Although he supported his son, Dwight looked at him with obvious distaste and put him away from himself as soon as Ted could stand at all. Nila was more compassionate. She stood beside Ted, helping him lean against a pew. The action, small as it was, drew her husband's ire.

"This is all your fault," he said to Nila, waving his arm toward where Maria still stood. "You're the one who brought that slut into the house!"

Zeb and Ernie had quietly begun to usher Uncle Simon, a sobbing Lupe, and the two bewildered children out the side aisle. People made way for them, alternately embarrassed for them and sympathetic with their duress.

As soon as he realized that Rory was caring for Caroline, Jake took Hannah's arm and escorted her down the center aisle with all the aplomb they could manage. They saw no one, not even Maria, who had cringed back into an empty pew at their approach.

Once he could stand firmly and command his legs, Ted looked around for Caroline. He had lost sight of her, but he did not want to lose her. He walked contemptuously around his parents and the ineffectual minister and went after Caroline. She had to be in the back. She had to believe him. He would make her believe — make it up to her. Reason told him it was impossible. Caroline Farnsworth was not a woman to trifle with, but dear God, he had to try.

The room was empty. He flung open the door to the small corridor leading outside and saw her. Rory was outside, drawing her to the narrow stairs there.

"Caroline."

She turned, her face as white as the gown except for her reddened eyes. The evidence of her tears gave him courage. He rushed forward to take her hand from the doorjamb.

"It's not true, Caro," he said, giving her his most winning smile.

Before he could say another word, her brother loomed up in the doorway. Ted bit back the twist of fear in his gut. He had survived her father; he could survive this. Rory wasn't a real brother, even if he was bigger than Jake. He spread his hands in a placating gesture, trying for a certain man-to-man stance that he hoped would not be offensive to Caroline.

Rory's face took on a feral eagerness as he moved past Caroline in the narrow passageway. "I'll handle this."

Ted stepped back before the threat, but Caroline intervened. "No, Rory. I want to talk to him." She spoke firmly, her voice giving the lie to any previous weakness. She looked past him to the empty room and indicated that she would follow.

246

So did Rory. He stood in the doorway, filling it completely, it seemed to Ted, as if he were waiting to snatch Caroline away again.

Ted stopped in the middle of the room, mindful that the way he'd been forced to move looked like retreat. Caroline strode to the other door and shut it, ensuring their privacy. She tilted her head at him, looking like a teacher offering a recalcitrant student a moment of explanation. She didn't even lean back against the door for support.

Ted jerked his head toward Rory. "Send him away," he said, trying to equalize the scales.

"Not a chance," Rory said before Caroline could answer.

Nothing in her expression indicated that her reply would have been different or offered hope.

"I love you, Caroline."

"So you said," she responded coldly, still waiting.

"There is no baby." He lifted his hand to her, then lowered it. "Maria is lying."

"You took precautions?"

Rory.

Ted saw Caroline's eyes go past him to meet Rory's. He wanted to turn and confront Talmage, but to do so would distract Caroline from his plea.

"Maria hates you. She wants to ruin your life. Are you going to let her win?"

"This isn't a question of winning or losing, Ted."

"It is to her."

"I don't *care* about Maria," Caroline said emphatically.

Ted felt a surge of optimism. "Neither do I. Let's just go out there and get the minister and finish the ceremony. None of this matters." He started toward her.

"I didn't say that." Caroline's voice nailed his feet to the floorboards. "It matters very much to me. I want to know if you've been bedding Maria."

"And don't bother to lie again, Jasper," Rory said

247

before Ted could draw breath to answer. "The ranch hands at your place—and ours—have a lot to say about you two."

Ted lost his temper. He swung around and challenged Rory. "I suppose you're going to pretend you've never slept with her?"

"My activities are not under question right now, Jasper."

"No, of course not," he said sarcastically. "But you've had her too, and you know it."

"I take it, then, that your answer is yes?" Caroline asked from behind him.

He whirled around to confront her, furious that he'd been tricked. She stood there in her pure white wedding gown, looking down her nose at him. So cold. So composed. Suddenly it occurred to him that Maria was right. Caroline wasn't woman enough for him. Of course he'd slept with Maria. Any man would. But he'd intended to give her up for Caroline—fool that he was!

"Of course I slept with her. Just as often as I could! A man has needs, you know, and Maria is a real woman who knows how to please a man, not a frightened little virgin mouse who doesn't even know how to kiss!"

He had more to say—much more—but Rory spun him around and hit him. He went down hard, his ears ringing. He struggled to get up, but something was holding him down. His mouth began to fill with blood. His tongue—he had bitten his tongue!

He opened his eyes and staggered to his feet, holding his jaw. Caroline stood right there, watching him, her eyes cold as the stars and just as far away. But she was keeping Rory away from him. If she hadn't had her damned bodyguard he would have knocked her across the room. But she did have him, and Ted didn't dare open his mouth for fear he would spew blood in every direction. If he saw his own blood he would be sick. He could feel a broken tooth. . . .

When Ted's eyes finally focused on her face, Caroline was shocked by the hatred she saw there. She refused to acknowledge it. "I feel sorry for you, Ted," she said in as even a voice as she could manage. "You're an utter fool. You and your needs. You could have had anything."

He started for her and almost fell.

She stepped back neatly. "Women have needs too, you should know, Ted. The need for a man with honor and decency, a man whose word is worth something. Needs a man like you can never fill."

Ted made a gurgling sound as Rory grabbed his shirt-front.

"Don't hit him again, Rory," she said, putting her hand on his arm. "I'd hate to see a grown man cry."

Rory laughed and pushed Ted backward. His knees caught and buckled. He fell as they walked out, Caroline first. Rory shut the door and hurried after her, aware that she was functioning on pure nerve and backbone. She would collapse soon, but not, he hoped, before he got her home, where she was safe and protected.

He shielded her as much as he could from the knots of people standing in the churchyard, herding her to the carriage he'd come in. It wasn't the family's best — she'd come in that — but neither of them cared. Giving only a quick glance around to be sure he wasn't stranding any-one without a ride home, he helped Caroline up onto the seat. He thought of putting her inside. Her dress de-manded it, but he couldn't do it. She needed company — and so did he.

Rory stopped the buggy once on the way home. He grinned at her inquiring glance and tore off his tie and high, starched collar. Next, with a ferocity that brought a reluctant smile to her lips, he took off his black coat, folded it and stuffed it under the seat. Then he rolled up his sleeves.

"Hannah will kill me for that."

"No, she won't."

He studied her face for a moment. It was too . . . something. Too composed and cool. "You were real fine back there, sweetheart, but if you want to cry and scream and hit someone, now's your chance."

She shook her head. "Thanks, but I've already given him too many tears."

Gently, Rory laid his hand against her cheek. "Not for him. For you."

Caroline drew back far enough to break the contact. "Don't feel sorry for me, Rory. I couldn't stand that."

He wanted her to cry, not so he could comfort her but so he would get it out of her system. The sooner she was over Ted Jasper, the sooner . . .

He snatched up the reins again, furious at himself. He was a selfish bastard. She'd just had what should have been the happiest day of her life turned into a freak show, and he was thinking about how long it would be before he could pick up the pieces behind Ted!

Caroline saw the way Rory's jaw tightened in anger, and her misery doubled. She wanted to howl then at her foolish pride. How long would it take before she drove away everyone who loved her? She could see herself turning into one of those strange old ladies Mr. Dickens wrote about. She could dress forever in her wedding gown to remind herself of her great disappointment.

She almost smiled at the thought, but it felt wrong to smile. She felt numb, miserable but numb. She put her hand on Rory's arm, meaning to apologize. She felt the leap of warm muscle under his sleeve and pulled back her fingers as if she had been scalded.

Her touch had gone through Rory like a plow in tillable soil, laying back his skin all the way to the quivering nerves. He looked down in time to see that he had startled her. She was staring at his arm as if it had turned into a snake. He had to do better than this!

250

He shifted both reins to his left hand. The horse knew the way home from here as well as he did. *Brotherly,* he cautioned himself, and held out his hand to her.

Caroline took it with both hands and brought it to her mouth. She laid a soft kiss on the back and nestled it briefly against her cheek. She could smell the horsey-leather scent of the reins on his fingers and feel the tuft of golden brown hair that sprang up from his strong wrist. It all went together in her mind as one word: Rory.

She let his hand fall to her lap but didn't let go. Her silky white dress slid back and forth over the supporting layers of petticoats as the carriage swayed and bumped along. In spite of her hands, in spite of the clothes, what Rory felt was the long line of her thigh under his forearm.

He had seen her thighs encased in revealing work pants, and he had seen them emerging from her bath water. He had felt them clench around his leg when he had dared to hang her on the wall, as she had put it. What he wanted now was to shake off her hands and touch that slim, firm thigh.

For a moment he imagined it all. The slide of silk under his palm, the warmth . . .

He lifted his hand and put it down on his own thigh.

Caroline had been lost in her own contemplation. Beside her, his body radiated comfort, giving off rays of it like a cookstove. She could have held out her hands to warm them if she'd been willing to let go of his hand. She wasn't.

She studied the contrast of his one large hand and bare forearm to everything it touched. Her own hands were not delicate or small, but his hand made them seem so. Even the underside of his forearm was darker than the backs of her hands; it was also corded with muscles that moved like separate ropes bound together under the surface. His rolled shirt sleeve, starkly white and starchily crisp, seemed the essence of masculinity next to the muted sheen of her gown.

It came as a shock to find her left hand resting against his thigh under his hand. She clenched her right into a fist and put it into her lap. The subtle pressure of his grip told her he didn't want to relinquish her hand, and she was content — until she realized that the stretched cloth of his pantleg communicated every shift of his leg muscles to her hand.

Fascinated, she wanted to turn her hand and stroke the warm hardness she rested against. Instead, she wove her fingers into his and clung.

They rode that way in silence until they approached the ranch. Caroline gave Rory's hand a squeeze as he released hers. She didn't say thank you. The words were unnecessary.

She had already begun to heal.

Or so she thought.

At home it was another story.

The house was a maelstrom of activity. Hannah had put every able body to work. Ranch hands, still in their "good" pants, had discarded coats the same way Rory had. Their ties dangled out of their back pockets or flapped loosely from under opened collars. They were all intent on destroying every scrap of evidence that a wedding reception had been planned for this afternoon.

Until they spotted Caroline. Then they stopped. Embarrassed. Guilty. It was almost funny. It was as if she were a corpse who had just climbed from her own coffin and caught them — doing what? Not celebrating, that was certain. Their shamefaced expressions bespoke more of the mourning after the celebration.

Rory tried to shield her with his body for as long as possible, but he couldn't stand there forever. He gave her over to Hannah who circled her waist protectively. "Darling girl, I'm sorry," she said softly.

"I know." She hugged Hannah back, and then they looked at each other — or tried to. Even the way they went inside was awkward. Caroline moved stiffly, as if she were encased in ice that would break off into cutting pieces around them. She was too conscious of everyone's sympathetic glances, too aware of her beautiful dress — now a mockery of all it was meant to symbolize.

It was better with Papa. Caroline went into his sheltering arms with a feeling of relief. Like Rory, he made her feel cherished, protected. But over his shoulders she saw Rusty struggling with a pile of beautifully wrapped wedding presents, and the reality of the day hit her again.

She backed away from his embrace, blinking back tears. "I'm going to go to my room for a while, Papa. If you don't —" She broke off and ran down the hall to her room.

Her going was a relief to everyone left behind, Rory included. He had come in just in time to see her dash away. He stood and watched her go, awash in helpless rage. He strung together every bunkhouse expletive he could think of. That he said them softly only made them louder. Hannah glanced over at Rusty, then shrugged.

"Amen," Jake said with mock reverence.

After that, except for the occasional sigh or anxious glance toward Caroline's room, everything went smoothly. Of those left behind, Abby was most visibly upset. She'd had her heart set on a party, and even the adventure of hiding everything from Caroline didn't seem to compensate for its loss. Worse, she'd been told to take off her wonderful new dress.

Seeing her distress and Hannah's momentary inability to meet her daughter's need, Rory went after Abby to help her. He was glad that her room was in the opposite wing of the house from Caroline's so that they wouldn't bother her. He didn't hurry Abby out of her dress, but let her go at her own speed. Finally, she let him undo the tiny buttons she couldn't reach.

"You know, Abby," he said, struggling not to tear any loose, "you were as beautiful as a bride yourself today."

"I don't think I want to be a bride any more," she said sadly.

"Today didn't turn out very happy for Caroline, I know, but I remember the day your mother and father got married. That was different."

"Was I there then?"

Rory chuckled. "In spirit maybe, little one." He kissed her neck noisily and she giggled. "That was a happy day. You ask your mama to tell you about it sometime. But not today," he cautioned as she turned in his arms to hug him. He lifted the dress over her narrow shoulders and held it out of harm's way. "If you hurry and find a dress that's not too hard to wash, you can go with me to take the cake out to the bunkhouse."

In her squealing haste, she poked her arm into the wrong sleeve and had to be helped. As Rory was turning the dress for her she said with sudden vehemence, "I hate Maria!"

"I'm not too fond of her myself," he agreed drily, even as his heart asked, *Aren't you?* He shook his head at the thought. He wanted Caroline to be happy.

He had gone through hell worrying about whether or not to speak out about what he knew about Ted. He'd kept his silence—just barely—because he knew he had no right to condemn Ted. His own past was not spotless. Promised to Caroline, he would have wanted no one else, but that wasn't true for most men. His anger at Maria came from her desire to hurt Caroline; at Ted, for compounding the injury.

"She made Lupe cry and cry all the way home," Abby went on fiercely.

"I know," he sighed, giving her a consoling pat. "Zeb will be nice to her, though."

"And Ernie. He's nice, too."

Rory agreed again. Today he had only two villains.

254

That was enough.

While Rory took Abby and Rusty to the bunkhouse to enjoy the special cake, Caroline lay on her bed, staring up at the ceiling.

She had taken off her wedding dress and the lovely silk underthings, torn by conflicting needs. They were too beautiful to mishandle and too tempting a target for her pent-up emotions. She did want to rend and tear something, but not these clothes. She had hung them out of sight and pushed her overnight valise with them.

She and Ted were to have spent their first night together at his parents' home before they traveled to Santa Fe for their honeymoon. Her trunk, packed with lovely new clothes, was thankfully elsewhere.

Her eyes burned with unshed tears. She wanted to cry, but somehow she couldn't. She felt crushed by guilt. She had brought disgrace to her family. Maria was part of it, the instrument, but she—Caroline—was the true cause. She had not loved Ted enough. All her fine reasons and good intentions came down to exactly that.

The real, honest-to-God love Papa called the only reason for marrying was missing between them. Ted knew it, sensed it somehow, and had turned to Maria for what she had meant to give him. Was that why he never pressed her for sexual gratification? Because he didn't love her either? Or was it because he was getting that from Maria already and didn't need her?

Did it matter anyway? She rolled over and got up to finish dressing.

When Hannah tapped on her door she was sitting on the bed again, fingering the folds of her blue gingham skirt. Hannah hesitated only a moment before she took her place beside Caroline. Putting her hand over the two nervously working ones in Caroline's lap, she stilled them.

"You were right, Hannah."

"I didn't want to be. I wanted you to be happy."

255

"I know." A sad little smile turned up the corners of Caroline's pale mouth. "It's funny. Even now, I'm sure I would have been. I wanted it to be right so very badly."

"I know." Hannah made a small move toward Caroline, wanting to hug her close and comfort her. Her distance and air of dignity prevented it.

"It's all my fault," Caroline said.

"It certainly is not!"

"Yes, it is. Ted knew I didn't really love him. That's why he . . . slept with Maria."

"Caroline, that's utter nonsense."

"No, no, it's not. I've been thinking about it. If I'd been . . . more of a woman, he wouldn't have needed anyone else."

"There is nothing wrong with you, Caroline," Hannah said fiercely, more angry now than she had been all day. She clutched Caroline's shoulders, almost shaking her. "Do you hear me? Nothing! You're a warm, beautiful woman, a woman any man would be lucky to have for his wife," she finished vehemently.

"But Ted didn't want me."

"Of course he did. He was marrying you, wasn't he?"

Caroline shook her head. "He was *marrying* me, but he didn't *want* me! Don't you see? I told you he was . . . respectful. Well, he was. That's all he was. Sometimes he seemed to get steamed up a bit, but he'd stop. I never stopped him, Hannah. Maybe I should have, but I didn't want to. I wanted that. I wanted to be loved and wanted . . ." Her voice began to break apart, cracking like ice over a swift-running stream in spring. "Like you and Papa—"

Hannah gathered her to her breast, her arms tight around Caroline's back. She was glad to feel the tears soaking the front of her dress. Crying would help her heal. She stroked the long fall of her hair down her back, rocking her body lightly back and forth as if Caroline were Abby. This was more than a skinned knee,

256

but hurt was hurt, and comfort was comfort.

Caroline didn't cry easily or prettily. Not today. But finally the storm subsided and she was spent. Hannah eased her down to the bed. She needed rest now more than reassurance.

That could come later. And it would. Caroline was strong and resilient. She wouldn't wallow in misplaced guilt. Hannah wouldn't allow it, nor would Jake.

She pulled up the light blanket folded at the foot of Caroline's bed, fitting it over the limp form there before she tiptoed out.

She had to talk to Jake. They had some planning to do.

Chapter Twenty-three

It was dark when Caroline woke. She opened her eyes, not moving, and lay for several seconds, trying to figure out why she felt so strange. She was fully dressed in bed, covered by a blanket. She moved her hands over her too-warm body, pushing off the cover.

Then she remembered. Everything.

She sat up, rubbing her eyes. Her lashes were stiff with dried tears. As soon as she moved she realized that she was hungry. She had missed supper. That was just as well, she decided, grimacing at the thought of sitting down with everyone for what would have been a supremely awkward meal.

She found her bedside lamp and lit it. Then she discovered the tray of food next to it. She had not been forgotten.

She walked stiffly to the window and looked out into darkness that seemed total. She had to peek out obliquely to avoid her reflection. That was something she wasn't eager to encounter. Her hair was disheveled, her dress wrinkled. She shook out the dress, brushed her hair and washed her face and hands. Better.

Lifting the napkin from the tray, she felt her appetite stir. Nothing on the plate was fancy enough to remind her of the buffet Hannah and Lupe had planned for their guests, but she recognized the beautifully sliced ham anyway.

Sitting down to tuck it away, she decided it didn't matter. Food was food. She was definitely going to live.

With that thought came a question: But how?

She could go on living here as her father's daughter. She could erase the months of Ted's courtship from her mind and go on. In time people would forget; the sympathetic looks would fade—especially here on the ranch. The men were too busy to coddle her for long. Although no one would actually forget, the shock and wonder would lessen with time and the intervention of other events.

Caroline's appetite was easily appeased. Within minutes she set the tray aside, the food only sampled. She went to her chest of drawers, curious about the time. The house seemed utterly still around her. How long had she slept?

Grampa Lunig's gold watch said two-thirty. She shook it, then put it to her ear. She had forgotten to wind it. Now she had to know the time. Carrying the tray to the kitchen first, she went to check the time on the handsome parlor clock. A gift from Uncle Simon, that timepiece was never neglected.

Dismayed, Caroline discovered that it was after ten o'clock. She had slept for hours! No wonder everyone was asleep. It had been a hard day for them all. As hard as for herself, she didn't doubt, knowing how wearing it was to be helpless when someone you love is hurt.

She sat on the bed for lack of anything else to do. Sleep was impossible now. She was more wide awake than she had been for days. If she tried to sleep she would only brood. Already her brain was beginning to replay Ted's words to her. They were like the refrain of a song that lodged in her mind and haunted. He had slept with Maria as often as possible. She was a real woman, not a frightened virgin mouse who didn't even know how to kiss.

Didn't she? She had asked Rory to teach her. She'd opened her mouth with Ted the way she had with Rory. Was there more? It hadn't felt the same with Ted as with Rory, so maybe she hadn't been doing it right.

What did Maria do, anyway?

That question hit rather too close to home. Caroline

jumped up from the bed, disgusted with herself. She blew out the lamp, then groped for her cloak. She would go for a walk. It couldn't be as dark outside as it seemed here. It never was. There were stars and a moon. She would walk until she felt tired—however long that might take.

She stood just outside the kitchen door, a shadow in the shadows, until her eyes adjusted to the darkness. As she expected, the night sky was strewn with distant pinpoints of light and a narrow crescent moon. Thin clouds drifted, blown by the sharp wind that presaged winter.

It seemed bad luck to Caroline that she needed activity—work—just now at the fallow time of year. She had wanted to marry in spring, but Ted couldn't wait.

She chuckled nastily. Well, he hadn't, had he?

She gathered the cloak around her and began to walk. Every inch of the ranch was familiar to her, not just the well-worn paths to the outbuildings. She followed the corral fence and skirted the bunkhouse. It too was quiet. Following the fence again led her to the stable and the thought of riding. She had ridden early this morning, at dawn in fact, but now that seemed as remote as last year. She'd taken Hannah's mare Dancer to the boundary of Colby land, thinking how perhaps someday she and Ted would buy that property.

Now they never would.

She had no horse of her own, for she had refused to let Jake replace her fallen birthday gift. Trying to decide which horse she would choose for a ride at this time of night, Caroline slipped soundlessly into the stable.

Again she stood still, waiting for her vision to adjust to a different kind of darkness. It took a moment for her to realize it wasn't necessary. Someone had left a lamp burning above one of the back stalls. It cast light in a small golden circle that fell far short of where she stood, but would help her find the lamp that always hung by the door for emergencies. Groping for it and coming up empty, she realized it was the one already in use.

Because she was wearing moccasins under her dress, her step barely disturbed the broken straw under her feet as she moved over the worn floorboards toward the light. The sleeping horses paid her no mind, but the stable was nevertheless alive with small sounds and potent smells. Here and there a horse shifted or snorted, and a cat stalked a mouse through the straw.

Caroline breathed in the peaceful atmosphere, knowing she had been wise to come here. She wouldn't even have to ride. She could groom one of the horses and find comfort in the exercise and the soothing motions required.

As she approached the lit stall she heard a sound, a low murmuring voice, and drew up short, setting her cloak to swirling about her ankles. She thought immediately of Ernie, recalling his habit of talking softly to the horses as he worked among them. But it was late for Ernie to be working.

Looking up, Caroline saw the hat hanging on the post at the end of the stall and knew who it was. Rory. Not Ernie. Then she remembered that when she had first heard Ernie talking to the horses he had reminded her of Rory. She had come full circle. Back to Rory.

She moved closer, just far enough to see into the stall without revealing herself. The cloak helped her blend into the shadows, particularly as it covered her hair. Perhaps it wasn't fair to spy on Rory, but she didn't feel that she was spying, more that she was simply studying him without interference.

He was grooming Duchess, using a curry comb, his arm moving in long, gentle swoops that told Caroline he was doing it as much for himself as for the horse. He had changed from his dress pants and shirt into the male equivalent of her gingham dress, worn but clean denim work clothes. His left hand worked in counterpoint to the right, following behind the curry comb occasionally, then stroking open-palmed over a shoulder or flank. His hand looked golden against the dark red mare. Shudders of pleasure moved over the horse, traveling just under the hide surface. When Duchess turned her head as if to nip at his hand, Rory laughed and scratched her neck, reaching up behind her ears.

"You like that, old girl?" he asked unnecessarily.

He stepped around the back of the horse and bent to retrieve something. Only then Caroline saw that Duchess stood with one foot in a bucket.

Unable to stop herself, she stepped closer. "What's wrong with Duchess?"

Rory's head snapped up and he dropped the hoof he had been lifting. It plopped back into the pail. "Good heavens, Caroline! You startled me." He straightened, regarding her warily. "What are you doing out here? I thought you were asleep."

"I woke up." She made a face. "Now I can't get back to sleep."

He nodded and bent to his job again.

"What's wrong with Duchess?"

"Old age, mostly." He moved the bucket and put a different hoof to soak. "This is Ernie's cure." Rising, he considered her across the swayed back of his horse. "She likes it and it doesn't do any harm. Makes me feel useful."

Caroline put out her hand to let Duchess nuzzle her palm. "You're very useful. You're the only person who makes me feel . . . human now. I feel like such an *embarrassment*."

"That's crazy. You didn't do anything wrong."

"Didn't I? Come on, Rory, you heard Ted."

Rory exploded "Christ, Caroline! You didn't fall for that, did you? That's the oldest trick in the book. Blame someone else—preferably someone innocent!"

She shook her head. "Not so innocent, Rory. I was dead wrong—about everything." She saw the way his hands had knotted into fists and realized that she was compounding her offenses against Rory. She had not waited for him to speak up, she had lied to him about her true feelings, and now—when he had retreated here to find comfort with his old friend Duchess—she was invading his sanctuary and taking away his hard-earned peace.

She backed away. "I'm sorry, Rory. I didn't follow you here and I should have le—"

He nearly vaulted over Duchess in his haste to prevent Caroline from leaving. He caught the hood of her cloak as it fell from her head, then transferred his grip to her arm when the tie around her throat threatened to choke her.

"Don't leave," he said when she turned her frightened-looking eyes up to his. He eased his hold but didn't let go. "I'm well aware that you didn't follow me. Did you intend to ride?"

"I thought of it."

She looked wary enough to bolt if he released her, so he didn't. "So did I, but you're not dressed for it." Rory made a decision. "Come with me on Brutus. We won't go far, just out of here for a while. Then you can help me groom him."

Caroline was tempted. Brutus was big enough to take both of them to the ends of the earth. She couldn't go back to her room. She just couldn't. "All right, but not for long." It was a silly restriction, but she had to say something that sounded reluctant.

Rory let her go and went to saddle Brutus.

He understood Caroline's need to escape from the house. He'd done the same thing as soon as possible. Supper had been understandably glum, with everyone's mind on the one person missing from their circle. Afterward, Uncle Simon took Rusty and Abby outside. Rory soon wished he had gone, too. Staying had been his own idea, the product of his loyalty to Jake and Hannah.

263

They might need his company. Or so he had thought.

The reality was different enough to be embarrassing. To have something to say in the wake of quiet left by the children's departure, he asked. "Was it your idea or Caroline's to say that both of you gave her in marriage?"

Hannah's face bloomed with pleased color. "Yes, Jake, that was so sweet."

"It was the truth, that's all. You've been all the mother she's ever known," Jake answered in a suspiciously rough voice.

With Lupe gone to her own place, incapacitated by her shame and remorse, they had all pitched in to deal with the meal and cleanup. Hannah put aside her apron and went to Jake. "You've been everything to her. You were all she ever needed."

He faced her, thumbs hooked over his belt, a slow grin spreading over his face. "Is that right?" He lifted his hands to her shoulders. "Funny, but I remember hearing a different story once upon a time."

Hannah knew what he was leading up to and she tried — not very hard — to push him away. Her color deepened as she also fought down her own smile. "Jake—"

"I remember hearing that I'd ruin the life of a young girl if I didn't also provide her with a mother to counsel and sympathize with her—"

Jake bent back to avoid the hand she tried to put over his mouth. They were both laughing now, lost in memories that were as real and close to them as yesterday. It was their heritage, the story of how Hannah had pursued Jake to Pennsylvania, trying to convince him that marrying her would ensure his daughter's happiness. Jake went on teasing her until she got her hand around his neck to bring his mouth down to hers.

They hadn't even heard him when Rory excused himself, mumbling about seeing to something in the bunkhouse.

He slapped the saddle onto Brutus with the mindless

ease of long familiarity with such chores. He was glad that Jake was himself again in all ways, but being around such happiness could hurt like hell. Once he'd told someone that the way they acted made his teeth ache like too much sugar. Now it was worse. For Caroline, it would be impossible.

Leading Brutus, they walked together outside. Already Caroline was having second thoughts, but when she tried to express them Rory wouldn't listen. He swung up into the saddle, then lifted her to sit sideways in front of him—no easy task, for Brutus stood at sixteen hands, and she was no lightweight.

Peering down at the ground, Caroline laughed a little. "No wonder I've never liked a sidesaddle. It feels very strange."

Rory eased her back against his chest, fastening one arm around her tightly. "I've got you."

Indeed you have, Caroline thought, relaxing tentatively. For herself, it was ideal. But for Rory? Was she hurting him? She did not think she could bear adding to his pain.

"Remember when you brought Brutus here for the first time and Duchess was jealous?"

His chuckle warmed her ear. She had not replaced the hood of her cloak, and his face was very near hers. "Poor old Duchess. She thought she'd been replaced."

"Well, she *had* been. No matter how you tried to dress it up, you had a new horse."

"I suppose. But she's still first in my heart. He just gets to lug me around."

"A rare privilege," Caroline teased. "When I was away I thought of her and wondered if she'd still be here when I got back."

"Was it so bad being away from here?" Rory asked.

Implicit in the question was another: *Was it so important that you live here that you'd marry Ted?* Caroline wanted to answer honestly, but what was the truth?

265

What she thought yesterday? Or what she believed to-day? Now that she knew Ted had deceived her, her view had necessarily changed. But how to express that to Rory? She didn't think it was possible.

"No, it wasn't terrible. Not at all. At least not until Papa was hurt. Then it was torture for me. I felt help-less." The horse was just walking along a well-used path to one of the pastures, the motion like that of a giant rocking chair. "When I was away I was sure I'd be able to help if only I were home. Then I *was* home and he got hurt again," she said, picking her way through her thoughts as carefully as Brutus picked up his path. "I saw that I couldn't make a difference, and I fell apart. Does that make sense?"

"And Ted was here and I wasn't."

Was it really that simple? Was *she* that simple? That . . . shallow?

"I thought I was doing what was right," she said on a thread of sound. His arm tightened reassuringly, and they rode on in silence until Caroline found the courage to ask the question that had been burning on her tongue. "Did you ever . . . go to bed with Maria?"

"No," he answered so promptly she wondered if he had expected to be asked. Had he known she would interpret hesitation as deceit?

It was the answer she wanted, of course, but it meant she couldn't ask the rest of what she wondered. "Oh."

She hadn't been leading him with that deflated reply, but he went on anyway. "I could have. She doesn't play hard to get. Quite the opposite. Has for years. Under other circumstances I might have. I can't throw any stones at Ted."

Worse and worse. "What other circumstances?"

"I love and respect Lupe. I wouldn't hurt her."

Caroline chewed on that awhile. "Then you mean Ted didn't—doesn't—love and respect me, don't you?"

"That's not for me to say, Caroline."

266

"I know he doesn't."

Rory pulled back to peer down at her face. "Then why the hell were you marrying him?"

"I only just found out. Today. He looked at me with such hatred."

"I don't know, Caroline. I'm no expert on Ted Jasper, but you may have mistaken anger and guilt for hatred."

"Then why did he say such hurtful things?"

"Even Jake and Hannah hurt each other."

Caroline fell silent. They both knew Papa and Hannah were the last word in devotion. Rory directed Brutus back toward the stable at last, Caroline soothed enough to let her head rest on Rory's shoulder.

For Rory it was a mixed blessing. He was pleased that she felt better, but holding her had brought his body to aching life. She came down into his arms like a boneless doll, warm and soft. He was glad to have the horse to care for, or he would have been tempted to carry her to the empty stall next to Duchess and make love to her. He was tempted anyway. Calling himself every bad name he could think of helped, but not enough.

"Why don't you go back to bed now, mite. You'll be able to sleep."

Just the thought of her empty room brought Caroline out of her trance. "I want to help you with the horses."

"There's nothing much to do. Brutus isn't worked up and Duchess is done."

"Please, Rory. I want to stay. Even if it's only make-work."

Her pleading blue eyes got to him. They always did. Make-work it was, but they did it together, soothing animals that didn't need soothing because *they* needed soothing.

When the job was done, stretched out as finely as the tension between them, Rory carried the bucket containing Duchess's soak outside and dumped its contents onto the ground. He lingered awhile in the crisp night air,

267

finding it a necessary antidote to the pungent fragrance inside that was so evocative of life at its most earthy.

The first thing he noticed when he came back was that Caroline's cloak was gone from the peg where she'd hung it on their return. The second was the stillness. Caroline was gone. Disappointment chased relief through his body.

Good, he told himself, letting out the breath he hadn't known he was holding. It came out as a sigh of such longing as to negate his thoughts.

All for the best, he reiterated, reaching to take his hat from the post next to Duchess's stall. Plopping it onto his head, he turned away, then stopped, frozen into an exaggerated attitude of attention. He heard a small sound from the empty stall. Hoping it was a mouse or cat, he whispered, "Caroline?"

"Umm?" came the sleepy answer from the stall.

Oh, God.

He pushed the stall open and saw Caroline nestled into the hay, wrapped in her cloak. She lay curled so that even her feet were covered. Although there was nothing provocative about her position, desire went through Rory like flame up a straw.

"Caroline, you can't sleep out here." He didn't move closer. He didn't dare.

Rory's voice came to Caroline from far away, an annoying buzz like the sound of a fly against a distant window. She rolled into a tighter ball and put her fingers over her ears to deaden the noise. She was almost asleep. If she could keep him at bay a little longer—and not think—she would be asleep.

"Caroline!"

She didn't answer.

Rory tried to think. What was wrong with leaving her here? She would be safe. No one who came to the stable early in the morning would harm her. Wake her, yes. But then she would return to the house.

Hannah or Jake might miss her from the house and be worried, he argued. But not if he put a note on her bed and in the kitchen.

All that was very logical, but there was nothing logical about the way she looked to Rory. She looked small, forlorn, and very, very hurt. Obviously the thought of returning to her room was repugnant to her, so much so that a pile of rough hay in a stable was preferable.

Who was he to wake her and send her back to that just because the sight of her tore at his guts?

He was so quiet, standing at the gate of the stall, lost in deliberation, that Caroline came to believe that he was gone. Suddenly the thought that she was alone became insupportable. It was what she wanted, but it was unbearable.

A tiny sob caught her by surprise. She clamped her hand over her mouth to contain the rest of the ones she could feel building inside her. She wouldn't cry again! She wouldn't! She was tired of tears.

The small sound of a muffled cry decided the issue for Rory. Instantly he was at her side, pulling her up into his arms. For a few moments she fought him, struggling for something he didn't understand.

Caroline fought herself, not Rory. She had prided herself on being strong. She wasn't. It was all sham, all surface. She rode like a man, worked like a man, even shot a gun as well as most men; inside, she was the complete opposite. She had made a mess of her life, hurt the people she loved, and now she was bawling about it all — again.

"No!" she protested fiercely. "No more!"

Rory held her against his broad chest, soothing her back with the same long stroke of his hands he'd used on Duchess. Her hood fell back, but the rest of the cloak was as binding as a shroud. "Don't, Caroline," he said tightly. "Don't fight me. I'm only trying to help."

She gave in then, letting the tears flow, hating every

269

minute of her weakness. Like Duchess, she reveled in Rory's touch, in his gentleness.

When she was spent she had soaked the front of Rory's shirt. She smoothed it with damp hands and said, "I hate crying. I'm so sick of doing it—especially when I don't have a handkerchief."

"After all these years, Gramma Lunig's teachings still haven't taken?"

Caroline laughed. "You remembered that?"

"I remember every word we've ever said to each other, starting with that conversation. Until then you were just Jake's kid, a girl. I'd had a sister, you remember—"

"Betsey?"

"Yeah." His voice was raspy with emotion. "Poor old Betsey." She had died of cholera as a child of twelve. "Funny thing, now that I know Rusty and Abby, Betsey's dearer to me in memory. But then I didn't have much use for girls. You, though . . . well, you were different. You were straight. You said what you meant. What really won me over, though, was the day we went to Gettysburg and you told me about Gramma Lunig's rules for young ladies. Do you remember?"

Caroline's tears were drying fast, and her few sniffles were, too. "I remember the rules, of course, and I remember Gettysburg." She moved back just enough to see his face. His smile was heart-stopping.

"You started reciting off the rules: a lady sits just so, a lady stays out of the sun—I don't remember them all."

"Neither do I," she said, chuckling. "I haven't been very ladylike."

"Then you said, 'And a lady *never* blows her nose without a handkerchief.' You were grinning from ear to ear when you confessed that you'd tried that after seeing one of your grandfather's field workers do it."

"I did?"

"You did. You were terribly proud of your daring, even though you admitted that it was pretty disgusting. I began to love you right then."

Caroline was amazed and delighted that he remembered something so trivial about her. Her arms went around him and tightened. "Oh, Rory."

"Well, I was only sixteen myself, you remember. I didn't have very good taste in women then."

It was banter, the teasing wordplay that had been their life together, but it was also different now. Fuller. Deeper. Like a simple tune picked out on a piano that had been enriched with chords and harmonies into a complex composition.

She laid her palm against his cheek. "Oh, Rory, I hurt you. I'm so sorry."

"Hush now, don't say that. You've been hurt."

"I deserved to be. I was so wrong."

Rory couldn't help himself. He kissed her. Her mouth was soft and yielding. It tasted salty, like tears, and sweet, like Caroline. She deepened the kiss and he was lost. He had thought her lost to him and here she was, in his arms.

A feeling of safety and homecoming stole over Caroline, warming her and making the humiliation of the day fade away. Here she was secure.

Quickly, though, her feelings spiraled beyond security. There was urgency as well as tenderness in Rory's kiss. He was not kissing the child who had amused him with her shocking ways. He was kissing the woman he said he loved, and for Caroline, for a moment, this kiss was a continuation of his last one. Then, he had been trying to convince her that she loved him. She hadn't permitted herself to show her response, but now she could. Now she was free of her promise to Ted, free of Ted. She could erase the time between and give Rory all that her heart held for him alone.

Slowly, slowly, she melted into his embrace, letting him feel the quiver of need that ran through her body. His hand, resting on her waist, slid slowly to the outer rounding of her breast, and she moved to give him access. He hesitated, and then his big hand closed over the fullness, shaping it gently to his own design. Caroline couldn't contain her surprised whimper of pleasure as her nipple puckered to hardness agains his warm palm.

Instinctively, she arched her back, her hand slipping up to hold his head when she feared he would pull back. There were feelings building inside her that she didn't want to lose. She wanted him closer. She wanted . . . something she couldn't name. She touched her tongue to his lips and, and at his yielding, followed his tongue into his mouth.

She felt his groan as well as heard it and sank back into the hay, bringing him down upon her. The cloak was half under her and half discarded, no longer needed for warmth or comfort. Rory settled in a kneeling sprawl with his face in her neck. His breath came in rough gusts that excited her.

She wanted to protest when his hand deserted her breast, but then he began to kiss his way down the side of her neck to the modest front of her dress. Button after button opened as he nuzzled lower and lower. He displaced her camisole with a deft flick of his hand, and one breast was bare.

Caroline gasped softly, in delight and in astonishment, as he cupped the underside to lift the already straining bud to his mouth. She had not known she could feel such longing or such joy. Just the touch of his moist breath made her nipple tingle and tighten painfully. Like a promise too quickly withdrawn, Rory touched his mouth to the peak just briefly before he began to nibble and nip at the aching center. It was sweet torture to Caroline, who knew only that some fulfillment he could give her hovered just beyond her reach. Each teasing touch of his gentle teeth and hot tongue increased the frantic yearning of her body even as it ultimately disappointed, making her toss mindlessly before him.

Finally, *finally,* his mouth closed over the engorged nipple. Instead of being relieved, after a few moments Caroline felt the coil of desire tighten around her.

"Oh, Rory," she pleaded. It was pleasure—she knew that—but pleasure so pure that it was unbearable. Like looking at the sun, pleasure like this burned.

He seemed not to listen. Using his teeth, he tugged back the folds of cloth covering her other breast so that he could repeat the same treatment there. Because Caroline was senseless to everything else, she didn't notice that he was raising her skirt at the same time. But then he touched her restless thighs, and she found there was more in store for her.

Even as Rory touched her and gloried in the knowledge that this was Caroline, that he was finally giving rein to his need for her, he hated himself for what he was doing. He was taking advantage of her at a time when she was hurt and vulnerable. He could give her pleasure, but at what cost? She needed assurance that she was desirable, not an attack on her innocence.

But he couldn't stop. Not yet. Soon, though. Oh, God, yes. Soon.

Caroline didn't help him. She couldn't.

"Please," she whispered urgently.

If she'd been able to think she could have offered perfectly good justifications for the fact that she didn't resist or protest a single thing Rory did. She was beyond thought, however. All she knew was that she would finally have what she wanted. She lifted her hips and wriggled out of her underclothes, even kicked off her moccasins to facilitate the process. Her hands were clumsy as she tugged on Rory's clothes, yet her every touch excited him in ways more experienced women never had.

She wanted him. Caroline wanted him. *Caroline.*

Caroline had never seen anyone more beautiful than Rory as he stood briefly in the spill of golden light from the lamp. His body hair was the tawny shade of a lion's, and he was as sleekly muscled. She had no time to be afraid of the swollen jut of his sex, and she wouldn't have been anyway. This was Rory. He would never hurt her.

When Rory stood to cast aside his clothes he filled his mind with the picture Caroline made, her slim body an offering of milky white against the dark cloak. Her hair was tumbled and loose, lying around her shoulders like the finest gold cloth. A thick strand curved around one pink-crested breast and pointed to the nest of curls at her thighs.

She lifted her arms in welcome and the picture came alive. She was real. This was really happening.

"You are so beautiful . . . lovely . . ." His hand swept to include all of her as he stretched his considerable length beside her. "All yellow . . ." He lifted the lock of hair to his lips. "And white." His fingers caressed her breast to its crest. "And pink." He kissed her there, and the power of Maria's taunt, "whey-faced," leached away, leaving her secure. Rory called her beautiful.

With her eyes begging permission to touch him, her hands fluttered to his chest. "And you . . . you're gold." She brushed one palm over the ruff of hair at the center of his chest. He held himself rigid before her caress, like someone luring a wild animal into trust with preternatural stillness.

When he didn't seem to mind her forwardness, Caroline, more daring now, with a mischievous gleam in her eyes, covered each flat nipple with a thumb. "And copper," she pronounced, toying with the small hard nubs.

In spite of himself, Rory stiffened in reaction. Caroline snatched back her hands in alarm. He caught them and drew them back to his chest. "That wasn't rejection, sweetheart. Quite the opposite, and I can't hide my reaction."

His laugh was rueful, inviting her confidence. She

buried her face in his chest, wanting to giggle and cry at the same time. He was Rory when he laughed and held her, but this man with the wonderfully exciting body was a stranger. Which was real? Or was he two people in one?

Before she could decide, or even think about the questions, Rory wrapped her in his arms. In just that movement he became one whole person again—Rory, the man she loved.

She cried out to him, "Love me, please, Rory. Please." Shutting her eyes tightly against tears, she clutched him desperately. "I want to *know!*" It wasn't what she meant to say, and it wasn't what Rory wanted to hear, but her plea struck his heart.

At the last moment he hesitated at the thought of hurting her. "Caroline . . . sweetheart . . ."

She was determined. Driven by instinct, Caroline took the pulsing length of him in her hand and drew him to her parted legs.

"Oh, God!" he cried. Her soft, yielding flesh felt hot. His initial thrust was cautious, and he moaned as if he were in terrible pain.

Caroline felt a sharp, hot sting, then nothing as he lay stiff as a board above her, unmoving on braced arms, barely touching her. She felt a quiver of effort course from his shoulders.

"Rory?" This was awful. How could he have wanted such agony? How could she?

She circled his back with her arms, stroking his rigidly held body, offering him comfort in his travail. The movement, small as it was, unlocked their mutual rictus. She could feel him inside her, filling her now without discomfort, so when he started to withdraw she clutched at him to keep him with her.

But he returned, this time with more force, and Caroline began to melt from the wonderful friction of hard flesh on soft. Harder, faster, he moved like one possessed by the devil, his face contorted by pain. She closed her eyes so as not to see his suffering. She heard the harsh cry that ended it, though, and then he collapsed on top of her. After a moment he rolled onto his side, taking her with him.

To her everlasting shame, Caroline found that she was crying again. She didn't know why. Not exactly. He hadn't hurt her, only himself. But that hurt her anyway.

"Damn," he said in a low, ferocious growl. Then, "Oh, Christ. I knew better."

"Don't . . . swear so, Rory," she scolded, trying to get free from his hold around her. Although she knew it wasn't possible, she felt more than just naked. She felt raw and more lonely now than before. And if she felt that bad, what must Rory be feeling?

He looked so utterly miserable that she wanted to hold and comfort him. Unfortunately, she knew what that would do to him. She might be forgiven once because of her ignorance. But a second time?

She scrambled into her clothes with guilty haste, not bothering with buttons at all. Then she realized that Rory was sitting on her cloak. His forearms were propped on his knees with his head resting on doubled fists. He was the picture of misery.

She went onto her knees beside him, careful not to touch him. "I'm sorry, Rory. It's all my fault . . . and . . . I'm sorry," she finished ineffectually, unable to find any other words. She ached to hold him as he had held her, but it would be wrong. She loved him too much to cause him more pain.

He rolled away and got to his feet, also careful not to touch her. He didn't accept her allocation of blame. In fact, it made him feel worse—if that were possible. He dressed as hastily as she had, noting that she looked away. As soon as he was off the cloak she had herself wrapped up in it, her fingers hooked into small white claws to hold it tight around her.

Her cheeks glistened with tear tracks that hadn't dried yet. "You're not to blame for anything here, Caroline," he said stiffly. "I'm totally to blame and totally sorry."

The way he stood, as if moving would make him shatter, drove Caroline to want to comfort him in some way. She took a step toward him. He backed up and she stopped. She was afraid she was going to cry again, so she tried to smile. "Anyway," she said in a small voice, "now I'm glad I didn't get married after all."

She hurried away, but the sound of his muted outcry made her pause at the outer door, then hurry on to her room.

Chapter Twenty-four

Rory spent the night in the stable.

When the men came in the morning, whistling, laughing and calling back and forth over their chores, no one noticed him, still in the empty stall. He waited until the place grew quiet again before he moved, grateful for his habit of changing his resting place often enough that no one would remark on his absence. At the house they would assume he'd slept in the bunkhouse, and vice versa. He brushed the hay from his clothes, considering his discomfort as inadequate penance for his crime.

He didn't doubt that it *was* a crime. He had selfishly taken his own pleasure at the expense of Caroline's innocence. What he had done to her was, in his eyes, worse than what Maria and Ted had done. He'd meant to give her pleasure and perhaps a healing sense of her attractiveness. Instead, he'd ruined her physically and hurt her so badly she now felt relieved *not* to be married.

Nevertheless, the experience would live within him to the end of his days—in spite of his guilt—as the most wonderful moment of his life. For a little while Caroline had wanted him enough to give herself to him. He regretted, bitterly and deeply, the ending, but not the beginning.

Dear God, no; never that.

He crossed the yard to the house, hoping to escape everyone's notice. Uncle Simon was leaving tomorrow, and Rory was going with him. He'd have to speak to Caroline again, if only to assure her that he would marry her in the off chance that he had made her pregnant and to absolve her of guilt.

The guilt was his alone. She had to understand that.

He made it to his room all right, but later, when he was washed and changed, Hannah came upon him in the kitchen.

"Oh, here you are, Rory," she said brightly. "We've been looking for you everywhere."

He put down the dish he was holding, careful not to break it.

They knew. Somehow, Jake and Hannah knew what he had done.

"Jake wants to talk to you," she went on. "And so do I. Can you give us a few minutes now?"

"Of course."

She was smiling at him, but there was something edgy about her movements and posture. If she knew, she wouldn't be smiling. He'd seen Hannah angry before, and she wasn't a woman to mince words. No. *She* didn't know. But did Jake?

"I don't mean *right* now. You can finish your breakfast."

"No, thank you. I'm done here."

"Did you eat? It doesn't look like it."

He hadn't, and now he knew better than to try. His stomach was churning. "Yes, ma'am, I'm fine on food."

"Ma'am?" Hannah grinned, arching one brow sharply. "Now where on earth did that come from?"

The smile he gave her was weak, and so were his knees as he followed her to the little room Jake used as an office of sorts. It was the only place in the house where he smoked his cigars, so the odor persisted. Consequently, Hannah, who did most of the record keeping, did the work elsewhere and merely stored everything in the office. Its main feature was a big rolltop desk with a comfortable, masculine chair before it.

That was where Jake waited for him, sitting back in the big chair, filling it and the room with his compelling presence.

Jake peered at Rory's face, then exchanged a swift

279

look with Hannah, who had followed him in. "You look like you had a bad night, too," he said. Shaking his head, he sat up straighter in the chair. "Just like Caroline. She looked like hell this morning—when she finally put in an appearance. And very brief it was, too."

Rory's stomach muscles clenched, making him glad he hadn't eaten. Gratefully, he took the chair Jake indicated. He was even more grateful when Jake went on to say, "That's what we wanted to talk to you about, Rory. Caroline."

Rory had to wet his lips before he could speak. "What can I do?" It was the only possible comment he could make.

"You can take her with you when you go tomorrow."

"Take her . . . ?" Every muscle in Rory's body tightened, making his motion jerky as he got back to his feet. "She'll never want to leave here," he exclaimed. "That was the whole reason for her marrying Jasper in the first place!"

Jake winced at Rory's blunt words and passed a hand over his face. When he looked back at Rory he looked more like the sick man of months before. "I know. I'll always regret that I had any part in that decision of hers, and God knows I don't want her to go, but we have no choice. Hannah tells me she's taken all the blame for Jasper's actions onto herself."

Rory knew that much was true. "He . . . said some things to her in the back room of the church," he told them, looking from Jake to Hannah. "It was totally self-serving, but she took every word to heart."

"She would," Hannah agreed.

Rory knew that, too. Hadn't she taken the blame for last night as well? How much blame could she absorb without breaking? He paced to the window.

"We're afraid that if she stays here Ted will try to patch things up with her," Jake said.

"As long as she's within reach of him, and lonely and

280

bored, as she's bound to be here this long winter," Hannah added, "she might succumb."

"Especially if Maria is lying."

Rory spun to stare at Jake.

Hannah put her hand on Rory's arm. "Maria's had 'babies' before. Babies that turn out to be miscarriages or 'mistakes,' " she explained softly.

"Ted will never marry her anyway. His father would cut him off completely."

Rory felt bombarded by their comments, all persuasive to him. The idea of Caroline with Ted Jasper sickened him. It always had. Last night, after she'd gone, he'd been racked with guilt to think of Caroline being ill-treated or misjudged by her future husband because of what he had done. He'd had enough trouble with the idea of a "mythical" husband for her; Ted Jasper was totally unacceptable.

But to take her away . . . She'd never go willingly, particularly with him and most particularly with him *now*.

"What does Caroline say about this?" he asked.

Jake cleared his throat. "We . . . ah . . . wanted to get your agreement before we . . . discussed it with her."

Rory had his out. Caroline would never agree, so he was safe. He could accept, knowing she would not.

He didn't like doing that, however. "You know I'm going to a rough mining town. Is that what you want for Caroline?"

Before Jake could respond, Hannah spoke up. "Frankly, *I'm* counting on the adventure of that outweighing everything else with Caroline. She's not the kind to mind a bit of a challenge."

"Challenge? How about outright danger, Hannah?"

"Uncle Simon believes she'd be an asset to your scheme," she answered calmly. "I'm sure he'd never suggest anything that would harm her."

Jake wasn't as certain. "He sent you off to Fort Kearney in the aftermath of the Civil War, Hannah. That was hardly a wise decision."

She spread her hands. "And look where I am. It was the best thing I could have done." That trip had, of course, brought Jake into her life. He had rescued her from the wilderness when her wagon train had been destroyed and all the other travelers murdered.

"You could have died a dozen times over," Jake argued.

"But I didn't, and my parents did, back in a safe little settlement in Ohio."

Rory had heard this argument before. It wasn't one either of them would win. "I won't be going to Colorado until spring," he reminded them. "What about the interim?"

"She'll be in Knoxville. Uncle Simon will take good care of her—of you both," she amended. "We care about you, too."

Rory knew that, but he wondered if Hannah's oblique remark meant they were playing matchmaker. If so, they would be disappointed.

"She can't stay here, Rory," Jake said, determination in every word. "Can you think of any other way?"

"No, Jake, I can't. I'll do anything I can to help." Including, he vowed to himself, letting Caroline know she was entirely safe from him. He would tell her that at his first opportunity.

Jake and Hannah exchanged a brief, relieved look; then Hannah said, "I'll go get Caroline."

Rory tried to follow her.

"No, no, Rory," Jake said. "Please stay. We need you for backup."

"I don't think so, Jake. You'll do much better without me here."

"Rory, please."

Something in Jake's voice stopped him, a note of genuine anguish. Jake asked for so little and gave so

282

much that Rory couldn't refuse him outright. "I really think she'd rather not have me here. How can she speak frankly in front of me?"

Jake made a wry face. "Are we talking about the same person?"

But that was Caroline before last night, he thought. *She's been hurt — again.*

Rory went back to look out the window. If Jake wanted him here, he'd stay. But he would be as unobtrusive as possible. Maybe she wouldn't notice him.

He was the first thing she saw.

Her first thought when Hannah had come to usher her into Papa's presence was that they had found out about last night. She had successfully fought down her initial panic, because Hannah was solicitous, not reproachful. Now she could feel turmoil rising inside her like water in a flooded creek.

Caroline's gaze bounced wildly from Rory's stiff back to Jake's concerned countenance to Hannah's encouraging smile. All three promised trouble.

But what? She was so busy trying to think and trying to discover what Rory's part might be that she scarcely heard her father's words. His tone was worried, kind, loving — all things Caroline felt herself unworthy of.

She gave him a distracted smile meant to be reassuring. "Please, Papa, I'll be all right. I assure you I'm not going to spend my life hiding in my room. I was just a little . . . tired this morning."

She had chosen the most innocuous word she could think of, in deference to Rory, but he took it like an arrow to the chest. He didn't however, indicate that he was other than insensible.

Her father was encouraged by the note of impatience in her voice. Perhaps a fight was just what she needed. He was prepared to give her one rather than let her stay anywhere near that bastard Jasper. As with Rory, he came right to the point. "Hannah and I have been thinking about what you should do now."

At Caroline's look of blank surprise he lost his momentum. He sent a wordless plea to Hannah. Suddenly the idea of sending her away had lost all its appeal, even for her own good.

"We know there's only one thing that could substitute for marrying right now," Hannah said, taking up Jake's dropped reins. "We don't want to have to give up your company for any reason, dear girl, but in this circumstance we know it's for the best."

Caroline felt faint. "I don't understand." She looked from Hannah to Jake, trying to read in their faces the meaning she couldn't find in their words. "What are you saying?"

Jake rallied. "Don't look like that, sweetheart. We're only thinking of you."

"Thinking *what* of me?" she demanded.

Rory was ready to jump out of his skin. Hannah and Jake were making hash out of the whole thing! He turned and fixed his gaze on Caroline's frightened face. "Relax, mite," he said with more composure than he felt. "They're not sending you to a nunnery. Uncle Simon thinks you could help me trap my uncle, as you heard him say. They thought you might like to try it."

"Go with you?"

Only Rory heard her slight emphasis on the last word. He concealed his slight wince. "And Uncle Simon."

"Will Uncle Simon be going to Colorado?"

"No."

"But I would?"

Rory consulted Jake and Hannah, still expecting disapproval. There was none. "It seems so."

Caroline's small bubble burst. She looked away from Rory, her emotions in tumult. "What's the real reason behind this, Papa?"

His flush told her more than she wanted to know. Her disastrous marriage ceremony had brought disgrace to

284

the family. They wanted her gone. And that without them even suspecting what she had done with Rory last night!

Hannah was more perceptive than Jake. She saw Caroline's flush of shame. "It's not what you think, Caroline. We are *not* ashamed of you! This isn't banishment, honey. It's escape for you."

"They're afraid Ted might win you back if you stay here," Rory said in spite of the fact that Jake flinched to have his motives brought into the open.

"But I wouldn't!" she cried out indignantly. "I know better than that now. I'm not ever getting married."

Rory didn't share the amused glances that flew between Hannah and Jake. He alone knew why she felt that way and knew it had nothing to do with Ted or Maria. He also knew he wanted a chance to change her mind. He wanted her to come with him. The trust Jake and Hannah placed in him might be misguided, but dammit, he still loved Caroline. He would take care of her and protect her, even against himself.

"Are you afraid of the danger in Colorado?"

Caroline didn't notice that he was goading her. She turned her indignation on him. "Of course not. And I can take care of myself. I won't have you bossing me around all the time."

Rory hid the smile that was fighting to burst over his features. He gave her a level look instead and said. "We'll see about that, won't we?" At the door he nodded to Jake, who was trying not to look smug, and added, unnecessarily, "We leave in the morning."

"How fortunate then that I'm already packed," Caroline answered tartly.

As soon as Rory closed the door Caroline sagged visibly, but Hannah was so happy to see her face full of color and animation she didn't care. She surged forward and took possession of Caroline, tugging her along out the door. "That was a wonderful answer, Caroline. Nevertheless, we *do* have a few things to do."

Caroline let herself be hustled away, because she had no energy to resist. She had been prepared to leave home to live with Ted; now she was going with Rory. But not to be his wife. He didn't want her with him, that much was abundantly clear. Sometime she'd get him to confess how Papa and Hannah had forced him into accepting her.

She consoled herself with one other thing besides the fact that, wanted or not, she would be with Rory. He had been honest with her. He had told the truth about her parents' concern. That was a comfort to her in spite of the fact that she knew she didn't deserve their continued support and love.

For whatever reason, she was getting another chance. Sometime before she left she would let them know their faith was not misplaced. As it was, she barely had time to visit Lupe that night. But she was determined to set her second mother's mind at ease.

Lupe began to cry the instant she saw Caroline, although it wasn't entirely clear that she had ever really stopped since the wedding. She had just one lamp burning low at the side of her chair, but at least she wasn't sitting in the dark of her bungalow.

Now that Caroline was grown she was inches taller than Lupe—which seemed odd. She remembered being cuddled against that broad bosom and finding peace and solace there. When they hugged this time it was Lupe's head on her breast.

"Hush, hush," she crooned, rocking gently. "Don't cry, *mamacita*. It's all right now. Dry your tears and let me tell you what I'm doing."

"Zeb, he says you're going away!"

"Because I want to, Lupe love." Caroline tried to peel Lupe back far enough to see her face. "Remember how I used to tell you my secrets and you'd never tell anyone?"

She felt a nod against her damp chest.

286

"I'm going to tell you another, and I'm not just saying this to make you fell better. You mustn't think that."

Lupe loved secrets. She was intrigued enough to begin composing herself.

"I found out something yesterday that makes me very happy I didn't marry Ted." Lupe's upturned face began to crumple again, so Caroline rushed on. "No, no. Not what you think! I found out for sure that I never loved Ted."

Lupe couldn't take it in.

"Maria did me a favor, don't you see?" What Caroline saw was that she shouldn't have mentioned Maria. "No, Lupe, don't cry. It was a mistake that I almost married Ted. I was mixed up. I kind of knew I loved Rory, but he went away and never told me he loved me. Then Papa got hurt and Ted was so nice and helpful that I got gratitude mixed up with love." She laughed at her confusing explanation.

Her laughter got Lupe's attention as nothing else could have. "You're . . . really happy?"

"Yes, yes, I am." And she was, she realized. Even last night didn't seem so bad to her now. Today Rory had been strange and distant, which, although it hurt, didn't surprise her. But then for a few minutes in Papa's office he'd been more like his old self. That had given her hope.

She was going to cling to that hope.

"What I'm trying to say, Lupe, is that I love Rory and I think he loves me."

"Rory?" Hope dawned in Lupe's beautiful dark eyes.

"That's my secret, Lupe," Caroline said simply. "That's why I'm going with him. That's why I'm happy to be going with him. Do you see?"

"You . . . and Rory." Lupe was putting them together in her mind. Two of her favorite people — together. She smiled a teary smile and reached up to pat Caroline's cheek. "He's a good boy."

Caroline giggled. To Lupe, Rory would always be a boy, even though he had been almost grown up when she met him.

"Your papa—" A cloud of doubt passed over Lupe's face. "He lets you go with Rory?"

"It was his idea. His or Hannah's." She gave Lupe a quick conspiratorial hug. "Now you know why what I told you is a secret. Papa would never—"

"No," Lupe agreed solemnly. "Never." Then she began to laugh with Caroline.

Their laughter bordered on hysteria, but it was shared and it was healing, cleansing laughter. Much better than tears for both of them.

Caroline left soon afterward, knowing that although Lupe wasn't over her "disgrace" yet, at least her heart was eased of its burden on Caroline's account. Her secret was safe with Lupe, and it made her feel good to know that someone who knew her feelings would be wishing her well from here. Besides Hannah, of course. Caroline was sure Hannah knew, but she wouldn't confide in her any more. She was too close to Papa.

Although it was early, hardly more than nine o'clock, the house was already dark and quiet. Caroline was supposed to be asleep herself in preparation for tomorrow's early departure hour, so when Rory stepped into her path as she hurried to the kitchen door she gave a small cry of surprise.

Recovering quickly, she said, "Don't you ever sleep?"

"I could say the same to you."

"I went to see Lupe."

"How is she?"

"Better." She almost laughed, then repeated, "Much better."

Rory nodded and took her arm. "Come with me."

She resisted reflexively, then was ashamed of herself as his hand fell away.

"Just to the fence. I have something to say to you."

288

His tone put her back up, but she followed.

His stance at the fence reminded her of the way he had stood by the window. One hand rested on a fence post; the other was crammed into the pocket of his pants. They fit so tightly she wondered how he managed it. She was glad for the dim light that hid the sudden heated color in her cheeks. She had not let herself think about Rory's body since last night, but all the lovingly stored images were still there, readily available.

She pushed back the hood of her cloak, then regretted the way its loss revealed her face to him. Her hair had a way of gathering all the available light, making her stand out like a torch. Fortunately, the clouds were thick. All she could see of Rory's shadowed face was the glitter of his eyes.

"I just wanted you to know that I didn't have any choice about these arrangements for you and that I'm sorry." The statement sounded well rehearsed and stiff, like a piece of odious poetry from a schoolboy.

"Then why did you agree?" She wasn't hostile, just curious.

He made an impatient gesture with his free hand. "You know I can't refuse them anything. Uncle Simon would have taken you anyway. For me to object would only arouse their curiosity or their suspicions."

She shrugged. "I thought as much."

"If you want to come home in the spring, they'll be happy to have you back. You're not committed to anything."

"And you? Are you committed to anything?"

His head snapped back as if she had struck him. "Caroline—of course I am. If . . . if you're worried that you might be pregnant—"

"No!"

"No? How can you sound so positive?"

"I just am." She turned away from him, hiding her embarrassment. She wasn't going to explain her certainty.

Just remembering was bad enough. Back in her room last night she had discovered blood on her underwear. She had washed away the evidence, assuming that it was her virgin's blood. But then in the night she had begun her regular flow. It wasn't her normal time, but with all the turmoil of the past few days it was hardly surprising that her body would also rebel.

Rory touched her arm gently. "Are you all right?"

"Perfectly." She didn't turn to look at him.

"Caroline, I will marry you if—"

"It's not necessary."

"If it should be," he insisted.

To get him off the subject, she said, "I understand."

He turned her to face him. Even in the darkness she could feel his concern. "I'll do whatever you want, Caroline. Please believe me. I'll take you with me in the spring or bring you back here. It'll be your decision. I promise."

"But you won't want me with you."

"That really can't be helped, and it has little to do with us. My uncle is not a nice man, and his wife is a ghoul. It's just no place for you."

"That's not what I meant."

"But it's what I meant," he emphasized. "All I can say is that I promise you'll be as safe as I can make you—even from me. There'll be no repeat of last night, Caroline." It sounded to her like a vow. She couldn't doubt that he meant every word. "I can't make it up to you, I know that, little one. But if I could, I would."

"Will you kiss me?"

He actually moved back. Out of surprise, of course, but Caroline didn't realize that.

"To show there're no hard feelings?"

"You mean . . . now?"

"I need to know you forgive me."

"There's nothing to forgive. I told you that."

"Then you can kiss me, can't you." It wasn't a question.

When she put it that way Rory didn't know how to deny her.

Caroline had already decided that some inner demon had made that demand, not herself. It was as much penance for herself as it was a test of his good faith. As such, she was determined to remain passive and calm. She would not be forward with Rory again.

He kissed her with all the enthusiasm of a small boy forced to buss Aunt Matilda, and she did nothing to enhance the exchange except to smile at him afterward. Radiantly. "There now," she said gravely. "Now we're friends again. Right?"

After she skipped away, leaving him at the fence, Rory decided that the gesture had provided just the right note to establish what their future relationship would be.

The next morning, after an agonizing round of farewells, with tears from both sides, Jake and Hannah had no such illusions. They stood in the yard, staring at the diminishing cloud of dust that was Uncle Simon's carriage, their arms around each other.

Zeb, Ernie and Lupe stood in the periphery, Ernie to the side and Zeb as close to Lupe as she would permit. Abby had clung to Hannah's skirts, watering them with her tears, and now she made for Lupe, who welcomed another excuse to cry. Rusty had sauntered off toward the corral, seeking release in physical activity. Of them all, Ernie was perhaps the most desolate, because he had no one to share his sorrow. He had pledged himself to Caroline. He wanted to follow her, had vowed to—but how? He owed his new life to her father as well as to Caroline. How could he divide his loyalties? Like Rusty, he drifted off, kicking at nonexistent rocks in his path.

"In spite of everything," Hannah sniffed, raising her face from Jake's shoulder, "I think she was happy to go, don't you?"

Jake tightened his grip on her arm. "God, I hope so.

291

And I thought it was bad sending her away before!"

"Her place is with Rory now. He'll be good to her."

"He'd better be."

"But they'll fight, Jake. They won't have an easy time of it any more than we did."

"I wish I could be sure—"

"Now you sound like your daughter," Hannah laughed.

"They looked like it yesterday, I'll admit. I could see the sparks. But today they hardly looked at each other."

"But that's part of it, my darling. They're new at it, and it goes in fits and starts."

"I don't remember a minute when I didn't want you."

"But it didn't always show," she reminded him. "Any more than it did with me."

"Oh, you," Jake teased. "You were transparent. Always chasing me—"

The old argument didn't have its usual result. Their emotions were too abraded for lighthearted teasing or even passion. They hugged for comfort instead, and when Hannah raised her face to kiss Jake, his eyes were wet with tears.

"She'll be back, darling."

"I know. She told me." This time Jake lowered his head to bury his face in her neck. They stood there together long after the others were gone.

Chapter Twenty-five

Rory tapped on the door. "Are you ready?" He cocked his head, listening to the silence on the other side of the door. Had Caroline fallen asleep?

Back in New Mexico, such silence meant only that small sounds were blocked by the heavy door and absorbed by thick adobe walls. But this house was made differently. Although it was as roomy and elegant as Uncle Simon's money could make it, the walls were flimsy, merely a netting of thin wooden slats over the wall joists, to which muslin or canvas had been affixed. The final surface consisted of wallpaper. There was no plaster at all. Consequently, sounds carried from one room to another with alarming ease.

They had been in Lake City, Colorado, for less than a week, and Rory felt the strain already. They had a housekeeper and cook, but she went home at night, leaving him alone in the house with Caroline.

In spite of all he could say, he hadn't been able to convince Caroline that it was in her best interests to return to Renegade Ranch when winter was over, rather than accompany him here. Having wronged her once, he was determined not to do so again. Nevertheless, he regretted his promise that she could decide where she was to go. Even more, he regretted the result, for here she was—a complication in his already complicated life.

He knocked again, louder, then opened the door.

"So you are ready," he said as annoyance flared. "Couldn't you have answered me? I thought you'd fallen asleep."

She roused from the chair, laughing. "Maybe I did. It's all I seem to want to do lately."

293

"It's the thin air. You'll get used to it."

"I'll have to, won't I?" She turned slowly before him, showing off her dress. "Will I do?" she asked over her shoulder.

The dress was beautiful, especially the color. Rory didn't know the name for it, only that it was between pink and red and that it made Caroline's cheeks glow.

"Very nicely. Uncle Joseph's wife won't be a patch on you," he said with heavy understatement. The dress made a sensuous rustling noise with her every movement. Rory knew he would spend the evening listening for that sound.

"You'll have to stop thinking of him as Uncle Joseph, *Royal,*" She had been calling him that since they left Knoxville, practicing, she said, so she wouldn't slip and give away his true identity.

"Don't worry about me." He was brusque because he *was* worried. Caroline was too clever to give him away. That would be his trick.

Her answering "I don't" was so soft it almost got lost in the folds of her new velvet cloak.

Rory stopped helping her into it to peer down at her face. Under her beauty, under the glow of her skin, he saw her confusion, her doubts. He hadn't been a bit gracious about having her here with him. Because of that, she now doubted herself.

He couldn't have that.

"Is this the same Caroline Farnsworth who took out a regiment of train robbers single-handedly?"

She considered that a moment. "You want me to poison the soup tonight?"

That was more like it.

He laughed and gave her a hug. "Not without warning me first."

It was the first time he had touched her spontaneously since he'd come to Knoxville to fetch her here. Caroline wrapped the cloak around her as though that would preserve the gesture and keep his warmth surrounding her.

In the six months they'd been away from New Mexico he'd more than kept his word about leaving her alone. A less stubborn woman than she would have given up on him and returned home. She was determined to see attraction in his avoidance of her. In Knoxville she'd taught school and read her way through Uncle Simon's library. She hoped the two activities had made her wiser as well as better informed. Only time would tell.

Rory regretted the hug immediately. Seeing her wrapped in that elegant cloak reminded him of the plain black one she'd worn back home. She looked regal and beautiful and unattainable now, but she had been far lovelier in the stable, lying before him just as God made her.

He pushed down the image and the urge that came with it like a dog following a butcher cart. He had to concentrate on the job at hand. His emotions were running so high it seemed impossible that Uncle Joseph wouldn't feel the spillover and recognize him instantly.

As if she read his mind, Caroline stopped at the door to survey him. "You look like a stranger," she pronounced. "Nothing like the Rory I used to know."

It was true. His new clothes were perfectly tailored to enhance the height and breadth of his superb body, completely erasing any remnant of the awkward or the homespun from his appearance. His hair, though still springy and thick, was probably darker and certainly longer. It brushed the collar of his starched shirt, falling in irresistible waves that emphasized the clean-cut thrust of his jaw.

Caroline's words were reassuring, but her tone, distanced and remote, raised the fine hairs on the back of Rory's neck. "I don't want to be a stranger to you, Caroline. Never that."

Her eyes warmed in response. "A handsome stranger?"

she teased. "An intriguing one? A *hairy* one?"

For, most disguising of all, Rory now sported a full mustache. Only his warm brown eyes, now sparkling with golden lights, were the same. He aimed a swat at her backside, missing completely as she sidled past him out into the crisp night air.

Caroline pulled the cloak tighter around her and tipped her head back to look up at the rising moon. It was round as a cookie. "Every time I step outside here I feel I should pinch myself awake. It's so . . . *vertical!*"

Lake City sat on a tiny plain at the base of some of the highest mountains in America, very near the Continental Divide, which was, according to Uncle Simon, somewhere beyond the next range of mountains. Or the range beyond *that*. Up here, where mountain piled on top of mountain in dizzying excess, preciseness didn't seem to matter much. Only the rivers could find their way out. Man had found his way *in* by following the rivers back toward their source. Here and there along the way, people had made settlements like Lake City.

The river here was a branch of the Gunnison River. It was called the Lake Fork, presumably because it led to Lake San Cristobal, which lay deeper within the mountains to the north.

Caroline found it easier to believe in Lake City during the day, when she could see the buildings for what they were: stores, liveries, saloons, hotels, banks and houses. At night, with only a few windows showing lights, even the most substantial structures looked flimsy, more like temporary scars on the land than permanent dwellings. Next to the grandeur of the mountains and the luster of the stars, what were a few wooden buildings lit by lamplight?

Her mood lightened considerably as soon as they reached their destination, the home of Wendell and Beatrice Davenport. There was nothing insubstantial about either of them. She had met Wendell upon her arrival and had liked him immediately. A spare man, he was so exceptionally tall that his shoulders were rounded from years of bending down to listen to what others had to say. He bent over her attentively, then passed her on to his wife.

Rory did not underestimate either Wendell Davenport or his wife. Beatrice resembled an overfed parrot, all garish plumage and raucous noise, but her eyes were both shrewd and kind. It was clear from everything Wendell said and did that his wife was his partner as well as his mate. Rory had seen enough of Jake and Hannah to recognize another such union. He was pleased to see it, believing that as soon as Beatrice took Caroline aside he would be able to relax and give his attention to Wendell's conversation.

But Beatrice had other ideas. She drew Caroline to sit beside her on a small couch covered by a Spanish shawl that clashed with both of their dresses. She kept one hand on Caroline, but she addressed her remarks to Rory.

"My dear boy," she trilled, "you've done the menfolk of Lake City the most *generous* good turn by bringing your sister here! We'll have her married off in no time, won't we, Mr. D.?"

"Now, Bea, settle yourself down," Wendell remonstrated. He spoke so gently that Rory knew he expected to have no impact on his wife's behavior.

Rory was stunned. It had never occurred to him that other men would consider Caroline fair game. Nor, to the best of his knowledge, had anyone else. Not Jake, Hannah or Uncle Simon.

He was amazed at everyone's stupidity. Particularly his own.

How could he have overlooked the most basic fact of frontier life, the scarcity of marriageable females, especially decent ones?

How would he stand it?

For a moment his glance locked with Caroline's and he saw that she, too, had overlooked the obvious. She smiled at him as though she were sharing a joke, and then she gave her attention back to Beatrice.

That lady was saying, "Now don't pay any mind to Priscilla. She's a perfectly *odious* woman, but her son is a gem. I think you and Gabriel would be lovely together."

Caroline didn't bother to look back at Rory. She knew he would not be amused at the prospect of having her paired romantically with Joseph Talmage's son. Nor was she. Odious or not, Priscilla was her quarry.

Before she could comment, Beatrice, spoke again, speculatively. "Your brother is a most handsome man."

Caroline concealed her surprise. Had Mrs. Davenport read something into her unspoken exchange with Rory? "I think he is, of course," she said stoutly, with what she hoped was a diverting smile. "Perhaps you can find a young lady to suit him as well. Someone who will tempt him away from his stuffy old business talk all the time."

Beatrice heaved a sigh of genuine regret. "Perhaps as the summer comes on conditions will improve for him. Mr. D. assures me that every day new families, not just single men, are streaming into the area, but I fear there are still far too few eligible ladies for a man like your brother. There are *women,* of course," she admitted, "and he might find one or two *tempting,* but not, I believe, for conversation. And certainly not for marriage."

She was scandalous, but Caroline couldn't help laughing; Beatrice looked so pleased with her daring. For herself, Caroline was heartened to think that Rory would not easily find another to love.

"You're sure Mr. and Mrs. Talmage haven't a daughter as well?"

"None that I've heard of."

"How long have you known them?"

"They arrived in the fall last year, just before we left for the winter. I'm only now beginning to renew my acquaintance, for we haven't been back long ourselves," Beatrice answered.

"They stayed through the winter here?"

"More and more people do that now. Particularly the very determined — like Joseph Talmage. Or perhaps I should say, like Priscilla."

Caroline pretended shock. "You mean Mrs. Talmage involves herself in her husband's *business?*"

Beatrice chuckled. "You'll see, my dear." She patted Caroline's hand.

Caroline did see.

Priscilla swept in on her son's arm, a woman who would always be the last to arrive in order to be sure of an audience. Her eyes flicked dismissively over Beatrice and Caroline to home in on Rory. She acknowledged his introduction with a regal nod and a coy smile. "Royal," she repeated, making the word sound like a caramel. "Such an appropriate name for a man who looks as majestic as a lion."

Caroline barely controlled a snicker. But Rory wasn't laughing. All his attention was focused on the man behind Priscilla. His uncle.

Because Rory was too nervous to notice, Caroline watched Joseph for a sign that he recognized his nephew. There was none. Priscilla's idiotic comment about his name had precluded any chance that he would connect this mature man with the boy he'd known back in St. Louis.

They shook hands without event, while Caroline reviewed Ernie's description of Joseph in her mind. An average man. Not tall, not short. Running to fat. He didn't look like Rory, and he looked even less like his black-haired son. Neither did he look like a villain.

Caroline smiled to herself at that thought. What did a villain look like anyway? Once she had believed she knew. Villains in her dime novels were hard-faced men with small, shifty eyes.

She knew better. She had seen three men who had been hanged for their crimes, Walt Stimpson, Moon and Baltimore Blackie; of the three, the one most responsible for their wrongdoing had been the best-looking. Most of the time Blackie had acted like a perfect gentleman, no more reprehensible than Gabriel Talmage or Rory.

Most of the time. That, she decided, was the key to villainy. It wasn't enough to be a gentleman most of the time, as Ted was. A good man had to be fine and caring all the time—like Papa and Rory and Uncle Simon.

At dinner Caroline was seated between Joseph and Gabriel, with Rory and Priscilla opposite her. Although she tried to engage Joseph in conversation from time to time, he was much more interested in talking to Wendell, who, as host, sat on his right at the head of the table.

Rory did better with Priscilla, so much better that Caroline was surprised when Priscilla suddenly addressed her. "Your name sounds familiar to me," she said in her deliberate way. "I just can't think where I've heard it before."

"Neither can I, Mrs. Talmage," Caroline answered with assurance she didn't feel. She didn't dare look at Rory. "Perhaps you knew someone else named Caroline?"

"Never." Priscilla's eyes narrowed to study her before she looked at her husband. "Help me out, Joseph." He shook his head, deflecting her appeal to her son. "Gabriel?"

"I would remember Miss Farnsworth, Mother."

"Not *her*," Priscilla corrected. "Her name."

"When I was in Philadelphia," she offered, making up her answer from whole cloth, "I heard of an actress named Caroline Farley. Perhaps that's the name you remember."

Priscilla wasn't convinced, Caroline could tell, but short of bringing up her involvement with Baltimore

Blackie's gang—which she wasn't going to do—there was no way to satisfy Priscilla. Rory said she had been in Dodge City at the time of Blackie's execution. Doubtless someone had bandied Caroline's name about within Priscilla's hearing.

Rory had called Priscilla a ghoul once, but even if she wasn't, Caroline didn't want that story to follow her to Colorado. Blackie was dead and so was that part of her life. She didn't want to revive it. Later, she and Rory could laugh about the fact that *her* name should ring a bell, and not his. She was feeling more and more useful to Rory all the time!

"This ham is simply delicious, Mrs. Davenport," she said, endeavoring to divert attention from herself. "I don't know what I expected the food to be like out here—perhaps beans and hardtack?—but I've been delighted to see such quality and variety available."

"It's much better now, isn't it, Priscilla?" Beatrice commented. "Did you suffer any hardships this winter?"

"Just the loss of my cook," she said petulantly. "And I brought the wretched woman here at my own expense."

"Is she ill then?" Caroline asked.

"She went and married one of the miners, and now *she's* going to hire someone to cook for her," Priscilla sniffed.

Caroline shouldn't have laughed, but it struck her as funny. "What a perfect story for this country," she enthused. "Everyone here is going to get rich!" Seeing Priscilla's displeasure with her, she quickly amended by way of apology, "Perhaps you could ask Mrs. Finn at the bakery for a recommendation. That's what I did. She sent me a Mrs. Larsen, and she's wonderful."

"*You* hired Mrs. Larsen?"

Puzzled by the woman's never-ending antagonism, Caroline stretched her courtesy to its limits and murmured, "I just said I did."

"I suppose you paid her the outrageous salary she

wanted?"

"She's well worth it," Caroline said. "She works very hard."

"It's people like you who give these ignorant immigrants ideas above their station and make life difficult for the rest of us."

"Actually, Mrs. Talmage," Caroline said firmly, "I think you'll find that 'ideas above their station' provide the impetus for all people who come out here prospecting for gold and silver. We're all immigrants here in the San Juans. And we're all here trying to better ourselves. I have no doubt that you and Mr. Talmage will succeed very nicely, just as I hope Mrs. Larsen and her husband do, too. Surely there's enough good fortune waiting for all of us to share it!"

"Now that sounds like the perfect toast," Wendell said, raising his glass. "Let's drink to that."

Grateful to be rescued from her soapbox, Caroline sent Rory a look of chagrin and lifted her glass. "To good fortune!" she proposed cheerily.

"And may good fortune also have a particular name," Rory added as he touched his glass to hers across the table. "To Little Josie!" That was the name Uncle Simon had given the silver mine he had bought. Rory was setting the bait for his uncle already.

Beatrice laughed, joining in. "To good fortune and Little Josie!"

When they had completed the ritual Gabriel asked, "Who is Josie, may I ask?"

Rory started to answer, then deferred to Caroline, saying, "You're better at explaining these family things."

"Josie was my Uncle Simon's sister. She died many years ago." She consulted Rory. "I guess that makes her an aunt, doesn't it? But she wasn't Uncle Simon's wife, I know that."

"If he's your uncle, then his sister may be considered to be your aunt," Beatrice told her.

302

Caroline didn't attempt to explain that neither she nor Rory was any relation to any of these people—much less to each other. It was all too confusing. Intentionally so, of course. But that was part of the plot and not to be revealed. Certainly not now.

"And Little Josie?" Joseph asked. "That's a mine?"

Before Rory could give whatever answer he thought appropriate, Caroline interrupted. "Just the best in the whole San Juan Mountains!" Then she looked guilty and crestfallen when Rory stared at her angrily. "I'm sorry." She sent a hesitant smile to Joseph. "I'm not supposed to say that."

"We *hope* it will be the best," Rory said, managing to sound stuffy, annoyed, and proud all at the same time.

Caroline went back to eating, looking as if she knew the world's biggest secret. She could feel Priscilla staring at her intently. Instead of responding to that curiosity, Caroline complimented Beatrice on the spiced fruit she had served as a side dish. Throughout their discussion of chutneys and glazes, Priscilla waited to ask her question.

Or so Caroline thought.

But Joseph spoke first. "Is Little Josie a new claim?"

Caroline let Rory answer. "It was called Golden Chance before Uncle Simon took over the claim," he said.

Joseph laughed then, sounding relieved and smug. "I hope he didn't pay much for it. That claim played out ages ago."

Caroline erupted. "Oh, but that's—" She clamped her hand over her mouth, stopping herself as if by force, and sent Rory another apologetic look.

"We hope not," Rory said judiciously, sounding as though what he really wanted to do was to strangle Caroline.

She settled back, chastised, to wait for Priscilla's question.

"Has your uncle . . . Simon, is it?" Caroline nodded

303

eagerly. "Has he much experience mining? Is he here?"

"He's never done quite *this* before," she admitted, trying for a blend of pride and reluctance, "but he's been very well advised." Caroline smiled at Wendell. "Mr. Davenport has been kind enough to act for Uncle Simon until now. Now, of course, Royal will do his best."

Rory harrumphed modestly.

For a moment Caroline worried that Priscilla and Joseph—or certainly Gabriel—would see through the charade. Surely they were playing their parts *too* well.

But no. Even Beatrice and Wendell seemed enthralled. Perhaps they too were hopeful gamblers. If not, what were they doing in Lake City?

"Uncle Simon's advisors are always the best," Caroline said with great finality.

"His name is Simon Farnsworth?" Priscilla. Doubtfully.

"Oh, no. He's Simon Sargent. He's my mother's uncle," Caroline said. "He used to be involved with the Union Pacific Railroad, back when it was just starting out. He bought his way out of that company of rascals, taking quite a financial loss for the time, because he found out that his partners were actually *buying* favorable votes from senators and congressmen in order to get the laws they wanted enacted. I'm sure you heard of them? The *Credit Mobilier?* That was the group."

She wondered if her voice took on added conviction now that she was speaking the absolute truth. Certainly it required no acting ability to portray her pride in Uncle Simon's character.

Once he had joked that he had ultimately made money from the loss just because withdrawing had enhanced his reputation for honesty. One of his maxims now went: Every man wants to do business with an honest man, even if he doesn't want to *be* an honest man.

For whatever reason, either because of her conviction or because she had acting ability she'd never tapped before, her audience was persuaded to believe her. The knot of anxiety that had been all but disabling melted away. Caroline relaxed and began to enjoy herself.

And to think that before tonight she'd thought herself ill equipped for subterfuge! She'd been rehearsing a speech for Rory earlier when he had knocked on her door at home, telling him she was too blunt and plain-spoken, too open of countenance to be any help to him. She'd never been a good liar, she had intended to say, so how could he expect her to play such an important role in his scheme?

But of course she had said nothing about her doubts. How could she? He hadn't asked for her help. She was the one who had insisted upon coming to Colorado, insisted on offering "help" where it wasn't even wanted.

Now she was glad. She chatted with Gabriel and Beatrice like the amiable ninny she had shown herself to be, all the while listening to Joseph make his first cautious move toward Rory.

His offer was elaborately casual. "Even with the best advice in the world," Joseph was saying, "mining is a risky venture. I've been quite fortunate, so perhaps I could be of some help to you and your uncle. And if you're looking for investors, I just might possibly be interested. I'll keep it in mind."

Rory pretended a diffident sort of gratitude, and that ended their discussion.

It was enough, though. Rory had presented the bait and Joseph had snapped at it. That fact was further confirmed for Caroline when Priscilla next spoke. Not only did she address herself to Caroline, she also spoke pleasantly for the first time to someone other than Rory.

"How did you happen to accompany your brother, Miss Farnsworth?" she asked in a purring drawl. "I'm afraid you'll find your social circle will be severely limited out here."

Caroline was prepared for the question. "Actually there

305

are a number of reasons, so you can almost take your pick from among them. My parents wanted to get me away from the young man next door, so to speak. It's miles away to the next ranch in New Mexico, but they worried that I'd choose to marry him against their wishes. Then Uncle Simon wanted me to be his hostess, and *I* wanted adventure."

She smiled at everyone, noting that Rory was glowering at her again, but not for effect with the Talmages. She decided to use that as well. Gesturing to Rory, she went on with a shrug. "As you can see, poor Royal is the only one whose wishes were not consulted. So he's stuck with me."

Beatrice began to laugh noisily. Gabriel joined her, asking, *"Would* you have married the boy next door if you'd stayed at home?"

"I really don't think so, but I was so *bored* there," she confessed. "I haven't been bored at all here, and now that I survived the trip over the mountains, I don't think I'll ever dare leave here. Not if it means climbing back up into one of those Concord coaches again!"

No one, least of all Rory, could doubt that she spoke from the heart.

"Oh, my dear child, how right you are!" exclaimed Beatrice. "Every year I tell Mr. D. I'm not making the trip again. Next year I swear I'm doing as you do, Priscilla. I'm staying for the winter."

"I'd rather ride a mule the whole way," Caroline said fervently. "And what made it worse for me was having to put up with Royal telling me what a marvel of modern engineering the coach was!"

"But it is," Rory insisted. "The suspension system prevents it from overturning no matter how bad or how steep the roadbed—"

"Roadbed!" Caroline scoffed. "There was no roadbed. There was barely a trail fit for a mountain goat!"

"But we didn't overturn," Rory concluded trium-

306

phantly.

"No. You're right, and I was warned. I just didn't believe anything could be so terrible."

Before the trip into these San Juan Mountains, Caroline had considered herself a seasoned traveler. She'd ridden every kind of animal and every conveyance, from a steamboat to a train to a rustic cart. But Rory's "miracle of modern engineering," the Concord coach, had humbled her of all pretensions to hardiness.

If careening along at the side of one precipice after another wasn't bad enough, there was the constant, sickening lurch and sway of the coach itself to contend with. Designed with no springs at all to cushion passengers from the jolts of the road, the coach hung like a giant egg from thick leather straps that stretched horizontally from the front to the back of the frame. Pendulum-like, the coach swung back and forth, tipping up and down in its never-ending search for equilibrium. Because it was free to seek its own center of gravity, no matter what the road held, the coach did indeed remain upright. But at what cost!

Of course, now she was glad they had arrived in one piece, but at the time of the trip she would have traded her life for suspended motion.

Caroline was unprepared for Rory's silence on the way home. At first she thought he was savoring their success, as she was, but when they were well away from Davenport's house she realized differently. Driving the rutted roadway might require his attention, but not such a deep frown.

"What's the matter, Rory? Did Joseph say something I didn't hear?" For the last part of the evening Gabriel had claimed most of her attention.

Without looking at her, he shook his head. "Later," he said tersely. "When we get home."

Caroline pushed down her uneasiness and concentrated on keeping her seat. Like everything in Lake City, the

307

material for their carriage had made the same perilous, expensive trip over the mountains she had bemoaned earlier in the evening. For that reason, their carriage was primitive, more supply wagon than elegant vehicle. Ordinarily Caroline appreciated such practicality, but not tonight. Successful or not, the evening had been a strain. She was tired.

She ignored Rory's tight-lipped silence when he helped her down. She was no longer curious about his mood, sure his discussion could keep till morning.

Rory had other ideas.

She was sleepily brushing out her hair, already dressed for bed, when he knocked on her door, back from tending the horses. This time it was no light tap, but a peremptory demand for admittance. She dropped the brush with a clatter he took for permission to enter.

"Can't this wait for morning?" she asked, turning to look at him. "I'm tired."

Rory knew he should have waited. He hadn't the self-control to confront her now, but he was ready to explode.

She had surprised him. Over the years he had prided himself on his understanding of Caroline. With the single exception of her decision to marry Ted, she had never said or done anything out of character. He had even understood that decision, wrongheaded though it had been. That mistake, at least, had been true to her character.

"What the hell were you doing tonight?" he demanded.

She picked up the brush, turned away from him and drew it down through her hair. The motion lifted her breasts and made them press against the front of her nightgown. "I thought it went rather well."

"Well? When did you become such a perfect little liar?"

"Is that what's bothering you?"

In the mirror he saw the way her lips turned up in a

smug smile. He grabbed her arm and tugged her around to look at him. "Shouldn't it?" he asked sharply. "I thought I knew you." He only just managed to control the urge to shake her.

"Did you want me to spoil the whole thing for you?"

"No!" Put that way, it was his only possible answer, but it wasn't the one he wanted to give.

"Well, then? Why are you complaining?"

He dropped her arm and stalked away. He had no idea what to say. She was so logical and he felt so . . . not *illogical*, just . . . upset. Disconcerted.

"If it's any comfort to you, Rory, I surprised myself, too. I was afraid I'd ruin everything." She waited for him to stop pacing and look at her. "Can't you just be pleased?"

He wanted to be, but he needed his anger. Otherwise he was afraid of what he might do. Coming to her room like this had been a gigantic mistake. "Should I also be pleased that you made a fool of yourself over Gabriel Talmage?"

"I did not!"

"No? That's what it looked like to me. *Priscilla* was supposed to be your target, not her son."

"They go together," she defended.

"Not from where I sat. She was looking daggers at you every time you smiled at him. He's completely unimportant. You're supposed to concentrate on Priscilla and leave him alone. See that you remember that."

With that, Rory marched out the door, leaving Caroline sputtering. She clenched the hairbrush and started to throw it at the door. She stayed her hand, first because she was afraid its bounce onto the wall might puncture the wallpaper. Then she thought of a better reason for self-control.

Rory was jealous.

The signs were unmistakable.

Smiling broadly now, Caroline went back to brushing

her hair, too happy to feel tired any more. She had hoped to please Rory tonight. Instead, she had pleased herself.

That was even better.

Chapter Twenty-six

In the days following their confrontation, Caroline saw little of Rory. He was up early and home late. Since he was indeed Uncle Simon's agent in booming Lake City, Caroline understood that he was legitimately busy — quite apart from the fact that he was also avoiding her.

She understood. There were unresolved issues between them, issues she was both eager to settle and terrified to tackle. The folly of her aborted wedding and its aftermath — particularly making love with Rory — had given her a different perspective on life. She'd come away from the stable shaken and torn and very much in need of guidance.

But from whom? Had she stayed in New Mexico she would have probably — eventually — consulted Hannah. That her questions would have revealed her loss of innocence didn't concern her overmuch. Hannah was not a censorious person. She could also be trusted. She would answer embarrassing questions honestly and not betray Caroline's confidence to Papa.

But Caroline hadn't remained at home. She had been gone long before she was able to work through her feelings of guilt to confront the questions she needed answered. Uncle Simon was sweet and dear, but he held even Hannah at arm's length.

That left Rory. He had been her closest friend for a dozen years. Once she had imagined she could say anything to him, ask anything of him. But no more.

What they had done together in the hay had been the most thrilling experience of Caroline's life. It had also

311

been the most costly. In exchange for a few moments of physical intimacy with Rory, she had given up not only her virginity and her heart, but also all the deeper intimacy she had shared with Rory for so long.

Being Caroline, however, she didn't give up. She turned to books for her answers. It took longer, but she had all winter to give to it. She had always read for pleasure. Reading for information was not so different, just harder, because she had no way to test the efficacy of what she learned. Now that she was again with Rory she intended to do that.

But not yet. The time was not right. They had to get reacquainted first.

In the meantime Caroline concentrated on learning about Colorado and silver mining, and on getting to know the Talmages. She took Rory's proscription against Gabriel very much to heart, but not to the extent of obeying him. She agreed that Gabe, as he'd asked to be called, was unimportant to their scheme. He had no apparent influence with Joseph and no financial ambition that Caroline could see.

Nevertheless, he was the key to Priscilla. Caroline had not observed his mother's overt jealousy at Davenports', but she didn't doubt it existed. Priscilla doted on her son. Ordinarily that would be cause for Caroline to *avoid* Gabe in the hope of winning the woman's friendship. But Priscilla was a special case. She was not a woman to have friends, particularly not another woman.

In Priscilla's case, Caroline decided that none of the normal rules applied. Priscilla would pay attention to Caroline only as a rival for her son's affections—unwillingly, perhaps, and never out of a desire to know and like her son's friend.

In making her decision to use Gabriel to get at Priscilla, Caroline thought long and hard. She didn't like to oppose Rory and wouldn't do so lightly. Nor would she encourage Gabriel to be anything more than a friend. He

312

was a Talmage, but he hadn't harmed Rory and she didn't want to hurt him. Fortunately, he seemed to feel the same way about her.

In spite of her happiness at discovering that Rory felt jealous of Gabe, Caroline didn't want to make Rory jealous any more. From what she knew of jealousy, it was a terrible thing. She wanted an honest, open, loving relationship with Rory—just as soon as he would permit it.

So on the rare occasion when Rory asked how she had spent her time, she told him, quite honestly, that she had visited Priscilla or Beatrice or that they had visited her. She didn't mention Gabe or the fact that he had driven her carriage more often than she had. Rory didn't need to know that because it wasn't important.

Rory informed her that Joseph had visited Little Josie twice and professed himself to be impressed. His offer to invest in the mine had been refused. Eventually, Rory would accept his money, but not so easily. First, he would whet Joseph's appetite for the venture by being reluctant to sell any shares. Each refusal, Rory reported, made Joseph more eager to invest. Already he had doubled his original offer.

Besides running the house, Caroline had found two small projects to help pass the time she was alone. The first involved teaching two boys to read. Lake City had a school, but these boys, both foreign-born sons of mine workers, one from Wales and one from Cornwall, England, didn't attend. They came to her irregularly and not always together, yet both were bright and eager to learn. She took them as they came, delighting in their humor and liveliness.

She expected less from her second enterprise, a small kitchen garden. She found it hard to imagine that seeds could germinate here within sight of mountains still deeply covered in snow. Nevertheless, when she went out to check she discovered several ragged rows of carrot,

313

bean and pea seedlings. Soon they would need to be thinned, but not yet. For now she could only stand and admire them. After a few minutes of that she felt silly and went inside.

And found Rory in the kitchen. "Is something wrong?" she asked, surprised.

"Wrong? Of course not."

"But you never come home so early. I sent Mrs. Larsen home."

"That's all right," he laughed. "I didn't come to see Mrs. Larsen."

"Oh."

"Where were you?"

"Outside." Laughing, she led him, unresisting, to her garden. "Isn't this wonderful? We'll have *fresh* peas and beans this summer."

Rory looked from the scraggly little plants to Caroline's glowing face. Did she really think she had to raise her own food? Trying not to hurt her feelings, he said carefully, "It's very nice."

Her face fell anyway. "Nice! Is that all you can say?"

He tried harder. "It's better than nice. You're right. It *is* wonderful."

"No, *you're* right. It's ridiculous, isn't it?" Her shoulders sagged as she saw the lovingly planted little plot realistically for the first time. "It'll be September before there's any yield. I must be losing my mind. It just seemed like such a good idea."

Rory hated to think he had been responsible for her loss of enthusiasm. He patted her arm. "If you enjoy it, that's all that matters."

She drew away from him stiffly. He meant it kindly, but that wasn't the idea at all. Although she had been filling her time, she'd also meant to do something useful. That was what he didn't understand.

Rory followed her inside, feeling helpless and mean. Did he always have to trample and crush what he loved

314

most about her, her spirit?

"Mrs. Larsen did up some fried chicken and biscuits for you. Would you like to eat now?"

"Maybe we could take it with us." He folded his arms and leaned back against a shelf. "Seeing your garden made me forget why I came home. I have something to show you. If you pack up the food we can have a picnic."

"Really? Where are we going?"

"It's a surprise. Why don't you go put on something so you can ride. Did you bring those scandalous pants you love?"

"No, but I have a split skirt." She was flying around the kitchen, gathering up provisions for a basket.

Rory was disappointed. Although he pretended disinterest in her work pants, the picture of her thighs and bottom encased in worn denim figured prominently in his fantasies of Caroline. He took the basket from her. "Go put it on then. I'll finish this."

"Don't forget napkins!" she tossed back, whirling away.

She was back before he had found where she kept them.

"What on earth are you doing?" she asked from the doorway.

He looked up from the drawer he was rummaging. "You asked for napkins."

She pulled out a chair and pointed him to it. Then she went around shutting the drawers and cupboard doors, smoothing ruffled contents as necessary to close them. The napkins were on the table in plain sight. She wrapped them around sturdy tumblers and added them to the basket. "Shall I bring a jug of water?"

"There's a stream up there."

"Then we're going up into the mountains?"

"You'll see."

Caroline asked no more questions, assuming that she

was at last going to be permitted to see Uncle Simon's mine, Little Josie. Always before Rory had put her off, saying the men were working there. She had accepted that explanation, knowing miners were superstitious, especially about allowing women into their province.

But Rory took an entirely different trail out of town, away from the massive Uncompahgre Range that dominated the skyline. "This isn't the way to Little Josie," she called to his back after a long, unsuccessful wrestle with her curiosity.

"No, it isn't," he said without turning.

Caroline vowed never to speak to him again. Within minutes she had broken her vow by saying, "Oh, Rory, look!"

They followed a tight switchback that dropped away on their right to reveal alternating stands of bull pine and quaking aspen, the chalky trunks of the white poplar vivid against the shadowed rocks and darker pines. A golden eagle circled above the trees, riding invisible currents in the air just below eye level.

Rory stopped to look back at her, not the scenery. He saw trees and birds every day. They were magnificent, but she was more so. A slanted shaft of sunlight spilled over her, highlighting her pale hair that was like the mix of gold and silver hidden in the folds of the mountains around them. Men killed for metal worth less than she was to him, he thought.

The eagle soared, wheeling close enough to show them its powerful hooked bill, then plunged out of sight into the ravine below. When it was gone Caroline sought Rory's eyes. She was pleased to see that he was as moved as she was.

"Thank you for bringing me here, Rory. I'll never forget this."

"We're not there yet," he said, turning away quickly.

Getting "there" involved leaving the broad trail that was wide enough for a team of horses, to follow a much

316

narrower way. It was no steeper, but the entrance to this path was so obscure only an informed person would discover it.

"How did you ever find this trail?" Caroline asked, looking behind in wonder. If she hadn't just passed through that opening in the rock wall beside them she would never have believed it existed.

"I didn't find it. Sally did."

"Sally?"

"Remember the burro I told you about?"

"The one you rescued?"

"That's an exaggeration. I had a use for her and Foster didn't." Foster drove the pack train between Little Josie and the Crooke Smelter, a mile or so outside of Lake City, where the ore was processed.

Caroline knew better. Rory had saved Sally from destruction just the way he kept Duchess alive years after her usefulness had passed. Foster would have pushed the injured burro off a mountain pass. It was a common— and inhumane—practice. Mule skinners were notoriously harsh. Unsentimental, they called it.

"You rode Sally up here?" she asked.

"I was exploring. That's why I wanted her, after all."

"Didn't your feet drag?" she asked, smiling at the picture of tall Rory on a burro. Big though he was, his two hundred pounds would be nothing for Sally after the usual pack animal's load of five hundred pounds.

"We looked pretty strange," he said, grinning. "She was thirsty, so she went through that opening in the rock. I guess she could smell the water. Anyway, she brought me here."

Dismounting, he lifted her down from her horse. They stood in a formation of rock shaped like a giant amphitheater. Although it was open to the sky, the light was dim because of the steep, slightly in-curving sides all around.

"It's magical, Rory. I've never seen anything like it."

Caroline turned slowly to look at everything. "What a perfect place for a picnic."

"You must be hungry if that's your first thought."

"Where's the water? I can hear it."

He led her around another rock curtain to where a small cascade tumbled noisily along the face of the mountain. "It's snowmelt, I'm sure, but it will do for us."

Caroline got the lunch basket while Rory spread a blanket. There was no vegetation, just loose scree to cushion them from the tipped rock base under the blanket. Rory filled the tumblers with water as Caroline unwrapped the food.

She touched her glass to Rory's. "Here's to Sally."

He laughed and took a sip. "Amen to that."

"Is something wrong?" she asked when he refused her offer of food.

He shook his head. "No, it's right. Everything is right." He found a way to settle the glass safely beside him and reached out to touch her arm with a gentle finger. "I want to remember this always. This place. You."

Deeply touched, Caroline put the food aside, untouched. She looked down at her hands, clasped tightly in her lap. "Does that mean you've forgiven me for forcing myself on you?"

"You've never done that."

"You wanted me to go home."

"For your own good."

She chanced a look at him as soon as she felt his eyes leave her face. The rocks made an appropriate background for his strongly etched profile. "We have different notions about what's good for me."

"You'd be safe there."

"Papa didn't think so."

"He was worried about the wrong man."

"I don't think so. I think he and Hannah want me to

marry you." She felt daring just saying it.

He didn't look at her. "Maybe they do. That doesn't mean we have to oblige them. People don't always get what they want."

"You will," Caroline said. "I'm sure of it."

He looked at her then. "Are you?"

"Look how well everything is going. Joseph can't wait to give you his money."

He wasn't convinced, she could tell. He drew up his knees and wrapped his arms around them. Everything about his posture proclaimed his separateness, his aloneness.

"Have you changed your mind about Joseph now that you've seen him again?"

"No. He's as much a bastard as I remembered."

"You don't feel sorry for him at all?" she questioned softly, probing—gently, she hoped—for the source of his unhappiness.

His look was hostile, a reprimand for a backslider from the true faith. "He didn't feel sorry for my father."

"You misunderstand me, Rory. I'm only trying to figure out why you're unhappy." Then she realized. He hadn't been unhappy before they began this discussion. What had she said to disturb him? "It's me, isn't it? *I* make you unhappy."

"If you do, would I have asked you to come here with me?"

"I don't know. There's so much I don't understand."

"About me?" He laughed harshly. "I'm clear as glass."

"Not to me, you aren't. I used to think I knew you, but since . . ." She couldn't bring herself to mention their lovemaking.

He knew anyway. "Caroline, I told you that would never happen again."

She bowed her head. "I know. I just wish there was someone I could ask. . . ." Again her voice faded as she lost courage.

"Ask what?"

She wiped her damp palms on her skirt and stayed stubbornly silent. She wanted to know, but she was so afraid of what he might say.

"Is something wrong with you?" Alarm sharpened his voice.

"I don't know."

"Tell me, Caroline. Jesus, you have to tell me what it is!"

Rory didn't let her hide. He caught her shoulders and turned her to face him. The look on his face convinced her she had to speak, if only to relieve him of *his* worries. She could bear her own, but not the fact that she was frightening him.

She licked her lips in a futile attempt to combat the dryness in her mouth. "You're the only one who can answer that question, Rory. I've thought and thought about it, but I don't know what I did wrong."

"When?"

Her skin began to heat. "You know . . . when we . . ."

"When we made love?"

She nodded.

He stared at her, uncomprehending.

"I thought men enjoyed . . ." His harried expression forced her on. "But you didn't," she whispered finally.

His hands dropped from her shoulders, and she sagged. She wanted to bury her face in her hands, but pride prevented it. She had put him on the spot. But whatever discomfort he felt, he had to understand that it was worse for her.

"Please be honest, Rory. I really need to know."

He raked his fingers through his hair, his expression disbelieving. "Let me get this straight," he said at length. "You think I didn't enjoy making love to you?"

"I know you didn't."

Incredibly, he laughed. Or she thought he laughed. It was a strange, choked sound. *"How* do you know that?"

"By the way you acted." She could see he was going to force her to elaborate. His unkindness when she had expected at least compassion made her angry. "All right," she said, "I'll spell it out. You looked like you were in pain and you sounded it, too." Embarrassed, she raced to finish before she expired on the spot. "Now I'm not so ignorant about that any more—"

"Why not?"

"I read some books Uncle Simon had and I learned . . . well, I guess that's common to men. Perhaps." She wasn't clear about that, however, and didn't want to be deflected from her most telling point. Nothing could be worse than what she was going through now. She wanted it over, but complete. "Then afterward . . . you were even *more* miserable and you didn't touch me again . . . or want me to touch you."

"Because I felt like the lowest piece of slime for what I'd done to you."

She couldn't let that pass. She remembered everything much too clearly. "What I asked . . . no, *begged* you to do."

"You were innocent, Caroline. It was up to me to—"

"I was ignorant, Rory, not innocent. I knew what I wanted."

"You wanted comfort, not lust," he said severely.

"And because it was lust you couldn't enjoy it?"

Rory worked to contain a shout of laughter. He pulled her into his arms, her face against his chest so he could at least let himself smile. "Caroline, this is the damnedest conversation I've ever had in my life." He held her head in place with one hand and tried to set her straight. "I did enjoy myself, as you so quaintly put it—enormously, in fact. Whatever was wrong about what we did wasn't your fault. You have to believe me. You're a beautiful, wonderful woman and you did nothing wrong."

"But something was wrong," she said, trying to understand. She pulled her head back against his slackened hand, able to look up at his shadowed face. "Please, Rory, I don't have anyone else to talk to."

"I'm sorry about that, too."

Caroline shook her head. "You're too hard on yourself." Her hands were flat on his chest. She raised one to his chin and let it touch down lightly. His mustache tempted her. How would it feel? Under her fingers? Against her lips?

As if he read her thoughts, he pulled back.

"You're doing it again," she said.

"Doing what?"

"Not letting me touch you."

"Caroline, I'm a man, and when you touch me I get . . . excited."

"So do I," she said softly. She put her hand against his cheek. "Your skin feels different from mine, even on your face. Harder, rougher . . ." She moved her hand slowly over the clenched contour of his jaw. She saw that a muscle jumped under the surface and rejoiced. He wasn't indifferent. Not at all. "I thought I might hurt you somehow when I wanted to do this before. I didn't understand."

Her whispery voice was like the slither of satin along his skin. Rory held himself absolutely still. He reminded himself that she was still innocent. Although she didn't realize what she was doing to him, she needed to know that her touch wasn't repulsive. He knew now that in making love to her before he had not only taken her innocence but also robbed her of confidence in her femininity. Of the two losses, the second was the more profound, especially coming as it did on top of Ted's rejection.

"How did you think you could hurt me?" he managed to ask.

"Not physically—well, at least not physically *afterward*."

Laughing helped relieve his tension. "I was trying not

322

to hurt you, but I did."

"No, you didn't. It was just a twinge and I was prepared for that. I mean, I knew about that. It was the other I wasn't prepared for."

"What other?" Her hand rested—at last—on the side of his neck.

"We had been so close, like . . . one person." She looked up from his chin and met his warm brown gaze. His eyes were beautiful, eyes to get lost in, but her face heated, and she went back to addressing his chin. "Then you pulled away from me and I felt . . . worse than before. Lonely. Exposed, I guess." She laughed self-consciously. "Well, I was, too."

"Caroline—"

"I wanted to comfort you, but I was afraid to touch you. You were so stiff and cold."

"You were crying. I thought . . . I *knew* I'd hurt you."

"No."

"You said you were glad you hadn't gotten married."

She had forgotten that. She looked up quickly and saw that he was waiting. He needed reassurance as much as she did. "I thought I'd just proved myself to be as . . . unwomanly as Ted said."

Rory let his breath out slowly, savoring the relief he felt. But there was one more thing he had to say. "Caroline, I don't believe Ted meant what he said to you. That doesn't excuse his cruelty—not entirely, anyway—but I'm sure that was just his pride speaking."

Caroline moved back to look at him. "You defend him. Why?"

"You wanted to marry him. If you still feel that way, you shouldn't let a stupid quarrel stand between you."

"You think that's what it was?"

"Maria could have been lying."

"That's not what he said."

"If she had been," he persisted, "would you still want to marry him?"

323

"I don't think I ever did. I can't remember why I agreed. That sounds shallow, doesn't it?" She pulled herself away from Rory's embrace, feeling strange in some vague way. Not guilty, just . . . unworthy. She had made a mistake. She couldn't blame Rory for bringing it up. She had been about to *marry* another man. That wasn't a small transgression that he should overlook out of charity. In his place she wouldn't easily forgive, either.

Rory felt her withdrawal and let her go, wishing he'd cut out his tongue. Every time he mentioned Ted, she wrapped that figurative cloak of separation around her. When would Ted lose his power over her? Ever?

"I wish you could forget about Ted," Caroline said wistfully. "I know it's a lot to ask, but I hate talking about him."

Rory put his hands on his knees for safekeeping. If only he'd kissed her instead of being so damned noble. "Fine with me," he said. In trying to sound brisk and unconcerned, his voice rang hollow. He rubbed his hands up and down his pant legs, brushing them off. "We should get to that lunch, don't you think?"

With heartiness as false as his, Caroline turned to the forgotten food. "Of course. Leave it to me to natter on so and keep you from eating."

He looked at what she offered, wanting to refuse and draw her back into his arms, where she belonged. Her eyes were guarded, but they held something else, too. Was it longing?

He took the chicken reluctantly.

Caroline couldn't help herself. She put her hand on his arm. "I'm glad we talked, Rory."

He nodded. Talked. He bit savagely into the chicken, calling himself every kind of fool. He had ruined the day. Next time, he promised himself, he would use his tongue to better purpose and kiss her senseless.

She passed him a napkin; then, before he could take it, she leaned up and brushed it lightly over his mouth.

"I like your mustache."

Rory lifted the back of his hand to his mouth, hiding a smile. There would be a next time. Her tender smile told him so.

Chapter Twenty-seven

The Silver Spur was full—full of smoke and noise. Saturday night. Maria Martinez looked over the sweating, red-faced cowboys and wanted to scream. She would not stay in Rio Mogollon. She would not.

How many times had she said that in the last month? She meant every word of it, but meaning it and doing something about it were two different things. She needed money first. She had the money her father had sent her, but it wasn't enough. Thank God she hadn't used it to go to Mexico as he wanted. Now that he was dead she would never go there again.

She frowned, thinking how different her life would be if her mother had not left her father, Miguel, to come to the American Territories. Miguel would not have taken up with that bitch Hernanda and she, Maria, would be his only child. Hernanda wasn't even her father's wife. Her children were illegitimate, but did she care? No.

Maria laughed harshly. She wouldn't care either if she had Miguel's money as Hernanda did.

"Maria! You got customers," Vinnie yelled. "Hop to!"

Hop to, Maria mimicked, mouthing the words silently. She was supposed to smile. She would not.

Next week, she vowed. Next week she would go.

She poured watered-down beer, giving scant rations exactly the way Vinnie ordered, not because she wanted to please him but because it pleased her to cheat men. Men—all of them—were responsible for her troubles. Her father by dying, Ted's father by dying, too, and Ted . . . Yes. Most of all, Ted. Everything was his fault.

She plunked a glass in front of a wiry-looking dark-haired man. Beer slopped the sides of the glass and puddled on the table. She paid no attention until the man's hand lashed out and caught her arm.

"Take it back," he said, his deep voice cutting through the whoops and hollers around them. "I paid for a full glass."

Maria took it to the next customer and gave him another. She smirked her lips in imitation of a smile that made him laugh. He was pale in comparison to the leather-faced men around him, but the lines radiating from his eyes made her think his pallor was new.

He was new, she noticed. Probably a hand just hired on at some ranch. Exactly what she didn't need, another cowboy.

She spent the night ignoring him in spite of the fact that she was aware of him all night long. She knew everything he did, everyone he talked to. She knew he asked Mitch Cooper about her because of the way Mitch's eyes swung around to look at her after the stranger spoke to him. It wasn't hard to guess what Mitch told him. She was a local joke.

She had done only one thing right. She had stopped Ted from marrying Caroline Farnsworth. That still delighted her. All those people in the church. Her mother weeping. Jake Farnsworth shoving Ted across the aisle into his father's arms. And, especially, Caroline Farnsworth's face bleached whiter than her dress, looking ready to cry.

Remembering her triumph still had the power to soothe her spirits, but it wasn't enough. It wasn't done yet. *She* wasn't done yet.

Although Maria didn't realize it, the stranger was exactly the man to appreciate her story. He was attracted to more than her voluptuous beauty. Her restless, obvious discontent drew him even more.

Indicating Maria by a subtle shift of his shoulder and head, he said to the man next to him, "The *señorita* doesn't smile much."

327

Mitch guffawed and swiveled to look first at Maria, then at the man beside him. "Maria? Naw, she don't talk to pe-ons and cowboys. She's meant for better things." He parodied drinking tea with his meaty small finger crooked incongruously on his beer glass.

"What's she doing here then?"

"She's a little down on her luck. Temporary, I reckon for her. She's had a few ups an' downs awready, though."

"She's local?"

"More or less." Mitch wiped his mouth on his sleeve and looked pointedly into his empty glass. When the stranger had it refilled, he went on. "She come from Mexico years ago with her mama. Lupe, she works for Farnsworth out to Renegade Ranch, but Maria ain't never liked bein' somebody's do-mestic. Ever' once in a while she disappears down to Mexico, visitin' her pappy. Now I hear he up'n died on her."

The man listening waited for the story to continue. What he saw in Maria's face wasn't grief for a dead father. It was malice. "So she's all alone in the world, is that it?"

"Jest temporary, like I say. Old Maria, she lands on her pretty little feet. She thought she had it all figgered out once, but that didn't quite work." Mitch chuckled, his shoulders shaking as he remembered the wedding. "She sure did make it excitin' for a while 'round here, stoppin' the weddin' like that."

"She was getting married?"

"Naw, Miss Caroline over to Farnsworth's was marryin' Ted Jasper. We all knew he was foolin' with Maria, but Miss Caroline didn't. Not till Maria jumped up in church and yelled out, 'He can't marry *her*, he's gotta marry me!' "

"That right?"

"Then she told ever'body how old Ted had put a loaf in her oven."

"When was this?" the stranger asked sharply.

328

"Let's see, 'twas back 'fore Christmas, 'bout November sometime."

"She doesn't look pregnant."

"Weren't no baby, I 'spect. So did the Jaspers. But Miss Caroline, she didn't care. The weddin' was over. Her pappy 'bout killed Jasper and ever'body figgers the shame of it all killed *his* pappy. So now Jasper runs his own ranch, but he don't have no wife. Jest his mama. *She* sure is a nice lady!"

"So Jasper didn't marry Maria. Why? Because there was no baby?"

"He wouldn't of cared if there'd been ten. He wasn't never gonna marry Maria. She was a damn fool, that's all."

"Jasper couldn't patch things up with Miss Caroline?" He carefully referred to Caroline the way Mitch did.

"She took off next day for parts unknown."

"That right? No one knows where she went?"

"I don't, that's sure."

"Where do you work?"

"I work for that bastard Jasper. If you're lookin' for work, that's the place. Somebody's always leavin' there. Thought it was bad with his pappy, but now's worse. I ain't stayin' much longer."

"What about Farnsworth's? They got work?" He already knew he wouldn't learn more about Caroline's whereabouts at Jasper's ranch. Perhaps he'd do better at her home place.

"They got work, jest don't need no workers. Nobody ever leaves there. Gotta wait till somebody *dies* to get a job there. I been tryin' for years."

"I see."

Mitch watched the man's eyes follow Maria while he finished his drink. "What's your name, fella?"

"Al."

"Well, Al," he said confidingly, "if'n you're interested in Maria, I'd say you got more chance than anyone I

329

seen in a while."

"That right?"

Mitch nodded vigorously. "You been watchin' her pretty good, I notice, but then I notice somethin' else. She's been noticin' you right back, and Maria don't do that."

Al had noticed that, too.

"Could be 'cuz you look a whole lot like Ted Jasper. Not 'xactly, but you're the type. You could be his cousin, if he had one. Mebbe a brother."

Al smiled to hear it. He clapped his companion's shoulder and got up to leave. "That's good," he said. "I look like a bastard, do I?"

Mitch raised his hands, spreading his palms in a show of innocence. Standing up, Al looked menacing all of a sudden. "Looks ain't ever'thin'," he said with an ingratiating grin.

Al's hand left his shoulder abruptly. "Fortunately," he said.

Then he was gone.

Maria watched him leave, experiencing that strange tug of awareness that had been with her all night. But for Mitch Cooper, the man would have talked to her. He hadn't been pleasant, but his voice was compelling. She wanted to hear it again.

Instead, she heard more of Vinnie's "Hop to." She gave Mitch Cooper a dirty look that sent him away. That was fine with her. Mitch worked for Ted and she didn't care to be reminded of him. But then Ernie Coogins slid into Mitch's chair, and that was worse. Coogins was Zeb Prentiss's best friend. Zeb, her mother's skinny lover. It made her sick. Now that her father was dead, would Lupe marry Zeb?

She slammed a glass in front of Coogins, who smiled broadly. "Good evening to you, too, Miss Martinez."

Maria tossed her head and whirled away. She'd be away from here by next week. For the rest of the night

330

she concentrated on the thought. She would add tonight's earning to her stash and be closer to her goal. She didn't worry about where to go. Anywhere would do.

Ernie didn't come often to Rio Mogollon. He wasn't much of a drinker, and too much smoke made his eyes burn. Lately, though, now that Lupe's husband was dead, Lupe had stopped pushing Zeb away. They would get married sooner or later. Already, Ernie was in the way. He was glad for Zeb and Lupe, but without Zeb's company he was lonely. Again.

Funny how he had taken to Zeb right away. Except for being thin and loose-limbed, he and Zeb had only one thing in common: their devotion to the Farnsworth family. He had adopted Zeb as his father, or been adopted by him. He'd never had a father, and Zeb had had too much father by the sound of what he'd told Ernie. Yet they balanced out nicely, because Zeb had a lot to give, most of it just what Ernie needed.

Families sure were funny things, Ernie thought as he drank the flat beer slowly, just a taste at a time. It was so watered-down he found himself wishing they'd left out the beer. Then he would have enjoyed it more.

He'd been thinking about families lately, what with Zeb fixing to marry Lupe and with the branding they'd been doing all week. Putting that back-to-back set of R's on the hide of animals made him think that way. His real name was Boyd Kellogg, but the name had less meaning for him than the brand had for a steer. He liked being Ernie Coogins just as well. It served his purpose.

But family—that brand on the soul—was behind everything he did. What made it all ridiculous was that he had no family left any more.

Once there had been three Belascos back in Virginia, Priscilla, Boyd and Ida. As the oldest, Priscilla was in charge. When she fell in love with Thomas Yarborough and followed him west, Boyd and Ida went along. It was a fatal move for Boyd, because when Thomas became Baltimore Blackie, bank robber, Boyd became Kid Belasco, his accomplice and, ultimately, his fall guy.

Ernie didn't know what happened to Priscilla. Ida, his mother, died of consumption after a life of hard knocks, bringing up an out-of-wedlock boy by working as a hotel cleaning woman all over Kentucky, Indiana and Illinois. He had been told his father's name was George Kellogg, but the only man in his mother's life was Boyd.

Christmas for them came whenever Boyd sent them a package or money from his ill-gotten gains. The packages were always wondrous, containing something little Boyd, Kid's namesake, craved so badly he hadn't dared breathe word of his desire. Now he thought perhaps his uncle knew because he was still, inside, a small boy himself. His own childhood had been as deprived as Ernie's. Out of memories, perhaps, the aptly named Kid Belasco produced the occasional marvel for his nephew.

Ernie drew out his pocketknife, fingering it under the table. Of all Boyd's presents, it was the only one he still had. It was a wonder to him still. And a link.

Boyd Belasco, that hero-worshiping kid who had never grown up, had been killed in Kansas by a mob, blamed for a murder he hadn't committed. He'd trusted and obeyed Baltimore Blackie and paid for it with his life.

With Boyd in jail, the last years of Ida's life had been hard. Ernie worked, helping his mother as he could. In her final bout of sickness she had been fired by only one thought—that Blackie should pay for what he had done to Boyd. Over and over she had begged her son to find Blackie.

Ernie always refused. Blackie was trouble. Why should he seek out someone who would only ruin him? He wasn't the kind to murder someone, even someone as deserving of death as Blackie.

But Ida had insisted. "Don't kill him," she instructed, "only make sure he gets caught. He's a wanted man.

You'll get a reward, then you can use it to start a new life."

He never promised his mother. In the end, the fact that he hadn't given her the one thing she wanted acted as more of a spur than any pledge he could have given. Once she was dead, once those reproachful eyes finally closed, he became obsessed with Baltimore Blackie. More obsessed than Ida had ever been. Sometimes he wondered if, at her death, her soul hadn't climbed into his and taken it over.

He'd changed his name and gone looking for Blackie. When Caroline Farnsworth came into his life he'd just succeeded in infiltrating the gang. Now he thought it was Fate stirring the pot that brought him there at the right time.

Blackie got his, and Ernie found a new life. He didn't have the reward money his mother hoped for, but he had something better. He had good people, friends and a family—even if it was borrowed—to love.

Just before closing time Ernie gave up his place rather than order another beer. Inside, he craved a breath of fresh air; then, outside at last, he wanted a cigarette. Laughing at the perversity in him that made him crave smoke only out in the clean air, he paused in the doorway of the butcher shop next to the Silver Spur.

He'd have a smoke, he decided, while he waited for two hands from the ranch he'd seen earlier. Hank and Eli would be drunk as coots, but they'd be company for the ride home. He sat down on the stoop in the darkness to roll his cigarette. He didn't need to see; it was something he could do in his sleep just by feel.

Absorbed in his task, Ernie paid no attention to the traffic of men and horses as more and more customers left the Silver Spur. His cigarette was smoked down to the loosely packed end before he realized he'd probably missed the men. He ground it out under his bootheel.

Just then he heard a voice that made his skin crawl. It

came from the alley between the saloon and the butcher shop, projected to him by some accoustical quirk of the passageway. In leaving by the back entrance, Maria had met an admirer. She sounded surprised. Ernie was shocked. He didn't care about Maria, but he cared desperately that she was talking to Albert Humphrey.

Humphrey had either done his time for robbing the Santa Fe and kidnapping Caroline or he had escaped from prison. Either way, he was here for only one reason. Caroline.

To make matters worse, he had somehow managed to connect immediately with one of the few people in Rio Mogollon who would help him — cheerfully.

Because of Lupe, sweet, innocent, kindhearted Lupe, Maria knew where Caroline was.

Together, Maria and Al Humphrey would hunt down Caroline. It was up to Ernie to follow them and try to stop them from hurting her.

Fate again, he thought. He squared his thin shoulders and set off after the absorbed couple. He was safe enough now. The two vipers had just found each other. They would be busy for a while. The dangerous part would come later.

He hoped he would be ready.

Chapter Twenty-eight

Colorado proudly called itself the Centennial State. In the year the nation celebrated its hundredth birthday, Colorado had become the forty-first state in the union. For the people of Lake City, that made the Fourth of July doubly special. This year they would celebrate one hundred and one years as a nation and one year of statehood.

Although Lake City mine workers were not as oppressed as miners in some parts of the country, traditionally the Fourth was one of only two days a year when mine operations were totally suspended. The other day was Christmas.

Joseph Talmage, in his role as public-spirited gentleman and philanthropist, had taken charge of planning the celebration—which meant that his son Gabe had numerous duties to perform. Caroline had elected to help him wherever possible. They divided the work along traditional lines so that Caroline arranged for donations of food and materials from businesses and organizations, while Gabe solicited money from the rowdy—and vastly successful—saloons, dance halls and billiard rooms that catered to off-duty miners.

The work kept them busy, together and separately, frequently at Gabe's house, where his mother was always their chaperone. Since Caroline had no desire to be alone with Gabriel, she never thought to resent Priscilla's presence, although she often found her comments difficult to tolerate. Caroline's limited forbearance was enhanced by her knowledge that Joseph was now heavily invested in

335

Uncle Simon's mine, Little Josie. Because she knew that eventually Joseph and Priscilla would get their just deserts, she was willing to let Priscilla's barbs go unremarked.

Still, they rankled, sometimes to the point that it showed. Then Priscilla would smile with satisfaction. She had never given up trying to place Caroline's name and figure out why it sounded familiar. Knowing that her connection to Baltimore Blackie had no relevance to Priscilla, Caroline never minded those attempts. What she did mind was Priscilla's occasional speculation about Rory. Although he was sure Joseph's wife could not remember him from his brief time with the wagon train from St. Louis after his father's death, Caroline was not so certain.

Priscilla had only to look at Caroline assessingly as she did while she and Gabe were comparing lists of sponsors to raise alarm in Caroline. Accompanying the look came a remark: "You and your brother don't look much alike to me."

The purring challenge of Priscilla's voice made Caroline put down her pen and give the woman her full attention. "You're quite right, but then our parents don't look much like each other, either. What we share," she said, warming to the truth of her subject, "is a heritage of values, I would say, and a certain sameness of outlook. We're both pretty stubborn, too, and people have said we have the same chin."

"Is that right? I declare, I don't see any resemblance at all between you."

Pushed that way, Caroline decided to go on the attack a bit. Her glance flicked to Gabe long enough to find inspiration there. "That may be," she said. "Families are funny. For instance, Gabe doesn't look like Mr. Talmage, or you for that matter. Yet I don't doubt that he's your son."

Gabe laughed good-naturedly, while Priscilla's face

336

grew red. "Mother's always said I look like her family back in Virginia."

"You sound like Virginia, anyway," Caroline admitted, wanting to smooth things with both of them. "Did you ever live there?"

"I don't remember any place but St. Louis. Not until we left there. After the war, wasn't it, Mother?"

Priscilla didn't answer.

Later, when they were on their way to the business district for one more sweep, catching up with the few proprietors who had so far eluded them, Gabe took it upon himself to apologize for his mother's prying.

Caroline tried to wave it away.

"I don't know what's gotten into her this past year. She's changed. She used to be . . . nicer," he said sadly.

Caroline didn't know what to say. She couldn't bring herself to defend Priscilla, although she wanted to ease Gabe's embarrassment. When he spoke again she realized that he was talking to himself, not to her. He wouldn't have heard her if she'd spoken.

"I remember the day I noticed how oddly she was behaving. It scared me." He looked over his shoulder, not at her but at the cart he drove. "I was driving a wagon just about like this in Dodge City, Kansas. Have you ever been there?"

Caroline started as his eyes fixed on her face. "Um, yes. Once."

"It's a place pretty much like this, isn't it? But flatter." He looked around and said it again. "Flat and primitive. I didn't want to go at all, but she insisted. They were executing three criminals, and she wanted to see it. Can you imagine that?"

Caroline shuddered. That was when Rory had discovered how to find his uncle. She had to be grateful for whatever had brought Gabe and Priscilla there that day, but she hated being reminded of Blackie's execution.

Gabe noticed the shudder. "You're repulsed, and so

337

was I. But not Mother. She wanted to get as close to the gallows as she could. You'd have thought those men were her worst enemies the way she stared. And she watched the whole thing. I couldn't. Maybe I'm not manly enough—"

"No, Gabe, don't think that," Caroline rushed to say. "It's not manly to rejoice in another's misfortune."

"It's not womanly either, Caroline, but my mother loved it. I looked at the ground, at the horses, at my feet even, trying to remove myself from the scene. Every once in a while I'd peek at Mother, hoping to find she'd fainted or something. But no. She never took her eyes off those men. Especially the middle one, the ringleader. He was called Baltimore Blackie. She wouldn't leave until he was cut down. He was in the middle and they did the two others first. We'd be there still if they hadn't—finally—taken him down."

His evocation of the scene was so vivid that tears came to Caroline's eyes. She forgot that they were sitting on a wagon seat in broad daylight. He had stopped the team at the side of the main street where they had left it on each of their trips to town. It would serve as their collection point and meeting place when they finished their separate visits to merchants.

"Gabe . . ." She put her hand on his arm, trying to convey sympathy.

"She's been different ever since," he said, giving no indication that he had heard her speak or felt her touch. "Sometimes I think she knew that man. He was from the South, from Baltimore. Maybe she knew him."

He looked at Caroline then, and through the slight haze of her tears, Caroline saw another pair of dark eyes staring at her wonderingly. Her heart lurched into her throat and began hammering to get out. Even his voice . . something powerful tugged at her memory and she clutched Gabe's arm, needing to know that he was real.

She blinked and cleared her vision.

338

What she saw was a Gabriel so different from the one he had just been that she was forcibly jerked back into the present.

"What the hell . . . ?"

Caroline barely had time to see that he was looking past her to something happening at ground level. Then he scrambled past her, pushing her aside roughly to climb over her legs. She turned, trying to help and to see, as he jumped from the wagon and ran off.

Caroline followed with no clear idea why. She heard cries, both male and female, as she ran into the shadows next to the Draper Mercantile. It took her too many seconds to realize that Gabe was fighting with another man, pulling him away from a woman. She was huddled into a protective ball and thus useless to Gabe, who needed help.

The man Gabe fought was bigger and stronger. He was not angrier than Gabe, who reminded Caroline at that moment of an enraged terrier, but he was obviously an accomplished fighter. He shook off Gabe's blows with ease and landed his own just as easily.

Caroline saw that unless she could aid Gabriel quickly the unequal contest would soon be over. The collapsed woman was no help and a glance to the street showed no one coming. They were in a storage area, little better than an alley, but full of barrels and stacks of broken building materials. She grabbed up the first implement she could lift and turned back to see how Gabe was faring. The man had gone from defense to offense, and now he had Gabe trapped against the building.

Being smaller, Gabe was having some success dodging the big man's blows, especially to his head, but others were taking their toll on his body and on his stamina.

Caroline dragged her weapon to within striking distance of the man's back and lifted it with both hands. It was unwieldy, and with both men bobbing and feinting she was as afraid of hurting Gabe as she was of failing

339

to hit her target. She held the cudgel high, prepared to swing it at the back of the man's head, when he raised his meaty fist for the downswing into Gabe's face. He held Gabe by the collar with his other hand, ensuring his success.

Caroline swung the board, surprising a shrill scream from her own throat with the effort it required. Had she not screamed, the blow would have fallen harmlessly on the man's raised shoulder. Instead, he turned toward the sound and the plank caught the side of his head.

He went down in a heap, crumpled at her feet, with Gabe on top of him. It took her as much by surprise as it did Gabe. She fell to her knees, pulling at Gabe, not sure until he moved that she hadn't also struck him.

"My God! I killed him! Gabe!"

Gabriel crawled to the side of the building, there to be violently sick to his stomach. Caroline heard him retching and the woman, forgotten until now, crying softly behind her. All her attention, however, was fixed on the man she had felled. She knew he was dead. She was a murderer. She would go to prison and be hanged. She would never marry Rory and have his children. She would never see Papa and Hannah or Abby and Rusty again.

She knew she should do something, call someone, go somewhere. All she did was stare at the unmoving body.

Gabe came to her side and knelt. "Caroline. It's all right."

"No, no. He's dead."

"He's out cold, but he's alive. We have to get away from here. Someone will come."

Caroline stared up at him. Alive? The man was alive?

Gabe took her hand and put it on the man's throat. At first she resisted, but then she felt the pulse of blood under the warm skin. "He is! He's alive!"

"More's the pity for that then."

Caroline and Gabe looked up as one to see the inspiration for all this violence staring down at the unconscious man. She was utterly composed now except for the hatred in her clear blue eyes and the reddened mark of a man's hand on her left cheek. That side of her lip was split and bleeding. The disfigurement gave her a sneering look that was all the more obscene for the pure loveliness of the rest of her features.

Caroline struggled to her feet after first stepping on the hem of her dress. She paid no attention to the ripping noise it made. "You're hurt," she cried.

"We've got to get away before he comes to," Gabe said urgently. "It's a wonder we haven't been discovered already." He had one arm looped protectively over the woman he'd rescued, steering her back to the street.

"What about him?" Caroline asked, torn between fear that he would wake any second and humanitarian duty to someone she'd injured.

Gabe paused and turned back to where she hovered, halfway between her two objectives, flight and charity. "You help her," he said. "I'll take care of him."

Caroline went with the woman. Although she favored her left side, she walked more or less upright and declined assistance until they reached the wagon. Two women came out the front door of the store farther up the block and picked their way across the unpaved road just as a loaded dray passed them. No one gave them a glance.

When Caroline had the woman seated and was boosting herself up beside her, Gabe dashed around the back and leaped to the reins. The lurch of the wagon put Caroline onto the seat with a thud.

"What did you do with him?" she asked when they were all away from the scene.

"Don't ask," he answered.

Between them, the woman said nothing. Caroline looked at her curiously. Sitting, she appeared to be several inches shorter than Caroline, and she was sure other inches would disappear when they stood side by side because so much of Caroline's height came from her long legs. This woman was petite.

The side of her face presented to Caroline was perfect, the features delicate and finely drawn. Gabe, of course, could see the damage the man had inflicted. She was dressed in vibrant green that mocked the pallor of her complexion. Her bright red hair tumbled like fire down her back. Compared to the rich auburn of Hannah's hair, this looked bold, but it was too streaked and too shot-through with pale gold not to be real.

"Who was the man?" she asked.

Instead of answering Caroline, the woman asked, Gabe, "Did you kill him?"

"Good heavens, no. What do you take me for?"

The woman shrugged and looked ahead again.

"What's your name?" Caroline asked.

She didn't answer for so long that Caroline was sure she wouldn't. Finally, she said, "Darby."

Caroline tried to interpret the lack of a last name — or was that one? — and the small shrug that again accompanied her speech.

"Where do you live, Darby?" Gabe asked.

"Nowhere."

Caroline was beginning to be annoyed. "Everyone lives somewhere, Darby," she said briskly. Then she had a thought. "Was that man your husband?"

She got no answer, but close inspection of the woman's face revealed tears sliding down over her cheeks.

"She may be in shock, Gabe. We'd better take her to my house."

"What about Mrs. Larsen?"

"She's very kind," Caroline said, her answer questioning his objection.

"Is she discreet?"

"I've no reason to believe otherwise. You think we'll have a problem?"

342

"We could. That's a violent man. I don't want to endanger you."

"I wonder who he is?"

"Mick Garrity," Darby said.

Caroline was startled. They had been talking over Darby's head as if she were a child or insensible. Then Gabe swore fiercely. "You know him?" Caroline asked.

"I know *of* him," he corrected. "He's not a man I want to know."

"What did you do to him back there?"

"I piled lumber on him. He'll be a while getting out from under it."

Darby laughed softly, but her face showed no amusement.

Caroline touched her gently, noticing that the cloth of her gown was rich, although it was torn. "Are you all right?"

"I'm fine now. You should let me off anywhere along here."

"We'll do nothing of the kind. You're coming home with me."

"You'll be sorry," she promised.

"I don't think so." Caroline hoped she was right. The man hadn't seen her, but he'd held Gabe at close range. If he found Gabe he could find her, too.

But what *really* worried her — to her everlasting shame — was what Rory would make of such a lovely woman. Seeing Darby's effect on Gabe, Caroline dreaded to have Rory meet her. She was everything Caroline was not, small and dainty, with all the voluptuous roundness any man could desire. If only Priscilla were different, she thought for a craven moment, she could send Darby home with Gabe. Then Rory would never see her.

At least Mrs. Larsen didn't disappoint. She took one look at Darby's battered face and bundled her off to the spare bedroom outfitted for Uncle Simon at the back of the second floor. Caroline consoled herself that the room was not close to Rory's. Perhaps it would be days before he knew she was there. Perhaps she would be healed and gone before he found out. . . .

Caroline forced herself out of her selfish reverie. Already, Gabe was edging his way to the door. She stopped him with a question. "What do you know about Mick Garrity?"

She saw Gabe struggle with something and come to a decision. For the first time Caroline doubted him. He still didn't *look* like Joseph or Priscilla, but something closed in his face reminded her that he was their son after all.

"He's a tough. Everyone in Lake City knows him and tries to avoid him."

"I've never heard of him."

He ignored that. "Will your brother mind?"

She smiled, trying to look unconcerned. "I can't imagine any man turning Darby away."

"Don't be too sure of that," he answered cryptically.

"Where are you going? Are you going back there?"

He grimaced. "Not today. I have some things to do, though. I'll be back later."

"I could go with you. We didn't make our collections."

"I'll get Wendell and Beatrice to take over the rest. It would be better."

Caroline followed him to the door. "You're worried."

"Cautious. It's best to be." He gave her a smile that didn't reassure her. "Thank you for helping. She's going to need a friend like you—and so will I."

After Gabe left, Caroline went to see Darby. Mrs. Larsen had her in bed, dosed with the soothing herbal tea she swore by, a compress on her face. She put a plump finger to her lips and drew Caroline from the room with ponderous stealth. "Poor lamb," she whispered to Caroline when they were in the long hallway. "She'll need to be abed for days. I hope Mr. Talmage horsewhipped the brute who did that to her."

344

"I'm afraid not. We were lucky to get away."

"Well, she's safe now, and you're an angel from heaven for helping her. She'll be black and blue and yellow and green before this is over."

Caroline trailed Mrs. Larsen downstairs, thinking morosely that all those colors would look beautiful on Darby. She made several trips upstairs to check on her guest after Mrs. Larsen left, finding Darby asleep each time. Gabe didn't return as he promised, and somehow she wasn't surprised. She ate her supper and found some clothes she hoped Darby could use. Most would need alteration, but there was a robe she could wear until Mrs. Larsen could help her remake the dresses.

She was waiting up for Rory when Darby came down the stairs so quietly that she was startled. "You shouldn't be up, Darby. Did you need something?" She put her book aside and hurried over to the stairway.

"Only to be moving. I'll be stiff otherwise."

She was wearing the sapphire blue robe, and Caroline's heart plummeted at the way she made the simple garment look elegant. Caroline had never experienced such a sharp bite of envy and hated herself for being petty. It made her doubly solicitous. "Please come and sit with me. Do you think you could eat some supper now? I have—"

The sound of the door opening on Rory cut off her list of available foods. "Oh, here's my brother now. . . ."

She ran to meet Rory just as if she wanted him to meet Darby. But she didn't. He looked tired, and she wondered again what drove him to work such long hours. Since their trip to the mountains he'd stayed later and later from home. More than once she'd asked him if he was avoiding her. His denial never rang true.

Every explanation for Darby's presence she had worked out in her mind had been concocted with the idea that they would be alone while she delivered it. She'd expected Darby to remain in bed and not be a silent

345

witness to her tale. She'd even believed she could pass her off as a new acquaintance who merely needed shelter for a while. And she'd no intention of bringing Gabe into it.

All that changed, Caroline began her story thankful for one thing. Rory would never be rude to Darby. She was too harried to wonder why she expected him to be displeased, but she did. Was it because Gabe had planted the idea or because Gabe had been involved?

"Royal, come and meet our guest." Calling him Royal reminded him of his role and begged his cooperation at the same time.

Absorbed as she was in her mental dilemma, Caroline forgot the impropriety of introducing Rory to Darby when she was not fully dressed. By the time she realized her gaffe, Darby's poise had made her feel silly and immature for even thinking of such an unimportant issue.

"You sister has been extremely kind and brave today. I'm grateful to her."

Caroline noted with admiration that Darby didn't try to hide her injury or seem flustered in any way by Rory. Then she saw why. Rory looked to her every bit as smitten by Darby as she had feared he would be. Rory said all the right, kind things, and Darby did, too.

For her part, Caroline sat like a lump, looking from one to the other while they talked, feeling totally extraneous. She didn't say another word until Darby excused herself.

"But you didn't eat," she protested, following Darby halfway to the stairs.

"The soup I had earlier is all I need, thank you." With similar, perfect courtesy, she also refused Caroline's help going upstairs, leaving her nothing to do but go back to face Rory.

"You would have done the same thing," she said immediately, taking the chair before her nervousness showed.

His frown didn't change. "I'm sure you're right. You weren't hurt?"

"No, Gabe was, but he'll be all right, just sore and black and blue."

"Damn it, Caroline, I don't like this." He got up and paced around the room. "Why didn't he take her to his house? Why you?"

"Oh, come on, Rory." In her impatience she never thought to call him Royal. Besides, they were alone again. "You know as well as I do that he couldn't take her home to Priscilla."

"Caroline, she's a prostitute."

She jumped to her feet in protest. "Rory, no! Don't say such a thing!"

"Look, it doesn't please me either, but it's the truth."

"I don't believe you!"

"There are women like that, you know. Lots of them here and in all the mining towns."

"She couldn't be, Rory. She's beautiful and . . . well-spoken! You heard her. Her manners are better than mine."

He grinned at that. "She wasn't as nervous as you were."

"That doesn't mean anything." She glared at him. "You're teasing me, aren't you?"

"I wish I were, mite. Who was the man?"

Darby had told him she had been saved from an attack. Caroline hated to say the name Gabe had recognized. If Gabe knew, Rory was sure to. Rory was closely woven into the mining community by now. "She said he was Mick Garrity."

He whistled, then shook his head. "I should pound Gabriel Talmage into the ground for this. He knew, and still he brought her here."

"He's that bad?" Caroline asked tremulously, referring to Garrity, not Gabe.

"How can you ask? You saw what he was doing to her."

"I thought maybe he was her husband. Not that that *excused* him," she rushed to say. "But when I asked Darby she just began to cry very quietly. It's the only time she cried, come to think of it."

"I don't know what it means, Caroline, but Garrity isn't married and he runs a string of prostitutes. Maybe she was trying to run away or holding out money on him. I don't know. But he'll want her back. Her looks make her valuable, and that makes her dangerous to you."

"What about Gabe?"

"What about him?"

"Garrity didn't see me. He probably doesn't even know I was there, but he saw Gabe face-to-face. He's the one in danger."

"That's his problem. You're mine."

That rankled. Caroline didn't want to be a problem. She had come to Colorado to help Rory—at least that was her stated reason. Being a nuisance didn't help either his cause or hers, but she wouldn't apologize. She lifted her chin and said, "I can take care of myself."

To that Rory chuckled. She was never more appealing to him than when she was feisty and deeply involved in more than she could handle. He shook his head and tried to look forbidding. "Just lay low for a while, all right? Stay home and nurse your little refugee. *Don't* try to handle this yourself, all right?"

Feeling she was getting off easy, Caroline agreed. But there was one more question she had to ask. "This doesn't make the thing with your uncle harder, does it? I mean, how could it? Garrity has no connection to the Talmages, isn't that right?"

"I don't think so. The problem is that just because he doesn't mix in polite society, that doesn't mean he doesn't mix with them in business. My sweet Uncle

Joseph has some very strange and profitable connections."

Suddenly Caroline felt cold. "Oh, Rory, hold me, please. I'm so afraid."

Rory drew her into his comforting embrace, and upstairs, Darby made her silent way from the darkness at the top of the stairs to the bedroom at the end of the hall. She slipped into the bed so quietly that the headboard, which had a tendency to creak, never made a sound.

Neither did she, although it was a long time before she sorted out all that she had learned.

Chapter Twenty-nine

Mick Garrity came out from under the pile of lumber like a raging bull. His head felt as if every bell in Christendom had been set loose inside it, but he knew exactly who to blame for his pain.

He got to his feet too fast, then had to lean against the side of the building while his blood settled. He had a goose egg above his ear that oozed and dripped blood. He wiped it off his hands onto his pants and worked his way along the wall to the street. It was full afternoon. He squinted up at the bright sky, disregarding the stab of pain that shot through his right eye, then looked for a cart on the street. He had trailed Darby on foot, but he wasn't walking from here.

Of three wagons on the street, only one, a dairy cart, was headed the way he wanted to go. It wasn't fancy, but it would do. Within minutes he had liberated it and was cracking the reins over the back of the plodding team. He took the River Road out of town to a grove of cottonwoods near the Lake Fork, cursing each bump on the way.

"She'd better be there," he muttered out loud, knowing she would be. Pris always waited. She couldn't get enough of him.

By the time the river was in sight he was glad the way had been so arduous. He had his temper under control again. He'd been so furious at first he would have torn into Priscilla without thinking twice. He'd do it someday, but not until he had what he wanted from her. And it wasn't what she thought he wanted, that was for damned sure!

In spite of his headache, Mick laughed aloud at the

idea of him being in love with Priscilla. She had an appetite for abuse, it was true, and he enjoyed feeding it, but what he wanted from her wasn't satisfaction. He could get that anywhere. The picture of Darby's beautiful, arrogant face flashed across his mind's eye. He pushed it away. He wasn't ready to think about her yet.

One thing at a time, he counseled himself. He knew where she was. He could get her back any time he wanted. She couldn't work for a few days anyway, so those two fools could take care of her for him. He'd get her back and fix them at the same time. It would be easy.

But he didn't want to spook Pris. She was feeding him information he could use about the mines. He was going to win it all, and then he'd dump the plump little Priscilla and take his revenge on her Milquetoast son.

But it wasn't the son's face he saw when he fingered the lump on his head. It was the girl. Caroline Farnsworth. He knew who she was. She had a rich uncle. She also had a look he was crazy for, a wild, nobody-touches-me impudence that made him hotter than blasting powder. He'd have her—and soon—and then she'd pay for taking that board to the side of his head!

As he expected, Priscilla waited deep in the grove, her light carriage, one of the few smart ones in Lake City, well concealed. Her impatience was less hidden, but the sight of his vehicle instantly restored her humor. "Now I can see why you're late," she laughed. "You had to do your milk route first."

Mick let her enjoy herself before he growled, "Watch yourself, woman, or you'll be up here flat on your back on these wheels of cheese."

"That might be a novelty—for you."

Her barb made him laugh, too. He didn't doubt that once in her life she'd flipped her skirts for some man just about everywhere it was physically possible to do so.

She was wild. Old, but wild. He got down from the cart slowly, waiting for her to notice the contusion on his head.

He didn't expect sympathy, and she didn't disappoint him. Her eyes widened in reaction. She reached out to touch the lump. He caught her hand and twisted it away.

"Someone doesn't like you," she jeered.

"Besides you?"

"Oh, I like you."

"Just the way I like you."

Priscilla laughed throatily. "One of your girls?"

He twisted her arm, forcing her down to her knees. "She will be," he vowed.

"She won't be as good as I am."

"That so? You'll have to prove that to me."

"You have blood on your pants," she said nastily.

He grabbed a handful of her hair and pulled so her face turned up to him. "Virgin's blood," he taunted.

"Your own. You bleed like a stuck pig."

He leaned back against a tree. "Don't you have something to do?"

"You're messing up my hair."

He released her and closed his eye so he could see whatever he wanted. Darby's long red hair . . . Caroline, pale and silky and blond . . . Caroline . . .

At the first raucous rooster crow, long before true daylight, Darby came awake with a start. She had to be up. The girls would be awake soon and . . . A sharp pain in her side straightened her with a gasp. She turned the sob into a rueful laugh. It was this bed, this room, that took her back to the farm in Iowa and to her sisters.

Lucy, Mary and Dorothy. She tasted those innocent names again, savoring the feel of them in her mouth. She had been Dorothy then, the oldest sister, the girl

352

who stood in for her mother when little Timmy's birth ended her life. Somehow, Timmy had made Darby out of Dorothy and everyone took it up, even Da.

She flexed her left shoulder, hoping for another obliterating pain, anything to keep her from remembering the rest. Early morning hours were always the worst. She'd have to get back to work; that way there'd be no more long quiet hours like this to make her think.

She had a bruise on her left arm and her ribs hurt there. How instinctive it was, she thought bitterly, to protect one's soft parts. Women covered their breasts and men curled around their groins. In every fight she'd seen, and she'd seen too many, that was the target, especially on the opposite sex. Or was it just that men always wanted to get their hands on breasts? Anyway, Mick had missed—this time.

Again she moved, providing distraction for her mind. She wouldn't think about Mick any more than she would dwell on the past. She couldn't change any of that, but perhaps she could do something with her present situation.

Yesterday was gone, but there was today, wasn't there? And tomorrow? She was here now because she had decided to be a victim no more. And look where she was—in a beautiful room in a soft bed. And she was by herself. Couldn't she *use* this situation?

She reviewed the facts she'd learned yesterday, starting with her first surprise, Mrs. Larsen. Surely that was Nils Larsen's aunt, the woman he lived with, along with his cousins, Erik and Hal. And Nils was her one true friend in the whole world. If she'd married him after Pete had been killed she wouldn't be in this mess. He'd offered, but she'd known it wouldn't be right. It would have been like marrying a brother.

Darby didn't think Mrs. Larsen knew her. Nils hadn't been exactly pleased with her this last year. But if she

353

talked about a redheaded fallen woman her employer, Miss Caroline Farnsworth, was sheltering, it wouldn't take Erik or Hal long to figure out her identity.

That wasn't Darby's choice, though. If Nils rescued her he'd only bring down the wrath of Mick Garrity onto his own head. And he worked in mines Mick controlled. She didn't want that—not for any of them.

Today she'd speak to Mrs. Larsen and make her promise to keep her a secret from Nils and his cousins. If Mrs. Larsen was as discreet as Gabriel Talmage hoped, she'd understand and accept Darby's reasoning.

Gabe. Gabriel Talmage. Her angel of mercy.

She sighed, her eyes closed over the picture he'd made coming to her rescue. If she hadn't been watching him over Mick's shoulder, she would have ducked the blow to her face. As it was she had scarcely felt the hit. Even now, with her lip split and her face discolored, she would call it a fair exchange; her pain for the greater comfort of knowing that someone could get that angry for her sake.

The other Talmage, Rory or Royal, would have done the same thing, she knew. Being bigger and stronger, more of a match for Mick, this Rory might not have needed the girl's help as Gabriel had. But what she loved about Gabriel was his passion. The other one was cold. He wouldn't have cared the way Gabriel did.

Darby eased slowly to a sitting position on the side of the bed. She wanted to walk to the window and watch the sky grow light. She could think about all these Talmages there. She pulled a chair over and sat down. It was still June, the time of long days. Farmer's days, Da called them. If only Pete had been willing to farm . . . She brought herself up short. No more of that. She had to think, not daydream.

This Caroline called Rory Talmage her brother. At least that meant she was Gabriel's cousin and no competition for her there. Darby laughed to think how quickly—and how foolishly—her heart had settled on Gabriel when, as Joseph Talmage's son, he was hardly in the market for a prostitute-wife.

The important issue for Darby, however, was finding out all she could about Rory Talmage and his plot against his uncle and aunt. That meant, whether or not he and his sister intended it, a plot against Gabriel, too. Her Gabriel.

Today she would find out all she could about Caroline and her brother.

Or was he her brother? She had said to him, "Hold me, please." Would she ask that of a brother?

Darby paced from the window. Her feet were cold. She was cold all over suddenly. What was she into here? She was a prostitute, but she might very well be the more innocent of the two of them. Wouldn't that be something?

She got back into bed, shaking with spasms that weren't entirely physical. She pulled the blanket tight around her and swiped at the tears dripping into her hair.

Oh, Pete, she wept miserably, *why did you die on me? Why, oh why?"*

Caroline put down the tray and hurried to the bed.

"Darby," she called. "Wake up. You're dreaming." She was afraid to touch the woman's battered body, afraid she'd hurt her more. She placed her hand gently on Darby's right shoulder, then cupped the joint and gave it a small shake. "Darby!"

Darby's eyes opened, wide and unfocused for a few seconds before her gaze settled on Caroline.

"You were having a nightmare. Did I hurt you?"

"No, I'm all right now. I just didn't . . . know where I

355

was . . . am."

"Take your time," Caroline said. "I brought you some breakfast."

"Oh, you shouldn't have." Darby sat up and tried to straighten her twisted nightgown. She put her hand to her heart. It was still racing. "I'm sorry. I hope I didn't disturb your sleep."

Caroline laughed. "Oh, my goodness, no. I've been up for hours."

"Is it so late?"

"Just midmorning. Don't worry. You're doing what you should be doing. I just wake with the sun. Back home I didn't get to go out with the men unless I woke myself. No one wanted me there, so they'd leave without me every chance they got." She put the tray beside Darby. "I didn't know what you'd like, or what you can eat. Is your mouth sore?"

"Only when I try to smile."

"You haven't much reason to smile, I'm afraid. Would you like your robe?" Without being asked, Caroline put it on the bed. She was fussing too much. "I'll leave you now and come back for the tray later."

"Is Mrs. Larsen here? That was her name, wasn't it?"

"It was, but she won't come till tomorrow. Then we'll fix up some dresses for you. I mended your green one, but Mrs. Larsen is the clever one with a needle." She was talking too much. She did that when she was nervous. The only way to stop herself was to leave. She did, saying a last, "Call me if you need anything."

Caroline upbraided herself all the way downstairs. She had let Rory's words get in her way. So the woman was a prostitute—*if* she was! That didn't mean she wasn't a human being. She was a woman who had been hurt, that's all. Caroline would put everything else out of her mind.

By the time Darby came downstairs, Caroline had

356

succeeded in doing just that. She was once again herself; at least she was until Darby asked, "Will you tell me about your brother? Royal, is it? Is he Gabriel Talmage's cousin?"

Caroline dropped Darby's coffee cup in surprise. "His name is Royal Farnsworth, Darby," she said, smiling brightly to cover her awkwardness. "We're from New Mexico. Gabe is the Talmage, and he's no relation to either of us. He's my friend, although Ro . . . my brother isn't too happy with him just now."

"Because of me," Darby acknowledged. "I can't blame him for being afraid of Mick. I'm afraid of him, too. For good reason, as you can see."

Caroline felt on safer ground here. "I can't believe a man would hit a woman the way he did you. It's uncivilized!"

"Well, you see, he doesn't think of me as a woman—"

"He should," Caroline interrupted slowly. "There's no excuse for such inhumanity. None at all." She turned back from putting the kitchen to rights with unnecessary vigor and faced Darby. "Let's go sit and be comfortable, shall we?"

They sat, but it wasn't comfortable. Darby asked about New Mexico, letting Caroline talk and talk until she was embarrassed—and needed to be.

"I'm terribly sorry, Darby. I don't know where my manners are, running on at you so—"

"Your manners are excellent, Miss Farnsworth. That's the trouble."

Caroline looked up from her clasped hands to say, "Don't call me Miss Farnsworth, please. Just Caroline."

"The problem is, Caroline," Darby said with a crooked smile, "like me, you're a plainspoken woman, and manners are keeping you from talking plainly about me."

Caroline didn't know what to say, as her flaming face signified.

357

"Let me put you at ease. It's no secret what Mick Garrity does. I was trying to run away from him." This time Darby looked down at her hands in confusion. "I wasn't always a prostitute, Caroline. I was married to my sweetheart back in Iowa, where I grew up. I'd be there still if I could be, but Pete didn't take to farming. He wanted to come out here and find his fortune.

"He staked out a claim and worked it. It came to nothing, as did the next one, until finally he was losing money he didn't have. Then he got a job working the pack mules that take ore up to the smelter, and I worked at the Grand Hotel. It was terrible at the time, I thought. I wanted to go back to Iowa, but we had nothing to go back to. Pete had sold his share of the farm to his brother. He'd be a farmhand back home, a failure, he thought."

"What about your family?"

"They all died, of cholera."

Caroline thought of Rory's real family, his mother and sister, dead of the same dread disease. "Pete wouldn't go back?"

"We talked about it." Tears glistened in Darby's eyes, making the brilliant blue look new washed. "Let me give you some advice. If there's something you want, something you want to do, don't wait. Do it now. Go after it. Because if you don't, you may never have it."

She stopped, struggling to find her voice.

"You don't have to tell me," Caroline said, squeezing her hand.

"No. I do. I want to." Her strange, two-sided face made each word compelling as her voice picked up strength from her determination. "If we'd gone before the snow, we'd have made it home, I know. It would have been hard but we'd have been together. Pete wanted to wait till he had more money. He worked harder, taking on dangerous jobs that paid more. He went with pack

358

mules in the snow, and he didn't come back. He and some mules fell off the trail when a snowslide hit them. He was never found."

"How horrible."

"Yes. People tried to help me. I could have married, but I didn't care any more. I gave up just the way my Da did after Mama died. I never thought I'd be so weak. I have a friend—Nils—he says I took the Irish solution, and I did."

Caroline looked at her blankly.

"Whiskey," she said succinctly. "The Irish comfort. The Irish way out. Mick Garrity kept me supplied with whiskey; then he supplied men. At first I was horrified, but it was done, wasn't it? Who'd have me after that? I drank to forget and to keep all the demons away."

"But you said you were running away," Caroline said. "You meant it, didn't you?"

"Oh yes, I meant it. I just didn't get very far, did I?"

"You're here. You're safe now. You don't ever have to go back."

The right side of Darby's face smiled. "It's not that simple. Mick is a powerful man. He could send someone after me. He won't give up."

"My brother will help you. He'll—" Darby's harsh laugh stopped her. "Why do you laugh?"

"He didn't like me."

"Ro-yal?" Amazement made her stumble over his name. "Oh, but he did! I could tell. He . . . thinks you're beautiful."

"That doesn't mean he likes me."

"But he'll help you. I'll ask him."

"I don't see how anyone can help me."

Help came sooner than either of them expected, and from a source Caroline had not considered. One look at Darby told her *she* at least had never doubted Gabe.

Watching them together, Caroline found herself com-

359

paring the open adoration she saw on Gabe's face when he looked at Darby with Rory's expression. Last night she'd thought him smitten. Now she wondered. He had watched Darby closely and listened attentively. Her own jealousy had seen that as attraction. Perhaps it wasn't. Darby didn't think so, and wasn't she more knowledgeable about men than Caroline was?

At that thought, Caroline felt her face begin to heat with embarrassment. She yanked her mind back to the conversation.

"I don't know, Gabriel," Darby said.

Caroline heard her doubt without knowing what had prompted it. Before she could ask, Gabe said, "My friends call me Gabe."

Darby shook her head. "No," she said firmly. "I don't want to be your friend. To me, you are Gabriel, my rescuing angel."

Caroline fought the impulse to giggle by saying, "In the *Bible* Gabriel was God's messenger. Do you have a message for us?"

Gabe had to tear his eyes away from Darby. "Just what I told Darby. Garrity isn't chasing her, isn't even asking about her, or about me. Maybe that bump on the head knocked the whole incident from his mind. He was seen driving a dairy wagon out of town, and the wagon was found abandoned down by the river."

"That doesn't make sense," Caroline said.

"No, it doesn't," Darby agreed.

"But it does! He crawled out of the alley and stole Windsor's cart because he didn't know who he was. It has to be that. You beaned him, Caroline. I've heard of people not knowing who they are after a hit like that."

"Not Mick Garrity," Darby said. "His head is harder than granite."

"Even granite can be broken."

"It's too easy," Darby insisted. Reluctantly, she ap-

360

pealed to Caroline.

"I'm afraid I agree with Darby. Even if you're right, Gabe, it's safer to assume that you're not. I'll ask Royal tonight."

She didn't have to wait that long. Rory came home early. She didn't have to ask why, either. He went right to work on Darby.

"How long have you been off the bottle?" he asked briskly.

"Royal!" Caroline protested.

Darby ignored her to answer him calmly. "Six weeks."

"Word has it, it's only been two."

She smiled. "Word has it wrong, but not entirely. I pretended for a month first, to be sure I could handle it."

"Why would you pretend to drink?" Caroline asked, genuinely curious.

"I didn't want to attract Mick's attention until I was strong enough to fight him off."

Caroline could see that the answer satisfied Rory even if she didn't entirely understand it. Compared to Darby, she felt young and naive.

"Where were you going when he caught you?"

"To the stage."

Caroline understood that. The Barlow and Sanderson Overland Stagecoach, the same one she'd maligned to the Davenports and Talmages, made three trips a week in and out of Lake City. "Did you have money enough?" she asked.

"Someone I know had a ticket waiting for me. I gave him the money to buy it." By turns, her face registered comprehension, then anger. "So that's how Mick found out! I thought I could trust Duffy!"

"It wasn't Duffy." Rory's voice was softer now. "Garrity has long arms. The stage is a busy place, and Duffy is well known."

361

"Gabriel says he's not looking for me." There was no need for her to identify the "he" she spoke of.

"Because he knows right where you are," Rory said.

Darby deflated slowly. Like Caroline, she had resisted Gabe's easy explanation, but she had hoped he was right.

"Do you want to go back?" Rory asked.

She stiffened. "Of course not."

"There's no of course about it. If you're going to fold after one foiled attempt, you might as well go back now," he said with brutal frankness. "Before innocent people are hurt." His glance skated to Caroline's face. "If anything happens to Caroline because of this, I won't forgive or forget."

Caroline wondered if she was becoming ghoulish. Darby seemed to prefer Gabe's easy assurances and unrealistic optimism—and if she were being grilled as Darby was, maybe she would, too—but Caroline found Rory's grim determination infinitely more exciting.

To have such a champion! It was enough to make Caroline envy Darby again, fallen woman or not.

"I don't want others hurt," Darby said, her head bowed.

"You might not get another chance," Caroline reminded her gently. "Remember your advice to me?"

"You don't know what he's like."

"I saw him."

"You're not afraid?"

"Petrified," Caroline answered honestly.

"Being petrified makes Caroline bold." Rory threw her a grim smile. "But not this time. This time she's going to follow directions."

Her cocky "Yes, sir!" convinced no one, least of all Rory. His smile promised more discussion later. Instead of the kiss she wanted, he gave Caroline a curt nod and the back of his head. "Don't wait up for me," he ordered.

Because Caroline was too exasperated to disguise her feeling of baffled abandonment when Rory was gone, she found herself the object of Darby's scrutiny.

"He's not your brother at all, is he?"

"What?!"

She was as relentless as Rory. "I know men, Caroline, and there's nothing brotherly about the way he looks at you."

Caroline found her feet again. "You may know men, Darby, but Royal Farnsworth isn't like most men."

"Only to you, because you love him."

"Well, of course I do—"

Darby cut off her attempt to keep their pretense intact with a crude expression. Caroline had heard it before—from men. Hearing it from this delicate-looking woman revived her like a blast of cold air.

She made an instinctive decision, that she would trust Darby—but only a little bit. Her face, with one side ugly and one side beautiful, seemed to Caroline indicative of the woman she truly was, a beautiful and perhaps innocent person who had been badly damaged. Caroline would admit to what she couldn't hide and no more.

She took a deep breath. "You're right, of course. I do love him, I think I have ever since I met him."

"Then he's not your brother."

"Not physically. He's adopted. I was just a little girl when my parents took him in. His parents died, and he was alone. So, in a way he's my brother and in a way he's not. You can see the problem."

"Actually, I can't," Darby said. "If he loves you, and I think he does, what's the problem?"

"There's more," Caroline added haltingly. "I almost married someone else, and I don't think he'll ever forgive me."

"How almost?"

She grinned. "I was jilted at the altar, very dramatically. My parents sent me here with Royal so I wouldn't have to live with my shame."

Darby looked off toward the space where Rory had stood to cross-examine her and spoke as if she could still see him. "He's not an easy man, is he?"

"No." She knew she sounded proud.

"Maybe he hasn't forgiven you yet, but he will. Take my word."

Caroline did; she was that desperate for encouragement.

Chapter Thirty

That night Caroline proved how well she could take orders from Rory. She waited up for him. At least she tried to.

He found her asleep in her favorite overstuffed chair. She was wearing a dusty rose robe that gaped enough to prove to him that she wasn't naked under it. The glimpse of ruffled pink and white cloth wasn't as steadying as he hoped. Her hair was tied back with a pink ribbon that should have looked childish but didn't.

He stood for the longest time watching her sleep, fighting the rage of hopeless possessiveness inside himself. He wanted to lift her into his arms and feel her burrow under his chin. She was so trusting and warm—sweet. He could take off her robe and put her into the bed beside him. She wouldn't even wake up. He could hold her next to his heart all night. Nothing more. It would be enough.

He turned away without touching her. He was getting too good at lying to himself.

He kicked the leg of her chair, jarring it. She murmured a protest and slid to a new position. Her lips parted invitingly. . . .

Rory bumped the chair again. "Come on, Caroline, you're snoring the house down."

She sat up with a start that became a glare, then a short laugh. "I do *not* snore, Ro—" Then she remembered why she had waited for him. "What time is it? I was doing so well waiting. . . ."

"Two o'clock, I'd say."

"You've been drinking."

"Yes, Mother. Now what's this about?"

"I told Darby about us."

"*What!?*"

She expected his reaction, but not hers to *his*. His voice was no more than a whisper, but the heat of it raised blisters on her skin. She put up a placating hand. "She knew . . . guessed, that we weren't brother and sister."

"And you confirmed it?"

"I did and I didn't. I said you were adopted."

His next words were close relatives of the one Darby used.

"I think it will be all right, Rory. I told her about being left at the church and being sent here to get over it. It makes a good explanation—besides being true. I think it's best not to lie any more than necessary."

"Oh, you do, do you?" It was a low growl of warning before attack.

Caroline leaped to her feet, staggered by this reaction. She had evidently added to his fury! Because she sounded pompous? She did, but dear God, it wasn't *that* bad.

He paced the room, fighting an intense physical need for violence that frightened her. "Rory . . . I'm sorry—"

"Sorry!" He turned and came back to stand with his nose inches above hers. "Caroline, if I didn't know your screams would bring that bitch upstairs down here, I swear I'd put you over my knee and paddle some sense into you!"

She didn't back down. "I wouldn't scream."

It wasn't the answer he expected. "What?"

"I said, I wouldn't scream. I'd just grin and bear it." She tried to sound haughty.

He was the one who grinned. "Now that's an idea. *I'll* grin and you bare—"

The joke had done its work, relieving their tension— tension Caroline unwittingly reinstated with her next words. "She's amazingly perceptive, you know. She was

366

right about who we are and about how you feel about her. She said you don't like her."

"She's a whore."

"She's a woman who's had a miserable time since she came here."

"I know the whole sob story, and I'm not impressed."

"I can see that. I didn't think you'd be so . . . hard."

She was looking at him as if she no longer trusted him. And it hurt.

Actually, she wasn't revising her opinion of him, only wondering how he could be made to forgive her for almost marrying Ted if he couldn't forgive a grieving woman for slipping off into oblivion.

"I'm not saying I won't help her, Caroline."

"I understand."

"Do you? Whatever happened to 'actions speak louder than words'?"

"It still applies. I know what a good man you are. It's just that, as your sister, I also reserve the right to worry about your soul a bit."

"My soul?" He pulled a face at the word.

"Rory, it's two o'clock in the morning. I'm tired and you've had a drink or two—"

"Hours ago, Caroline. I'm perfectly sober and you've had a nap. You're not going to leave me hanging like this. You started something and you'll damn well finish it. Now."

Caroline shrugged. She had tried to back off once; she wouldn't try again. She walked away from him, making it look as idle as possible. She needed the distance. He tempted her so. Big as he was, there was in him still something of the boy she had first known. But boy or man, she loved him completely—enough even to speak her mind.

"Maybe soul isn't the right word. It's the one that comes to mind, that's all."

"Your point, Caroline?"

"My point is that I wish you'd give up the idea of swindling Joseph."

"May I ask why?"

She wasn't fooled by his restraint. "I'm afraid for you."

"Do you know something I don't?"

That did startle her. "I don't think so. How could I?"

"Very easily. You're close as a tick to a longhorn with Gabe Talmage."

"And you object?"

"So far I haven't. Should I?"

"No, you shouldn't." She was hurt that he could doubt her loyalty. Then she saw what he had done. He'd turned the tables on her, neatly throwing her from offense to defense. She made herself smile and acknowledge the trick. "But we're not talking about me now. At least not directly."

"Aren't we?"

Caroline lost her temper. He stood there like a great big human wall, bouncing everything back at her, skewing her every thought. "Will you stop doing that? I'm trying to explain that I'm afraid you're going to end up hurting yourself more than anyone else! And I don't just mean physically or financially, although that's also a possibility."

"But you know of no specific threat?"

"Of course I don't! Gabe doesn't have anything to do with Joseph. I swear he knows less about his father's business than I do."

"That could be a clever ruse."

"I don't think Gabe could pull it off. He's very . . . open."

"Ah."

She glared at Rory. "What does that mean?"

"It means 'I see.' "

"Do you?"

"I think I'm beginning to, but go on. Finish what you started."

Hounded by a feeling that was worse than futility, Caroline drove herself on. "I just can't see that you need to ruin the Talmages. They'll do it to themselves. Why should you bring yourself down to their level? You'll be doing to Gabe exactly what Joseph did to you: cheating him out of his start in life. Won't that return to haunt you someday? Won't you regret it?"

"Not as much as you will, evidently," he said.

"What does that mean? Am I supposed to defend myself again? Well, I won't. I'm right. I know I am. Even if everything goes the way you want it to, your success will really be a moral failure, Rory. You'll be diminished as a person, don't you see?"

"I see that you plead very . . . passionately, shall we say? But do you plead for me or for Gabe."

She was going to cry. She knew it. Determined that he shouldn't see, she started out of the room. She wasn't fast enough. He caught her arm and used her own momentum to swing her around to face him.

He was her tormentor, so how could the breadth of his chest look like sanctuary to her? But it did. Oh, God, it did.

With a sense of homecoming that shook her to her toes, Caroline threw herself against his strength and clung. He held her by her upper arms, his hands hard as hooks, frozen in indecision between the heaven of embrace and the hell of rejection.

With her face hidden in the front of his unbuttoned waistcoat and shirt, Caroline couldn't watch the battleground that was his face. She fought her own war, for dignity, not to cry, unaware that she had already lost.

As her tears soaked into his shirtfront, Rory, too, gave up. His arms went around her, rocking her gently, soothingly. He'd been so careful not to take advantage of their proximity. Had he been—again—too damned honorable? Had he waited too long to let her know how he felt?

Gabriel Talmage was a man much like Ted Jasper, it

369

seemed to him. Had Gabe now replaced Ted in her affections? He wanted to believe she had spoken tonight out of concern for him, not Gabe, but how could he be sure? She might not know herself.

Part of him didn't care, but the rest of him cared too much. He wanted Caroline, but only if he could have all of her—heart and soul as well as body. There was too much torment in the kind of partial possession he'd known with her before.

Caroline lifted her face from Rory's chest. She had angered him, yet now he was being brotherly again. And she hated it. If only she hadn't cried. It made her seem like a child to him even though she had hardly ever cried then. Being a woman made her weepy—and unattractive. No wonder he was put off.

Nevertheless, she put her hand to his face. She hated to plead with him. Still, wasn't that what Hannah had done with her father? Maybe all men were blind to what was right before them, plain as day.

"Rory, I know I made a mistake before, with Ted, but I know better now. I love you. Please don't keep on punishing me for that mistake." As though it had a mind of its own, her thumb strayed to the edge of his full mustache, there to toy with the soft, bristly sweep of hair. The feeling of it slid up her arm until it seemed she could feel its brush against her face.

Punishing her? Rory barely controlled a groan. What did she think he was doing to himself? Her eyes, sparkling with tears, were framed by spiked, wet lashes of extravagant length. Weren't blonds supposed to have fair eyelashes that were stubbly and sparse? Not Caroline.

Her fingers brushed his tightly held mouth. "Caroline—"

Just then the lamp sputtered out, the wick burned away as completely as his willpower. He lowered his mouth to her softly parted lips. She hadn't moved, and he needed no light to find her waiting mouth. It was as sweet as he remembered. Sweeter.

Caroline closed her eyes and settled into his arms. He was perfect for her. His height. His breadth. His hardness. Every part of him fit against her the way God intended. His mustache felt just the way she hoped it would, like a silky brush sweeping her face. She clutched a handful of his hair in a futile attempt to hold him still. His mouth tantalized, making forays to her eyes, ears, chin and nose, then coming back again and again to take biting kisses from her mouth.

"Rory," she said on a sigh.

He put her from him, his hands on her ribs, holding her away. She opened her eyes, now adjusted to the dim light. Even in the darkness she could see the intensity of his expression. Once she had mistaken that look for displeasure or unhappiness. Now she knew it for what it was. Her heart seemed to swell within her in recognition of his passion.

For one heartbeat she was afraid he was putting her away from him in order to leave her. Instead, he swept her up into his arms as easily as if she were still the child she'd been when they met. He carried her up the broad staircase to her room. The door yielded, then nicked shut behind them, sealing them inside. Moonlight streamed in the unshaded window, silvering the sheets she had turned back earlier.

Rory let her feet touch the floor just long enough to peel away her robe. He started to remove the nightgown, then thought better of it. He liked it. The ruffles were soft cascades that fell just shy of her breasts. Moonlight bleached away the pink of the ribbons that tied the neckline together, making them silvery. Her bare arms gleamed as she reached to draw him down to her.

All the care that had gone into placing her on the bed vanished as Rory pulled back and tore off his waistcoat and shirt. He dropped them to the floor next to her robe and devoted himself to his boots. They fell on top of his coat with a muffled thunk.

Raised onto one elbow, Caroline watched him straighten and change his mind about taking off his pants. She wanted to ask him why, but she didn't get the chance. He came to her in a rush, as though he feared she would evaporate. His kiss was a desperate claim that pinned her to the bed under him.

In time his mouth gentled. He released her and rolled to his side to let his hands play over the ruffles at her breast. Each time he stroked down, he stopped just short of touching her nipples as they peaked against the cloth. He fumbled with the first ribbon, finally untying it with a tug of his hand she felt to the soles of her feet.

"I thought you'd never want me again," she whispered.

He raised his eyes to look at her face and smiled. The sweetness, the tenderness of his expression pierced her to the quick. Then he bent to put his face into the opening he'd made in her gown. A second bow came apart to bare her body to the waist. He nuzzled into her softness, letting his hands coast, sometimes reverently, sometimes playfully, over the plains, valleys and crested mounds he had uncovered.

He took his time, kissing, tasting, sucking and nibbling until her head lashed from side to side. Her frenzy undid the restraining ribbon around her hair to spread it over the sheet in glorious disarray. He sat up and pushed the gown down over her shoulders, lifting her to take it away completely. One section of hair fell like a curtain over her shoulder. He let it slide through his fingers like sand, watching the gleaming length.

"I can't decide if your hair is gold or silver," he said, wonder in his voice. "Like you, it's precious."

It wasn't a declaration of love, but it warmed and soothed the part of her deep inside that was frightened at the chance she was taking. Thanks to her reading, she knew more about what she was doing. She knew Rory would marry her if she conceived a child with him, but

372

she didn't want their life together to begin under such a cloud. He was so honorable. She would always wonder if he really loved her for herself. He had done so once. But that was before she hurt him with Ted. If she gave herself to him now, freely and without constraint, wouldn't that erase her mistake?

She was betting everything that it would.

Caroline skimmed her hands over his shoulders and down his arms. The muscles there bunched under her fingertips, rippling like knotted cords under the silk of his skin. His forearms were lightly furred, reminding her of the golden brown crest of hair on his chest. She touched him there and pushed him down onto his back, leaning over him, first to kiss his mouth, then to stroke and fondle his chest hair. She brushed her fingers through the swirls and followed the line down to the buckle that had gouged at her abdomen and hip before.

He sucked in a breath that made room for her hand under the waist of his pants, but she didn't take advantage of it. She tugged briefly at the buckle, then abandoned it for the greater fascination concealed below. A flap of cloth covered buttons that strained to hold the bulge of his masculinity. She laid her hand over the heated mound and felt him stir and press back at her. His whole body straightened as his legs scissored and twitched.

"You're . . . killing me," he croaked softly.

She knew better. "Only with kindness."

He rolled up and undid his belt, then swung his legs over the side of the bed to stand. In seconds he was back, a beautiful, naked god-man. She rose to her knees to meet him, matching his desire with hers.

"I've wanted this for so long, Rory."

He took her in his arms, kneeling with her, face-to-face, all but joined from the knees up. The bed gave a creak of protest as he pushed his weight against it to put her down. From somewhere outside the room he heard an answering squeak.

Another bed.

Rory's head came up.

"What's the matter?" Caroline whispered.

Darby, he realized in dismay.

How could he have forgotten that they weren't alone?

It came again, faintly—the creak of Darby's bed frame as she moved. In sleep? Or was she awake—and listening?

"Rory?" Caroline rolled up as he had a moment ago, reaching for him in confusion and desire.

Damn that bitch down the hall. She was only a prostitute. She wouldn't care, but he did. He wouldn't let Caroline be subjected to Darby's crude interpretation of what they were doing. He loved Caroline. He would not sully her good name.

He grabbed his pants from the floor and jammed his feet into the still-warm pant legs. "We can't," he whispered fiercely, looking back over his shoulder. "It's not right."

The walls were only made of paper. Darby could hear every tell-tale sound of their lovemaking.

"Rory!" Caroline wailed.

He put his hand over her mouth. "I'm sorry, sweetheart. Not now. Not here. We can't." He started to take his hand away, then changed his mind when he felt her fill her lungs, ready to protest. "I know it's not fair and I'm sorry. I just can't." He patted her shoulder and found the sheet to draw up over her.

"What did I do?"

"It's not you, sweetheart. I promise you." He saw the tracks of tears on her soft cheeks and kissed her. "Don't cry. *I'm* the one who wants to cry," he said with a twist of a smile.

Caroline didn't get the joke. It wasn't funny to her.

From outside the door Rory heard the bed protest noisily as Caroline threw herself over onto her stomach to muffle the sound of her sobs with her pillow. He even heard the soft cries she made.

He had been right to leave her; he knew it. But that was no comfort at all — to either of them.

Chapter Thirty-one

Although the crowd in the Big Swallow Saloon had been thinned by the announcement of a high-stakes game in the back room, Ernie Coogins wasn't afraid to stare openly at Maria Martinez. Every other man in the place was doing the same thing. He would attract more attention if he didn't watch her, and even in disguise he wanted to blend imperceptibly into the blur of miners and mule skinners, gamblers and drunks around him. He didn't expect Maria to notice him. She made a point of ignoring her audience.

To Ernie, Maria was transparent. Her alliance with Al Humphrey would be brief. Neither one had any loyalty. She had been looking for a way out of New Mexico, and Humphrey had needed information she could provide. Now that they were in Lake City they were already bored with each other. He was a gambler and a thief; she was . . . a whore? Ernie considered that and decided it wasn't quite right. Maria was self-centered. Totally. While Humphrey was plying his trade in the back room, Maria was setting up her future out here.

She kept a cool head, he could see. Man after man approached her now that she was alone, trying to buy her. One or two tried to charm her. She refused their drinks and their advances, which only increased the competition and goaded the men to heights — or depths — of foolishness.

When he didn't watch Maria directly, he used the mirror behind the bar to keep his eye on her. Now and again he encountered his own image there. It never ceased to startle him. His clothes as a miner were only slightly different from his cowboy gear, but he felt altered beyond belief. His own mother wouldn't recognize him, he thought with a chuckle. Then he took that back. She *would* know him, but only as Uncle Boyd.

Before he'd dyed his hair and grown a mustache, he'd never realized that he looked like Boyd Belasco, the Kid himself. What he'd been was a bleached-out version. Now, his hair and mustache darkened, he was so much like the old Kid Belasco that, if his uncle were still alive and still wanted for his crimes, this disguise would be unsafe for Ernie. As unsafe as the name he was using now—his own name, Boyd Kellogg.

He still thought of himself as Ernie Coogins. He missed using that name because it had served him well. He'd taken the name to hide from Baltimore Blackie in his gang. Now he had to take another name because Humphrey and Maria both knew him as Coogins. He'd considered another alias and decided against it. Uncle Boyd was dead. Humphrey hadn't known him personally or heard of him as anything but Kid. There was no one left to keep him from being himself. He'd get used to it soon.

While Ernie decided whether or not to order another whiskey in order to keep his place at the bar, something changed in the room behind him. He felt it like a cold draft down his neck. Two men came into the room. They talked affably, as if they were great friends, but they eyed each other with distrust. And both of them looked at Maria while pretending to ignore her.

No one ignored *them,* Ernie noticed. Even Maria's eyes were drawn to the men. One was Joseph Talmage, the man Ernie had seen in Dodge City and remarked upon to Rory and Caroline. He knew now that his chance mention of that occurrence had set the stage for nearly all of them to be here.

Ernie knew the other man by reputation. Mick Garrity. He owned this saloon and two others. He owned most of the whores in Lake City. For all Ernie knew, he probably owned Joseph Talmage as well.

The men shook hands and parted. Garrity headed for the back room, moving slowly. Joseph, trying to look casual by sauntering on his way, walked past Maria. Or started to. As if he had just noticed her, he paused and spoke to her. Ernie watched them in the mirror, gratified to see that he got no further with her than the lowliest mule driver.

Ernie saw it all. The contemptuous curl of Maria's full lips. The angry tightening of Joseph's smiling mouth. The amused twinkle of Garrity's watchful eyes. Joseph walked on, pretending disinterest, and Garrity left the room, breaking up the tableau and scattering all the focused energy in the room once again.

The scene had decided Ernie on another drink. What he had seen was only a preview for other scenes that would follow. He intended to watch all he could. The more he knew about the principals involved, the better he could do protecting Caroline. That was his purpose, and he tried never to forget it.

His patience was rewarded long before the drink was gone. Mick Garrity came back and made his way directly to Maria. Unlike the others, he didn't try to ingratiate himself with her. He took a seat at her table and restrained her with an ungentle hand when she sought to leave. Whatever he said to Maria, he said it bluntly; that much was plain from his expression. At first Maria held herself haughtily, but she quickly gave up her aloof pose.

They left together soon after, and Ernie wondered what it meant. Had Mick Garrity acquired a new mistress? A prostitute? And what about Al Humphrey? Would he care for Maria's defection?

His doubt about that was proved within minutes when Humphrey emerged, grinning, from the back room. His grin never dwindled when the men were quick to point out his other loss. Another man might have taken offense, but not Humphrey. He had won what he wanted

378

to win. Maria had already served her usefulness. She no longer existed for him.

Ernie saw the men's inability to understand. Some respected him for his coolness. Others, just as mistaken, saw it as weakness. Only Ernie — and Humphrey — knew it for what it was, a matter of total inconsequence.

Except to Maria.

Sunrise in the San Juan Mountains was a precipitous affair that Caroline hated to miss. One minute the sun was obscured by massive angularity; then, abruptly, it was *there* — up — free to soar above the jagged peaks.

The morning after Rory had fled from her bed, she didn't wake until the spectacle was over, nor did she give a thought to what she had missed. Her eyes felt gritty and her head clotted. It throbbed to the dulled beat of her pulse. Sometime after Rory had left her, naked and alone, she had pulled on her robe as protection against the cold night air and dragged herself back to bed. She woke in bedclothes twisted around her like a winding sheet, with her thoughts just as tangled.

Why had he gone? What was wrong with her? He had wanted her. He had! Until . . . something. But what? She had been too forward. That had to be it. But why did he mind that? She knew men paid money for the chance to do what she had been eager to do. Only with Rory, of course, but was that what he minded? Her eagerness?

She kicked off the robe and washed, scrubbing viciously at her unpleasing body. Rory liked her hair; he always praised its color. It was the rest of her that disappointed him. If only she were smaller and rounder, less angular. She thought of Darby's petite voluptuousness. That was what a man wanted. Rory might not like what Darby was, but he must want the way she looked. The thought didn't please her.

If only she didn't have to remember the way she had thrown herself at Rory—and the way he'd been forced to flee her advances, half-dressed and apologetic, manfully trying to absolve her guilt and take the blame upon himself.

She bypassed her most attractive dresses, seeking out the darkest, drabbest she could find. The plain navy blue had buttons that marched to her chin with never an ounce of enticement. To her, it was unrelieved boredom and practicality, suitable for a mourning costume.

In her militant mood she didn't see how the rich color deepened and intensified the blue of her eyes to a heart-breaking indigo. Nor did she guess that a man—the right man—might see challenge in the crisp line of buttons that went down into the narrow valley of her breasts as well as up to her throat.

She brushed her hair until it crackled like her temper and tied it back with a ribbon to match the dress. Childish. Spinsterish. She hurled the words at her image in the mirror, angry that her *hair* pleased when *she* didn't.

If she was blind to her attractiveness, Darby was not. She looked up from the book she was reading, the one Caroline had fallen asleep over, and took in everything. Caroline's energy and her tension. Her unhappiness. "Oh, my," Darby said.

"Good morning," Caroline said brusquely, stalking to the kitchen without pause.

Darby trailed her distantly, her eyes watchful. "Your . . . brother left early," she ventured. "He said Mrs. Larsen wouldn't be coming this week. I hope it's not my fault?"

Caroline stared, trying to follow what she had said. She heard Darby's need for reassurance in the questioning way she conveyed the information. "No, I'm sure it's not. Mrs. Larsen was quite taken with you. It must be something to do with her family. There are a lot of them."

"I made coffee," Darby said. "It's strong, though. That's the way Da liked it. And Pete," she added softly.

Caroline felt a twinge of real sympathy—finally. She got down a cup and saucer. "That's fine. Just what I need." She added cream and watched the mixture roil, then blend with her stirring.

Could she ask Darby what she had done wrong? She turned the question over as she stirred. Would she be offended? Would she laugh at her? Somehow it seemed wrong to talk to someone else about what was so intensely private. Rory had been angry that she'd told Darby that they were not physically related. He'd never forgive her for disclosing something so personal.

But she needed to know. What did men do to learn about women? She tried to imagine Rory seeking advice from another man. The very idea was ludicrous—and mortifying. What would he say? I just couldn't go through with it. I tried, but I couldn't.

If he *ever* . . . but he wouldn't!

And neither would she. It was her shame. Darby wouldn't know any more than she did. How could she? She was so lovely no man had ever run away from her. They *paid*—

She put down the spoon with a clatter and drank a long swallow. Darby was still watching her when she looked up. "How are you feeling?" she asked. "Your bruises are—"

"Colorful," Darby supplied. "*I'm* better, though. I can smile now."

So could Caroline, albeit a bit grimly. "I'm glad." She finished her coffee quickly, casting about in her mind for occupation. "I'm sorry Mrs. Larsen won't be here to help with your dresses, though. I can try it, but I'm likely to botch the whole thing."

"There's no need for you to do anything, Caroline. I can wear my own clothes. They're all clean and mended now."

"No, no, you'll need more. Did I tell you Royal has promised to help you?"

"That's kind of him," Darby said politely.

"I don't know how exactly," Caroline admitted. "He's not the most . . . forthcoming man in the world. But he *is* trustworthy. If he says he'll help, he will."

Darby didn't dispute the claim, nor did she ask the questions Caroline knew *she* would have wanted to ask. To keep her silent, Caroline suggested brightly, "Why don't we see what we can do with the clothes?"

Darby could do quite a bit. More than Caroline, who only marked the seams for alteration. After that, Darby took over, as skillful as Mrs. Larsen. With every accomplishment, Darby complicated Caroline's picture of her—and cleared it at the same time. No matter what Rory thought of Darby, Caroline felt more and more sure that she was a badly wronged woman, not a common prostitute. Her speech and manners, the fact that she could read—everything except what she had seen in the alley—pointed to a charitable view of Darby.

They worked steadily all morning, or at least Darby did. Caroline's attention was fixed elsewhere, although she sat with Darby, sometimes watching her sew, sometimes framing questions she didn't ask, believing them unanswerable anyway. Several times Darby started to ask what was troubling her, but she never did. Caroline didn't notice either her curiosity or her sympathy.

A knock at the front door startled her. She jumped up in confusion and looked worriedly at Darby. "I didn't hear a carriage. Do you suppose you should hide?"

"If you're thinking of Mick, Caroline, he wouldn't knock."

"It's not Gabe. He does a little . . . tattoo."

"I'll go to the stairs and be ready to hide," Darby offered. "Go see."

It was Stu, Caroline's little Cornish pupil. He stood

there grinning up at her. " 'Ello, Miss Farnsworth," he caroled. "I've come fer a lesson, if ye've time today." The way he said "today" made it into "to die." It was just the touch to restore Caroline's spirits. She laughed loudly in relief.

"Oh, Stu! Of course I do. Come in, come in." He was just what she needed. A quick glance over her shoulder told her that Darby had slipped away upstairs. An unnecessary precaution, perhaps, but one Caroline appreciated. Stu was outspoken, and a woman with black and blue marks on half her face would intrigue him. If he spoke of it — well, who knew? Rory said Mick Garrity knew where Darby was. If he really thought that, wouldn't he post some sort of guard? She'd ask him later.

While she thought of all that, she brought Stu into the parlor and fetched their parcel of school materials. On an impulse, she said to him, "Why don't we take our classroom outside today? We can walk down to the stream behind the house and make a picnic of it."

She had two — no, three — reasons for the suggestion. She wanted to be out of the house so Darby could move around, and she liked to see that the boys got some solid food as often as possible. Stu would be sure to tell Owen, her more infrequent pupil, about the picnic, and that would bring him around again soon.

For all those reasons, they left as soon as Caroline packed a suitably nourishing lunch for a growing boy of nine. At the bottom of the stairs she stopped to ask Stu when he had to be home. It was a foolish question, for he was never properly supervised, but she translated his answer into a loud message to the unseen Darby that she would not be back until midafternoon.

Darby came down wearing the most becoming of the dresses Caroline had given her. There were three, each chosen to suit Darby, either in color, style or fit. Their vastly different coloring and body type had eliminated

383

many choices from Caroline's wardrobe, but in this vivid blue all three elements came together to flatter Darby's bright beauty. The dress was already resewn except for the hem, which Darby had only basted in place. It would hold that way while she worked on the other dresses.

It was a familiar process to Darby, like making over clothes so many years ago; hers for Mary, or Mary's for Lucy. Caroline's dresses were nicer than any she had owned as a girl in Iowa. Most of those had begun as hand-me-down from the church ladies, not as dressmaker originals of fine fabrics like this heavy faille. With each stitch she caressed the silk, reveling in the feel of it under her fingers. She knew better than to consider herself lucky, yet that would not keep her from savoring the few compensations she found in her present situation.

When she heard the knock at the door she knew why she had dressed and fixed her hair. That "tattoo," as Caroline called it, signaled Gabriel—the man she had been hoping to see.

"Darby!" he cried when she opened the door. "You look wonderful!"

"I'm much better, thank you. Caroline has taken her pupil for a walk, but perhaps you could keep me company while I sew?"

He could indeed. Darby recognized her own eagerness in him and knew instinctively that no matter what the rest of the world called her, to Gabriel she was as wondrous and magical as he was to her. Their rapport bypassed convention and let them communicate on a level usually available only to children.

He didn't doubt or question her, so Darby could tell him her deepest feelings. His sympathy was complete and nonjudgmental. He was like Caroline, only better. He was a friend she could love.

He told her about growing up in St. Louis, about his mother's sudden marriage to his "father" after years of being called a bastard. He poured out his heart to her

384

and found ease in her acceptance. Unlike Caroline, Darby didn't demand strength from him, so—for her—he could find reserves of fortitude he'd never suspected he had.

Darby's hands fell still over her sewing. Now and then she reached out to touch his arm in a gesture of consolation. He put his hand over hers to show that he appreciated and accepted her kindness. Soon their hands were in a tangle.

Darby noticed and drew back. "Oh, my," she said in dismay. "I haven't even offered you coffee. What can I be thinking?"

She got to her feet. How long had they been talking? It seemed like no time at all and forever, all at once.

Gabe stood at the same time. "I don't need coffee," he said in a voice that throbbed with emotion. He touched her cheek gently. "Your poor beautiful face, Darby."

She turned into his hand, her lips seeking his palm. She had to hold his hand in place, not because he was repulsed by her but because he feared hurting her. She smiled against his hand. "I've never known a man like you."

Sudden consternation made her draw back. She closed her eyes against a black, defeating tide that rose inside her. She had forgotten!

"Darby, Darby." Gabe surged forward to wrap her in his arms. "That wasn't you! It doesn't matter to me. None of it. You're sweet and good and beautiful."

"Gabriel, I'm not. I've been weak and foolish. I wanted to die."

"For good reason." He smiled his angel's smile at her. "But if you had, who would ever love me?"

"Oh, Gabriel, a thousand girls would love you."

"I've never found one, until now."

"But it's too soon for you to know."

"Is it too soon for you to know?"

"No. I knew when I saw you coming over Mick's

shoulder."

"Can't I have the same privilege?"

"But I'm—"

He kissed her, gently but thoroughly. "You're mine."

She was. He was her Archangel Gabriel.

Gabe held her shoulders. "I want to love you, because I *do* love you."

Darby hesitated. He was too good to be true.

"Let me say this once, because I can feel your questions and I know you're afraid. I'm not an angel, despite my name. I don't want you because of your past or in spite of it. It doesn't matter. I'm not pure either. I'll never throw it up to you or doubt you. I want to love you now to make you mine as I will be yours. We'll both become new—together."

Her mouth fell open in wonder. Gabe touched her chin, lifting her mouth to his reverently. Before he sipped from her he said, "I'll work for you and care for you. Please have me, Darby."

"Dorothy Andersen," she said gravely. "My name is Dorothy Evelyn Peters Andersen. My brother Timmy called me Darby and it stuck. I was Darby Peters until I married Peter Andersen." She paused. "Would you really marry me?"

"Would you really have me?"

"Yes. For forever."

"And for now?"

"Oh, yes!" Somewhere along the way she had begun to cry. Now she laughed. The two blended into a confused mix of tears, sighs and finally, hiccups.

Gabe lifted her carefully into his arms and carried her to the stairs. He kept the wall at his shoulder so he could lean on it and stop frequently to kiss her. A cure for hiccups, he said. At the top of the stairs her hiccups were gone, and so were her tears. He shouldered open the first door he came to, kicked it shut, and put Darby on the unmade bed.

386

Darby tried to bounce up, "No, no, Gabriel."

He kissed her. "I won't hurt you, my love. I'll never hurt you."

"I know, but—"

"Shh . . ." His hands sought the fasteners she had resewn that morning, opening the back of the blue dress. "You're so soft and sweet. . . ."

"It's Caroline's," she managed on a quick intake of breath.

"The dress?" He drew it down over her shoulders. "It never looked so lovely on her."

"No, no," Darby moaned. "The . . . room . . ."

Gabe heard a groan that could have been anything. He didn't care. He was barely rational. She was perfect. She was Darby, his Darby. She gave him courage and determination. For her, with her, he would break away from the foolish prison he had built for himself out of his loyalty to his mother. That woman was no more. Now he had Darby. He needed her, and she needed him as his mother never had.

Darby, Darby, his blood sang. And hers answered.

While Gabriel and Darby were finding fulfillment in each other's arms, while Caroline was finding satisfaction of a different kind, teaching Stu to put "s" and "h" together to make "sh" and form words like "shoe" and "shirt," Rory was not faring as well. He had arranged passage for Darby on the next stagecoach out of Lake City and hired the Larsen boys, Nils, Erik and Hal, as round-the-clock guards at his house, but he'd been uncustomarily abrupt with his uncle, who had come to pester him with his seemingly never-ending questions about the mine.

Putting off Uncle Joseph had been a mistake, but Rory had had no patience. Joseph reminded him of Gabe Talmage and of Caroline's—what? Accusation? That's what it had felt like, that plea of hers that he not bring ruin upon innocent Gabe in his father's name.

Rory had not defended himself. He had never confided the details of his battle against the Talmages on the grounds that Caroline was safer not knowing. He told himself he trusted her, but did he? He wanted to. Desperately. His heart believed that Caroline could not have given herself to him last night unless she loved him. His heart told him she was not a woman like Darby. She was true. She was good.

His heart also told him he'd hurt her last night by leaving. He'd done it to protect her, had he not?

But had he? Hadn't he also doubted her? Hadn't he also grasped at the chance to protect them both from making another mistake? She was close to Gabe, and he was so much like Ted Jasper. He had the same build, the same black hair, the same kind of bland pleasantness. Did Caroline still yearn for Ted or someone like him?

Rory had to know.

Things were coming to a head. He could feel it, and not only with Caroline.

Darby's presence was more than just a complication. Mick Garrity would make a move to get her back soon, and he was already causing Rory troubles at Little Josie. Garrity's relationship with Joseph Talmage was no secret, and if he found out how thin the new deposits of silver being worked so diligently really were, he could warn Joseph that he was being bilked.

Wendell Davenport, the superintendent at Little Josie, had double crews working now, as Rory put the final squeeze on Uncle Joseph. He needed only one more week to complete the process. Then, when Little Josie went bust, it would be Joseph Talmage who would lose his too-eager investment in the mine.

Rory would be sorry, but Joseph would not be able to fault the advice he'd given over and over to his dear, greedy uncle. Joseph would know that he had done it to himself by his insistence upon investing in what he'd been warned was a marginal mine.

Uncle Simon had laid the groundwork well, of course, setting out bait and traps for a man like Joseph Talmage, whose greed would always make him willing to believe that tycoons could never go wrong. Determined to be one himself, Joseph had proceeded, sure that the reluctance he met was only a rich man's desire to keep all the profits from the mine to himself.

Joseph would find out the truth, and soon, but by then Rory wanted Caroline safely away. He would not send her with Darby. He would take her himself. Even if she loved Gabe Talmage, Rory would take her to safety. Then she would learn that, whatever his personal feelings for his cousin, he had not stolen Gabe's birthright from him.

It hurt Rory that Caroline could believe that of him, but he knew he had given her no reason to trust him. What he wanted from her, of course, was unreasoning, blind trust, the kind she'd once given to Ted Jasper.

Out of the corner of his eye Rory saw Wendell approach. Without a moment's hesitation, he ducked out of sight. When Rory wasn't on hand Wendell did a fine job. Let him do so now.

Rory was going back to the house. He needed to put everything right with Caroline. He could not demand of her the kind of trust he himself had never given her. He would explain; she would understand.

What he was doing to Uncle Joseph was not "mere revenge." It was justice. His last trip to St. Louis had produced solid evidence that Joseph had caused his father's death. But what good would revenge, or even justice, be to him if Caroline wouldn't have him? He loved her more than he hated Joseph.

It was that simple.

Riding back to town, Rory practiced what he would say to Caroline. He would lay it all out for her and let her decide. He had faith that when she understood the full story she would support him the way she had from their earliest days. She was still Caroline. He had to believe she loved him.

He took a shortcut through the backyard to the stable. Noting that Caroline's little garden was fenced, he simply loosened his mount's girth and let the horse go right there by the back door. The animal would not wander away from so much tender young grass.

Rory let himself in the back door, moving quietly. He wanted to surprise Caroline and avoid Darby, who, after being up so early, had probably gone back to her room to sleep the day away. The house was dark after the bright afternoon sun. Dark and quiet. He went through every lower room, looking for Caroline but not calling out.

He started up the stairs, pausing as he heard a sound from Caroline's room. He smiled. She was resting. She had not slept well last night, he knew. With no Mrs. Larsen to require her attention, she would naturally go back to bed to catch up on her lost sleep. With Darby down the hall, he still couldn't finish what he'd started last night, but he could kiss her and let her know his feelings. He went on, purposeful now.

By the time he reached the top of the steps, the sound coming from Caroline's room had taken on shape and meaning. The bed spoke with an unmistakable rhythm.

Rory stopped with his breath caught in his throat. Who the hell . . .?

But he knew. He knew even before he heard the voice. Gabe.

"Oh, God . . . oh . . . my love . . ."

Rory clenched his fists, ready to batter the door.

A female moan halted him, and Rory put his forehead to the door.

Caroline.

Dear God, if he went in there he'd kill them both!

"Sweetheart, sweetheart," Gabe said. "I've waited all my life for this moment."

"Gabriel . . ."

Rory turned away before he heard more than that soft, gasping sound. He didn't want to hear, to know. God, no!

He ran down the stairs and fled back the way he had come.

Chapter Thirty-two

Guilt made Darby stir long before she was ready to leave Gabriel's arms. She sat up and tugged at him. "Gabriel, please, we must get up. This is so wrong."

He arched a finely curved dark brow at her choice of words. "Wrong?"

"Being here." She indicated the room with a wave. When he failed to react to her suppressed urgency she explained, "this is Caroline's bedroom, not mine. I tried to tell you—"

He sat up, laughing. "Caroline's bedroom?"

Darby watched him look around, feeling jealousy surge. "You've never been here before?"

That made him laugh harder. "My sweet Darby," he murmured, drawing her to his chest. "Do you think I'd bring you here if I had?"

She tried to look severe, but Gabriel looked so pleased, so young and handsome, that she found herself smiling back. "No, my love, I know you wouldn't, but that doesn't mean we can stay. Caroline will be back, and I wouldn't want her to know that we had breached her hospitality this way. How could I explain?"

"It doesn't matter. We'll go to your room."

"We'll do no such thing, Gabriel. You mustn't tease me so."

He drew her down on top of him. "I want to tease you and please you. Oh, God, Darby, I want everything with you. I've never felt this way before in my life. Do you know how wonderful you are?"

"I know how wonderful *you* are." She couldn't resist giving in to his tenderness, kissing him back. She was so utterly happy that too many minutes ticked by before she remembered where they were and scrambled determinedly away from Gabe. He tried to catch her with one outflung arm, but she eluded him and began to dress.

Seeing that she was serious, he took the clothes she tossed his way and followed suit. He had not doubted her before, but seeing this display of scruples in Darby, this concern for another, made him proud of her all over again. He had not mistaken her quality. He helped her refasten the neckline of her dress, nearly overcome by his own feelings.

"You will marry, me, won't you, Darby?"

"You're sure?"

"I've never been surer of anything in my life."

She blinked away her tears and smiled, offering a chaste kiss. "But only if you hurry and go downstairs now. I know it seems foolish, but Caroline has been good to me. I wouldn't offend her for the world."

As soon as Gabriel left she straightened the bed, embarrassed to find she had no idea whether or not it had been made before. The rest of the room was neat, however, so she smoothed and tucked the sheets and covers. She looked back from the door, imprinting the room on her mind so she would be able to remember this place where she had experienced love once again after so long without it.

Gabriel waited for her with her altered dresses bundled in his arms. "Take these and put them with everything that's yours. I'm taking you with me now."

"Gabriel, no. I can't . . . just leave."

He put his arms around her. "My darling, you must. It's not safe here. Garrity knows you're here. He could come after you any minute."

"Caroline told me her brother will help me."

Gabe snorted derisively. "Is he guarding you now?"

Darby smoothed his brow. "I'm glad he's not."

"I'll take care of you, but I can't do it here, and frankly I'll never have a moment of peace unless you're with me from now on."

"Where will we go?"

He patted her hand. "Let me worry about that. You get your things."

"I haven't much." She indicated the dresses she held. "These are Caroline's. I shouldn't take them."

"Of course you should. They won't fit her now and she wanted you to have them."

Darby was persuaded. "I'll write her a note. I don't want her to worry." Good sense, which Darby had in abundance, told her to remain where she was. She trusted Caroline and Royal to continue providing practical protection. She didn't doubt Gabriel's love or his intentions, only his ability to deliver on his intentions. Reason told her that this move was impulsive on his part, that he had no plan.

In spite of all that, Darby was going with him. To refuse would mean turning her back on his gift of love, and she wouldn't do that. She couldn't. She had once given Pete control of her life, following him here to Colorado. That had turned out badly, but she would do it again. She wasn't like Caroline, who steered her own course. Darby knew herself. She had fallen apart after Pete's death because he had been the source of her strength. Gabriel was offering her another chance. She would take it with both hands—no matter the outcome.

Gabe looked up from his pacing at the bottom of the stairs when she appeared. She gave him the bundle she had fashioned out of the cast-off robe.

"That was fast," he approved. "Mother would have taken an hour."

"Just let me find paper for my note and we can go."

She didn't see his frown as she went around him, but she felt his nervousness as he trailed after her to the secretary in the parlor. To distract him as she found pen and ink, she asked, "How well do you know Royal Farnsworth?"

394

"Not well."

"Do you trust him?"

"With you? Not at all."

Darby passed him the bottle of ink to open. She smiled as the stuck cap released immediately for him. "Not with me. In general, do you trust him?"

"I don't know." He wanted to hurry Darby, not philosophize about another man, one he couldn't help but think was a rival for Darby's affections.

She paused with her pen poised to write. "You don't know him well?"

"Caroline was my friend, not him."

"He's not your cousin?"

Gabriel laughed. "Whatever gave you that idea?"

Darby wrote her note before she answered, giving herself time to think. Grateful as she was to Caroline, Darby was leaving her behind and casting her lot with Gabriel. That meant he now commanded her loyalty, particularly in areas of possible conflict. She sensed that there might be many such areas in the future and wondered if perhaps she was speaking too soon.

She stood so Gabriel could not read her message to Caroline, pleased that he hadn't tried to dictate her words. That display of confidence in her did a lot to restore her lost self-respect. She closed the envelope. "I'll put this here on the chair where she can't miss it," she told Gabe as she turned back to him. "Now I'm ready to go."

He watched her intently. "You didn't answer my question."

Darby had made her decision. What she had overhead between Caroline and Royal was too important to keep from Gabriel. He already doubted his own parentage, and she felt certain he felt little affection for Joseph Talmage. Shouldn't he know as much as possible about what Royal was doing? And Royal *was* doing something, something that even brave Caroline found frightening.

Caroline had been kind to her, but in a choice Darby knew her friend's loyalty was to Royal, not to her.

So it was with Darby. Gabriel was her man. She would not keep anything from him.

"The first night I was here," Darby said, "I overheard Caroline and Royal talking. They spoke of an uncle. I thought it might be your father."

"Their uncle is a financial wizard named Simon Sargent. He's the man behind all this." He indicated the house with a gesture. "My father only dreams he'll be as rich as their uncle."

"You don't dream of riches?"

"I haven't the stomach for what they do to gain it. I want a good life, but I'd be much happier running a store somewhere. A mercantile with clean, orderly shelves full of useful products—that's my dream."

"Why, Gabriel, that's wonderful!"

"Wonderful? No, Darby, it's much too ordinary to be wonderful."

Darby didn't agree. This was just the assurance she needed from Gabriel. It proved beyond doubt that he was the right man for her. It made telling him easier.

"Royal called the man 'my sweet Uncle Joseph' in a very sarcastic tone, Gabriel. And Caroline called him 'your uncle' to Royal," Darby said, choosing her words carefully. "She was worried that Mick was connected to your family. I wasn't wrong about the reference. The discussion centered around you, because you had rescued me."

Gabriel was stunned. "That doesn't make sense," he protested. "I've never seen either of them before we came here."

"Caroline has little to do with it. She's not really Royal's sister."

"What?"

Darby smiled. "Shocking, isn't it? Especially since they're in love with each other."

396

"You're making this up."

"No, I'm not. Caroline confirmed that Royal isn't her real brother. She says he was adopted after all his family died of cholera during the last of the war. I didn't let her know I had overhead her conversation. It was easy to guess their relationship from the way they look at each other," she said.

Again she had shocked him. "I don't mean they sleep together. They don't. That's why I could see that they weren't really related. They're frustrated, so it shows more. At least it did to me, living among them as I did."

Gabe shook his head, confused. "Why are you telling me this?"

"I thought you should know," she answered simply. "I don't know what it means, if anything, but Caroline spoke of something Royal was trying to do that concerned your father." She shrugged. "I guess the real question is why I'm telling you now—when you say we have to hurry. Do you still think I should come with you? Now that you see what a good spy I can be?"

"Don't be ridiculous. Whatever you heard, it hardly concerns us. I want you with me. Nothing will ever change that."

Her talk of being a spy had been a poor joke. Nevertheless, she was relieved that he hustled her up into his mother's carriage. Moved, she took his hand and vowed, "I love you, Gabriel. I'll never let you down."

For a moment his expression was pained; then he dashed away, back into the house. In view of her faith in him, it seemed wrong to scan Darby's note, then tuck it into his inner waistcoat pocket. Caroline would worry, but he wanted nothing left behind that would lead Mick Garrity to him. If Gabe would walk in and out like this, what was to keep Garrity's men from doing the same thing?

That done, he rummaged further until he found something to take with him. It was a hat, plain and unstylish, probably one of Mrs. Larsen's. He gave it to Darby. "To hide your hair," he said. "Now no one will guess you're not my mother."

His claim was absurd, but Darby had no way of knowing about his mother's obsession with fashion. She was pleased that he had foreseen a problem and done something to circumvent it.

"Where are we going?"

Gabriel grinned. "Where else would I take my mother but home?"

When Caroline returned home, much later than she expected, she wasn't surprised not to see Darby. The tidy kitchen and parlor told Caroline that her guest had finished altering the dresses, eaten what she chose, and gone to bed. An intelligent move, Caroline decided with a yawn.

Her lesson with Stu had turned into a ramble that had cleared her mind and relaxed her body. She left the lunch basket and packet of books and papers in the kitchen, deciding for once to put her own needs first. She would nap, then deal with everything else, and that included Rory as much as Darby. More, in fact. Darby took care of herself, at least domestically, better than Rory did.

Once she got to her room and saw her neatly made bed, Caroline couldn't help smiling. Darby, it seemed, also took care of her. Her last thought as she pulled up a light cover was a reminder to herself to thank her efficient and kind friend in the morning. Although she had only taken off her outer clothes, choosing to sleep in her shift rather than search out proper nightclothes, she knew she would sleep right through the night. She was that tired.

It wasn't to be. The next thing she knew rough hands pulled her upright and a harsh voice demanded, "All right, Caroline. What have you done with her?"

"What?"

Light, brighter than daylight, glared in her face. She pulled back from it and from the smell of whiskey.

"Rory?" She put up her hand, warding him off. "What's wrong?"

"You tell me."

That was easy. "You're drunk."

He wasn't. He had stopped at three drinks hours ago. He'd eaten, too: a bowl of stew the alcohol had evidently preserved in his stomach. It sat there still, a bowl of rocks in his middle. "What have you done with her?"

"I don't know what you're talking about, Rory." She squinted around her arm. "Would you please turn down that lamp?"

He pushed it away instead. "Darby's gone."

She sat up. "Gone?"

"Gone."

"But she can't be." Caroline tried to scramble out of bed, but Rory was sitting on the covers.

He didn't move. "Looking for her won't do any good. She's not here. I've looked everywhere."

"You're drunk," she repeated, and this time he moved aside so she could get up. He watched her find her robe and run out, only to come back for the lamp. He followed to the door, where he leaned, waiting until she had inspected Darby's empty room.

She walked back slowly. "I don't understand. What could have happened? I didn't hear anything."

Rory took the lamp and returned to her room. "Maybe you shouldn't have exerted yourself so much this afternoon," he said sarcastically.

Caroline sat down so hard the bed squeaked. Locked in her own misery, she didn't see Rory flinch at the sound. "Maybe I shouldn't have," she said angrily, "but I needed it. I didn't sleep well last night and—" She broke off, suddenly aware that she was revealing too much to Rory.

He came to stare down at her, revulsion in every line of his face. "Jesus, Caroline how could you do that? I don't understand you at all."

Confused, Caroline stared at him. He looked *hurt*. Wounded. "Do you care so much?" she whispered. She thought he disliked Darby!

He turned away without answering, but not before she saw his deep pain. She got up and followed. He wouldn't let her near him.

"I'm sorry, Rory," she said helplessly. "Really, I am." He held himself stiffly erect, as remote from her as the man in the moon. "We'll get her back for you, don't worry. Even if Mick Garrity has her, he won't be able to keep her hidden away forever, and she's a lot stronger than she seems." Talking to his back was hard, but eventually she saw him move. She had his attention, anyway.

Rory looked at her blankly. "Do you think I give a damn about *Darby?* After this?"

His incredulity puzzled Caroline. She extended her hand. "Come sit down. You look like you're going to fall over." He had to be drunk. He wasn't making sense. "What time is it, anyway?"

He passed a hand over his face. She was right about the falling down part. He drew out a chair and sat, having no stomach to join her on the bed. "It's after two by now."

"And you just came home?" she scolded.

"And you care?"

"Of course I care!" Caroline's temper ignited. "Rory, I told you I'm sorry. I fell asleep. Is that a crime? She's my friend, too, you know! In fact, *I* was the one who brought her here. I didn't know you cared."

"Let's get this straight, Caroline. I *don't* care. Not really. But I hired men to watch the house and—"

"You did? When?"

"Tonight. Nils Larsen is sitting out there now, guard-

400

ing—"

"Since when?"

"Six o'clock. He said he'd watch all night tonight.
Tomorrow he and his cousins will start a sensible rotation
of eight-hour shifts." Rory started up. "I'd better go tell
him to go home."

Caroline stopped him. "Then she must have gone before six, or Nils would have seen her leave. Wouldn't
he?"

"He should have."

"Then she was taken this afternoon—while I was out."

"Out? Is that what you call it?"

"Well, it started as a picnic, then we walked all over. I
was reading—"

Rory surged out of the chair to put his hand over
Caroline's mouth. "I don't want to hear it!"

Her eyes widened. She drove her elbow into his stomach, surprising him into releasing her. She jumped to her
feet and confronted him. "Look, Rory, I don't know
what your problem is—"

He rose to tower over her. "Don't you?" he sneered.
"You're my problem! Before you run on and on with a
pack of lies, it might interest you to know that I came
home this afternoon. I know exactly how you spent the
afternoon!"

Something was wrong here. "How did I spend my
afternoon?" she challenged.

Again he looked mortally wounded. "You're going to
make me say it?"

"Of course I am. I didn't do anything wrong."

"If that's the way you see it, then you're no better than
Darby."

She couldn't mistake his meaning. "Tell me."

"You were making love—"

"Oh, yes, of course I was," she threw back at him. "I
was rolling around in the grass—"

"Here. In this bed."

401

"I wasn't here, I tell you. I took Stu Treggar on a picnic—"

"Stu Treggar? Who's that?"

"My pupil. The Cornish boy. I told you. I have two boys I'm teaching to read. . . ." Caroline groped for the chair and sat. "You heard someone making love . . . here?"

"Not someone. Gabe Talmage."

"Gabe?"

"I started up the stairs and I heard the bed. Then I heard Gabe and—"

"Not me, Rory. It must have been Darby." She started to laugh. "Of course! They're crazy about each other!"

"But I heard . . . you. A woman's voice. You . . . she said, 'Oh, Gabriel.'" He imitated a female moan of passion.

"That's what she calls him," Caroline laughed. "Gabriel, her angle of deliverance or something. Oh, that's funny!"

"Funny!" Rory exploded. "You think that's funny! You tear my heart out by the roots and you think that's funny?"

"Tear your heart out? Oh, Rory, did I do that?"

He couldn't respond to her soft manner. He was still angry. "Of course you did. What do you think?"

"You left me last night. You tore my heart out and didn't care."

"I did care. I didn't want to leave you. I did it for you."

"That's not what if felt like."

"Caroline, these walls are paper. Darby was just down the hall. She could hear—"

"Why didn't you *tell* me? Explain?"

"I did explain—"

"You said, 'I can't. I just can't.' That's an explanation?"

"My God, woman, I wasn't coherent. I wanted you! It

402

was all I could do to walk. You expected me to talk at the same time?"

Caroline's heart began to do a little jig. "Why did you come back this afternoon?"

He paced away. "I wanted to talk to you."

She smiled. "Talk?"

"What you said last night, about stealing from Gabe, bothered me. I've never told you all the particulars of my plan. I was going to tell you." He took a breath, like someone about to jump into deep water. "It's not really what you think, you know. It's—"

"Irrelevant," Caroline finished for him. She put her and over his mouth, much as he had but softly. "It doesn't matter, Rory. I know you. You'd never do anything to hurt Gabe—or anyone," she added rashly.

"Don't be too sure of that." Rory's mouth was a grim line under his mustache. "I didn't dare come back until I was sure he was gone. I was afraid I'd kill him."

"So you got drunk."

"Don't keep saying that. I got drunk once over you, when you told me you were going to marry Ted. Once was enough. It didn't change anything."

Caroline heard his bitterness. She framed his face with her hands and peered up at him earnestly. "Rory, please, can we put all that behind us? I made a mistake then. It was terrible, but really, so was this today. Imagine! How could you think I would . . . with Gabe? It's ridiculous. I could never love Gabe."

"He's very much like Ted."

"No, he's not. He's like *someone* I know, but I can't think who. It's something about his voice."

"His mother?"

"No, she just talks slowly. It's the tone, or something." She shrugged indifferently. "The important thing is, Gabe has Darby with him, don't you think? That means she's safe."

Rory smiled slowly. "Yes, that's the important thing.

403

Darby's not here now. That's the most important thing in the world to me now."

Caroline felt herself grow light. "Does that mean you'll love me now that we're alone at last?"

For answer he took her hand and kissed her gently. "Not here," he said, drawing her along with him.

She followed, feeling resigned and a little indelicate. Was there something wrong with her that she didn't worry about their surroundings the way he did? She wanted him so badly she didn't care for the circumstances of their mating.

Still, she could understand—partly. He had overheard Darby and Gabe there in her room. She appreciated his sensitivity.

He took her to his bedroom. When she saw the room she began to laugh. "Oh, yes, Rory, this is much better."

The room was in a shambles. Discarded clothes lay everywhere, and the bed was unmade. Rory looked around as if he'd never seen the place before. He found a place for the lamp, frowned and hitched at his belt. "Mrs. Larsen hasn't been in here for a while."

While she went on laughing, he marched to the bed and yanked away the covers and top sheet.

His glare back at her increased her amusement. "I'm sorry, Rory. It's just that I was wondering about myself, trying to figure out why I don't care where or how you loved me, as long as you finally do. I thought perhaps I was being unwomanly again." She put her arms around his shoulders and leaned into him. "Now I think maybe it's a good thing I'm not too delicate."

He gave her a sheepish smile. "I'm a real clod, aren't I?" He lifted her face to his. "Can you just close your eyes and let me make it perfect for you this time? I want you so much."

She shook her head, giving him a small smile. "It won't be perfect unless I can see you. But if I can see you," she added, "I won't see anything else."

404

"Show me," he said. His hands dropped away as he indicated his willingness to let her do as she would with him.

With a wicked, daredevil gleam lighting her eyes, she began to undress him. She took his waistcoat and shirt off as one, dropping them to the floor and nestling her face in the golden fleece on his chest. She inhaled deeply. "Now you smell like you," she said, giving him little love bites on his shoulders and upper chest. The whiskey smell was gone with his coat; something spilled, she realized. Not Rory.

He pulled off his boots for her and submitted to the tantalizing business she made of taking off his pants. He wasn't passive, though. No, indeed. He was all waiting power framed by tensed and ready muscles.

Caroline skimmed the pants down his legs and stepped back so he could kick them off. He straightened and nodded to her. "Show me how pretty you are."

She expected to be self-conscious, but with Rory approving every move she made it was easy to cast aside her robe. Her hands trembled as she slid the shift down her shoulders. Although it settled at her waist briefly, by then Rory was helping her, reaching to touch the pale gleam of her skin.

Rory couldn't wait. He lifted her from the rest of her clothing, releasing the magical creature that she was from the dross around her. She was pure loveliness with open arms. Just for him. Once before he'd thought he'd lost her to Ted. Today had been a repeat of that terrible day, her wedding day. This was his second miracle, finding out he had been wrong. This time he would make her so completely his that no one could ever challenge him again.

He placed her on the bed, moving over her slowly. Conqueror and protector both, he sheltered her body with his own, resting for a moment in the cleft of her legs. "Trust me, my heart. This time there'll be no pain," he whispered.

"Not even for you?"

Her caught her teasing grin and smiled back. "Let me show you how brave I can be." He rolled to the side and took her hands, placing them on his chest, holding them there. "Touch me," he urged. "Do your worst. Make me suffer."

Caroline's eyes sparkled. "Like this?" She traced the slanting line of a ridge of muscle in his chest, her touch firm. "I've wanted to touch you for so long, Rory."

He sucked in his breath in answer as she explored his body. The tangled curls on his chest that narrowed to almost nothing at his lean waist. His hips that had none of the soft flare she knew from her own body. His legs that were indeed "limbs," the word Gramma Lunig used to be proper.

Caroline was not proper. She rubbed her palms down those sturdy limbs, relishing the feeling of soft, springy hair over treelike hardness. He flexed his leg muscles restlessly and groaned. Her glance flicked up to his face. "Ah," she murmured. "You're not so tough after all."

Rory caught her hands and put her onto her back to nuzzle a line from her breasts down to her thighs. Heat from her body made his head swim. "I give up."

It was pure ecstasy for Caroline. This time Rory held nothing back. He gave and took from her in an endless upward curl. Each touch gave pleasure and joy as her body was lost to her control. Each nip of his teeth, each stroke of his hand, drove her spiraling up another flight of stairs. She clung to him in supplication as the stairs grew steeper and the height more breathtaking. At each plateau he gave her less time to recover from the climb until she was swept away by delight. He persuaded her, wooing her from within her own body, overpowering her with her own blind need.

She wanted to shout her love and pledge eternal vows she had no breath to utter. It didn't matter. Nothing did.

Her pledge had been given with her heart and body. She loved.

It was enough.

Late the next morning Caroline came awake with a start. She was alone in Rory's bed. One look at the room told her she had slept through a lot of activity. Her clothes were neatly folded on a chair by the bed, and Rory's were put away. All of them. She pulled free of the sheet that was her only cover and sat up, wondering how she could have slept while he had done so much unaccustomed labor. Why hadn't she heard the clothespress open or close?

She remembered sleeping in Rory's arms. He had stroked her hair back from her face and kissed her eyes closed. She'd been so at peace. How could she not have woken the instant he left her arms?

Caroline pulled on her robe and went to her own room. She would bathe, dress and eat — physical creature that she was — and then she would go to Gabe's and talk to Darby. She was still worried about her. Rory would be checking into her whereabouts and safety, but he had other, more pressing matters to attend to as well. Darby was more her concern than his.

Then, too, she and Gabe had never finished their work for the Fourth of July. Even if Beatrice had taken over their abandoned project, there would be jobs for her to do. The celebration was tomorrow.

Caroline hurried to dress. She felt restored and filled with energy. Rory loved her; she could do anything, move anything, accomplish anything. Laughing, she put down her hairbrush and twirled across the bedroom, hugging herself with joy.

With her back to the door, Caroline never saw the two men who rushed into the room at that moment. She heard the door open, but before she could turn, one of the men clubbed the back of her head.

The other, a small man who was nearly hairless, bent to pick her up. "I thought she was supposed to be a redhead. This ain't no redhead."

"Whatever," came the answer.

Together, they wrapped Caroline in a blanket from the bed while the bald man continued to worry. "What if we got the wrong woman?" he asked. "Mick won't like it if we got the wrong woman."

"You see any other?" the big man asked.

Stymied for an answer but still unhappy, his partner picked up his end of the blanket without further comment.

Chapter Thirty-three

The scene unfolding on the street before him was the culmination of years of planning and scheming. It should have meant everything to Rory Talmage.

He knew odds well enough not to gamble, yet here was Uncle Joseph, learning about his total financial ruin in full view of the man who had arranged it, the very nephew Uncle Joseph had cheated and made an orphan so many years ago.

Rory could not compute the odds against that happening. Neither could he calculate the likelihood that it would mean so little to him at this moment.

He watched from deep shade next to the mine office, amazed that he could have forgotten that today the Little Josie mine was closing for good. He had come from a meeting with the Larsen boys, who were coordinating the search for Caroline.

Caroline. Her name was a raging ache in his heart.

He had left her this morning, never thinking that she would be in danger. Knowing that Darby had left, he had called off the guard on his house just in time to open the way for Caroline's abduction. Full of happiness and foolish beyond belief, he had failed to protect Caroline. Now he saw everything, even Uncle Joseph, through a blinding haze of regret.

Joseph Talmage stood in sharp relief against the sun-washed building behind him. Rory could actually see his uncle's face drain of its normal ruddy color as he absorbed the blow.

The man giving the news to Joseph was unimportant, although it was clear from the way he spoke that he knew the impact of his message. He said it cheerfully, the way people do when they know they themselves will not be adversely affected. "You've heard the bad news? That Little Josie's gone bust?"

He said more, but neither Joseph nor Rory listened. Joseph put out his hands as though to ward off a blow, then folded them over his sagging middle.

Rory turned away. Once he would have hurried back to the office. He knew how it would go. Joseph would charge in, demanding an explanation. Wendell Pendleton would say the words for Rory.

"We're so sorry, Joseph. We knew it was a risk. We hoped to pull it off, but the vein just flat-out disappeared—dwindled down to nothing."

Wendell wouldn't gloat. He was not a party to the scheme Rory and Uncle Simon had perpetrated. Wendell was honest. He didn't know that the secret shifts of workers—usually a sign that a big strike had been found—were decoys. Wendell would apologize and commiserate with Joseph—if Joseph would let him.

Rory didn't care. His triumph tasted of ashes. Caroline was right. He had broken Uncle Joseph, but who was Joseph? He was a mean-spirited shell of a man. He was nothing.

Rory went back the way he'd come. He had men everywhere looking for Caroline, but there was one person he hadn't sought yet. Maybe . . .

He broke into a run.

The sounds coming from the next room were so familiar to Darby that she resisted waking. She burrowed under the pillow. The silky feel of the pillow cover brought her up sharply, reminding her that she wasn't at Mick's place any more.

She sat up, affirming herself and what she knew. This was Gabriel's room in Gabriel's house. She was in

Gabriel's bed, where she had slept last night. He was hiding her from Mick, just as she'd told Caroline in her note. She'd not been specific, because she hadn't known Gabriel's intention. And she could never have guessed how easy it would be.

Gabriel had two rooms to himself, rooms no one else entered except at his request. His mother left housekeeping to hired help she had trouble keeping. Darby hadn't met Priscilla Talmage; she wasn't sure she wanted to—ever. She loved Gabriel, but his mother sounded like a dragon. Even with the best intentions, Gabriel painted the forbidding picture of a selfish, harsh woman with perhaps one redeeming quality—her love for Gabriel.

Almost two days of virtual captivity had not blunted Darby's pleasure in her accommodations. If she had to hide away, this was the way to do it. She had heard from Gabriel that Caroline's uncle was a man of fabulous wealth, but by comparison with the Talmages, Caroline and Royal Farnsworth lived modestly. Everything here was fancy. She had food, shelter, clothing and amusement. When Gabriel wasn't with her she could read, sew or nap. He was even teaching her to play chess.

Another sound froze Darby half-in and half-out of bed. She hadn't seen the room next door. Gabriel told her it was his mother's sitting room, a room much like his own parlor. Now she understood why she woke from this nap thinking of Mick's Palace of Pleasure. She moved soundlessly, muscle by muscle, pulling a blanket around her suddenly cold shoulders.

That groan—

No one had used the room before. A maid? No. Gabriel said his mother had a male cook and no maid. But—

"Say it!" urged a low female voice.

A muffled groan. "Ah . . . Pris . . ."

Pris!

411

Even through the wall Darby heard the lascivious glee in the voice that forced Mick Garrity to repeat his praise of her accomplishments. "Nobody . . . ah, God—" He started again and finished in a rush. "Nobody . . . does it better."

Mick Garrity and Priscilla Talmage. Darby tried to understand.

Did Gabriel know?

What did it mean?

When Mick spoke again Darby could imagine the satisfaction on his face. His voice was lazy and clotted—dangerous, she thought abstractedly, listening hard. "I heard something about that girlfriend of your son's the other day."

Darby's reaction was no less sharp than Priscilla's. "My son has no girlfriend!"

"No?" He chuckled nastily. "Does that mean you don't want to hear my news?"

Darby smiled. How beautifully Mick played Priscilla.

"I have a little girlfriend of my own, one who used to know your son's friend, Caroline." He lavished emphasis on the words he knew riled Priscilla Talmage. "She's working as an exotic dancer for me. She's a regular hot tamale. The men go crazy for her, especially for her high-and-mighty airs. She came here with a man named Al Humphrey. Does that name mean anything to you?"

Darby felt the escalation of tension right through the flimsy wall.

"I don't believe it does," Priscilla answered.

"And I don't believe you," Mick replied.

"I don't require your belief."

"That's a good thing," Mick laughed. "That way I don't have to remind you who Thomas Yarborough was."

Desperately, Darby wished to be able to see into the next room. Priscilla said nothing, but did she react to Mick's taunt?

The silence was thick as molasses.

"Or do you know him better as Baltimore Blackie, Pris?"

"I . . . may have heard that name . . . somewhere."

Darby racked her brain. The name meant nothing to her.

"Doubtless you remember seeing him hang in Dodge City last year."

"I may have." Priscilla's effort to regroup was obvious. "But what does all this have to do with Caroline Farnsworth?" Her own mind gave her the answer, and she gasped. "So *that's* where I heard her name! She was the one who captured Baltimore Blackie's gang!"

Priscilla had given up all pretense of not knowing Baltimore Blackie. A convicted criminal, recently executed, Darby reasoned out, but what else? Darby knew Mick Garrity. He had a reason for bringing up Priscilla's knowledge of this man. What was it? What did he know?

"More than that," Mick urged. "Think, Priscilla Belasco!"

Gabriel's mother was absorbing one jolt after another. Darby knew that. What she didn't know was the background. What did these names mean to Priscilla? Because, she realized, if they meant something to Priscilla, they also meant something to Gabriel. But what? Could she use this information to help Gabriel?

She stored the names away. Yarborough. Belasco. Perhaps Gabriel would understand.

"My, my, Michael," Priscilla said on a soft laugh. "How thorough you've been."

"Thorough enough to know that your precious son is not Joseph Talmage's 'get,' as they say in the horse business."

"If you think you'll terrorize me with that information, you're wrong."

413

"Me? Terrorize you? I know better than to try. I only want to do you a favor. My little Mexican friend Maria tells me that Al Humphrey came here to kill Caroline Farnsworth. I thought you might want to help him."

"Why?"

"You don't want to avenge your lover's death?"

"I traveled long and hard to watch him die," Priscilla said with chilling sincerity.

"Because of Kid?"

"Yes. He killed Boyd just as surely as that mob did. Boyd was a fool, but he was a sweet fool and he was my little brother. Thomas should have protected him. He never did. He let him get caught robbing that bank in Independence and—"

As Priscilla broke down in tears, Darby found evidence that Gabriel's mother had once loved another person besides Gabriel. Not the man who had sired her son, but a brother who was now dead. Boyd. Kid. Another criminal nickname?

Mick's voice broke into Darby's thoughts. "And who caught him in that bank in Independence?" he asked Priscilla.

"Some little girl and her father," she answered angrily. "They were—"

"Caroline Farnsworth was the little girl," Mick said. "She's the one who killed your brother Boyd."

"No!"

"Yes," Mick insisted. "Blackie knew. Twice she fouled up his life. And yours. That's why Humphrey is here. He promised Blackie he'd get the girl. And he will."

"Why do you care?" Priscilla demanded.

"She's an interfering little bitch. She and your son stole one of my whores. But I've got her back now, and *she's* going to lead Miss Farnsworth right to me. Humphrey can have her when I'm done with her, but I get first crack at her."

Darby put a hand over her mouth. She was so full of information and fear she was sure it would bubble out noisily and give her away. She listened to Mick and Priscilla, knowing that all the time she'd been lounging here in comfort and safety, Caroline had been in danger. Her danger would grow worse—particularly when Mick found out that the woman he thought was Darby—his decoy—was really his prey.

Darby had to hurry. But first she had to wait for a chance to steal away from Priscilla and Mick.

Caroline considered her situation again. It was still bleak. Nothing had changed all day, not even the throb of pain emanating from the back of her head. There was nothing else to do, however; thinking and planning passed the time.

Physically, there was little she could do. *Correction*, she thought wryly. *Make that nothing.* She was bound and gagged. She wasn't guarded, though, at least not obviously.

The lack of anyone nearby weighed on her mind heavily, in fact. Was she to be left here indefinitely? If, as she suspected, she had been taken by Mick Garrity's men in place of Darby, why hadn't she been taken to him? What did he intend for Darby? That was the biggest puzzle to her.

She was in a small, rough building, probably one of the storage huts where mining equipment was kept. She and Stu Treggar had picnicked next to one of these outbuildings just yesterday. They were dotted around the area like outcroppings of rock in a meadow. With the mines closed for the Fourth of July, no one would come here for days. She wouldn't die in that time, but she'd probably wish herself dead many times before anyone discovered her accidentally.

She had tried without success to roll over to what looked like a pile of pickaxes and cut her hands free. Tonight she would be glad for the warmth of the blanket around her, but now it impeded her progress. It wasn't dark yet, just very dim because the shack had no windows.

It was late afternoon before anyone came. Caroline was amazed to discover how quickly she could change her mind. After hoping and praying she hadn't been forgotten, her first sign of company terrified her. She found she didn't want to confront Mick Garrity after all. The hammering of her heart set the back of her head pounding to the same rhythm, and between the two of them all she could hear was her own fearful pulse.

Then the door opened and she could see more of her untidy surroundings. The man who unrolled her from the blanket was untidy, too. She smelled him before she saw him. He was as large as Mick Garrity, with long hair that hung down his back like the strands of a dirty mop. He untied her and let her stand, but didn't answer any of her questions.

He led her outside with one ankle tied by the rope he continued to hold. Although he played it out far enough to give her a modicum of privacy to relieve herself, she knew her chances of untying it and escaping were slim. For all his size, the man seemed agile.

She decided to be a model prisoner in the hope of being left alone again. She hadn't long outside. He brought her water in a dirty jar and two slabs of dry bread. She needed all the water just to lubricate her dry mouth after being gagged. She asked for more water, finally pantomiming the need to wash. She concluded from his silence and lack of response to her questions that he didn't speak English. He did get her the water after securing the rope to a hinge of the door. He was back with it quickly, so quickly she wouldn't have been

416

able to run away.

She had no intention of running. She thought she could do better as a docile victim. The man attending her wasn't vicious. There was even a look of dumb sympathy in his eyes. Acting totally cowed, she let him retie her, making sure she had as much play as possible between her wrists. He didn't replace the gag when she struggled against it, nor did he tie her ankles again.

But when he left she became despondent. Here she was, locked inside the same dark shack. Even if she could cut her hands free, how would she get out? And who would find her here?

She thought it was the same shack where she and Stu had rested during their hike, but Stu wouldn't come here today. No one would. She disgraced herself with some uncharacteristic tears before she brought her errant emotions back under control by focusing her mind on Rory.

He was her hope. He loved her. He would rescue her.

Darby had to endure most of a second sexual exchange between Mick Garrity and Priscilla before she was ready to leave Gabriel's rooms. Once she was dressed, she started to make her escape while they were busy with each other. But they were interrupted.

Something—some instinct of Priscilla's or a fortituous glance out the window—alerted her to Joseph's return. At another time Darby might have enjoyed Mick and Priscilla's scurry to make themselves presentable. They just made it, although Darby could tell from her listening post that Joseph was too upset to notice anything beyond his own dilemma.

He burst into his wife's parlor, proclaiming his catastrophic news. "We're ruined, Priscilla!"

Only Mick was equal to the occasion. "I just got here, Joseph," he said smoothly. "I came as soon as I heard

417

the news." Then *he* told Priscilla about the close of Little Josie!

Darby could imagine Priscilla's fury that in all the time he had been with her he hadn't seen fit to mention something so important to her. He'd been toying with her, literally and figuratively, during their long, intimate exchange.

Darby knew about Little Josie. Some of her customers worked in the mine, and she knew it was vital to Gabriel's future. If Joseph was ruined by the close of Little Josie, so was Gabriel.

She heard Priscilla's outcry with half her mind, trying at the same time to gauge her chances of fleeing the house. Her need for Gabriel was extreme. Caroline was in physical danger, and Gabriel's whole future was in disarray.

She took a deep breath at the door, poised to make a run out of the house, then froze as Mick spoke again, rooting her feet to the floor.

"You know who did this to you, don't you, Joseph?"

Priscilla answered before Joseph could. "Royal Farnsworth."

"You have the man right," Mick said, "but not the name. Didn't you recognize him, Joseph? He's your nephew."

"I don't have any nephew," Joseph denied quickly.

"Rory Talmage?" Mick goaded. "Surely you remember your nephew Rory!"

"He's dead."

"He didn't die. He's been looking for you for years, looking for revenge on you."

"How do you know so much?" Priscilla challenged.

"It's my business to know about people, Mrs. Talmage. One of my employees, a dancer, comes from New Mexico where the Farnsworth family lives. She's been most informative."

418

"I don't understand," Joseph said.

Darby had heard enough. She eased the door open and slid through the crack. Everything in her life had come apart. For Caroline, for Royal . . . Rory, and for Gabriel.

If she didn't do something, find someone—Rory or Gabriel—Mick Garrity would win everything and own everything.

She ran down the hall for the back entrance, the one Gabriel had used to bring her here. At heart she was still a country girl. She could—and would—ride anything with four legs she could find in the stable.

She wanted Gabriel, but instinct told her that Rory was the man she needed now. In spite of everything, she still trusted him.

Priscilla gave scant attention to the plans Joseph made with Mick. She was lost in the past.

She remembered the newspaper picture, grainy and yellowed, of Caroline Farnsworth and her father after their capture of her brother Boyd in Independence. At the time the name hadn't been important to her. She had hated the smug, proud look on the girl's face to the exclusion of everything else. Would the words in the article have meant more if she could read? She didn't know. She'd felt so helpless then. The girl had been gone, out of her reach. But Thomas—Blackie—was close to her, as close as Gabriel. Every time Gabe spoke she could hear Thomas and hate him anew.

Love and hate. They were so mixed. She had once loved Thomas. Then she hated him. She loved Gabe, but with him her love reminded her of her hate. It was too complicated.

She pressed her hands to her head. The ache was so much worse these days. It throbbed and pounded like a living thing inside her brain, making it hard to think. She could safely leave Rory Talmage to Joseph. But Caroline? What should she do about Caroline?

How entangled their lives were—one with the other. She had instinctively disliked Caroline on first sight. Now she wondered how she could have overlooked that blondness. Shouldn't she have suspected her identity? Had she?

The honest answer was no. She had disliked Caroline because Gabe liked her. Gabe was *hers*. Everything she did, she did for Gabe. He was her life. Earlier, she had worried about Gabe and Caroline, but then she'd sensed that there were no hidden currents racing between them. Caroline really wasn't very feminine, in spite of her looks. She didn't seem to flirt or have any wiles. A very boring young woman, Priscilla had decided.

There *was* something about Gabe of late, however. An air of suppressed excitement that didn't bode well.

Mick left, and still Priscilla could not rally. Their plot was simple, as all the best plots are. They were careful men. Both of them would be far away from the mess, surrounded by Fourth of July celebrants, and thus innocent of blame when Caroline Farnsworth and Rory Talmage died. That was the way they always operated.

Priscilla almost laughed at Joseph. How he talked! And how little she cared.

He left, came back and left again. Her head ached on. Lately, one powder she relied on for relief didn't touch the pain even at double strength. It was dark when she woke, still dressed, still in her chair.

Where was Gabe?

She never went to his room, but now she did. His empty bed had been slept in. Her giddy sense of relief lasted only until she saw the bright green dress on the floor. She fell on it with pain shrieking through her head. He'd had a woman here! In her house!

420

Priscilla sat, holding the dress, until the first streaks of light replaced her guttering lamp. She had fallen into a near trance of pain and anguish. And hate. Hate prowled through her head, pushing at the boundaries of her skull. This was more of Caroline Farnsworth.

Pushing onto her feet, Priscilla went to find Joseph.

He was a sorry sight. In sleep, his mouth was slack, with snores rattling in and out, punctuated by an assortment of whistles and groans. She pushed him onto his side and thrust the dress at him, demanding to know whatever he knew about the woman.

Caroline. She wanted it to be Caroline, but everything about the dress was wrong for Caroline. The color. The style. The scent clinging to the fabric.

Incredibly, Joseph laughed at her questions. His explanations fell over her like an avalanche, burying logic, sweeping away reason.

A whore! Her Gabe and one of Mick Garrity's whores! She couldn't take it in. She heard the story in bits and pieces as her concentration ebbed and flowed. Caroline was involved. Hadn't she known that? Caroline was involved in everything.

"He thinks he's fallen in love," Joseph scoffed.

"With Caroline?" Priscilla asked.

"With Mick's prostitute. Her name is Darby. She's quite a favorite with the miners, they say. So of course Mick got her back."

Priscilla looked at the dress. Why was the woman's dress here? "I don't understand."

"Weren't you listening to Mick?" Joseph asked irritably. "Your precious son and Caroline Farnsworth worked together to rescue her."

"Your precious son" was what Mick called Gabe. Priscilla shook the words off. She had to concentrate. This was important.

"Mick is using this Darby person to lure Caroline

421

Farnsworth to the mine. She's such a do-gooder, she'll fall for it," Joseph explained.

"The mine?"

"Little Josie. Al Humphrey's going to blow up Little Josie with Caroline and Rory Talmage inside."

Through the satisfaction in Joseph's voice, Priscilla heard another question. What about Gabe? Did no one care about Gabe? She knew him; if he loved this Darby—or believed he did—he would do anything for her. Even fight Mick Garrity. Hadn't he already done it once?

Who would warn Gabe? Who would keep him away from the mine when he thought this Darby person was there? Who would save her Gabe?

Chapter Thirty-four

"Be you Miss Caroline's brother?"

Rory's heart kicked over at the question. A boy in shabby, outgrown clothing stood before him. Rory's tired mind couldn't place the child's accent. A lilt. A singsong. Ireland?

"Do you know where she is, son?"

"I kin help you, if you kin help me," came the enigmatic answer.

"How?" He would bargain with the devil himself at this point. He couldn't remember where he'd slept — if he'd slept — and yet, well into the day on the Fourth of July, he was still no closer to finding Caroline.

"You've got to promise not to hurt my pa."

"I wouldn't harm your pa, son. Who is he?"

"People think he's crazy," the boy said. "But he's not!" Rory shook his head. "Your pa has Miss Caroline?"

"It was supposed to be someone else. He didn't know!" The boy was pleading for . . . what? Understanding? Pardon?

"Miss Caroline," he said again. "Please. Do you know where she is?"

It took many such gentle proddings before the boy could tell Rory where Caroline was. Where he *thought* Caroline was. According to his pa.

The boy was Owen Llewellyn, son of Daffyd Llewellyn. Rory had heard of Owen's pa. He was a dynamite specialist, reputed to have endured a few blasts more than was good for a man. He spoke little English and was presumed to be deaf. He was Welsh, not Irish, and this boy, his son, was one of Caroline's pupils. She had rarely spoken of him; or rather, Rory had barely

423

listened when she spoke of him, but here he was, bringing information to Rory.

Daffyd Llewellyn had been told to care for a woman tied up in a shack up near the mines. He'd been told who she was, but when he got there he knew he'd been told a lie. This woman had silvery gold hair, and Daffyd knew who she was. Owen had talked his ear off about Miss Caroline. She was teaching him to read, teaching him English. She gave him nice food and read stories to him. He'd told Daffyd those same stories, translating them into Welsh to share the magic with his father. Last night he'd told Owen about the lady in the shack. It had taken Owen this long to find Rory

Rory considered trying to get the Larsen boys to go with him as backup, but he didn't want to delay. He was armed. According to Owen, Caroline was not guarded. Getting to her quickly took precedence over force, he decided.

But all his haste was not sufficient. Caroline wasn't in the shack. The door wasn't even latched, let alone locked. Fearing a trap, he opened the door without showing himself in the doorway, then darted in, bent low to the ground. It was all for nothing. Inspection of the shack by candlelight revealed a cleared area on the floor where Caroline might have been, but nothing else.

Mulling over his options and the likelihood that Owen had lied to him, Rory was less careful coming out. He stood in the shadowed door, thinking, then stepped around it without precaution. Only his quick reaction to a faint sound behind him saved him from being knocked senseless by a blow to the back of his head. He put his shoulder into his assailant's midsection instead, at the same time eluding the downswing of a makeshift club. He raised his fist, prepared to smash down at the man under him.

"Rory!" the man choked out. "No!"

Without letting him go, Rory tugged the man's head

424

up to see who he had.

"Sorry . . . didn't know you."

"I don't know you either," Rory said, still holding on.

"It's me. Just Ernie . . . Coogins."

"Coogins?" Rory's hands went slack, letting Ernie roll up onto his knees.

"Yeah. Just let me . . . get my breath."

"What the hell are you doing here?"

Ernie remained bent over, shaking his head and rolling his shoulders until he could function; then he sat back onto his haunches. "Sorry. You caught me just right. I thought you were one of them."

"Who?" He didn't take the hand Ernie offered. "What's going on here?"

"Al Humphrey showed up a while ago in Rio Mogollon, lookin' for Miss Caroline. He hitched up with Maria Martinez right off, and I followed them here."

"Humphrey? What's he got to do with Caroline?"

"Nothin' good."

"You look different." Rory had just gotten over his surprise enough to notice Ernie's altered appearance.

"So do you."

"For good reason," he said brusquely.

"Yeah, I know about that. Your uncle."

"The one you saw in Dodge City." He gestured to the shack. "A kid told me Caroline was here."

"Humphrey took her to the mine a while ago."

"The mine? Little Josie?" It was the nearest mine.

"I was watchin' this place and the mine. I saw you sneakin' here and figured I could take out whoever's helpin' him."

"What's he doing? And why?"

Ernie told him what he knew about Blackie and about himself and his family as quickly as he could. "I was just gettin' ready to go in there after Humphrey when you came. He hasn't had Miss Caroline in there long, but he's been busy, goin' in and out."

"What's he doing?" Rory demanded.

When Ernie told him what he suspected, Rory cursed. They made their plans, speaking tersely. As Rory started to leave, Ernie held him back to ask, "You got a knife?"

"A gun."

"She's tied. Take this."

It was a pocketknife. "You have a gun?" At his nod, Rory asked, "You been inside?"

"No. I would've, but I'm glad you came. I hate dark holes."

"Better for me anyway. I know the place."

"Take good care of Miss Caroline."

Rory heard the unspoken "for me" and gave Ernie his hand. "Take care of yourself, too. She'll want to thank you herself."

Ernie nodded and waved Rory on, watching as he disappeared into the mine. He patted his empty pocket, trying not to feel naked without Uncle Boyd's knife.

He had known for a long time that Miss Caroline and her father had caused his uncle's capture. Unlike Priscilla, he didn't hold it against them. How could he? The blame was not theirs; it was Blackie's and Boyd's. And the Farnsworths had given him a home as well as their trust. If he had to give up his lucky knife, there was no better cause than this, saving Miss Caroline.

When Rory was gone Ernie moved back to wait for Al Humphrey.

Joseph Talmage raised his gun, counted off to himself, "Three, two, one," and fired.

A cheer went up along both sides of the street as the burro race began. Joseph put the gun back into his belt and joined the rowdy men, yelling and waving his hat as the braying, bucking animals charged down the road. It was more stampede than race, but no one cared—least of all Joseph Talmage.

This was a tough town. By carrying out the role he'd taken on weeks ago, Joseph was proving to everyone that he was as tough as they were. Last night Wendell Davenport had offered to relieve him of his duty here if he was too upset by the failure of Little Josie to carry it out. Joseph had promised to do the job. He basked now in the admiration he saw around him. Everyone knew about Little Josie, and everyone knew he'd lost his shirt. They admired gumption, though, and he was proving he had it.

He ran along to the finish line, following the ropes and struggling to stay upright in the crush of men and animals. He was used to the struggle. As he saw it, his whole life had been a struggle. No one had ever credited him with the brains or the will to succeed.

It had always been Robert, his older brother, who got credit for everything. Robert started the foundry. Robert married well and had his perfect family. But where was Robert now? He was dead and gone, killed in an accident just like the accident that would finish off the rest of his perfect family today.

"Hey, hey!" yelled the miner next to him. "You won! Look at that!"

Joseph tried to dodge away from the filthy hat the man clamped onto his head. Others pounded on his back, offering congratulations.

"Must mean your luck's gonna change!" one shouted close to his ear.

"Of course it will!" he yelled back, pleased by the omen.

It wasn't luck, however, that determined Joseph's fate, now or ever. It was planning. Already he'd start turning yesterday's misfortune into tomorrow's triumph. This time he had some help from Mick Garrity, but that was all right. Their needs coincided. Mick wanted a crack at Caroline Farnsworth, and she would deliver Rory

Joseph couldn't believe he'd failed to recognize Rory.

Royal was such a stupid name. He should have known it wasn't real.

The fact that Rory had fallen into Simon Sargent's gravy boat years ago was going to be what saved Joseph as well. When Rory was dead he could go to Rory's adopted "other uncle" and use that connection as leverage to get in on the ground floor on another deal of Sargent's. He wasn't afraid to borrow money to invest in something Sargent backed. Even another mine.

Sargent would be bound to be impressed that Joseph had taken this loss so well. A lesser man would give up or whine about losing so much capital. Joseph would prove he could keep up with the biggest and best — and Rory would set him up for all that just by dying.

No one would be able to connect him to Rory's accident. He would be trying to rescue his adopted sister — or whatever she was — from the abandoned mine where that crazy Welshman had taken her. The Welshman couldn't speak English, so it was the perfect setup. Justice was swift here in the mining towns. When people found out that Daffyd Llewellyn had hidden Caroline Farnsworth in her brother's mine and blown it up, Llewellyn would hang. Half the people in Lake City were scared of him already. He was known as a fair hand with dynamite, and that was tricky stuff.

Of course, Llewellyn wouldn't be the one to blow up the mine. That job was going to be handled by a man of Garrity's. Because he was a stranger, too, no one would defend him either. Besides, according to Mick, Al Humphrey had done time for robbing trains. The little work he'd done around here had also been with explosives, and for some reason he wanted Caroline Farnsworth dead. In getting her, Joseph would also get Rory, thanks to Mick's plan.

There had been only one change, and that was unavoidable. In order to make the plan go smoothly, Mick had to give up having Caroline. There just wasn't time.

Not if he wanted an alibi. Like Joseph, Mick was going to be prominently visible at all the day's festivities.

Miners loved to set off explosives on the Fourth. With all the explosions up in the hills today, no one would pay any mind to one more. And no one would miss the Farnsworths—or whatever their names were—for days.

It was simple.

Surrounded by miners and mule skinners, Joseph made his way to the next event of the celebration. He collected money all along the route, his winnings on the burro race. He had two hundred dollars by the time he got to the greased pole. He had donated the five-dollar bill at the top. Filthy black axle grease from the mine wagons coated the slender pole and would soon be smeared over half the men swarming at the base.

Joseph picked out a slim lad with husky shoulders. "Who wants to bet five dollars that this fellow will win?"

He shook hands with the takers and raised his gun again. At the signal, the first man leaped to the pole and slid down. He was pulled off to make room for the next. Laughing, Joseph watched. That was the way it went. One man failed and another took his place.

Today, when everything was over, Joseph would be the one at the top of the real greased pole that was success. He knew it.

Caroline heard the footsteps and held her breath. What now? She was bound and gagged again, but she still feared some inadvertent move would attract Humphrey's attention. He was going to blow her up. Wasn't that enough?

Bad as it was to face death, she knew listening to Al Humphrey's vileness again would be worse. In the explosion to come she would at least die quickly. It was hard to wait, though. She couldn't help but hope someone would find her before Humphrey could complete setting the charges.

He'd told her all about the explosion and what it would do to her body. That was sickening enough, but he'd said other things as well. Personal things that made her stomach roil, and things about Blackie and Kid Belasco. Humphrey held her responsible for everything, as perhaps he should. She couldn't change any of it now except—maybe—this ending.

She didn't want to die, and she wanted Rory.

"Caroline."

The half-whispered voice seemed to come from everywhere at once, sounding so eerie that prickles of fear crawled over her skin. She held herself still, listening with every sense. It was Humphrey, wasn't it?

But then, he knew where she was. He'd come to her twice before without calling out. Was he trying to frighten her? Or . . . her heart hammered harder, making it impossible to hear . . . was it someone else?

Rory. *Oh, God, let it be Rory,* she prayed.

It came again, that echoing call, hoarse and insistent. This time she made an answer deep in her throat. Whoever it was, she was sure it wasn't Humphrey. She would take her chances with anyone else. Her gag prevented a true cry, but she could make noise and thrash her body. She kept it up until she felt hands on her shoulders.

She knew at once it was Rory, and at once her eyes began to fill with tears. Unfortunately, her nose also filled at the same time, and for a moment she thought she would suffocate in the time it took him to release her gag.

Gasping for breath, Caroline began to cry in earnest as he cut the rope from her hands and feet. She used the cloth that had held the gag in place and the front of Rory's shirt to mop up, wishing all that moisture could be rerouted to her mouth instead. It was a long time before she could talk, and then Rory didn't want to listen.

"Come on. We've got to get out of here."

"He's going to blow up the mine."

"No, he's not, but we're going anyway."

"Did you stop him?" Caroline asked. She stumbled on feet that were too numb to walk.

Rory scooped her up into his arms, hissing, "Don't talk."

But Caroline couldn't help herself. She swung her head to look where he was taking her. "This is the wrong way!"

He stopped dead and put her onto her feet just long enough to gather her against him. Bending his head, he kissed her. Although her mouth was dry, it wasn't a problem. His tongue stroked hers as thoroughly as if they were back in his bed. He didn't let her go until every sense was singing. Then he turned her to face the yawning darkness of the mine and said, "Walk."

Caroline walked.

Mick Garrity and his partner were winning the drilling contest just as they were supposed to. Joseph watched complacently as the sweating men, stripped to the waist, worked drills into the stone, one holding, the other hammering with the huge sledgehammer called a double jack, making a deep hole in the flat rock before them. At the call of each minute the men changed jobs so rapidly they missed no more than a single beat of the hammer.

This was his day from start to finish. He'd won every bet he'd placed so far, and this one would be no different. Chuckling, Joseph lifted his hat, resettling it against the glare from the rock, and let his eyes rove over the crowd. He was utterly relaxed, in contrast to the crowd around him.

The drilling contest elicited the most interest of all the

day's activities because it was a test of what the men themselves did in the mines. Each man took pride in his skill and endurance at making the holes that would, in the mines, hold the dynamite charge that blasted ore from the ground. It was a dangerous and unequal contest of man against nature; the tiniest slip of the hand could mean the loss of that hand—or of another's.

Joseph didn't know which struck him first, the face in the crowd or the groan from that same crowd when Mick's blow landed wrong, breaking the drill off while it was stuck in the hole. The two wrongs fell on him in the same instant. The crazy Welshman, Llewellyn, was watching the contest when he was supposed to be up in the hills. And Mick was out of the contest. Two signs of disintegration that Joseph couldn't ignore.

He began to work his way back from the crowd. Leaving everything to Mick had been a mistake. He knew that now. If the Welshman wasn't up there at the mine, was the other man there instead? What was going on at Little Josie?

Joseph grabbed a burro and got on. Alibi be damned! He had to be sure. Didn't he know by now that the only things that worked for him were the things he did himself. How could he have been so stupid as to let someone else manage this accident? A hundred people saw him ride away. He'd say he was going to Rory's rescue. Being seen didn't matter; getting the job done was all that counted.

He was soaked with perspiration and had lost his hat by the time he got to the clearing at the entrance to the mine. He dropped off the burro and staggered to lean against a tree and catch his breath. There wasn't a sound to be heard, not even a bird's call. Where was Humphrey? And Rory and Caroline? He couldn't call out or just blunder into the mine.

Good God, he had to think. He sent the burro back with a swat on the rump and tried to get his bearings.

432

Waiting was excruciating agony. For the longest time he heard nothing but his own labored breathing. Then he saw a flash of movement off to his left. He slid around a tree and found a rock to peer from.

The moving form became a man in dark clothing. Al Humphrey? It had to be. But there was something about the man . . . It plagued him. Damn. The entrance was obscured, like so many in this area, by the rock formation of which it was part. The mine wasn't a shaft down into the ground but a tunnel into the rocks. It was part of what had sold him on investing in Little Josie, this formation that would make pumping out water unnecessary. Maybe he could get closer.

He moved, but so did the man and so did another shadow, this one at his right. They moved together toward the mine. The man went inside. Quickly. One second he was there; then he was gone. In that second Joseph saw the other person clearly. It was Priscilla.

Priscilla! She ran after the first man, holding up her skirts. And then he knew why. The man was Gabe. He'd seen just a glimpse, but it had been enough.

Joseph ran awkwardly after Priscilla. He could hear her calling to Gabe. Her voice pulled him deeper into the looming darkness of the mine. Echoes of her scream beat at him from all sides as he stumbled forward. He couldn't see the hand he held in front of himself to feel his way. Then, suddenly, Priscilla stopped crying out and Joseph halted to listen as the last reverberations of her shrieks died. All he could hear was his own breathing, loud in his ears.

"Priscilla!" he called. "Gabe?"

He heard footsteps. Not Priscilla's, he knew.

"Gabe? Answer me, son!"

The footsteps came on, relentless, firm.

Joseph turned and began to work his way back to the opening. He found his way to the wall of rough stone. It was cold and damp. He stumbled over loose rocks at the base of the support timbers, trying to find his way back to the light. His heart was hammering so loudly he couldn't hear the footsteps. Had they stopped?

He stopped and spoke one more time. "Gabe?"

Before the echo of his cry died away, Joseph crumpled to the ground in a heap, felled by a solid blow to the head.

Caroline stopped when she heard the distant echoes of Priscilla's screams, but Rory urged her on. "Never mind," he said. "We have to get out."

"How much farther?"

"Just a bit."

"What was that noise?"

"An animal," Rory muttered.

Caroline knew it wasn't, but she didn't argue. The passageway was narrow and low, the floor littered with debris. Rory carried a candle with his hand cupped protectively over the flame, yet they moved forward mostly by feel.

"The air is getting fresher," she whispered.

"Soon," he answered. "Next corner should do it."

It didn't, and they staggered on, but the next turn showed light. They stumbled toward it.

Ernie waited outside, so frustrated he didn't know what to do. He'd been about to tackle Humphrey when the woman had appeared. He hadn't known it was a woman at first. All he'd seen was a blur. While he'd been unsure, frozen in place by shock, she'd gone running inside with a man after her! That meant there were four people inside the mine with Humphrey. Rory would be bringing Caroline out any minute, he hoped, but he couldn't count on that. The passage they sought might be blocked. They might get lost. Humphrey might discover them. Anything could happen.

He had to wait for Humphrey to come out, and he

had to prevent him from setting off the dynamite. He couldn't just shoot him for fear of setting off the charge himself. He didn't know much about explosives. Just enough to be terrified.

Ernie crept to the entrance and flattened himself next to the opening, hand poised for his knife, to be ready to jump Humphrey as he emerged this time. He could wait no longer. Too many lives were at stake. The waiting went on and on until his nerves were stretched to the breaking point. He listened with his whole body and kept his eyes busy, skimming the area. He hadn't expected those last two people. Any more and—

Suddenly Humphrey was there. Surprised in spite of his vigilance, Ernie's jump came two beats late to catch Humphrey off guard. He curled and rolled to one side and came up with a knife.

Ernie crouched and grabbed for his knife as he circled, facing Humphrey. His hand groped and came up empty. He'd forgotten! Rory had his knife.

He kept his eye on the gleaming blade before him and found his gun. Just as he grasped it, Humphrey charged him. He twisted away from the knife and lost his footing. The fall saved him that time, but when he got up Humphrey caught him. The knife sliced his right arm to the bone. He fell to his knees again, almost dropping the gun. Instead, he took it with his left hand and tried to fire. But Humphrey was on him again. This time he plunged the knife into his back and Ernie went down. The pain was excruciating. Hot. Sharp.

Ernie fell. He couldn't breathe. On one knee, he raised the gun with both hands aimed it at Humphrey. He saw the flare of a flame and fired the gun.

A scream. A woman?

Caroline.

Ernie crawled toward the flame he could see burning its way along the fuse to the mine. He reached for it through scalding pain. It flickered, and he threw himself

435

onto it with his last breath. A shadow rose beside him and a shot rang out.

Ernie and Humphrey fell together just short of the flame.

Rory just had time to throw himself on top of Caroline when the explosion rocked the mine and echoed like thunder in the mountains around them.

Chapter Thirty-five

Caroline had just worked it out in her mind. "Do you realize," she announced in a voice full of wonder, "that Ernie Coogins was your cousin, Gabe?"

His smile was thin, a mere stretching of his mouth that conveyed no pleasure. "If so, he's the only relative I had with the remotest claim to decency."

Although Caroline sympathized with the shock and outrage he'd felt upon learning the truth about his parents, Darby consistently refused to let him brood about it. "I know it's hard on you, Gabriel," she said, "but I can't help but be a little pleased. If it weren't for your outlaw father, I'd be the only sinner in our family. This way we balance out. Neither of us is better than the other. It makes me hope we can make a good new life together."

"Of course you can," Caroline said stoutly. "I can tell you firsthand that Blackie was anything but a monster, and the evidence about your Uncle Boyd indicates that he was more feckless than bad. If I had it all to do over again, knowing how much misery would follow, I'd probably not urge my father to capture him in that bank. On the other hand, a lot of good came from that act as well. Papa was able to buy land in New Mexico and marry Hannah. It gave my family a new start — one we needed as badly as you need yours."

She looked to Rory for confirmation, but it was Gabe who answered. "They were outlaws, Caroline, not you. Someone would have stopped them eventually. It might as well have been you."

"What I regret," Rory said, speaking at last, "is taking it upon myself to right the wrongs of the past. *That* was wrong."

"I don't blame you," Gabe put in immediately. "I'd have done the same thing in your place, or wanted to."

Rory acknowledged Gabe's support with a glance but remained adamant. "You warned me, Caroline, and you were right."

"I was only afraid for you. And I misjudged your intent."

She had not known that Rory had arranged for Gabe to be compensated for half of every dollar he and Uncle Simon swindled from Joseph Talmage. It was money Gabe was now reluctant to take, even to finance the store he wanted back in Iowa with Darby.

To Caroline, that was just one of the many details they had yet to work out in the aftermath of the explosion at Little Josie. That mine was now truly defunct, just as Joseph had been told. Uncle Simon would retain ownership, according to Rory, in the hope that a new process would be discovered someday for separating the abundant remaining silver from its tenacious alloys. In that eventuality, which Simon believed was only years away, Little Josie might yet enrich Gabe, Rory and Wendell Davenport, all of whom remained in partnership with Simon as owners of the mine.

In the meantime, there was another mine to be worked. Rory called it Silver Sally. Sample ore taken from the site where Caroline had picnicked in the mountains with Rory had assayed well. Caroline considered it only fitting that Sally, the burro Rory saved from death, had rewarded him so handsomely.

Before Rory could argue the moral point of his revenge with Caroline, Gabe said, "If only I could understand my mother, then maybe I could forget. But I can't imagine any reason for her to be in that mine. I

438

know Joseph took her there once, by why then? It was so unlike her!" It was not the first time he'd worried the question aloud.

Ernie had lived just long enough after the explosion to warn Caroline, "People . . . in there!" At the time she and Rory had believed he meant themselves, fearing that Ernie hadn't recognized Caroline. She'd been anguished to think he hadn't known her or heard her profuse thanks. But of course she'd also been hysterical, holding Ernie and trying to stanch the flow of blood from his fatal wound. The miracle was that he'd lived to speak at all.

Then others had come on the scene, people who had seen Priscilla and Joseph riding to the mine. The Larsen boys told what they had learned from Mick Garrity's men, and the digging began. Priscilla and Joseph had been found near the entrance of the collapsed mine, their presence there a mystery to everyone, and particularly vexing to Gabe, who still wrestled with the problem.

This time, however, Darby spoke up. First, she shot a warning glance to Caroline, for she had told her friend about overhearing Priscilla and Mick. Caroline had agreed with Darby that Gabe did not need to know about his mother's relationship with Mick. Now Caroline held her breath, wondering if Darby had decided otherwise.

"From what I overheard between your mother and Joseph and Mick," she said, "I think only one thing could have sent Priscilla to the mine. I think she was trying to save you. I heard her speak about your uncle, Boyd Belasco. She blamed herself for what happened to him. I think she couldn't bear to fail you as she had failed her brother."

Caroline was proud of Darby for what she was doing for Gabe. He had doubted his mother, and Darby was giving her back to him as a person he could love. Darby's words erased the ugliness of Priscilla's last months and restored her as a loving mother. "I'm sure that's true, Gabe," Caroline added. "She would have done anything for you."

"I wish I could believe that," he said, speaking almost to himself.

Caroline loved the way his eyes came to rest on Darby. He might address someone else, but invariably he looked at Darby, who was now his wife.

Darby smiled back at him, then turned to Rory and Caroline. "You're coming to see us off in the morning, aren't you?"

"Of course we are." Caroline went to the door with her guests. "We wouldn't miss it for the world."

Darby looked around one last time after hugging them both. "I'll never forget this house and all that happened here. The good and the bad." She and Gabe had been imprisoned for eighteen hours by Garrity's men on the Fourth, each in a separate room of the house, each unaware that the other was so near.

That was the bad. But Darby didn't know that Caroline and Rory knew the good she referred to was more than being taken in by them. They exchanged only a quick glance of understanding, saving their amusement until the Talmages were gone.

Caroline's humor didn't last long. She had not been alone with Rory since the night before she'd been kidnapped. So much had happened since then that she felt unaccountably nervous with him now.

No, not unaccountably, she corrected. She knew exactly why she was nervous. Everyone else's life had been settled in the week since then. Darby's, Gabe's; even Mick Garrity had left, taking Maria Martinez with him.

Caroline tried to take heart from the fact that she

440

was now back with Rory, but she was afraid that was more her doing than his. She'd spent all week with Beatrice Davenport, suffocating under that woman's kind but overwhelming care. It had taken all her guile to win her release, and now she worried about Rory's reaction to her plans.

One look at Rory was enough to make her decide that tonight wasn't the right time to talk to him. She headed for the stairs, giving him a faint smile. "I guess I'll go to sleep now," she announced foolishly. "We have to be up early."

Rory followed and took her hand, stopping her. "Beatrice said you have nightmares."

"Oh. Well." She moistened her lips in order to smile. "I did, but I'm sure I won't any more. Now that I'm home."

"About the explosion?" His eyes were warm and concerned.

"And Ernie. I . . . feel so responsible."

"I know, but he also had a personal score to settle with Humphrey, for his uncle."

"But he was helping me, protecting me. In my dream I keep trying to save him—and I never do."

"I was wrong about him. He loved you. He was a good man."

"And so modest. He always called himself 'just Ernie,' do you remember?"

"Yeah, I do. He said that to me, too. It's hard to let go of someone like that."

His understanding helped. She smiled her thanks and tried to ease away. He didn't let her go.

"We have to talk, Caroline."

Her heart skipped a beat, then began to march to a hasty new rhythm. She wanted to plead that she was tired, but she wasn't. Upstairs, she would only worry. It was better to have it out now. She straightened her

441

shoulders and said, "I think so, too. I've been doing a lot of thinking this week."

He didn't look pleased, so she blundered on, filling the awkward silence with words. "I've decided to stay here in Lake City. Children like Owen and Stu need someone to teach them even though they won't go to regular school. I could do that."

Rory couldn't believe his ears. "But what about your family? The ranch? Don't you want to go home?"

Not without you, she wanted to say. But she couldn't. Instead, she said, "They'll understand. I mean, it's not as if I'd never go home again! But now I want to stay here. I've found something worthwhile to do with my life, and I'm sure Papa and Hannah will accept my reasoning. After all, they sent me back to Philadelphia for an education. They can't object to having me put it to use."

"You could teach in New Mexico."

"But I'm here and I want to stay. There are so many needy children here, with more coming every day."

Rory moved away from her uncertainly. Everything she said was true. He had already set up a fund to help the families of the miners, using the other half of Uncle Joseph's money, the share not going to Gabe. He'd decided he owed it to Owen Llewellyn—and to Caroline. Without the good she had been doing in the community, he would never have learned where she was in time to save her from Humphrey's explosion.

Still, he was shocked. He thought of the letter they'd had from Hannah. Her news . . . .

"It's Ted, isn't it?" he said finally. "You don't want to go home because he's not there any more." Ted had sold the ranch to Jake. His story had been that ranching was something he'd done because his father insisted. Now that his life was his, he wanted out.

"Of course not. I'm glad he's gone. Now Papa and

442

Hannah don't have to be embarrassed any more."

"But you are—embarrassed to go home, that is."

Caroline was getting desperate. "No, Rory. Can't you understand? I like it here, and I've found something important to do—"

"Something more important to you than I am?"

He sounded as desperate as she did, and finally she dared to look at him. There was misery in every line of his face. "More important than you are *how?*" she whispered.

"I don't want to leave you. I love you, Caroline."

"Leave?"

"I thought after all we'd been through, and especially after the night we spent together, that you loved me, too."

"I do, Rory."

"Then you have to marry me," he said, starting to smile at last. "You see, I had a hard time getting you back from Beatrice. Someone told her I wasn't really your brother, and she was determined to protect you from me. To get you back, I had to promise to marry you tomorrow morning."

"Tomorrow!"

"I know that's hurried, but I've been waiting so long already."

"But . . . the mine! What about Silver Sally? I thought you would stay here and work your claim!"

Rory laughed. "Oh ho! So that's it! You wanted to stay here because you thought *I* would stay here." He caught her up in his arms, hugging her so hard she could barely breathe. "That's it, isn't it?"

Rory looked so handsome and so happy, Caroline found him irresistible. Still, she tried to tease him. "No, it wasn't that at all," she laughed. "It's that coach trip over the mountains! I couldn't face that ride again."

"Liar!" His kiss stopped her laughter—and his. When

he lifted his head he wore an earnest look that moved Caroline deeply. "Will you marry me? Really?"

"Yes, Rory, oh, yes! I love you so much!" She kissed him again. "Are you sure you want to go home? What about the mine?"

"Wendell will manage it. I trust him. I only came here for one reason, and that's finished. Perhaps I wouldn't do it again, knowing the cost, but I can't undo it."

"You weren't wrong, Rory."

"I think I was. Now. But except for Ernie, I'm satisfied. Maybe I shouldn't be, but I lived too long with anger not to feel glad that it's gone. My father was a good man. He didn't deserve to die that way. Now I can go home."

"Will we go to St. Louis then?"

Rory grinned and hugged her again. "Not unless you're crazy to go back there. I, for one, would like to see Rusty and Abby again before they're all grown up. I'm going to buy Jasper's ranch from Jake. Once, you were ready to move into Jasper's house. We can live there or tear it down and start over."

"You don't have to be a rancher for me, Rory. You can go anywhere, be anything. Just let me live with you and love you."

"It's what I want, but if you want to go home to be married, I suppose I can wait."

"But can Beatrice?" Caroline countered, teasing again.

"I don't want to deprive you of having your family with you, or of all the fixings you deserve."

"I had that once, Rory. Now I'll have what really matters — you."

"You know, when Maria spoke out at your wedding she was only saying out loud the words I was saying to myself."

444

"She did me a great favor, Rory. I knew it in my heart. Coming down the aisle, I couldn't bear to look at you. I was afraid I would cry. I've always loved you and I always will."

Now you can get more of HEARTFIRE right at home and $ave.

Preview
Four Brand New
ZEBRA
Heartfire
Romance Novels...

FREE for 10 days.

No Obligation
and No Strings Attached!

♥

Enjoy all of the passion and fiery romance as you soar back through history, right in the comfort of your own home.

Now that you have read a Zebra HEARTFIRE Romance novel, we're sure you'll agree that HEARTFIRE sets new standards of excellence for historical romantic fiction. Each Zebra HEARTFIRE novel is the ultimate blend of intimate romance and grand adventure and each takes place in the kinds of historical settings you want most...the American Revolution, the Old West, Civil War and more.

FREE Preview Each Month and $ave

Zebra has made arrangements for you to preview 4 brand new HEARTFIRE novels each month…FREE for 10 days. You'll get them as soon as they are published. If you are not delighted with any of them, just return them with no questions asked. But if you decide these are everything we said they are, you'll pay just $3.25 each— a total of $13.00 (a $15.00 value). **That's a $2.00 saving each month off the regular price.** Plus there is NO shipping or handling charge. These are delivered right to your door absolutely free! There is no obligation and there is no minimum number of books to buy.

TO GET YOUR FIRST MONTH'S PREVIEW… Mail the Coupon Below!